THE ARK 47 LIBRAE

BORIS STERN

The Ark 47 Librae

leta
CAPITAL

This is the first and limited edition done on behalf of LETA Capital

ISBN 978-989-53701-5-3
DL – 522855/23

Design, typeset and prodution by GRACAL,
at Rua Moinho de Vento 44, Caldas da Rainha, Portugal.

Website: gracal.pt

Website: leta.vc

The book belongs to the genre of hard science fiction. It concerns the colonization of a habitable—but initially dead—exoplanet, sixty light years from Earth. With this, the author has attempted to stay within the framework of known physics, with many thousands of years of flight time and tens of thousands of years involved in running a program for the "revitalization" of the planet. The colonization of the planet begins successfully enough, but then the story of the new world begins to unfold in an unforeseen manner...

INTRODUCTION

Boris Stern is a well-known Russian astrophysicist, Dr. Sci. in Physics and Mathematics and a leading researcher at the Institute for Nuclear Research (INR) of the Russian Academy of Sciences. His new hard science fiction book immerses the reader in the story of the colonization of a distant planet located sixty light-years from Earth, and all this in the absence of any scientific compromises, because there is literally no place for teleportation, hyperspace jumps or superluminal speed. It is impossible to surpass the speed of light given that at near-light speed you will be fried by cosmic radiation. The project to prepare for departure takes as long as one hundred and fifty years, and the flight itself is another ten thousand. Not a bad planning horizon, is it?

We at Leta Capital VC realized a long time ago that we can implement any ambitious project, and in fact it is not as complicated as it initially seems, if we give it enough time and resources. And what is most important is that the project team is highly motivated, and they believe that their project will make the world a better place. I am inspired by the belief in the triumph of reason and the creative power of science for the benefit of humanity. The book you are holding in your hands is about such concepts as humanism, the flight of thought and the search for something more. For this, the author can be forgiven for violating the laws of the genre when no love story, scenes of betrayal, canonical villains and heroes can be found in the book. Instead, the writer appears as a scientist and visionary, whose scale of ideas and, more importantly, values are so lacking in today's world preoccupied with crises and wars.

And isn't his plan to find and populate a new world not for the sake of valuable resources, like locusts, but so that more intelligent beings can enjoy the beauty of the universe? Doesn't a scientist, who is ready to put all his talent, all his life into a project, the result of which he will never see, deserve admiration? What the author writes about is probably the only thing in this world that is truly worth living for. I do not know if genius and villainy are really incompatible. However, people like Boris Stern make me believe again that the words "scientist" and "noble" are almost synonymous.

Immerse yourself in the world of this book. Despite the detailed description of complex physical phenomena, it is written in simple language. The author does not forget about lyrical digressions with detailed descriptions of nature. There are also amazing details in the work emphasized with gentle realism. What are worth only the fragments in which scientists openly fool around, while letting the reader into the life of a scientific team that has forgotten about the assumed seriousness! The smallest details of the narrative give a full understanding of the realism of the project at the current level of scientific development, making it finally clear that this book is a kind of inspiration for scientists and visionaries from all over the world. Plot twists and, of course, the ending will not leave anyone indifferent. Along with the author, experience all the ups and downs of a universal scale project lasting ten thousand years, it really is worth it.

Enjoy!

Alex Chachava

Founder & Managing Partner at LETA Capital

www.leta.vc

TABLE OF CONTENTS

"And that is about the same thing! The devil forced me to take up such a beaten topic!"
"If you write badly, you will be beaten."
"But if you write decently, you'll have an eternal theme."

From a conversation overheard on a plane

PART ONE

While the salty sea gently laps the warm sand...

The places in our narrative cover vast expanses of time and space. They are without doubt worthy of and deserve several paragraphs. The place where the salty sea gently laps the warm sand for the entire day and only occasionally irons out the surface of the wide beach with heavy waves is one such example. Beyond the beach a strip of sand dunes quietly sits, while further on granite slabs take over, in some spots crossed over by moraine ridges. Once long ago, in time immemorial, a wide glacier flowed over this area, apparently flowing from the blue mountain range that dominated the view of the landscape visible from the dunes. It had probably happened a hundred or two hundred million years ago as the continents were shifting, but now there is a warm and stable climate here. Judging by the snow caps, the mountains are very high. In such a climate, at a latitude of forty degrees north, eternal snow lies at an altitude of over four and a half kilometers. Some of the jagged ridges of these mountains would certainly be of interest to intermediate climbers. However, the fact is, there are no climbers here.

At one point, the dunes part and allow the river to flow into the sea. The mouth of the river is marked by an unforgettable rock sticking out of the sand about a kilometer from the confluence (to the left when viewed from the sea). The rock looks like a hundred-meter-high dog's fang with its vertical side facing the sea. It is obviously not limestone but either gray granite or basalt. What stands out the most is that as far as the eye can see, there are no other such rocks anywhere.

Most of the year, the trade winds prevail here, predictably like clockwork carrying with them the weather. In the mornings the air is so transparent that the blue colored mountains become multi-colored, full of

pinks and grays, and the snow caps turn golden in the sunlight and change to blue in the shade. At noon, cumulus clouds appear and grow, swirling higher and higher above the belt of granite ridges between the endless sea and the towering mountains. They are then blown away by the damp breeze that soars up over the granite and is heated by the midday sun.

The rain-swollen-clouds suddenly let loose a heavy downpour and a double rainbow rises over the land. Despite the pouring rain the sun still shines over the shore, and the sea licks the warm sand. Suddenly, from the blue-black sky beyond the rainbow, lightning begins to strike and thunder starts to peal. A rainbow and lightning, both at the same time, about ten strikes per second, each time breaking and branching, accompanied by the eerie unceasing rumble of pealing thunder.

All of it then stops as soon as the granite cools down from the cold shower. A golden evening comes and with it a holiday of water, crystal clear and warm. The water that has fallen from the sky, having accumulated in low areas, depressions and gulleys, receives the warmth of the granite and runs along winding routes to the river valley that cuts through smooth rocks. This would be a paradise for teenagers, jumping into huge granite baths filled with clear water, climbing under warm waterfalls, swimming down streams along smooth winding chutes. However, there are no teenagers here. In the distance beyond, the mountains are golden, sporting newly refreshed snow caps.

The clear transparent river flowing through the pebbly valley is cold as it originates from the remnants of a former glacier and small glaciers hidden in the upper reaches of the mountains above the valleys. There should be trout here, but there is not, and there's a lot more that is not: there are no mosquitoes, no trees and no grass, despite the warmth and abundance of fresh water.

Not a single blade of grass! No lousy ciliates! There is nothing at all that even with a stretch of the imagination could be attributed to or classified as wildlife.

Why? What happened here? Was it environmental poisoning, or perhaps radiation or a supernova explosion? Maybe it was a case of self-destruction or an apocalypse? No, none of these of course! The matter is that the question "What happened here?" has been applied incorrectly.

The real question is: "What didn't happen here?" The answer to that is that there has never been an event whose probability we have no idea about. The answer: life never happened here.

We still do not know how it arose on Earth.

As biologists concerned with the origin of life like to say: "The probability of life arising under the right conditions is equal to the product of two quantities: zero and infinity."

Even today we still don't have a clearer estimate. Zero to infinity... The only thing we know is that the result of any calculations is not exactly zero, and that is only for the sole reason that we have one example before our eyes. There are optimists who say that the probability is close to one in infinity being as life appeared on Earth very quickly, during the first half a billion years. However, the pessimists have objections: they say that if life had not appeared when the environment of our planet was much more volatile and active volcanically, chemically and electrically, it would never have appeared on our planet at all. After that the window of opportunity then closed. Therefore, from the point of view of pessimists, life on a planet can appear either quickly or never. However, nowhere in the world does there exist a judge to arbitrate and competently judge both scenarios.

It gets dark there very quickly and the nights are usually clear and starry. A person lying on their back on the still warm sand of the beach would be delighted with the unfamiliar constellations, among which is an almost perfect semicircle of five bright stars which catches the eye. It is true though that in order to calmly enjoy the spectacle of the unfamiliar sky, a person would have to use a breathing apparatus to deliver them oxygen. The atmospheric pressure there is only slightly higher than that on the earth but oxygen exists only as an insignificant fraction of a percent of the atmosphere. Almost all of the "air" is made up of nitrogen mixed with a little CO_2 and water vapor. Obviously without photosynthetic life, what possible oxygen could anyone mention?!

Even if someone was wearing an oxygen mask, a person who remembers the sky of the Earth very well, would see something familiar. Of course, there would be the same bifurcated Milky Way but that's not all. One would recognize the Pleiades although they appear a little smaller there, seeing a pair of very bright stars, one bluish and the other reddish in hue, in principle one could recognize Betelgeuse with Rigel only without Orion and Deneb would shine just as brightly but only without the Swan.

Two small moons would be seen and when they rise they would appear to be ascending towards each other, both rotating in the same direction as the planet itself, one of them at an altitude of 20 thousand kilometers overtaking the rotation of the planet and the other at a distance of 56 thousand kilometers circling counter to it.

No one can really say why life never appeared here. Where there some missing connections? Was it a shortage of quiet lagoons saturated with organic broth? Did the lightning not strike hard enough? Or was it simply that even in the presence of everything needed, the insignificantly small chance for the correct assembly of the combination of molecules (zero) never occurred even with the gigantic number of related interactions (infinity). It appears that the window of opportunity really did slam shut here a long time ago, and now for six billion years sterile clear dawns have risen above the coast and the barren sea guiltily licks the warm sand.

Sixty Human Years

There may be nothing more serene than a long summer day on the banks of a large river. Mark Selin lay on the hot sand of an island overgrown with plant life and willows. A smooth looking steep mountain stretched into the sky beyond the river, its ridge covered with forests from which limestone cliffs protruded here and there. Mark looked at the mirror-like surface of the river at a spot where the mountains slowly floated above the clouds. The day seemed to have begun in time immemorial and would drag on indefinitely until the evening coolness came. With it would come brutal hunger and he would have to swim back through the canal, pull the bike out of the bushes and go home. When he got there, he would have to listen to the grumbling of his parents about a long absence and only then would he have his blessed dinner.

That would be later, while the sun was still high, he could think and dream for a long time, and there was much to dream about. Mark has just entered the International University of Advanced Studies which was a university that had earned the status of "legendary" in only fifteen years of existence.

Of course, he, being a creature of this wonderful outback, was incredibly lucky. He was lucky for the three teachers he had had in physics, mathematics and literature. He was lucky for having such wonderful parents, who slipped him good and fascinating books that made him think. Yes, and he himself, through the sweat of his hard work had nurtured his luck, which honestly deserved a rest in the day's serenity.

True it was one of the last days of rest and relaxation. Soon he would have a five-hour flight which would take him to a new life: one which Mark's imagination painted vague but disturbing pictures about, as he would be *at the forefront of world science*.

Perhaps he was also lucky with the times into which he had been born, such luck rarely occurs with the inhabitants of these backward places, and it was not only the locals... The world, having gone through a severe crisis, seemed to have woken up and rubbed its eyes. Talk show stars, the news heroes whom Mark's father called "fiery lackeys", "chain patriots" and "obscurantist courtiers", all disappeared from sight as if hiding in some secret cracks. Instead of them smart normal people began to appear in such numbers that he had to ask: "Where were they before? Where had they been hiding for decades?" The changes did not stop there, finally after a seventy-five-year hiatus; people actually returned to the moon and have already delivered equipment and supplies there for a Mars expedition that will be launched in six months.

An exciting life lies ahead, thought Mark. *How important it will be to succeed in this life and to become a real scientist!*

Looking at the reflection of the mountains in the clear water, he said to himself: "I must definitely come back here when the main events of my life have already happened. Come back here in sixty years and give myself an accounting: whether what I am thinking about now has come true. Did I become a scientist? Did wisdom come with age? How great it would be if everything I planned worked out and how nice it would be to lie here with a great life behind me...

In our youth we often make all sorts of stupid promises and vows and almost always quickly forget them, but there are exceptions, some things get stuck in memory for life, perhaps due to some bright detail, like the reflection of the mountains for example. So as it were, sixty years later the now accomplished and wise Mark Selin, a man of moderately wide renown, got out of a rental car on the banks of that very river. After a continuous three hours of driving, the usual five-minutes of rehabilitation were necessary. When he got out and attempted to stand like a decent human in a vertical posture, his knees and back screamed out in pain. In order not to waste time, in a half-crooked state, Mark took the boat out of the trunk, connected the hose and turned on the compressor. Now he had time to walk around the car five times, shaking the stiffness and pain out of his legs and in turn gradually straightening out his back.

Every time Mark asked himself: Where does this idiotic pain come from? Are my joints or ligaments causing the pain? Is there some kind of rubbish that accumulates in them while I'm driving?

The fact was that Mark, with his ability to quickly understand any area of knowledge where he had previously been a complete layman, in half an hour could have easily and thoroughly figured what kind of idiotic pain it was and what kind of rubbish built up, but the question was more of an idle rhetorical one, just to keep his mind busy while recovering from the drive and not really worthy of investigation. And after five minutes Mark finally straightened all the way up, and said to himself: "Well, now I'm going somewhere!" He picked up the boat, carrying it with his shoulder, and went to the river.

Before returning here he had studied satellite images and already knew that his beloved island had long been washed away by floods. As an acceptable alternative, he chose a place on the left bank opposite the mountains, a spot from where the view should be almost the same as it was then. It was necessary to row five kilometers upstream, but since Mark had no problems with his shoulder girdle, no *rubbish accumulated* there, he did it easily and rather quickly.

The weather was the same as it had been then, sixty years ago. Mark had followed the weather forecast and chose a time accordingly. He lay down and began to look at the river, where the mountains floated above the clouds in the same way but, so far, the past had refused to revive itself. Then, lying on the sand after an eight-hour flight with the corresponding jet lag and three hours of driving, Mark fell asleep. When he woke up, he felt the poignantly familiar smells of a hot day by the river: the willows, beautiful plants with long soft needles and round red berries, hot sand, silvery burdocks with a name unknown to Mark, and then the smell of the river itself. And the past gradually came to life.

"Well, how did it go with you becoming a scientist?" asked Mark Jr.

"It seems to be that I have become one. At least a lot of people think I am."

"Have you discovered anything important?"

"Yes I did in fact, but it's a bit of a sad discovery. I discovered the reflection of a star in the ocean of a distant planet, the reflection of the sun of that planet, sixty light years away. The sad thing is that there is no life there. There is a huge ocean which extends over two-thirds of the planet's circumference at low latitudes and one third of the planet is occupied by a continent. All of this I found thanks to the reflection of the star. There is land, there is sea, an atmosphere of nitrogen and a warm climate. Clouds float around there no worse than these and there must be rivers, almost like this one, but there is no oxygen. So there is no life."

"But maybe there is some other life out there that doesn't need oxygen and doesn't provide oxygen?"

"I had hoped so, as did many others, but biologists have dashed those hopes to smithereens. If life appears capable of evolution, it will certainly begin by using oxygen photosynthesis. Evolution must stumble upon such a valuable find but yet on that planet there are all the conditions for photosynthesis: light, liquid water and carbon dioxide, which we also see. And as soon as photosynthesis begins, life blooms and creates an oxygen atmosphere. However, all of that does not happen right away, on Earth it took a couple of billion years, but that planet is already six billion years old. That's the law, I do not know in detail how it was proven but in general terms I understand that it is true, so if the inevitable trigger of life is not present, then there is no life."

"Are there other planets where life has been found?"

"No. There are three more planets with the right temperature and with what appear to be decent atmospheres with water vapor, except that the glare of the star is not yet visible on any of them. There is no oxygen anywhere, but this does not mean that there is no extraterrestrial life anywhere at all, just that so far only four suitable planets have been found. So as soon as I get back, I will start to process the data for two more. What we already know for sure is that even if all of the conditions are right, life does not necessarily arise."

"It's really sad. Life loses 1:4. How did you find the reflection? Has the planet been seen?"

"Seen in detail? Of course not! The planet is visible only as a luminous dot and is very faint and to see such weak points of light I had to spend a lot of time, work and money. Even in your time, they wanted to resume long-buried projects, *Darwin* and another one, abbreviated as TPF, you seem to have even read about it. Some of the projects were really renewed, united and improved and given the name *Darwin*. It took a long time, but they did it in the end. Do you remember what *Darwin* is?

"Three space telescopes, it seems..."

"Now there are seven, a whole flotilla. They are capable of accuracy within fractions of a micron, which is necessary to nullify the light from a star but at the same time see the planets around it. Light from six telescopes is added to and mixed in the central unit, the seventh. From a star, whose light is in an opposing telescope there is what is called an antiphase, that is, it is subtracted and the light from the planet is added. It may seem incredible, but the star which is billions of times brighter than the planets truly vanishes and the planets appear to us as separate points. All together it is called a null interferometer."

"Can't you see the planet anyway?"

"No, of course not, this requires a whole armada of cyclopean telescopes and they have not been developed and will not be developed in the nearest coming centuries. Therefore, we see only one weak point, but we can measure their spectrum using infrared rays which are emitted by the surface of the planet. There are a lot of interesting things: the atmosphere lets something through, and absorbs something else but since physics is the same everywhere, we know that at such and such a wavelength there must be a dip in the frequency and the like. And we see all these dips and in such and such a place there should be a dip from oxygen, more precisely, from ozone. It is visible in the spectrum of the Earth but in the spectrum of that planet, named 47 Librae it's not. There is not the slightest hint! And in the spectra of four more known exoplanets, which are similar to the Earth in everything, it is also not visible."

"Did you take the spectra readings yourself? How did you see the reflection of a star?"

"No, not me. Spectra readings are exactly what the experiment was started for. Obtaining the spectrum is like skimming cream, it's what everyone wants. I took aim at what was hidden deeper and used it for temporal analysis in visible light. It is more difficult to observe the planet in visible light than in the infrared range, the star interferes even more strongly. If you just look at the light curve of the planet, you will not see anything there, only noise. I forgot, do you already know what the Fourier Transform is? It is powerful stuff. If we conduct a Fourier Transform for the light curve, then if there is even a weak periodicity hidden there, drowning in noise, it will come out in the form of a peak in the Fourier image, and if the noise is huge, and the periodic signal is negligible, it will still come out if you watch for a long time. Something showed up for me, a rather wide bump with a center at a period of twenty-seven hours. These are the clouds of the planet, twenty-seven hours is its day. Where there are more clouds, the planet is brighter. They rotate with the planet and give out a period of rotation, but clouds are impermanent, they move. Therefore, the Fourier Transform shows a bump, not a narrow peak. After a year and a half of pure observation time, something interesting appeared: a weak but narrow peak on a period of twenty-seven point two hours, it could only have been caused by something firmly attached to the surface of the planet. This is by far not the end of the story but let's take a breather. Ask me anything if something is not clear."

"Why is the planet called that?"

"It's named that way because it is the 47th star in the Libra Constellation. There was such a contemporary of Newton named Flamsteed, he numbered two and a half thousand stars. The star is like the sun, although its mass and luminosity are a little less and its life expectancy a little more."

"Why planet b? So is there also an a?"

"Heavens no! For some reason, they decided to reserve the letter 'a' for a planet behind the star itself. People had some vague arguments for such a rule and this has been customary since the 1990s, when the first exoplanets began to be discovered. However, there is a planet c, it's cold like Mars. There are also d and e, those are gas giants. In general, the system looks a lot like ours, which is not so common.

"Sixty light years?" Does this mean you are now studying the light that was emitted when I was lying here before?"

"Yes, that's what it means... Listen further... When I discovered this peak, they decided to close the project. The *Darwin* had been in operation for more than twenty years. The fuel for the micro thrusters was running out, the solar panels were dying out, some of the electronics had already totally stopped functioning. We needed a two million kilometer space expedition by the service team. It didn't seem like that God awful much, some one and a half billion, cheaper than a flight to the moon in both directions. Then a global whining began: the economy is in recession, there are more pressing needs, life still has not been found, the goal of continuing the experiment is incomprehensible..."

"How can such a goal be incomprehensible? What, are they crazy?"

Both of them sat and thought, looking at the river through the eyes of the elder Mark. A three-deck tourist ship was sailing far off the right bank. Exactly the same ones sailed here in the time of Mark Jr. against the backdrop of the same mountains and under the same clouds. The same smells, the same peace. Nothing seems to have changed in sixty years. No matter how everything else had!

"Crazy, you say... No, rather, they just all went stale. It was you who lived during good times, when the goal was always clear and bright, but good times tend to pass, like youth. The flames are not enough for many generations. So the global whining about incomprehensible goals began. In short, if the project had been closed, I would have remained with my barely hatched peak at a period of 27.2 days, but we won because we spoke wherever possible, and explained and finally convinced everyone. As a result, volunteers organized a special fund to support the expedition, where people contributed a hundred or even twenty dollars. Of course, one and a half billion cannot be collected in this way, but the governments of the countries participating in the project were apparently ashamed and chipped in for a service expedition."

"The team has done an excellent job since then, *Darwin* has been working for fifteen years now, better than before and for four complete years out of those fifteen it has observed 47 Librae. My peak grew and became unkillable, in other words, statistically significant. It told us that we definitely see something on the surface of the rotating planet. But what? I plotted an average daily brightness curve but still couldn't see anything! It already seemed mystical! But then I accidentally saw a picture of the Earth from space and on it, the sun's glare in the ocean. And in the glare, almost a quarter of the brightness of the entire image of the Earth! And how did I not guess before?! I ran to the computer and in ten minutes changed the starting point of the rotation phase. This task made it within your power to determine where on the planet the highlight should be, and count the rotation of the planet from that point, which changes with the seasons. After half an hour I had an expressive curve with a *trough* of one third of the day and a plateau of two thirds. This means that two thirds of the circumference of the planet is covered by the ocean, and one third by the mainland. The ocean and the mainland on the planet are sixty light years away, can you imagine?! However, this is all very approximate, the picture should depend on the latitude, after all the glare at different times of the year appears at different latitudes. We knew the parameters of the orbit, but we did not know the inclination of the planet's axis of rotation. And only by accumulating data for five years, two years before the expedition and three after, were we able to restore both the tilt of the axis and the approximate geography of the planet from twenty degrees south latitude to fifty degrees north. In the northern hemisphere there is one giant continent covering up to half the circumference of the planet. It narrows to the south, and another smaller continent appears in the southern hemisphere. However perhaps further south it becomes wider, we cannot see there. The reflection of the glare of the star provided us an example of the geography of the planet, like the beam of an ancient TV or more precisely a scanner beam. The rotation of the planet is like a horizontal scan and the seasonal movement of the glare along the latitude is like a vertical one."

"Awesome! And that's all I have to do?"

"You have to be, to be..."

"Did they name anything after you?" with timid hope asked Mark Jr.

"There was one anecdotal case, thank God, it did not take place. At a recent anniversary, a major science official suggested naming 47 Librae b, Selina. My hair stood on end. I did not expect such vulgarity and I was ready to collapse from shame. And all of the people supported it and applauded. Then, I half fought back and the story of renaming the planet quieted down."

"Why was it vulgar? After all, it sounds beautiful, like Selena."

"Yes, although you read good books, I remember that you had a serious problem with taste. God, what music were you listening to? Pop is bad! Oh well, it will soon pass. Let's talk about something else."

"What about Mars? After all, they should fly there soon!"

"With Mars, oddly enough, everything is in order. It's actually much better than with the Earth. There are already more than a thousand people living there, some of them were even born there and they are not planning on going anywhere. They predicted that life on Mars would be worse than a term in any earthly prison, but the fact is that a meaningful creative life in prison is better than the empty passing of time in the most beautiful paradise. They are creating a new world and are quickly expanding the walls of their "prison". They already have a nuclear power plant operating on Martian uranium, powerful earth-moving equipment and huge halls under ten-meter-thick roofs. The roofs are held up by pumped air pressure from below. You grew up during a good time, everything was advancing. Having lived the next sixty years, you'll understand this very well. Right now, there would not be the slightest chance of winding up the Martian epic. But the deed is done and the Martians almost have no dependence on us. There only remains rare flights with settlers and tools and to be honest, I envy them."

Mark Sr. also talked with Mark Jr. about all sorts of things that in fact lie outside the main stream of our story. Finally, the past did not so much dissolve as simply fell asleep in the memory of Mark Selin, but not without leaving a trace.

Wow, Mark thought, *he had just fulfilled his youthful vow, and it was great! He remembered so much! It was as if life had become longer. No, not really longer... How could he be more precise...?* Mark concentrated, looking at the surface of the river, where the mountains were still reflected above the clouds. *Here: it is wider and deeper! I just tensed up, came, felt and remembered, and life became a little wider and deeper. Too bad it's coming to an end...*

When he started heading down the river back to the car, Mark tried to shoulder the boat and realized that the sun had horribly burnt his shoulders and back.

What the hell was this? he thought. *After all, back then he did not burn at all! And it seemed this year he had already been in the sun quite enough... All sorts of protective creams exist for this. I wonder what they put into them. In theory, the heavier the element, the better it absorbs ultraviolet radiation. Lead? No, most likely harmful. Tungsten? It's a pity to spend money on such nonsense. Oh!*

They could probably use salt, cesium-iodine is a scintillator used in gamma-ray detectors... However, these were just idle arguments, designed to brighten up a hike that turned out to not be very pleasant with a boat that he could not hoist on his shoulder.

Here we have to leave Mark, although his life is far from over. He still has some things he needs to do. However, we are forced to say goodbye as our narrative jumps ahead forty years.

Mongolian Park

In what directions can the idle chatter of two cool professionals go to? Probably only God knows, but in general, much further than in their own business conversations. It all depends on the circumstances, their moods, their location and the stars above their heads.

In the mountains of Northern Mongolia, the summer nights are cold, but for a couple of hours after sunset, the earth retains some of the daytime heat and that is the time for the mating concerts of small living creatures.

On that late evening in the river valley, a combined chorus of frogs and grasshoppers could be heard in a cacophony of sound and an incredibly starry sky reigned over everything. It seemed that the stars were twinkling in time with the grasshoppers, or the grasshoppers along with frogs all in time with the flicker from the heavens.

Against this background, quietly, so as not to interfere with the frantic concert that was in progress, the conversation started: "...Yes, the universe is in its prime, you might say it's just an orgy of life."

"Well, a heyday is very relative. We sit here on a living island, among thousands of dead planetary systems, and rejoice."

"But what about Cygnus 68?" the younger interlocutor asked.

Note: Here the author is forced to apologize for the fact that he gives the direct speech of the characters without any adaptation and with all the terms and slang words they may us. The fact is that the "bird" language of professional scientists is expressive in itself, and when you try to translate it into a universally accepted one, it turns into a faded mess.

"Sorry," the slightly older interlocutor answered, "but the oxygen line there has only a three-sigma rating significance. Just a bunch of sad sobbing. Do you know how many three-sigma effects have faded into history?"

"I know, but it all depends on the context. A three-sigma was shown on only a dozen Earth-like planets where it was possible to capture the spectrum. This is a level of confidence somewhere in the two ninths, not really just sad sobbing."

"Well, let these two ninths warm our souls. The moral here is different, even with Cygnus 68, life in the universe has turned out to be depressingly scarce, especially intelligent life. So ours is priceless, and that's all."

"Yeah, but with what frequency do some of the alpha rulers of the gloomy people in our wonderful world start using nuclear blackmail? For little things every twenty years, for large ones once every half a century approximately and then another appears on the horizon. Try to explain to them about the pricelessness of life.

"This one has a thin intestine."

"And where is the guarantee that the next one will not be so thin? They look like they come off the assembly line! And everyone has something consoling and sacred for their subjects in their bosom: faith, rage, nation, hatred, victory or war, maybe a sacred state, sacred power and great teachings. All these sanctities, in fact, are needed to strengthen power and justify the right to beat heads. Only life for them is never sacred, it interferes with power. And nothing changes from century to century. All new well-armed chiefs and new Pharisees and new Goebbels, and there is no end to it. Sorry, if I say all this, they only change their sense of style and sense of humor. But how can I say otherwise, if sooner or later, alas, they shoot?! Why is there no hint of even the most shabby artificial radio signal from any direction? That's why. The lifespan of developed civilizations is short, that's the whole answer. Short, since all the technical power created by the sane minority is at the disposal of the powerful and other idiots."

The man, uttering this tirade, smoothly switched to a raised tone, which caused the surrounding grasshoppers to become quiet. Noticing this, both interlocutors fell silent until the grasshoppers resumed their party and he continued in an undertone.

"Old as the world, you are repeating back to the twentieth century. Carl Sagan and others. The first to say anything about the silence of the cosmos was probably Fermi. And now it's the middle of twenty-second century. For two hundred years we have been somehow getting by.

"In addition to all of that, Martians have appeared, who obviously will not be reached by some crazy leader. But in general, you are right when you imagine what can happen in a million years at the current rate of change... It is better not to think about it. All that is left is to believe in something. In some secret springs which will launch evolution. You know, in the first half of the twentieth century there was this amazing man, Teilhard de Chardin..."

"How could I not know?! The Omega Point and so on. In my youth it seemed to me that it was a gate to the astral, a portal in the form of a capital Omega, to where herds of mammals and crowds of people moved."

"So, being a Catholic priest and theologian by profession, he in fact turned out to be the most ardent singer about evolution, for which he received a ton of grief from his colleagues. By the way, he also got it from biologists at the same time. For him, man was only an intermediate link in evolution and the final point, the Omega Point, is God, roughly speaking. Of course, to be honest, all this has no predictive power and, from the point of view of science, is complete nonsense but from the point of view of philosophy it's a very good metaphor, in fact it's even optimistic. And good metaphors don't just lie around everywhere. Look how long the noise has been around for things like self-organization, synergy..."

"That's exactly what the definition of noise is. These 'synergists' cannot predict anything."

"Yes, but maybe it's not in vain that they beat around the bush, they feel something with their canine instinct, but they can't understand what. Maybe there really is some kind of powerful law that we don't understand, the opposite of the second law of thermodynamics, which inevitably produces more and more complex and developed systems? Then a being who does not understand this law sees it in action, and it might seem like a movement towards a total goal."

"Alex, any evolutionist would tear you to shreds right now! They tell you: Nature has no purpose! There is no question 'for what', only the question 'why'. There are causal chains and that's it!"

"Sorry, but there are laws regarding large numbers and their work is not traceable from direct causal relationships, the same with the increase in entropy. There are non-linear dynamics, look at the weather, where causal relationships are quickly broken, but laws of another level arise. What if the unknown Omega Point is something like an attractor, to which life aspires as a gigantic dynamic system?! Teilhard de Chardin writes that Omega sends out rays from the future, and these rays pull all living things towards them, a perfect metaphor for a dynamic attractor. To us, it may seem like a goal, because we do not understand the law, but we see the stubborn desire of nature to develop. I'm telling you that good metaphors are not just left lying around! And if so, then all the talk that man is a dead-end branch of evolution because of his overdeveloped brain is complete nonsense! If so, then humans are another step on some main path."

"You lay it out so beautifully. On a galactic scale that might work but such a law is unlikely to guarantee against the complete failure of even the greatest branch of evolution on any single selected planet. We'll just cut ourselves off and ask: Where is the great path?"

In the time between that phrase and the response, a breeze managed to quickly rustle up and subside – not a wind mind you, just a light breeze. The Earth was cooling down, sending its heat straight into cold space, heat that would never heat anything again, radiation from the Earth would forever travel through space, cooling down along with the expanding Universe.

"I agree. It would be nice to extend the growths from this branch onto other planets, which, in principle, is what the Martians are doing. Actually, they have already done it and now they don't need anything from us, except sometimes the occasional unexpected thing, which are in fact more like whims than necessities. By the way, one of the mechanisms of evolution is the isolation of parts of the same species from each other so that they do not interbreed and thus slowly and naturally diverge. In my opinion the Martians don't even understand how important they are."

"Damn, the *Darwin* flew and it worked great. If it had kept flying we *would* have already had three times as many Earth-like planets and full confidence in Cygnus 68. But they were so greedy just giving money for a second service expedition. Bastards! Oh if your grandfather were alive twenty years ago, I can imagine what he would have said about all this!"

The interlocutors fell silent but the frogs and grasshoppers kept on with their orchestra with all their might, interrupting the twinkling of the stars with their chorus. After a moment's pause, the older man continued: "Okay, don't get upset. We had it with us!"

"What did we have with us?"

"Eh, you don't know the classics... Russia, from the twentieth century, Mikhail Zhvanetsky. However, this is purely a national specificity."

The man took out a bottle of cognac, two glasses and two apples from his backpack...

"Well, a toast to the Omega Point!"

"To the Omega Point! Oh, that's good! By the way, this theory resonates well with the Purpose Postulate. Do you happen to know who the author is?"

"In my opinion, historically it doesn't have a single reliable author. I have heard one story that once in a student hostel there was yet another dispute about the meaning of life. As usual all of the participants were categorical, hot headed and stupid and it occurred after midnight. Finally, one student who did not participate in the dispute exclaimed: 'How tired

I am of all of you! The point is that as many intelligent beings as possible must observe and see the universe and perceive it in all its glory. And that's it, so all of you go to hell! Let's go to sleep!' That story is probably just a joke but it fits."

"By the way, all ten commandments, well, maybe except for one, also indirectly fit into this postulate. And what the Martians are doing is its direct embodiment. But listen, then there is Selina..."

"Listen, Roland, please don't use that name in front of me! My grandfather was furious every time he heard it and so was I. 'Don't waste your name in vain!' he said."

"Well, there is 47 Librae b, the closest of the convenient but lifeless planets. Is there a way to transfer our lives there? So that there will be a new branch of the Earth's evolution! It would be remarkably isolated there."

"Well, you turned it down... An ordinary ship would get there in about six hundred thousand years. A well-sterilized blank of whatever you upload onto it would arrive. Can you imagine what the dose from cosmic rays would have been once it got there?!"

"Well, if it runs on uranium, theoretically, up to one thirtieth of the speed of light could be obtained making the trip about two thousand years long.

"Theoretically is the key word there. Practically only one hundredth at best and that would take six thousand years, more like ten thousand really. A slightly worse sterilized blank would arrive. Some prokaryotes might survive but even that is unlikely."

Unfortunately, here the author is forced to interrupt the conversation and intervene with his own comments since someone out there might not fully understand the problems that are being discussed. The fact is that many readers are brought up on science fiction in the form of books, films and television series where the heroes fly from star to star in a matter of seconds using various bizarre ships and uttering science-like spells. Willingly or unwittingly, the reader might get the impression that sooner or later technological progress will make manned interstellar flights possible, if not in seconds then at least in years. This will not happen! Manned flights between the closest of stars, while purely speculative (and then under the influence of a number of wild assumptions), are just as impossible in practice as a supersonic city taxi. Manned flights over distances of dozens of light years would really only be possible if the pilots lived for many thousands of years. The limits on speed are bound by the laws of nature, ones that have about the same status as the one that does not allow you to pull yourself out of quicksand by your own hair.

What is more, science fiction writers like to pronounce all sorts of words like "zero time transportation", "teleportation" and "wormholes". The first two are just empty words, although "teleportation" is jokingly used as a metaphor for an effect said to be found in quantum physics. As for the wormhole, that is a completely hypothetical scientific concept, although it is possible that they do exist. What is more, if someone really found themselves near a wormhole (although hardly any of them appear to exist in the observable part of the universe) and sends their ship into it, then whatever remains of the traveler and the ship after having passed through the bottleneck of the wormhole in the form of some kind of exotic matter, may cause some kind of causal event to occur as a response in another universe where the hole leads. Can this be called a journey? Decide for yourself.

So please dear reader, forget about any tricks with space-time. Our world and ourselves, in relation to space-time, are like tiny light ripples on the surface of an endless sleeping abyss. Nature has placed man on a tiny island in terrible isolation, leaving within reach only a few dead planets and satellites and piles of "construction debris" in the form of asteroids.

To understand the full extent of our isolation, let's mentally reduce everything ten billion times, or ten orders of magnitude, at which point the Earth becomes a grain of sand with a diameter of 1.2 millimeters and the Sun is the size of an orange, located fifteen meters from the Earth. Let suppose this model is in the yard of the author in the Moscow Region. Where would the nearest star be then? Approximately in Krasnoyarsk about 4,000 km away, and where would 47 Librae be? Somewhere over 60,000 km away, but as there is no such remote place on Earth, another grain of sand and an orange would have to be placed somewhere in space about one-sixth of the way to the Moon. Now take that 60,000 km and stretch each and every one of them out ten billion times, then you may understand the true scale of things.

Back to the topic of science fiction, we in no way intend to accuse them of disinformation. They have interstellar travel but that is an artistic convention, sometimes helping to convey something good and important to the audience. We have a different task: to show humans in their true and real loneliness, isolation and helplessness, that is the real drama of the human race but it is not a death sentence! Nature, although having treated man cruelly, isolating him in space, also endowed him with reason, spirit and perseverance (at least selectively). Therefore, a person is in principle able to challenge their own isolation and even win. Only for this you need to show utmost perseverance and spend a lot of time, an amazing amount of time. However, let's return to the conversation between Alexander Selin and Roland Wolf, especially since he just turned the dialogue in this direction.

"So, what if we hide all the biology in a thick shell?"

"Not really a good idea. It would be too heavy. I think something more like a magnetic field. Place everything in the center of a superconducting solenoid. The Earth's magnetic field works very well: beneath the radiation belts, the background radiation is an order of magnitude lower than above."

"Wait, what about superconductivity?" If the windings have to be cooled, everything becomes meaningless. Do you remember what the average radiation temperature is in the Galaxy? Outside of the galaxy the equilibrium of the temperature with the cosmic background radiation is about two point seven kelvins; however, inside the Galaxy it should be much higher."

"I don't remember, I only know that at the Lagrange Points in the shadow from the Sun it is about forty. Far from the solar system it should be less, if I recall correctly interstellar dust is heated to about twenty kelvins."

"But there are already superconductors for such temperatures! That's really why people have been fighting over high-temperature superconductivity for so long! To be in outer space for a long time! All other uses are small compared to that."

"Wait to rejoice because the field must still be maintained purely at a mechanical level. It will also expand the windings. We focus on a field of ten Tesla, that is not a joke. H squared by eight pi, seven orders of magnitude down: forty joules per cubic centimeter, seriously. So... to calculate the force, it is necessary to express the energy field in terms of the circumference of the windings and differentiate along the length. So, Roland you are younger than me, so differentiate! Don't forget to express the magnetic field through the length of the winding under condition of maintaining the flux. The field outside the solenoid is allowed to be neglected as I'm still contemplating." I just keep on pouring.

"Uh, two pi per R square, instead of per R we substitute the circumference, L, divided by two pi... Oh, now I'm getting confused in these pis and twos... From H square, L appears in the fourth in the denominator ... we reduce it, there remains a minus to the second degree, so... Yeah, here is the answer in kilograms of force: the circumference in centimeters multiplied by two, divided by pi. If the radius of the solenoid is ten meters, then it turns out four tons per linear centimeter of the winding."

"Oh, that's quite reasonable! My old climbing rope holds four tons, is just sixty meters long and weighs, four kilograms maximum dry. There are far stronger materials than my rope but let's calculate with a margin of four kilograms per linear centimeter. A solenoid twenty meters long would weigh only eight tons. That is despite the fact that the junk that needs to be transported will be somewhere around five hundred tons. It's possible to make a radius of twenty meters and forty meters in length and that would be sixty-four tons."

"Well, there you go. Making all ends meet!"

"So it all works out... Good! Everything should come together, I think. We are plotting a charitable deed."

"Is it pleasing to God, I mean in the sense of approaching the Omega Point?"

"More like the Purpose Postulate."

"So that as many reasonable people as possible... See and perceive it... Yes, I agree, this is right on point. By the way, while you were counting the tension there, at the same time I figured out how much a solenoid with a radius of ten meters with a field of ten tesla would cut off the flow of particles. It will cut out everything below fifteen GeV and cut the flux down to fifty GeV. It will facilitate the suppression of radiation by hundreds of times. True, the holes must also be plugged along the central lines of force, into which particles might fly in at small angles to penetrate the axis. You can increase the radius a little. It is necessary to calculate, but I think that suppression by a thousand times, or even two thousand, is quite realistic. Frozen embryos will arrive alive, albeit a little irradiated."

"Well, that's what I'm saying: a charitable plan should be realizable!"

"What is the intention? So far, what we are doing is only fantasizing, albeit they are noble fantasies."

"Just think, if we came up with a similar concept at the park council, we would be laughed at. No question that money would be allocated or not, but simply laughed at. Well, we could assemble a team at our institute and write out an intelligible concept where all ends are made to meet, but where will we go with it? This is a project of absolutely unprecedented scale and to be honest civilization has not yet matured to such projects! It's not just the cyclopean costs, the idea has one very weak point, and that is the problem of motivation. Imagine, people will work hard all their lives, invest their souls and everything they have, other people will be forced to deny themselves something or other and no one will see the result. Even worse no one will be sure that everything will work out. Neither their children nor grandchildren will see the result. Only unknown descendants spanning dozens of generations may eventually find out whether it worked or not."

"Wait, but when Michelangelo started building St. Peter's Basilica, he also knew that he would not see the result and those who helped him and those who paid, they knew the same thing: neither they, nor their children, nor grandchildren would see the final cathedral."

"I'm afraid people have lost some important qualities since those times. Namely the ability to work for centuries, and then, there's this: after you look at everything, the cathedral is actually being built right on the ground that is in front of you. You will see what was done in your presence, the foundation pit, then the foundation, then part of the walls. And you know that it will eventually be built there, it will not go anywhere, it will all become part of a grandiose building, the contours of which you can already see. But in our case? They will put in a lot of hard work and talent and most likely they will have had to work for more than one generation. They then create a kind of miracle and then it is sent to nowhere, into the darkness of future ages."

"Wow, it took off and the Devil took it. Then it blotted out the stars, and then silence."

"They are cold-blooded, unlike you and me. In that regard we have warmed up to this but they have not. It's gotten colder and so it's gotten quieter and we keep chirping along as if nothing has happened. Maybe it's time to head for the tents?"

"Wait, we didn't discuss the most important thing. I mean about motivation, Alex, do you still have any left?"

"Of course, what else?"

"Well, pour another one."

"Hold on. So what's the motivation?"

"A toast! To her! I can't speak for others so I'll speak for myself. You know my style of working is as a lone wolf. I always choose my own task and terribly hate all kinds of scientific collaborations, with their publication rules, their subordination and their politics. The fact of the matter is that what you call fantasies, smell like business, for which you can drop everything else and harness yourself to for the rest of your life. Let there be less science than technology, let them have to work in large teams; consider it as the lone wolf smelling the trail of real prey and calling the pack, and as for me personally, I am not afraid that the work of half a life will fly away into a dark distant future. And you know what? Somehow I feel like I'm not the only one."

"No, you're not alone. I don't know how to express myself as artistically as you, but perhaps, yes, it's worth it. By the way, it's good that we settled in here in the Mongolian Science Park. There is always more freedom in the outback. In the Canadian Park, for example, the Canadian government is trying to keep an eye on the affairs of the council, although the park does not exist on their money. Here, they say, it would be nice if you worked in this or that promising direction, we can even provide additional financing. But for this there is no prospect of doing that and by the way, isn't it time to re-index the rent? And so on and so forth. This increases entropy and greatly interferes with work, nullifying the benefits of civilization. But here, the rent is paid and the Mongolian youth receive a first-class education on account of the fees. And no one else cares about anything and everyone is happy. Therefore, if there is a chance to push through a similar project at the level of the park council, then it is here. It is clear that starting at the level of the council of a park is ridiculous in such a case, but at least there will be some kind of seed."

"So, let's make a declaration of intent right now. We, the undersigned, form the 47 Librae Concept Development Team hereby declare.... You are older than me and have a higher status so you will be the boss."

"Well, adventures always adorn life. Let's try it. This means that we will have to sacrifice a three-day rest on the lake, we will not sit around there anyway. Then we'll go back tomorrow and start to gather people for brainstorming. And now the order of the chief: to the tents."

Auditorium B3

There was only one way to get to auditorium B3, where the brainstorming session was scheduled, and that was by walking along a six-kilometer-long trail and climbing 800 meters along the ridge. The trail wound through a fragrant larch forest, and from time to time it opened up and offered a view of the valley below and the Institute of Astrophysics, the Physics Faculty, the university campus, the lake and a scattering of houses along the slopes and the bottom of the valley. The way up, if one was not in a hurry and enjoyed the views while finding and picking berries, took about two hours, the way back, one.

The auditorium itself was built on a decent-sized larch frame on a stone plinth, all built on a rocky ledge. In principle, everything that was needed was there: running water fed by a creek in the gorge, electricity from solar panels and a pair of gasoline generators. It even had a sauna with a small outdoor pool, but the most impressive thing about the structure was the way it was built. Not a single mechanism larger than a chainsaw or circular saw was used. Not a single kilogram of cargo was delivered by any vehicle other than hikers. Everything, including the roofing, cement and double-glazed windows, was carried up on the backs of professors and post-doctorate and graduate students. For the rest of his life Alex Selin was proud that he had single-handedly dragged a ten-kilowatt generator weighing sixty kilos up to the site. As it turned out, it wasn't so bad: with a good solid backpack on the back, use the leg and the entire foot not bending at the knee, lean strongly on the ski poles, move slowly and evenly. And when you finally remove the load, take two steps or it would seem that you would leave the ground and take off.

Where does such irrational enthusiasm come from in serious people? Why did they need voluntary hard labor to erect a meaningless structure in a meaningless place? To understand what motivated the pundits, it is necessary to explain what the Mongolian Science Park is and how the civilized world lived in the middle of the 22nd century.

All of the major science parks of that time (and there were three more, Canadian, Argentinean and South African), if you call a spade a spade, they were reservations for the very smart. At that time, the more or less prosperous part of the Earth's population was very comfortable with the idea of the homeostasis of civilization, that is, a stable sustainable existence without rapid progress and economic growth but also without the problems and crises associated with them. It was a kind of civilized stagnation through the voluntary self-restraint of a responsible enlightened world community. The whole idea looked very logical and attractive from a strategic point of view: slow development without cataclysms and disruptions is better than development at a tenfold pace with global problems, crises and the risk of self-destruction. The easier you go, the further you'll get, as they say.

In theory, everything looked great. However, first and foremost there was a problem with the voluntariness of self-restraint as more and more radical methods of suggestion had to be resorted to. Secondly, the stagnation did not develop with enlightenment. The overly enlightened require movement, they can't sit still and they don't understand how it is possible not to do something new and interesting if doing so is possible. They had to hold back, and to slow down development means to slow down mental activity. They created a commission to control global TV channels: more positive, less analytical and less embarrassing information. They carried out reforms in the field of education, reducing mathematics, natural science subjects and literature, and they introduced new history textbooks. Most countries underwent reforms for the optimization of national academies of sciences. At the same time, they closed several space projects and froze the construction of the largest research facilities.

The results became visible ten years later and everything appeared to have worked out: the restless educated youth finally calmed down, society became simpler and calmer and life slowly became more measured and predictable. However, worrying signs began to emerge. The infrastructure of civilization began to deteriorate, everything seemed to be being repaired and updated, but minor defects accumulated due to the inability of staff to carry out independent thought, not everything fit into the instructions, but the most disturbing thing was that religious fanatics and fiery leaders began to raise their heads. They always raise their heads when prosperous humanity goes headlong into a state of quiet and warm well-being.

The globalized and stabilized world, feeling threatened, realized that it was necessary to keep the gunpowder dry, without real science, without new technologies, without first-class education, everything could end badly. Although doom was already beginning to loom over the horizon, the decision turned out to be a compromise, something like: "We urgently need to restore science and quality education but let them exist somewhere separated from everything else."

So that is how international scientific reservations appeared. They were well financed by international funds and talented youth from all countries flocked to them, then the leading scientists moved to them as well. And from all over the world, some, like an invisible substance, were drawn to science parks. Let's try to describe it with the help of the following metaphor: We might say that someone is "a person with a divine gift", everyone understands what that means, although it is difficult to express the same thing in other words. It's not really a talent and it's not exactly spirituality, and certainly it's not passionarity. It's not even at all religious but all the same, "God's gift" is clear and to the point. So, this concept is applicable not only to individuals, but also to the most diverse human communities. The carrier of God's gift can be an educational institution, a scientific institute, a club or even a city. The personal composition of the community in this case does not play a decisive role, the matter is in the atmosphere, gifts or not. If there are gifts then bright manifestations of intelligent life occur in the community which from the outside might seem redundant and irrational. The construction of Auditorium B3 was one of these cases.

Its creators hardly gave any thought to exactly what their activity was called, they just worked with joy and passion. They felled trees, dragged logs, stripped them clean, carved them to fit each other, cut down logs and finally raised heavy logs placing them on the frame of the building only with the help of ropes. High above the valley in the cool mountain air, basking in the sunshine under clear skies among the ridges where larch forests give way to alpine meadows, they worked hard together, giving them the feeling of a surge of strength and the ability to move mountains upon returning to their laboratories. Let us take the liberty of defining such human behavior as sporting unification.

Nothing lasts forever, and someday God's gift will leave the Mongolian Park too. Auditorium B3 will no longer be used for its intended purpose and will become dilapidated, or maybe it will turn into an expensive restaurant for tourists, to which a cable car will be stretched. This of course all depends on the fate of the territory. A long time ago, almost two centuries before the events described, the author sadly watched how the divine gift gradually faded away in scientific towns near Moscow: how the typical faces of random passers-by changed; how completely boring scientific seminars became; how the famous Physicist Days disappeared into oblivion; how collective meetings marking the New Year with sparkling skits turned into corporate parties with hired mass entertainers, gypsies and pop music, and then they disappeared altogether. Of course, someday God's gift will return to these parts, but not before the country becomes completely different.

In those days, the days which are being discussed in our story, the Mongolian Park was on its way up. Therefore, on a fine August morning, on the path to Auditorium B3, about thirty people with small backpacks came up to brainstorm. Some were carrying fuel for the generators, some had food, some had drinks, which was by no means superfluous after heavy brainstorming. The main issues on the agenda were the power plant and main engines for the 47 Librae Project.

The Storm

Lex Selin took on the role of moderator, immediately pulling in the reins sharply: "Let's start with the power plant. I propose to immediately forget about the controlled thermonuclear proposal. We are not engaged in fantasy but in a real project. I also suggest forgetting about the radioactive decay generator as it has too little energy output. The only viable option is a uranium reactor, and even with that a speed of three thousand kilometers per second will be a record if the weight of the fuel is halved."

"And how do you propose we reload the fuel rods over thousands of years?"

"This is not about re-loading fuel elements, there shouldn't be any moving parts at all!"

"What about generators?"

"Steam generator? Turbines?"

"Don't make me laugh!"

"What century do you live in? Haven't you heard anything about thermoelectric converters?"

"So why are they not used at industrial nuclear power plants? Efficiency is low, right?"

"Yes, efficiency is not very good, twenty-five percent. Apparently, the specific yield per unit area is small, and the price is high–"

"Stop, stop!" Alex intervened. "We don't care about the price at all. In any case, the project will cost so much money that everything can be made from platinum, this will hardly affect the cost. Better efficiency would be nice but there is no choice. The service life will still be a problem, right now it is dozens of years, but thousands are needed–"

"Wait a minute, this is complete..." began the red-bearded professor of the Department of Condensed Matter Physics Richard Waxman, nicknamed Red Waxman. However before continuing, he looked around, examined the audience and hesitated ... "This is complete... well, this is so full of... Well, you understand that," the professor muttered in embarrassment, and this embarrassment only emphasized the hopelessness that was evident in his words, he then became silent for several seconds. "Can you imagine what it's like to increase the service life of something from ten to many thousands of years? A thousand times! And what about the reactor core? With an engine? Yeah, and with electronics none the less! What are we doing here? Is this some kind of kindergarten! Why did I spend two hours dragging myself here, I don't understand..."

At that moment, everyone had been anticipating the most interesting part, and they looked at Roland Wolf, waving his hand.

"Come on, Roland," the moderator nodded.

"Sir," this address does not bode well, "if you don't understand why you dragged yourself here, then you simply didn't bother to figure out what this was about. Otherwise, with a clear conscience, you could have stayed at home. This is not about a project that is at the forefront of modern technology. For the sake of such a project, as you put it, I would certainly not "drag" myself here. We are talking about a project that goes far beyond the limits of modern technology and for which it is worth pushing the limits. We came up here to sketch out a preliminary concept that would fit into the laws of nature, and not into existing technologies.

So dear colleague," Roland addressed Waxman and it sounded softer than 'sir', "can you name the fundamental reason why the life of thermoelectric converters cannot reach ten thousand years?"

"There is perhaps no fundamental reason, but there are many practical reasons. Well, there is the accumulation of defects, diffusion, radiation swelling... This is not my area really, I need to contact Bob Price from the Canadian Park, he will explain."

"Explain why it is impossible, or how to approach the matter?"

"It depends on which foot you are standing..."

"As homework could you contact him and invite him here at our expense? We'll worry about getting him on the right foot."

Then we talked about the reactor. As one, everyone remembered about liquid fuel based on uranium salts, it would be enough to pump it in slowly and no overloads would be needed.

They were all set to appoint a person in charge and give them homework, but then someone suddenly waved their hands and shouted, "Stop, stop!" It was tall Jose.

He was known for his propensity for speaking nastily and taunting others, anyone in fact, for any reason. At the same time, he never actually did nasty things to anyone, quite the opposite really, he always came to the rescue without waiting for a request and helped and supported everyone while continuing to grumble and swear. This property in him baffled people: how to coincide the two? When a person says pleasant things and then does nasty things, is much more familiar. In the end, people got used to it and they began to joke: "Jose hasn't come after me for a month. I must be getting insignificant."

"My dears," began Jose, "what are you storming with here? Your brains or asses? Why pump fluid? There is a lot of ballast in the saline solution, except for the uranium! Let's take ordinary pure uranium two hundred and thirty-five rods, for example ten kilometers long, and we will pull them through the core at a speed for example, of one meter per year.

Even if they hang out ten kilometers behind, they won't interfere with anything and at the exit of the active zone they will evaporate and ionize and then go into the engines, as an already working substance. The core can be adjusted, made heterogeneous in length: the beginning is optimized for pure uranium two hundred and thirty-five, and the end for uranium that is pretty well-used up. One more thing: neutrons from the beginning of the core will go to the end and there they will help to burn out the spent rods. Oh, and a feed mechanism that gives one meter per year can somehow be built for a ten-thousand-year guarantee period."

"You are tormented by criticality to maintain a clean two hundred and thirty-five! It will go up a little and it will explode. You won't even be able to collect the pieces."

"Okay, we're tormented, but we'll do it. You think that's a problem! It's you who are all suffering, for the second year you cannot calculate the merger of neutron stars in three-dimensional space."

"Sorry," said the young post-doctorate Volodya Drake. "Why move all the rods in one direction, and then fight with the inhomogeneity of the core? Let's alternately move half of it forward and the other half back. It will be more homogeneous, and at the ends the neutrons from the fresh incoming rods will burn out the uranium in the spent outgoing rods."

Anguish appeared on Jose's face. He obviously liked the idea, while he could not in any way chide the young author. Finally he concluded: "Wow... It happened... Through the mouths of babes..."

"Yes, yes," Alex replied. "I guess I like that idea too. I really like it. It also appears like it will free up a couple of hundred tons of payload. So, Jose, are you taking on the development and trappings of a competent reactor engineer?"

"You, Alex, first of all listen: you don't know how to moderate shit. How much time has been wasted because of you on all sorts of nonsense! You appointed yourself."

Alex listened calmly and politely.

Jose then stated, "Well, okay, I'll take that, although to be honest I don't understand a damn thing about any of it–"

"Stop!" cried out a biologist named Gene (Eugene) Cooney. "Are you planning to build a biological defense zone around the cargo zone? After all, the precious embryos will fry there, not only from the cosmic radiation but also from the neutrons... And how much will such protection weigh?"

"No defenses!" Roland nearly screamed. "We remove all biological objects all the way to hell, release them on a line a few kilometers back. One kilometer back is better than any concrete of lead protection. It seems that many of those here view the ship as having to be a single structure. Why not let it be a caravan of separate parts connected with thin lines and cables! At the front is the engine and behind that is the reactor with the radiators and hanging rods. Behind them is the payload surrounded by magnetic protection. The acceleration is negligible, which means that the weight on the lines will be insignificant."

"So then it's decided! That's accepted as an obvious rational solution!" the moderator announced.

They then discussed the cooling system for about an hour. As it turned out the radiators would be the largest part of the ship in terms of size, about two hectares, although not so significant in weight. Here, area was what was required, for the tubes and the membranes of black foil between them. The discussion heated up.

"If you put water into such a radiator, all the pipes will shatter into a million pieces! Can you imagine what the pressure would be! It will be at least a thousand degrees in the active zone, what do you think the water vapor pressure will be like there? The horror!"

"What kind of water? You need to make two circuits. Let the radiators be filled with liquid metal, lithium for example. The pressure from water vapor would be absolutely off the scales."

"Lithium means that the minimum temperature will be about two hundred Celsius. The entire structure will be at around the same temperature. It that acceptable?"

"Why not? What will be damaged there at two hundred degrees?"

“The electronics will suffer at that temperature and really, in general, the colder the better for all structures and mechanisms, especially within the context of ten thousand years.”

“You can use gallium at about thirty degrees. However, the warmer, the smaller the radiator. The difference in area for thirty and then for two hundred degrees is significant.

“Wait, but if the reactor stops, then the end will happen right there, the coolant will freeze and everyone and everything is done.”

“Why on earth should the reactor be stopped? The easiest way is if it works with minimum power all the time. It accelerates for half the way then slows down for the other half.”

“It is useful to stop here,” Alex said, “because none of us understands what temperature conditions are comfortable for reactor structures. I think we need to use gallium and run it at the maximum allowable temperature, say, the same two hundred Celsius, less chance of a disaster if any. This should be given to someone as homework. Dick, are you up to it?” Alex turned to Red Waxman.

“I’ve already plugged in Bob Preece. It’s highly unlikely that he understands everything about the temperature parameters. Let me talk to him, and then he’ll recommend someone else who can help. Oh, and I don’t like all this! A problem on top of another problem, but since I promised, I’ll try to find something out.”

After that they argued for about twenty minutes about the physical geometry of the radiators, there were proposals for two wings on the sides (then the ship would resemble a gigantic butterfly) or three or four flat planes along the axis of the entire structure (then it would look something like a semi-sailboat mast several kilometers long). The dispute then turned into the purely aesthetic direction, some liked the butterfly more, some the mast. The decision was then postponed.

Finally, the participants started discussing the main engine. Alex immediately warned them not to hold back on any options or ideas they might have had in relation to the acceleration of particles in an electric field. Any significant volume charge would instantly kill any such engine design. The only option was a neutral plasma engine but what neutral plasma engines are in operation? Only the VASIMR? And what kind of creature is that? Heated plasma pushed in a magnetic nozzle? With a maximum speed of three hundred kilometers per second? Is that thermal speed? Well, that's completely inadequate, it won't do at all! We need almost ten thousand kilometers per second and running on uranium fragments. Has nothing else been invented?

And then came the Roland's stellar moment.

"How can you say it was not invented? Nature invented the necessary engine thirteen billion years before the appearance of man! Haven't you heard anything about space jets? About quasar jets? About protoplanetary disk jets? Or finally about collapsing supernova jets? There is the ready-made engine for you. The speed of the outflow is almost the speed of light. The Lorentz factor is up to seventy! As for the x-ray binaries, it is close to what we need.

"The idea is as simple as a felt boot. We take a magnetic field and start to rotate it, then we inject plasma into this field. What can plasma do there? Just slide along the lines of force. So it will slide like beads on a rotating spoke, gaining radial speed due to centrifugal force. This cannot go on indefinitely however: the Coriolis force will act on the plasma, and the magnetic field is not made of iron, it will begin to bend in the direction opposite to the rotation along with the plasma and twist into a spiral." Roland depicted what he was saying by rotating his hand, and to be more convincing he started squatting and jumping when depicting wide turns.

"The magnetic field along with the plasma will expand, like a once tightly twisted roll, pushing the environment apart. This is how some stars explode. What if the field lines form a cone around the axis of rotation, with an angle of, for example thirty degrees?" Roland twirled his outstretched hand, making a cone. "Everything will be exactly the same only a swirling field with plasma inside it will fly forward with continued acceleration until the energy of the particles exceeds the energy of the field. Here, look." Roland found the necessary pictures on the network in a few seconds. "The Eagle Nebula, what a handsome creature: the jet of the protoplanetary disk is a parsec long, and in this photo, it is one and a half parsecs in length. If for someone that is not enough, then here is the Cygnus A quasar: jets with a span of three hundred kilo parsecs. We can arrange exactly the same thing, only smaller. You need to take the magnetic poles so that the lines of force go out at forty-five or thirty degrees to the axis of rotation," Roland depicted the windings of magnets, twisting the fingers of two hands, stretching his arms forward to the sides, "then spin it," Roland described the circle with outstretched arms, "and inject plasma obtained from evaporated spent fuel elements into it."

"And how do you rotate the field? Moving parts again?"

"How does the field in an ordinary synchronous electric motor rotate? A three-phase current is supplied to the windings, and that's it."

"And the current from the thermoelectric converters is constant, which means that it needs to be transformed. Do we use high current transistors? For ten thousand years?"

"Does that run contrary to the laws of nature?"

"That runs contrary to common sense."

"What we have here is the primacy of the laws of nature over common sense!"

"So how do we achieve the desired speed of the outflow?"

"We have at least three things that can control the speed: the magnetic field, the size of the windings, and the speed of the rotation. Of course three-dimensional magneto hydrodynamics simulation must be done as well. I'll be taking this as my homework."

Finally, all of the tables were moved and set. A few people went downstairs and left so as to get home before dark but most of them stayed for the night, dinner was worth it.

By tradition, Alex turned from a moderator into a toastmaster. The first toast required an increased dose of pathos: "Well, today we have taken the first small step along the path, the length of which we can't even imagine. Many people know the feeling of enthusiasm at the beginning and the despair in the middle of a difficult path and that awaits us. The reasons why our endeavor may fail are in the thousands. These can be everything from money, to politics, to technological obstruction, to the immaturity of humanity and so on and so on. However, there is only one reason why it will succeed and that is the strength of the spirit of those who are involved and will get involved in this matter. So a toast! To the strength of the spirit!"

They drank while standing, saying things to each other like: "Well, how is the strength of your spirit?"

"Let's raise our spirits right now!"

The second toast was proposed by Roland: "Alex is right, but a miracle is still needed: money must appear. In today's rotten world, this will certainly require a miracle. Let's drink to the miracle that needs to be added to the strength of our spirits. Well, maybe let's put it a little milder: to luck! May we all be lucky!"

The third of the toasts which had been announced in advance was delivered by Gene Cooney: "I would like to wish all those present health and a long, long life. We will need them in order to hold out until the completion of the project. Not to see its result, God forbid, but until the moment when this colossus leaves the Earth's gravitational field and nothing more depends on us. I suspect that this will take a long time. So! To a long life for all!"

Then there came the unannounced toasts which arose with such frequency that if anyone conscientiously drank to everything that the speakers proclaimed, then there would have been practically no chance of anyone maintaining decent form until the end of dinner.

The dosage of pathos gradually decreased, and suddenly tall Jose stood up, looming menacingly over the table: "You are all monstrous villains! Look at this! There is a clean planet with beautiful ocean beaches, azure water and not a soul! Now imagine what will happen if your project comes true! In twenty thousand years there will be nowhere to step on the best beaches because of all the fat bodies of vacationers! Mothers will be clucking, their capricious children will be screaming... The horror! It would be wonderful if your project failed to hell. But it won't fail, you bastards, since I've gotten involved in it. And why did I get involved?" José knocked over a glass of grappa and a coffee cup of Calvados with these words, and then shouted: "What misanthropes you all are!" He then sat down and, resting his head in his hands, stared with a ferocious gaze at a point between the door and the window, beyond which, against the background of the fading sky, the neighboring ridges blackened into night.

Noah's Ark

A month passed and all of the participants in the brainstorming session received a special invitation: "On October 15th, at 19:00 in the large assembly hall of the Faculty of Special and General Physics, a solemn yet fantastic performance of 'Noah's Ark' will take place. The presence of the participants in the 47 Librae Project is strictly obligatory."

The last phrase sounded so intriguing that the participants came out almost in full force, but not only the participants. The hall was filled to capacity and more, there were not enough seats and people were standing along the walls. Finally the curtain opened.

The fanfare and drums from Richard Strauss' Sunrise sounded. A graduate student from the Department of Planetary Science came out onto the empty stage in sandals and a sheet wearing a gray disheveled wig with a beard hanging by strings, a plastic halo over his head and holding a huge staff. Looking around the hall angrily, he hit his chest with his fist and broke into a monologue:

"I, the patriarch, the virtuous Noah,
hereby protest
against the surging filth of the earth,
which has hidden all the land everywhere."

At the same time, Noah violently slammed his staff into the stage and to the amazement of the audience a third of the staff went into the floor. Noah tried to pull out the staff, but it was in vain.

The hall was filled with whispers: "How did they set that up?"

Apparently, they had made a hole in the floor and filled it with building installation foam. Noah, feigning a moment of embarrassment, waved his hand at the protruding staff and continued:

"Here you have Gomorrah, and here is Sodom,
one's a homophobe, the other gay,
here is a leprosarium, and there is a madhouse,
and there are no ideas.
"Vilely they sin! The Bushman, the Finn,
the Jew, the Greek.
A rod should be driven into them below their backs,
to insert spiritual bonds!"

Diligently portraying a brutal desire, Noah completed the ascertaining part of the monologue, walked around the stage holding his hands behind his back, looked around the hall intently and, raising his hand with his index finger outstretched, moved on to the constructive part:

"I announce that yesterday having made,
accurate calculations and cross-checks,
I have determined that the time has come
to build the great ark.

"For only it will save all from sin
forty righteous wives,
a thousand tons of creatures in pairs,
cattle and masters of science.

"And I won't give a penny
for the fate of the hopeless Earth.
To work, my children,
Shem, Japheth and Ham!"

Three students ran onto the stage, dressed up just like Noah, only without halos, two with black hair and beards, and one (Ham) with bright red hair. Each had a large name written on their sheets. Then the immortal melody from Disney's, the *Three Little Pigs* could be heard and all four began singing "we are building, we are building our ark, our ark", and they ran and got classroom tables from behind the curtains, folding them into the figure of a child's boat, almost the size of the stage. Having laid out the contour with the tables, they did not stop and began to put up the second row, tables on top of tables.

"Looks like they cleaned out all the classrooms on the floor," was heard from the hall.

Having finished the second row, they began the third.

"I think they cleaned out the other two floors as well," the front row clarified.

But Noah and his sons did not stop with the third row and began to pile up the fourth, for which they had to lift the tables on outstretched arms, standing on tiptoe.

Finally, the fourth row completed, Noah again addresses the audience:

"There it is! How handsome it is!
Ready to surf space on atomic steam.
All that remains is for us to load
pairs of all kinds of creatures into it."

This is where Ham comes in:

"Listen, father, even though our ark,
is made of oak, is heavy, large and made of steel,
in the holds, there are elephants and whales,
all creatures in pairs will not fit."

Noah tries to scratch the back of his head but the halo is clearly preventing him from doing so. He first shifts it around on his forehead, then irritably tears it off and twisting it, launches it into the hall. The halo is followed by all the eyes in the audience and to the light murmur of the public, solemnly glides over all the rows and smoothly descends into the gallery where someone catches it. Continuing to scratch his head, Noah measures the size of the ship from stern to bow in steps:

"Although he is a boor, he is right, the red-haired devil!
So let's lighten the load.
So, oh, children, on board we load
a seed from every creature."

The sons run backstage, take out boxes and kegs with tags. Then Noah announces the inscriptions on the tags:

- Red caviar
- Black caviar
- Pollack roe
- Whale caviar
- Seeds of field herbs
- Sports lawns
- Buckwheat
- Walnuts
- Seeds
- Poultry eggs
- Quail eggs

- The eggs of livestock and wild animals
- Canned spermatozoa.

All this is placed on the tables of different tiers. Finally, Noah crosses his arms, indicating that the loading is complete, and continues:

"That's it. Let's break the bread..."

(Pulls out a huge flask from under the hem of his robe, takes a gulp, snorts and shakes his head.)

"What good fellows we are!
The reactor is on fire.
Sim, give it up finally!

"The coldness of space and the darkness of the ages
are better than demonic darkness.
We are leaving the earth
to search for other worlds.

"To you who laugh at me,
God will send you a judge!
The righteous Noah sends you
to hell! Goodbye, adieu!"

At the same time, Noah tore the sheet off his chest and the fabric ripped with a crack, exposing his chest with its dense fake vegetation. Then all four put their hands on the structure, and an incredible thing happened: the 'Ark', being a shaky pile of auditorium tables weighing a ton, under the same fanfare and Strauss drums, sailed across the stage and disappeared backstage.

The audience rolled with laughter and sobbed with delight. The reader is unlikely to share that enthusiasm, since student humor usually does not stand the test of time: in retrospect, it all seems quite stupid. Such actions must be observed live, perceived in the accompanying atmosphere. Nevertheless, the performance left a mark in history that stretched for thousands of years, giving the project its full name.

The project participants gathered in a group in the foyer.

"Well, now people will hang the name 'Ark' on our project, and it won't be possible to get away from it."

"So, it means that Alex will be our Noah, only his appearance is rather weak. He needs to urgently grow bushy hair and a beard and dye it gray," said tall Jose.

"So then you will definitely be one of the sons, and we even known which one, Ham. Dye your hair red," Roland replied.

"Okay, I'm ready to be Ham with capital letters, and you will remain a boor with small ones," Jose retorted.

"I think I like that idea," Alex concluded. "There is something optimistic in the name Ark 47 Librae. A hint that Ark Cassiopeia 57 and so on should follow."

Press Conference

Lex came back from the Park Council meeting as excited as if after a fight. Roland, tall Jose and Gene Cooney were waiting for him.

"Well, how did it go?"

"Twenty."

"What?"

"Million. Bucks."

"That's not really that much."

"How can I put this? That's all I could shake out of them. At first, they

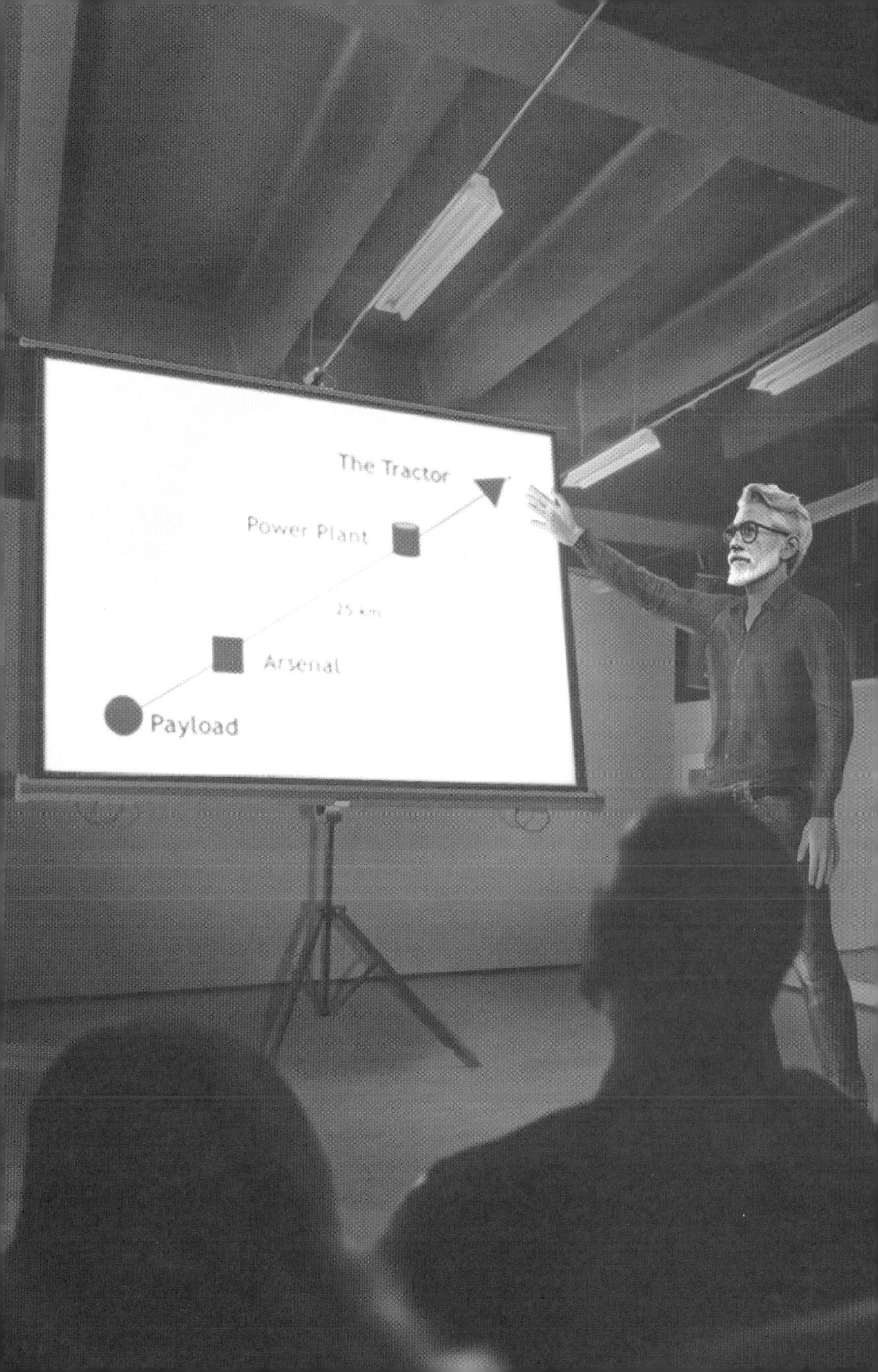
The Tractor
Power Plant
Arsenal
Payload

wanted to get off with two million, they tried to say: 'That will be enough for business trips, invitations and a couple of conferences, and then we'll see.' Not a single objection was raised. Everyone was silent. I told them that that was not even enough for the buildup. I then told them that they would then be using it as a banner project and repeating how they are involved in it. I asked them if that wasn't worth at least thirty million to start with. 'After all,' I said, 'if we convince the world, hundreds of billions will flow in!' That is, I resorted to demagoguery but of course it worked! In general, there is an interesting effect with them: each member of the council, individually, is a smart and decent person, but when they get together for a council meeting, their sum total turns out to be dumber and more primitive than the constituent parts."

"What can we meaningfully do with twenty million?"

"We can set in motion a certain tangible number of brains. We need to urgently arrange a press conference. Let the world learn about the project from us rather than from other people's words."

"Where do you think is better?"

"In my opinion in Europe, in the same Geneva where CERN is still showing signs of life. It is full of semi-unemployed physicists who are looking for an ecological niche. In particular, the lion's share of theorists is busy inventing theories that are allegedly competitive with respect to the standard supermodel, which can neither be confirmed nor refuted. Of course, they are literate people, and some of them will be glad to change their occupation and enlist with us. A literate person is always a literate person no matter where they may be."

"Which of us will speak at the press conference?" Jose asked. "I wouldn't mind talking frankly to the journalists."

"That's why you shouldn't be allowed anywhere near them. There is another worthy target for you, the talk show host of the Court of Reason on WWV. He is a leading obscurantist who, when he lacks arguments, becomes so inflamed that he drools. You pretend to be a felt boot, and he will swallow the theme of the Ark like a hungry wolf and then you will deal with him in such a way that his hysteria will not be simulated but the real thing will happen to him. You can do it."

Two weeks later, a press conference was held in the large CERN conference hall. No one expected that the hall would be packed to capacity. It seemed that the world had long lost interest in such big projects and as such, interest in general, other than certain personal ones of course.

"Did something in the world really change and these people also missed real deals?" Roland asked.

"Why not?" Alex replied. "Did you think you were the only one? Another issue is how representative is this sample? I mean those who have gathered in the hall. Let's go!"

"We are very happy to see so many nice smart faces all gathered in one room," Alex began, without even having to prevaricate. "Everyone has probably heard about the planet 47 Librae b with its oceans and continents, a dense atmosphere and a temperature comfortable for life. This planet has everything for life, except for life itself and the oxygen it creates. Many have probably thought that it would be nice to settle there! People settled on Mars, and life on that planet is much easier and more pleasant! The only problem is sixty light years.

"A person can overcome such a distance only in the form of a frozen embryo and only then if it is well protected from cosmic rays.

"Now let's step back a minute. Our idea is in line with the ancient theory of panspermia: life, once born, travels through the Universe in the form of the simplest of organisms. When it arrives at a hospitable planet it then takes root and evolves into higher forms and this continues to happen forever. A very beautiful idea, but it faded away when it was realized that the Universe is not eternal. Is there any sense in the theory that life did not originate on Earth four billion years ago, but somewhere else five billion years earlier and jumped over to Earth with great difficulty? And even earlier in the Universe there were no conditions for it at all. Thus, panspermia lost its status as the eternal sower of life. Its projection onto the past lost its meaning, but in the future, it has another role: the road to the future.

"How much time has been allotted for life in the Universe? At least tens of billions of years, that could be considered an eternity. Maybe hundreds of billions of years. And how much time is allotted for our civilization on Earth? This is a sore point. Over the past two hundred years, the world has already been on the brink of disaster several times. And what will happen to it in a million years with such dynamics? I don't even want to fantasize about that, but you can look at it from the other side. Man lives for an insignificant time but he gives offspring. And the human genus? We do not know, but there are serious suspicions that its lifetime is also negligible on an astronomical scale. Is the human race capable of producing a kind of offspring or branches that can survive earthly civilization? It has already produced one offspring, the Martian colony, which will soon become completely independent of us and if, God forbid, we commit total suicide, will be able to return and populate the Earth.

"Mars for its part is one of a kind. What if we, in the form of frozen embryos, jump to another planetary system? That will open an unlimited path for the expansion of life and mind! This could be called directed panspermia."

Alex stopped for a few seconds and looked around the room. Part of the public was clearly bored with all these revelations about panspermia, chaos theories and directional evolution; they were commonplace for most of the audience. People wanted specific ideas and assessments. Alex felt that he underestimated the audience and decided to omit a couple of general passages, quickly moving on to the point.

"Now is the time to drastically reduce the pathos. All such dreams and theories are shattered when one begins to imagine such an event in detail. That is why for a long time the idea was stuck at the level of dreams and general reasoning. To move the dream forward, someone had to decide to get into all these details, to try to push through them. Someone had to plunge into the task, and do so for the rest of their lives. So we plunged in, knowing full well that retreat would be a disgrace to us. Today's press conference cuts off the last chance to go back for us.

"So, we present to you the concept of the Ark 47 Librae Project.

"First of all, its general scenario: Assuming that uranium remains the most efficient and convenient fuel, a realistic travel time to a twenty-parsec target is twelve thousand years, that's with fuel weighing half the total weight. Any attempt to reduce this time dramatically complicates the task. Human and animal embryos are not capable of withstanding cosmic radiation for such a long duration but we can protect them with a strong magnetic field. So, for about seven thousand years the ship slowly accelerates, reaching a speed of three thousand kilometers per second, then slowly decelerates for five thousand years and finally finds itself in orbit around 47 Librae. It is also important that the power of the reactor and the engine's mode of operation are both maintained at the same level during the entire flight.

"Further, a part of the equipment being taken there will remain in space, in particular a radio transmitter with a parabolic antenna directed towards the Earth. It will transmit an arrival report and detailed images of the planet in the hope that there will be someone on Earth to receive the information. The payload lands on the planet somewhere near the coast. Robots, powered by solar panels, build a long-term station and begin to carry out a program designed to last ten to fifteen thousand years. The ocean and land are seeded with photosynthetic flora, after which all that remains is to wait.

"Wait at least ten thousand years until there is enough oxygen in the atmosphere. Then we can move on.

"In fact, ten thousand years is a mere moment. On Earth, tangible oxygen appeared more than a billion years after the start of photosynthesis, but we have very productive plants that did not exist then. Our forests emit so much oxygen that they could saturate the atmosphere in several thousand years. However terrestrial forests take back most of this oxygen when leaves, dead trunks and branches rot. Only what is deposited as peat does not bind oxygen. This means that all putrefactive bacteria, all woodworms and bark beetles must be kept in the strictest quarantine for the first ten thousand years. Let crumbling leaves be pressed together with fallen tree trunks first. The thickness of this carpet should be ten meters on average over the entire land. There has never been such a biosphere on Earth, even in the Carboniferous period. All this has to be modeled and tested experimentally and we have to start now. We have to create models and produce things that have never even existed.

"After a shock dose of oxygen, it will be necessary to act more subtly to make the planet's biosphere approximately equal to that of the Earth. To be honest, this seems even more difficult to me. Professor Cooney understands this better than I do and he can tell you more about the second stage in the questions and answers session after the presentation.

"All this time, the embryos remain frozen in nitrogen. They waited twelve thousand years to get there and they can wait ten thousand more. In general, the ability to wait patiently is one of the most important factors for success in such an endeavor. When the oxygen concentration reaches an acceptable level, the planet begins to remotely resemble the Earth and natural food grows on it, the program for raising animals and humans is then turned on.

"Behind the scenes of each item of this scenario are almost countless unsolved problems, but we noticed one amazing thing: as soon as you start to thoroughly understand any of these terrible problems, you first discover that there are no fundamental reasons why they cannot be solved, and then you find a specific solution. We even jokingly formulated the principle of the Ark: Every task related to the performance of a charitable deed has at least one solution.

"And now a few words about the vehicle. It will not be a ship, but a caravan, like a caravan of barges, with a tractor that flies in front for the first half of the journey and behind for the second half when it is necessary to slow down. The tractor's engine is based on a magneto-rotacin mechanism – this is a rotating spiral magnetic field injected with plasma which produces a jet capable of propulsion up to speeds of several thousand kilometers per second. We call the engine *Roland's Corkscrew* because it was designed by Roland Wolf, who is sitting right here in front of you. It is based exactly on the same principle that ejects the jets of quasars and protoplanetary systems. The only difference is that here you have to throw two jets in one direction; one inside the other, to compensate for the moment of rotation, otherwise the tug will spin. Naturally, in the inner and outer jets, the field will rotate in opposite directions.

"Somewhere seven kilometers behind the tractor is the power unit, a nuclear power plant to be exact. Its power will be ten times less than the power of current industrial stations, but the total energy that it will produce is an order of magnitude greater. There are a large number of problems associated with it; radiation swelling of materials, wear and so on, but they are all solvable. The power unit will be the most bulky structure thanks to the radiators, which look like the wings of a gigantic butterfly and have an area of about a hectare. In space, there is no other way to release heat other than to radiate it from a large surface. The "butterfly" will have long whiskers and a tail: uranium rods about six kilometers long will stretch back and forth from the power plant. They are continuously pulled at a rate of half a meter per year in two opposite directions through the reactor core. At the exit, the spent fuel will be crushed, transported to a tugboat, where it will evaporate, ionize and be injected into the engine's magnetic field as a working substance.

"Twenty-five kilometers behind the power unit is the useful non-biological load or the Arsenal. Such a large distance required to protect the reactor from neutrons.

"The fourth, so-called barge, of the ship will be five kilometers behind the Arsenal, that is the headquarters. In it will be the main processor, an observatory and a radio station with a parabolic antenna fifty meters in diameter, all the time directed towards the Earth. It will regularly report on the status of all systems and some scientific data. For all twelve thousand years the Ark will transmit messages reminding Earth of its existence, and pray to God that for all twelve thousand years there will be those who are able to receive and understand the signal of the Ark. Finally, the biological unit, the Incubator, is protected from cosmic rays by a superconducting solenoid.

"When all this reaches the target in near-planet orbit, the computer will select a landing site, two blocks with the payload will separate into dozens of landing modules, which will land separately on one patch. The tractor, headquarters and power unit will remain in space.

"With that said I would like to end my opening speech and move on to the discussion."

For the first ten seconds, not a single hand was raised. The host, looking at the huge hall, began to get a little nervous and was about to say thank you to the speaker when a dozen or so hands stretched out at the same time. The host with the microphone approached the nearest hand, which was being raised by a young man dressed in the style of the 1950s: a plaid short-sleeved shirt tucked into loose trousers with a high belt.

Ralph Alver (Associated Press): "What will the implementation of your idea give the inhabitants of the Earth?"

Alex Selin: "What does procreation give the inhabitants of the Earth? Why is it important for us to know that we will have not only children and grandchildren, but also great-grandchildren, and further generations that we will not see? The essence of our idea is to facilitate the birth of a child world, which genetically will flow from ours but will exist and continue to live its own destiny and evolve in its own way. To be honest, for some of the inhabitants of the Earth this is something they are indifferent to and perhaps their number is large, but there is another part of the inhabitants for whom a future child world will fill life with new meaning. Although this part is smaller, it is large enough to become a support base for the project."

Roland Wolf: "I would like to add a couple of words for the majority of the population that Professor Selin mentioned. Something will also be passed on for it (Alex looked sternly at Roland as if saying: be politically correct!). What I mean is that there will be tangible benefits for everyone from the project, in particular the development of new technologies, and not in the distant future, but in many of our lifetimes. These will namely be: machines and installations that can work for decades and centuries without repair and without human intervention, robots capable of reproducing themselves without human intervention, totally new building structures and assembling equipment, spacecraft engines for long-distance flights in the solar system and of course many other useful and pleasant things."

The next person the host looked at was a thin gray-haired man with a long face wearing shorts and a white T-shirt with the inscription Chaos Rules the Universe on it.

Chuck Mezner (CERN Theoretical Department): "Wouldn't it be easier to solve the problem of human abiosis and send ready-made people there along with all the embryos? After all, the conditions there are much better than on Mars. People would be much more successful than machines in dealing with all of the arrangements."

Eugene Cooney: "You see, it is possible to conserve human tissue and organs for such a long time, possible but difficult, and in the foreseeable future most likely the whole body, but alas, not the brain. There is a fundamental problem here; the brain must keep working all the time, it somehow even works when a person is in a coma. Otherwise, all memory is lost. Therefore, if you send a "canned" person, a vegetable will arrive. In addition, a heavily irradiated person is much more vulnerable than an embryo. The more scientists struggle with the problem of suspended animation, the more hopeless it looks."

Another person wishing to ask a question attracted the attention of the presenter by the fact that he did not just stretch out his hand but was nervously waving it. He was a small, quick-moving man with a beard and an emerging bald spot on the back of his head.

Oleg Verkhodonov (Troitsky Variant Newspaper): Is it possible to simplify the task by dividing it into two stages? First, we send all sorts of algae, bacteria and plants that will create an oxygen atmosphere. It will be easier and cheaper. And then human and animal embryos will be sent into a ready-made environment. While the atmosphere is being created and prepared there, there will be scientific progress and the second ark will be much easier to send."

R.W.: "Let me answer this question. We also discussed this option and it has remained with us as a backup plan if needed. Are you sure that in ten thousand years there will be progress here? Are you sure that in ten thousand years there will even be people here, including those who wish to carry out the second stage? Pray to God that there will be... Personally, I'm not sure of anything right now. We want to make sure that from the moment the Ark leaves the Earth's orbit nothing can stop its primary mission, so we want to send everything at once precisely because anything can happen to civilization. Our civilization, as a system is too dynamic and has too many strong connections that make it unstable, and as we see it, no homeostasis will take root in it."

Further, the host despaired in finding any intelligible principle regarding whom to choose and dejectedly wandered down the aisle, silently holding out the microphone to the nearest person. The next one looked like the definition of a pirate, wild black hair, a wild bear, raised eyebrows and a sharp wily look in his eyes.

Bob Trout (Der Spiegel): "You say forests will provide oxygen. But forests need soil. Where will it come from on a dead planet in such a short time?"

Y.K.: "Algae and bacteria will be the first to go into action. Algae will be spread not only in the ocean but also on land. Wherever there is a lot of rain, it will grow into thick wet mats, as has already happened on Earth, only it will happen much faster. The mats will act as oxygen cushions for aerobic bacteria and other organisms. Further on with the goal of expanding the oases, mushrooms and lichens will take over, digesting the surface of the rocks. After them moss will grow then cereals and all of this will set the stage for forests, thousands of times faster than on Earth because the slowest action necessary in this scenario, evolution, has already taken place. Plus we can create the necessary genetically modified organisms. All of this is, of course, a very approximate picture. It will take years of research to plan everything in detail and so it is reliable."

The next person the host gave the microphone to seemed to be from the 19th century, he was sporting a vest, a carefully combed beard with a mustache and had a wide forehead.

Bernard Darr (European Space Agency): "On Earth at first, all of the oxygen given off by algae went to oxidize iron in the ocean. On that planet the same thing should happen, until all the iron is oxidized, which can take millions of years. However, the oxygen content in the atmosphere will be negligible. How are you going to deal with this problem?"

(Roland looked pointedly at Jin and whispered: "You can't walk around this auditorium on an old goat! Come on!")

Y.K.: "We will win with high speeds. On ancient Earth oxygen was released in the oceans, but not as quickly, because most of it was immediately bound in the water by dissolved iron compounds. We propose doing it another way, through the forced release of oxygen by plants, thus oxidation will be faster. The sea will also be seeded, this will create an *oxygen barrier* at the surface. On land, oxygen will also be bound but even more slowly than in the sea. But you are right, for millions of years part of the oxygen will be used for the oxidation of minerals. In the oceans of the planet there will be less oxygen than on land, and thus consequently, less life. The settlement process will then be carried out in reverse order, first land, then sea."

The host, apparently, having decided to adhere to at least some principle, began to hold out the microphone exclusively to women.

Beatrice Winsley (Press Office of the Vatican): "The Creator settled man on Earth, he provided him with this particular planet. He reserved other worlds for some other purposes unknown to us. You are going to disrupt the Creator's plans. Will this lead to some unfortunate consequences?"

A.S. (quietly): "Roland, wait, it's better for me to answer here. (Into the microphone.) All three of us are here as atheists. But the question you raised is quite reasonable from our point of view, only it should be formulated in the language of ethics, not religion: do we humans have a moral right to expand beyond the solar system? If in our strategy we are like locusts, to devastate, pollute the world and flee to a new untouched one, then, of course, we do not. However, I will try to answer in your language. Are you sure you understand the Creator's plans correctly? Don't you think that perhaps he reserved the lifeless planets just for us? Or did he do so for other intelligent creatures lost in space and time? And the gigantic distances to those planets, is this not a test for the maturity of our kind? Perhaps the Creator has given intelligent beings the opportunity to spread throughout the Galaxy, thereby securing an unlimited future for themselves. Almost unlimited... Maybe this is what he had in mind? Maybe this is predestined by the Creator? However, in order to embark on this path, one must overcome the most difficult obstacle, which can only be done by those who are able to devote their lives to distant descendants.

This is not only an intellectual, but also a moral dilemma, fellow locusts will never overcome this barrier. Don't you think that this version of the Creator's plans would be more indicative of his wisdom than yours? I can repeat the same thing in another language without resorting to the metaphor of the Creator, but I think that there is no need."

After finishing the tirade, Alex took two deep breaths and wiped the sweat from his forehead with his sleeve.

Renata Hallosh (Nace): "The number of species on Earth is such that it excludes even the very idea of transferring the Earth's biosphere completely. Insects alone, not to mention bacteria, count for millions of species. How will you determine the worthy and unworthy to be allowed places in the Ark?"

Y.K.: "Of course, we cannot talk about the resettlement of the entire terrestrial fauna and flora. The challenge therefore is something like this: assemble a 'basic package', namely a set of species sufficient to allow many stable ecosystems to take root, together they will make the planet similar to Earth, not exactly similar, but overall the same picture. The problem is that many species will not survive in the new conditions. However, others will find new niches and begin to evolve and branch out. The main criterion for the basic package is that there should be enough species so that total diversity grows over time and does not fail. Right now, the basic package is an abstraction, we do not know what it should consist of. For example, do we need a variety of gnats in the basic package? Or parasites? The only way to understand this is to take into account the huge number of connections and model the development of different ecosystems. This is exactly what ecology does, but it has not yet reached such a level as to predict the evolution of any biocenoses from an arbitrary start. We have to work hard to take this science to a new level, something which will also be useful on Earth."

Eleanor Barbidge (New York Times): "How will the first man appear on a deserted planet? Will it be raised by robots? What happens regarding the psyche of the child? Will he become a man in the full sense of the word?"

Y.K.: "This is the least clear stage in the entire project. Robots that are able to take on the role of parents do not exist and it is unlikely that full-fledged artificial parents will appear in the foreseeable future. Robots that ensure the life of a child, although a problem, are completely solvable but the child needs communication and education, which is much more difficult. We have some ideas about this, but it's too early to announce them as they are still too raw."

The presenter suddenly changed the principle of selection and began to choose from the mass of raising hands by choosing people of exclusively non-European appearance.

Chui Ze Tai (People's Daily): "How much would such a project cost, and where would the funds come from?"

R.D.: "The cost is very difficult to estimate, because it requires technologies that are not yet available. The order of magnitude is somewhere in the area of a trillion dollars and perhaps even possibly more. This might be akin to the annual budget of an average country. A lot perhaps but for the whole of civilization it should not be so noticeable. Another thing is that there is no mechanism for accumulating or gathering this money. No country can afford such spending. We can only do it all together, but there is neither an organization nor a precedent for such an endeavor. Therefore, we are counting on a miracle and, in order for it to finally happen, we will begin to act in full force with the insignificant means that we do have."

Kazuhiko Kato (Yomiuri Shimbun): "You said a computer would choose the landing site. What criteria will it use to choose it?"

A.S.: "Thank you for the question. The first criterion is proximity to an ocean. The salty ocean will be a source of elements for the production of robots and structures. We will not be able to transport everything that is needed there and will need to produce many things on site. The materials needed are in fact few in quantity, but are of many types. A significant quantity of the necessary substances is in sea water and it is relatively easy to extract them. Moreover, the ocean is the first medium for planting flora. The second criterion is the proximity of a river as they will need fresh water. It would be especially good if the river flows from the mountains. Then its deposits should be filled with many necessary minerals and ores, up to and perhaps including uranium. In addition, the place must be safe, high enough to avoid flooding, and the ground strong enough, preferably rocky, to avoid erosion. The area should be seismically passive, away from characteristic volcanic areas. Moderately low latitudes are the best suited. We have enough of these places at home so the site selection program can be developed and trained here on the Earth's surface."

Jan Narligar (Times of India): "At present, the establishments of most major countries are pursuing a policy of civilizational homeostasis. Don't you think that your project is contrary to this ideology, and if implemented, it will destroy the homeostasis that has been maintained with such difficulty?"

A.S.: Our answer to that question will be the shortest one yet: Yes, we do. Yes, it will destroy it."

Silence reigned in the hall for a few seconds, and it was not clear how it would end. Then contrary to all expectations, it ended with a growing applause.

"Well, on this optimistic note, I propose finishing the questions and move on to behind-the-scenes communications," the host concluded. "Let's thank the speakers again."

After the press conference, a guy in his thirties with lush black hair approached the organizers.

"Rob Waksman, CERN researcher. I would like to enlist on your team."

"Well, tell me something about yourself."

"All my life I have worked with a variety of data, in which I have achieved a fair amount of professional success, namely in high-energy physics and astrophysics. I have run out of interesting data, but I found a new hobby in the field of artificial intelligence. I am struggling with a task which has the conditional name of *Human Replica*. For example, journalists pester you with requests for an interview. You give a dozen interviews and you get really bored. Then you give the recording of these interviews to me, I ask you an additional series of questions, after which I form your replica, a kind of database with which rather tricky software works, combining ordinary codes and trained neural networks. When the eleventh journalist turns to you, you will connect with him via a video channel but it won't be you but a replica. It will reproduce your answers to their questions so that they will not understand that they are not dealing with a living person but with a model of the person. Your logic, your intonations, your typical speech defects, everything will be adequately and appropriately reproduced based on what you have said before. It will not be a cut and paste of your words, roughly speaking, it will be your exact model. The journalist will be pleased and you will be pleased by watching or reading the interview, although at this point it's sort of a joke.

"Of course, in reality everything is somewhat more complicated. There is a 'skeletal replica', something like a generalized model of human communications. Then, when your conversations, statements and reactions are added to it, the model begins to acquire your features. Of course, you can't get away with doing a dozen interviews, you need months of pure recording time for a replica to become like you. This is very serious work. The more diverse that the recorded material is, the greater the similarity will be. I have already deceived one acquaintance, having slipped in my replica's remarks instead of mine into a response to a phone call. The friend did not suspect anything at all. It can thus be said that the Turing Test has been passed. However, so far only in a relaxed three-minute conversation and today I finally understood why all this is necessary.

"A replica can be put to work thousands of years later, after the original is long gone. A replica of caring parents will be able to raise a baby who was born twenty thousand years in the future and sixty light years away, it doesn't matter, they can be in the form of a hologram or an image on a screen."

"Enough. Please remind me of your name."

"Rob Waxman."

"Could you fly to Mongolia and speak at the seminar? We'll pay for everything. Just please, do it in person. Before that we will still have time to talk about your remarks."

"All right, go to Mongolia, so to Mongolia. I will come as my own person, and the remarks will answer any questions after I send you a report."

"Well, we already have a Red Waxman, now there will be a dark-haired one..."

"Oh and by the way there seem to be a few other potential recruits out there who want to chat..."

"Looks like the world has begun to change," Roland said.

"Yes," Alex agreed, "I didn't expect to see so many meaningful faces in one place. Something is really changing."

"We are sitting on our reservation and can't see anything from it. If we get out then we need to do so at a gallop, so they don't notice important changes," Jin added.

All three were wrong. The world as such has not changed. It's just that the thinnest layer has begun to crystallize in it, something which will change the world in twenty to thirty years. They saw part of it in the CERN conference hall.

We are always interested in how our actions and statements resonate in the world, so we dive into the Web, picking out statements and comments addressed to us there, we then rejoice or we grieve. There is nothing reprehensible in that, a person should get a sense of feedback. We surfed the Web and are most often disappointed, not because the reaction to us is negative, but because it is weak, usually weakly positive. This is exactly what our heroes discovered a few days after the press conference, looking through mentions of it. Major news agencies only mentioned the very fact of the event in one line, despite the fact that their correspondents were in the hall and even asked questions. Apparently, from their point of view, as a newsworthy event the information given turned out to be rather weak.

"The stone we threw into the swamp turned out to be too small," Alex summed up.

"Or the swamp is just too viscous," Roland added.

"I think it's just that you gave a mediocre press conference," Jose put forward his version. "However, even if you had done it wonderfully, the result would have been the same, since the world itself is mediocre as such."

"Well, that's what I say, it's a swamp! But in this swamp there are wonderful specimens. Here is a letter that came to the public mailbox of the Ark from a schoolboy. Should I read it?"

"Go ahead, maybe it will help us relax a little."

"Dear Professors Alexander Selin, Roland Wolf and Eugene Cooney!

My name is William Pak and I am a ninth grade student at Istanbul High School. After listening to your press conference, I firmly decided to dedicate my life to the Ark. I am fond of physics, mathematics and biology. Our schooling is poor but I study a lot on my own. I have learned to differentiate and work with simple integrals. Now I am training to solve ordinary differential equations on a computer. I've studied the special theory of relativity and I can solve problems in relativistic mechanics using four vectors. I have a question for you: where should I go in two years, so that later I will definitely get a job on the Ark? If I knew I would start preparing for admission right now. I will also keep reading literature on the project and think about what I can do in the future.

Sincerely, Bill Pak"

"The guy must be urgently pulled out of there and brought to us before his fire goes out. When are the boarding school exams for the physics department?"

"In a month, but there are often problems with parents."

"In this case, there is the correspondence school. In any case, we need to answer the guy urgently. Who will take it on?" Alex asked. "But wait a minute: Why am I inferior to such a child prodigy? I will answer him and take care of it myself, and how intriguing it sounds: Bill Pak from Istanbul!"

Personal Angel

Lex got a call from an unknown number.

"Professor Selin?"

"Yes, sir."

"This is Paul Dors speaking."

"Who? Who?!"

"Dors, Paul Dors. The very one."

Alex was silent for a few seconds, not knowing what to say.

"Yes, I am listening carefully."

"I understand perfectly how you feel about me. Therefore, do not try to comply with politeness. I have a proposal for you regarding the Ark. I think if you accept my offer, it will greatly increase the chances of your plan."

"Well, yes our relationship with you is really complicated. However, the Ark is above all. I am ready to discuss your proposal."

"For this, it is best for you to fly to my Tmutarakan place together with Professor Wolf. It's a long way, twenty hours by air, but I'll book you first class and you can fly in comfort. Choose a time that is convenient for you, but it is better not to delay. Soon you will receive a message with all the details. You only need to name the date."

"Thank you, I believe we can name a date today."

"Then I'll be waiting. Bye."

"Bye."

Alex immediately called Roland, who was also speechless for a few seconds. The fact was that Paul Dors was the richest man of all time, the only trillionaire in history. He had become so rich because he was the creator of the Personal Angel and had become an absolute monopolist in its distribution.

What is a Personal Angel? you might be asking. Well, imagine a car navigator, "Turn right, move into the left lane, etc...." which extends to all areas of the owner's life: leisure, communication with people, household tasks, medical treatment, study, work (if it is not too creative) and even sex. Well, okay, not for the whole process of sex, but let's say for finding a partner. That is, it works as a matchmaker or acts as a prompter in an exam. Schools and universities fought desperately against it but in vain. How could they deal with a device that picks up the quietest whispers or finger movements and transmits them through a miniature speaker that can be stuck to the owner's palate? The interface of the Personal Angel was varied and sophisticated, glasses, bugs and different sensors. At first glance, it was not easy to see that a person was functioning under the guidance of an Angel but it was possible. How can you figure out if a person is listening to the monologue of a partner during a telephone conversation through an earpiece on the go?

Roland, traveling to the mainland, often had fun watching people in a state of dialogue with an Angel. It was the best way to pass the time before a flight when it was impossible to work. The funniest thing you could watch in a public place was guided shopping. For example, you might see a woman looking at something and then pull it out in front of her so that the Angel can also see it (the video camera is in the frame of her glasses), then she brings the tag closer to the glasses. On her face you might see bewilderment and disappointment then she whispers something and goes to the next rack of clothes on hangers. Slowly she walks along aisles. Stops, takes another thing off the rack and shows the tag to the Angel. Another heavy sigh and she moves on.

On the third try the woman whispers something, more and more emotionally, finally her voice gets loud: "Well, I don't like this color, it's not my color!"

The Angel, apparently, does not insist very much, gives new instructions and the woman moves to another clothes rack, picks something out and hope appears on her face. She goes to the fitting room and soon comes out looking completely lost. But if you have time, you can almost always wait for a happy ending: the pacified customer is walking out and in a package she has the fruit of the final consent.

Naturally, Paul Dors' corporation received most of its income not from sales, but from consumer goods manufacturers. The Angel could imperceptibly push the client to buy the products of a certain company and at the same time, the system did not act rudely or impudently with the interests of the client always being first and above all, and only when the choice was not an obvious one, was the client-firm preferred. No, the brainchild of Paul Dors was by no means a cheap hack.

Moreover, as the Angel developed, different versions appeared. The toughest of them was called "the Angel of Success." This one never let the client down, it made them do exercises, not eat too much, get up on time, and do everything that was planned for the day. At the same time, "the Angel of Success" showed a fair amount of tediousness, attempting to achieve the complete submission of the client. It is clear that this version was not to everyone's liking. A more popular option was "the Angel of Happiness", which in fact referred to its owner more condescendingly. It also pushed the client towards the right way of life, but did so gently and kindly and was not too insistent, sort of like a loving mother. Equal in popularity was an even softer model called "the Angel of the Love of Life" and finally the lineup was completed by an Angel called "Personalized Companion".

It's no secret that the constant use of a navigator contributes to geographic cretinism. If the driver got somewhere with the help of a navigator, then the next time, in order to get to the same place they will be forced to use it again, instead of a memory of the area all that remains is scattered fragments and a vile mechanical voice (for some reason, usually female), "Move into the right lane... etc. etc." Now imagine the effect of a "navigator" dictating actions to a person in all spheres of their life. Even if a person himself sets the goals for the Angel, just as when the driver gives the navigator the final address, they only execute short unambiguous commands.

A person operating with an Angel is not something that turns into a zombie but just a little more stupid and simplified. Numerous studies were carried out on this topic. The anti-correlation between the usage of an Angel and IQ was so obvious that it was not discussed further. It turned out that the person's income also anti-correlated, even for the owner of "the Angel of Success", not to mention the rest. The benefit of the hints did not offset the harm from the accompanying dumbing down, but it did not stop the mass consumers. Moreover, the person who bought the system initially felt discomfort from the fact that someone was commanding them all the time but after a while they became accustomed to it and could no longer refuse. In other words, they became "addicted to the Angel." Not everyone was affected by this scourge, but the vast majority was, approximately eighty-six percent. Otherwise, Paul Dors would not have become a trillionaire.

Interestingly, even the fact that from time to time the Angel made serious errors did not stop the users. There grew to be a whole series of anecdotes about Personal Angels stemming from ancient jokes about the inner voice.

All of the jokes ended in basically the same way: "Holy crap!" says the Personal Angel.

The exclamation being uttered after the client either smashed into a cake, got into an extremely stupid situation or went completely and totally bankrupt obeying the commands. People told jokes, but continued to live under the influence of the Angels and happily follow their instructions.

It then should be clear that in the eyes of many, including some of the representatives of the eighty-six percent mentioned above, Paul Dors became known as a true villain. Of course, Alex and Roland understood that he was just a smart and enterprising person who filled a demanded niche and was prepared for the natural course of things. If not for him, then someone else would have made the unfortunate Angel, perhaps in a version that was even worse. Regardless of understanding this, it was hard to get rid of antipathy towards a person responsible for hooking the world on such a misfortunate thing, despite the fact that the world itself was more to blame than him. After all, even in the Argentine Science Park they made another Angel which had what they called a more "human face": a system that did not command, but informed; did not prescribe a ready-made solution but explained the situation and offered choices. It was a really wonderful system and it actually helped to develop a person. Alas all it was able to win was three percent of the market. People liked to receive ready-made solutions delivered in the form of a short imperative.

"Well," said Roland, "does he want to give us money?"

"It looks like that is what he wants. I can't think of any other reason for him to have called. The only question is: How much?"

"Yeah well even if he only gave us a billion it would be enough to make a small working prototype of our engine and run it in space. Then people would see that and other investments would try to catch up."

"Well, so are we flying there tomorrow?"

"Yeah we're flying there. But where to?"

"Oh, hold on! The message just arrived. My God... Wow!"

"What, New Zealand?"

"Much worse. Tierra del Fuego, the Argentinian part, Ushuaia Airport. There we will be met by a man in a tailcoat."

"In a tailcoat?!"

"Yes, in a black tailcoat, as elegant as a grand piano."

Tierra del Fuego

The plane landed on a small flat cape in the Beagle Channel which was surrounded by mountains whose tops were already white-capped with the first March snow. Actually, in the vile climate of Tierra del Fuego (+10 °C in summer and 0 °C in winter), there was always snow on the mountains. This snow however had only fallen yesterday over the old snow, the meadows and the rocks, and it was fresh and dazzling to the eye. Right at the hour of arrival, as if especially for Alex and Roland, the weather cleared up and while the plane was circling over the strait, they had to squint from the bright sun to look out the window.

The entire space of the cape was used up by the runway and other airport facilities. In the West hid a rounded bay, on the shore of which, stretching to the foot of the mountains, was nestled the city of Ushuaia, the only settlement in Tierra del Fuego which could be called a city without stretching the meaning of that word.

Alex and Roland saw the man in the evening attire instantly. In the arrivals hall there were a lot of people meeting passengers, some with signs and some without, some had backpacks, some were wearing waterproof jackets with hoods, others T-shirts, windbreakers and even just sweaters, but the man in the tailcoat was the only one formally dressed, and besides that he was two meters tall. The crowd in the arrival hall appeared to shun him, as if they were afraid, and everyone flowed around him, giving him wide berth. It was impossible not to notice such a greeter immediately upon entering the hall.

"Pleased to meet you," said the man in the tailcoat. "Let's go."

He led them through the parking lot to the heliport, invited them into the cabin and sat at the controls himself and lifted them off.

"Where are we flying to?" Roland asked.

"To Chile."

The helicopter flew along the fjords, past the ridges covered with snow and over the lakes. It flew into milky clouds and then emerged from them. They flew through the rays of the sun shining through the clouds, then a dense gray fog and then a deep blue sky. Red swamps and yellowish forests floated below, and to either side, steep grassy slopes or cold menacing rocks hidden by wisps of fog came very close, less than a hundred meters away, and they even saw a gray-blue glacier descending from the mountains directly into a lake. And at the helm a two-meter man in a tailcoat.

"Oh, how the 'Ride of the Valkyries' would serve for the completeness of harmony!" Roland remarked to Alex.

"As you please," the man in the evening dress responded, tapping on a keyboard and the cabin of the helicopter was filled with powerful militant Wagner chords, drowning out the noise of the engine. Despite the peaceful context, the harmony made everything so complete that the bewitched passengers did not utter a word until the end of the flight.

The helicopter, emerging from the low clouds, landed in a cozy forest valley in a clearing in front of a two-story house, under the circumstances surprising only for its ordinariness. Without a tailcoat, Paul Dors came out of the door himself, wearing sneakers and a jacket that was about the same as the one Roland was wearing.

"Make yourself comfortable," he said after the required greetings. "This is our guest house. Choose any room you want. There are no servants in the house at the moment, and well, indeed there are in fact none at all. Dinner, or breakfast for you, has been warmed up in the kitchen on the ground floor, you will find it by the smell. There is wine in the bar and I recommend taking a steam bath in the sauna, it will help a lot with the jet lag. A real steam bath with a wood burning stove. It has already been prepared for you, you will find it by the varied temperature gradient. And then in the morning you'll come to see me."

Paul pointed upwards, where a rounded glass structure opened up onto the mountainside in a break in the clouds.

"John will drop you off in the helicopter as soon as you call him."

"Is it possible to walk up?" Roland asked.

Of course, but it will take about an hour. Call before leaving if you choose to walk, and rest properly, serious conversations are best done with a fresh head. You probably thought that I wanted to give you money for your project, and in that case, you are right, however more on that in the morning. Till tomorrow then. Come on, John, let's go."

In the morning, Alex and Roland, with relatively fresh minds, hiked up the trail to the extravagant dwelling and did not regret at all that they had not taken the helicopter. The carefully laid path, not one that was trodden but precisely and carefully laid, first rose in a serpentine through the forest, then went along a steep grassy slope from where a view of a huge blue fjord opened up below in a valley between snow-capped mountains.

"Does this remind you of Auditorium B3?" Alex asked. "I don't mean the design, but the philosophy behind the buildings."

"It reminds me of a lot of things: the home of Fantomas, Dracula's castle and in the philosophy of B3, the main thing though is that we built B3 with our own hands and without technology."

"But the choice of location is somewhat similar. Have you noticed that there are no roads here? Apparently, everything was lifted in by helicopters. And there is also another quirk: apparently, he did not want to disfigure the landscape and perhaps the view will be far more grandiose than ours, majestic and cold."

"The perfect place for a misanthrope hermit."

The path passed under a glass gallery shaped like a thick hoop which stuck out over the slope of the mountain and led to the courtyard of the mansion where the owner was already waiting for Alex and Roland. After passing through a curving corridor, they ended up in a gallery overlooking the fjord where the guests settled in and they were numb from what they saw: between the towering snowy ridges and the striped rocks, ironed out by the former glacier, the remnants of which made its way down along the side of the gorge directly into the blue mirror that was the water in the fjord, a microscopic cruise ship, which looked similar to a white insect, made its way along the waters.

"What was it that brought you here?" Alex asked after two minutes of silence as they took in the panorama.

"The first time I came here was when I was a student. It was something like a juvenile romance, the diaries of Captain Cook and so on. For more than a year I saved money for a trip to Tierra del Fuego and then joined a group of the same romantics. We rented a boat, sailed through the fjords and climbed the mountains. When I found myself in this very place, my breath caught from the view that opened up before me, like what happened to you just now, only it was much stronger in my youth. I was dumbfounded and decided that here it was, my place on Earth, and that there was no better place for me! Probably everyone has their own place, so this one is definitely mine! I built a pyramid of stones because I definitely had to come back and find this place. I understood everything about the climate of Tierra del Fuego but a piece of my soul remained here anyway and I made the serious decision that if I ever got rich, I would settle right here. Well, I got rich and settled. By the way, the pyramid has survived."

"Aren't you bored here?"

"Well, I'm not alone. I'll introduce my wife at dinner. You have already met John. He works as a part-time pilot, but in general is an economist-mathematician. I also have a 'man's best friend here', he is sleeping in his favorite place in the backyard, and then there is a friend in the valley who also has friends and girlfriends. In addition to John, there are several other employees, good analysts who follow the market and the world in general. At the same time, they help with the housework along with their wives. All of them, like John, prefer to live in the valley and people come to stay regularly, children, friends and who have you. Yes, and we go out into the world from time to time but are always pulled home after a few days. By the way, this landscape changes all the time. Right now the sky is clear and the mountains are bluish-white and the fjord is blue. In a couple of hours, the wind will bring in wisps of fog which gives you the impression that you are flying on an airplane. Rarely, but sometimes there is also an anticyclone. When that happens the whole fjord and the valleys fill with thick milk-like fog but here it is sunny with blue skies and mountains stick out of the milk. In real bad weather, the wind howls and ice pellets pound on the glass, but here it is warm and cozy."

"Where do you get electricity from?"

"There is a small power plant down on the shore, an atomic one. It is almost autonomous as in your project. However, the autonomy extends for only a year and not for the thousands of years that you need. It operates without noise and or pollution and once a year a brigade sails in, does maintenance work and reloads the reactor. By the way, when we start cleaning up around the house and become overloaded with mud, I also call a brigade in from the mainland, and they bring us cleanliness and shine, enough for a couple of months.

"But anyway, let's get down to business. I have decided to take care of my obituary. Don't look at me like that, I'm not going anywhere yet... It's just like getting the sleigh ready in the summer. I would not want to go down in history solely as the father of my brainchild, the Personal Angel, who actually lowered the average person's IQ by several units. Therefore, I decided to support you. As I see it there is no other worthy cause on the horizon and neither is one expected. Just you watch, we will raise the average IQ by the same number that it fell, but seriously, I just like your idea. Who knows, maybe that is the main purpose and path of man?

"So, I'm selling most of my assets and allocating a trillion dollars to your project. The remaining hundred billion will be enough for me until the end of my days. Why are you shaking your heads? A trillion, yes you heard right, but not directly into your hands.

"Listen carefully and listen good, this money will form the basis of a fund. Such a scheme is called an endowment, and it will be well placed. I have an excellent manager and the main thing for you will be to not interfere with him, not to give him advice and not to try to pressure him in any way. You will earn interest and I think that even with the current global stagnation, my manager will squeeze out six to seven percent per annum. At first, you will not have more than sixty to seventy billion a year. However, at first you can save and build up the fund. You Alex, will be appointed the Managing Director of the Fund, and you Roland the Chairman of the Board of Trustees, or vice versa if you wish. In principle, with an adequate strategy, this money should be enough for the entire project. At the very end, it will be possible to squander what is left of the fund itself, but only when everything is clear to the last detail.

"I am sure you agree however I have conditions: First; you seem to be planning for the introduction of people on 47 Librae but somehow you are not very confident. As such sending birch trees and fish there does not inspire me, there must be people! I understand that putting people there is the next level up of complexity, but that is the main condition. You probably understand my logic. As soon as I see that the project is truncated, I will close the fund and the possibility of this happening will be included in the charter.

"Second; you must spread your project out beyond your leper colony and into the world. The main sites, the institutions and the production facilities should be located in the fairly densely populated areas of the so-called civilized world so they can suck up at least some good-for-something young people.

"Third; you must infect the world with your enlightenment and enthusiasm. Technically, this means that you will have to spend a couple of billion dollars a year on propaganda and education. In this regard you can gather the best filmmakers and television people, if there any good ones left, and give them jobs! Yes, and make it so they themselves do not disappear from the screens!

"Fourth; right now, I see that you are rushing into battle and hitting the ground running but fatigue always comes sooner or later. If this fatigue takes on such dimensions that it threatens the project, I will intervene, and do so harshly. My money will be hot on your heels!

"So, the fund will be ready in three months. Get ready to accept the first tranche by the end of the year. Do you have somewhere to take it?"

Over dinner and on the way to the airport, Alex and Roland didn't say a word, except about the talents of the hostess and the weather.

It was only at the airport back home before landing that Alex broke the silence: "So the miracle happened that you talked about at dinner at B3."

"Yes, I still can't get over it. To be honest, we were not ready for a miracle. It seems that his conditions only repeat what we ourselves were planning to do, but it's one thing when you yourself decide to do something and you still have ways to retreat, and it's another thing when you are ordered to do the same, and the path of retreat is taken away. Indeed, his money will be hot on our heels. I already feel them burning."

"Come on! You said yourself: '...to devote the rest of my life.' So dedicate and devote, the money has been blessed upon us. To be honest, I am especially troubled by his desire that we not get off the screens, although he is right, of course. We'll have to work on our image, especially you."

"Alex, you know what I was thinking? Why are such miracles possible in our rotten world? Yes, really! Simply glory to the Almighty! Not a single force in history has been able to bring this world to a common denominator. No matter how much they shout 'globalization', it remains diversified and motley. That is why the world is so tenacious and is still capable of surprises. Not a single bastard was able to build a unified global system for the extraction and distribution of resources, but how many were willing to jump in for the current 'homeostasis'! And if they had successfully built it, there wouldn't have been a trillion from Dors, they would have taken most of it away and divided it up amongst themselves and told us that for money for the project, please contact the appropriate authorities. These would have been hungry officials from science and technology with their own interests... No matter how unpleasant the oligarch-monopolists are to us, without them the world would have lost important degrees of freedom. Not to mention that we would simply continue to just suck our thumbs."

"You seem to sympathize with the moderate left? I think they would quickly short Dors, given free rein..."

"And I still sympathize. It's just that no one should be given free rein over the world, or even over its large pieces."

"Look, even though we made a big noise, we are in fact, only twenty or so people. We urgently need to assemble a large team."

"What big noise? You mean that press conference? It was a whimper not a noise. I suspect that noise will rise now."

Storm in the Swamp

The small Ark team only gradually began to truly comprehend their new status as the possessors of immeasurable finances and slowly grew more and more horrified. How would they make the money work when they were only operating at half strength? They only had access to the infrastructure of the Mongolian Science Park and there was no way even with all of its resources that they could spend more than a hundred million dollars a year. This was against the backdrop of the fact that it is only possible to launch such an enterprise from scratch by spending billions. In essence they all understood what needed to be done but in order for everything to take off, people, contracts, land and large-scale construction would be needed. The maximum amounts that Alex and his colleagues had managed in the past were grants worth several million. It was thus necessary to increase their level of responsibility by three orders of magnitude, and do it all at once! This was horror in its purest form.

Meanwhile news about the trillion dollars and items glorifying both the project and its authors spread almost instantly around the world. It was not just a sensation but a viral storm! Of course: someone gave someone a trillion dollars for nothing! Yes, and not just simply gave it to someone, but to some eggheads from a science reservation, and even worse not "just" a trillion, but honestly earned money paid by many hundreds of millions of workers for a Personal Angel. And what was it given for? For yet another bright future in many thousands of years! Give us a trillion for our present, why are we worse off than unknown descendants?! Why would anyone give someone a trillion on a whim?! Why does anyone even have a trillion?! This is contrary to the principles of social justice and offends the feelings of billions!

The wave of popular indignation was easily predictable but what did the administrative generals of the space sphere, namely the presidents and directors of all the world's national and international space administrations and corporations, have to say? It turns out that they said about the same thing, just not quite as straightforward as the masses.

Here are some excerpts from interviews conducted with senior administrators, omitting their names and positions:

From an interview with N1:

"How do you feel about the extravagant decision made by Paul Dors?"

"Well, how should I put this? In principle, the allocation of huge money for a space project is a positive thing. It is another matter entirely when we consider to whom and on what. In this case Dors, in my opinion, got a little too excited, allocating an insane amount of money to non-professionals for an ambitious but unfinished project. This particular case will most likely end in failure."

"Why do you call these people non-professionals? All of them are well-known scientists and each of them at the top of their fields."

"Yes, but they are not the right fields. We, on the other hand, are specialists in space expeditions, including long distance ones. We have a lot of experience in sending various types of probes into space and landing them on distant planets."

"I'm sorry but when was your last probe launched?"

"Seventeen years ago. However, the people who launched it continue to work on future projects, they have not disappeared anywhere."

"In your opinion, how should Dors have acted once he had decided to invest in such a project?"

"He should have acted through us."

"Yes but, if you'll excuse me for saying this, the concept and the initiative both come from Professor Selin and his colleagues."

"Yes, it is necessary to support their initiative, but their project should be developed further on the basis of specialized organizations. This means that their leaders must be represented on the board of the Ark Foundation. Never mind if Professor Selin is there as vice president."

"As an honorary figure?"

"Yes, even if he is just responsible for the scientific part, it won't hurt anything."

From an interview with N2:

"How would you care to comment on the greatest act of sponsorship in history?"

"This was not the greatest act of sponsorship but the greatest failure. It was an insane amount of money given to amateurs for the most insane and senseless undertaking of all ages in human history. The so-called 'Ark' is guaranteed to fail, discrediting the very idea of the private sponsorship of large projects."

"What would you recommend Dors spend that money on?"

"Buy cakes and hand them out to kids."

"A trillion cakes? With a billion kids living on Earth? A thousand per kid?"

"Well, maybe not immediately, stretch it out for three years."

"And what will be left after such an act? One hundred million tons of what?"

"Well, childish joy will also be left behind. Yeah well, the money will be eaten anyway and whatever is left will be exactly what you just had in mind."

At least a couple of dozen such interviews appeared. The armchair generals of space most often spoke along the lines of N1 rather than in the style of N2. However out of all of them there was one who spoke like the black sheep of the family.

From interview N3

"Do you subscribe to the opinion held by your colleagues that Dors, upon deciding to finance the Ark, should have acted through existing space related administrations?"

"If I answer honestly, I'll be violating corporate ethics. My first reaction was disappointment that it had passed me by. But then, by the way, I felt envy as well. After all, in my leisure time I was also thinking about the possibilities of an interstellar probe and whether it would be possible, even only in principle, to use it to send life to a suitable planet. Though they were idle reflections, it was still a little hurtful in a way. However, I tried to put myself in Paul's position (we know each other a little) and realized that I would have done the same thing. Yes, we may have a giant corporation and a lot of highly qualified people. But they, first and foremost, have initiative and a reasonable concept albeit it's a bit raw, and we have neither. However, the most important thing is that the Ark team has something that we have gradually lost and that is the fact that they have drive. In addition, they are acting scientists with fresher and more flexible brains. For those reasons they have a chance at succeeding. It may be small, but it exists. We wouldn't have that."

"You are still a really young man. How will you continue to work with the feeling that the most important and interesting things are passing you by?"

"That's a good question. How can I continue to work... So what, I'll just up and resign! Yeah really, you really gave me a good idea: I'll resign, there are a lot of people who want to take my place. I'm going to resign and join these guys. The Ark desperately needs good administrators. My brains may not be so fresh, but I have huge experience, I also have connections and know officials of all stripes like the back of my hand. I'll come in handy."

"You just made a very strong statement. Are you sure of what you just said? Can I publish that verbatim?"

"Publish it!"

Well, N3, to his credit, fulfilled his promise the very next day. Not only that, he brought with him a dozen associates from his older days when he was not yet an armchair general to the crew of the Ark. His name is Hank Orly.

The noise in the press and social networks did not subside, rather it moved to higher and higher tones, reaching up to the ultrasound. The smash hit of September was an interview with the Chairman of the Commission on Education of the Italian Parliament Ilona Stellar.

A fragment of the text of the interview was printed on a huge poster and posted at the entrance to the Physics Department of the Mongolian Park University. People constantly crowded around the poster, bursting into laughter or making cutting comments.

"How do you feel about the Ark Project in light of the funding that has come its way?"

"I think that the story about Dors' trillion is a very dangerous precedent, threatening indescribable consequences."

"Why does this story scare you so much?"

"The worst thing about it all is that a lot of money fell into the hands of the inhabitants of the so-called 'Science Parks', which are responsible for the fact that we are faced with a new kind of racism."

"Racism?"

"Yes, they treat the rest of humanity with contempt and consider themselves to be a superior race."

"Why do you think so?"

"They despise our culture, our way of life and our values. The schoolchildren and students from their parks always win international scientific competitions and then go around boasting about it."

"What does racism have to do with it? Don't you think that maybe they just learn better? Is our culture the highest example of what can be reached for all time?"

"With what right are they taught better? There should be no elite populations! Okay, outstanding students may appear, scattered among ordinary ones, that is tolerable, but specific territories with completely widespread elite education pose a threat to the rest of humanity."

"What threat?"

"The threat of hidden world domination and the hidden enslavement of the inhabitants of the Earth."

"What do you mean by hidden?"

"That is when everything seems to be proceeding in a normal manner but in fact every movement is inspired or instigated by a closed elite. That is when it seems to us that we make our own decisions, but in fact they are pulling on ingeniously woven threads and force us to act in their favor."

"Maybe you're just afraid of smart people?"

"I'm not afraid of them, I even love it when they are alone and nearby (the chairman of the commission flashed her eyes coquettishly), but when a lot of them appear in one place, do not expect anything good to come out of it."

Less famous but more unexpected than the rest was an interview with Harry Tavani, a former master of shuttle diplomacy who is famous for his ironic cynicism.

"You are widely known by the general public as a tough rational politician. How would you comment on the huge costs of the Ark project?"

"I think this is an example of an exacting project, the costs of which are now highly rational."

"However, the civilized world is in a difficult situation. Dictators with nuclear weapons and fanatics are sharpening their teeth on it. Maybe it is worth directing all our strength into repelling these threats, and not on a project that, God willing, will only bear fruit after many thousands of years?"

"In your opinion, who are these sinister characters that you call dictators and fanatics? They are just scavengers. When the so-called civilized world starts to rot away, that's when they show up. The best remedy for scavengers is to gather all your strength and rise to your full height and show them that you are alive and well."

"Yes, but what does it mean to rise and what does the Ark have to do with it?"

"It means getting up off the couch with the whole of civilization and doing something meaningful. Show that you have strong nerves, purpose and a future. In addition to aggression, there are other principles characteristics in people, a passion for creation and a craving for expansion into virgin territories. This is the best cure for aggression. The Ark combines both of these beginnings.

"Excuse me, but what do these fanatics and dictators care about the big picture? Will they lay down their arms? At minimum that sounds naive."

"They won't lay down their arms but they won't have the ammunition they need. Their main resource is our impotence, this is just the case when, against the background of all of us, these fanatics look sort of like a macho with a burning look. Let's show them that we are much cooler than they are! That's what we must aim for! It will then become clear to young people who are thinking about life, that these machos are just evil ignoramuses who have nothing but their own dreams of power and carrying out reprisals. If we show them that we are better, then the enthusiasm and energy of immature heads will switch towards a peaceful direction.

"But the enthusiasm of immature minds can hardly become a constructive force."

"Immature minds are like stem cells. Depending on the environment, they can become cotton-headed commoners, wedge-headed fanatics, or egg-headed homo-double-sapiens."

"Do you mean that this depends on the enlightening?

"Yes, I am. Now look: if we invested that same trillion in education, there would be an effect, albeit a small one. Since it has been castrated by the champions of homeostasis, enlightenment will remain without potency. For its part the Ark awakens feelings and it awakens them not only in immature youth, but, more importantly in the dying mediocre minds of the pedagogical class. After all, this is one hell of an educational project. There are so many areas of knowledge mixed up here and new breakthroughs are required everywhere, the mind dizzies at the thought! That is why I say that this is a very rational and effective investment of money.

The world made a lot of noise month after month, and it seemed that there would be no end to the noise. Everyone has voiced an opinion: TV presenters, writers, actors, scientists, singers, the question is who did *not* speak out about the Ark and its trillion. But the world has not argued, no arguments, just endless noise. Social networks and mass media were seething with rage and the foam from the boiling over covered up the very idea of the Ark, not a single glimpse made, not a single argument against or for, except for the numeral 'trillion', was visible from under the foam. When we say 'the Ark', we mean a trillion. The team members agreed: 'if we are offered an interview and the word 'trillion' is voiced in the opening or the first question, we give it a whack and leave'.

What about popular culture? Did it respond to the event of the decade? Of course, and how! Throughout November, the first place on MTV's ratings was held by a song with the words: 'If you want, I'll become an embryo, just take me to your Ark!'

In the meantime, things were slowly unfolding with the project. The arrival of such a seasoned administrator as Hank Orly removed one horror for Alex but another immediately took its place: no one from the team and no one on Earth understood at all exactly what should happen, or how, after landing the descent modules on the surface of the new planet. The only hope left was that people on Mars understood it a little bit better.

From the Mars STC

Goran Kirk was a long-time collaborator with Alex Selin, both of whom were involved in the field of exoplanets: among other things attempting to reconstruct the nature of distant worlds from scarce data and predicting their evolutions and destinies. Together they published fifteen articles and one book, but in life they never met and in fact could never meet, neither in the past nor in the future. This was for the simple reason that Goran was a Martian, something which, despite everything, did not prevent them from becoming good friends.

Therefore, Alex first turned to Goran, not only as a good scientist, but also as a member of the Martian scientific establishment. They did not have an academy of sciences ('they haven't evolved to the point of academies' joked Goran), but there was the so-called Scientific and Technical

Council (STC), which met once a week and worked almost to the point of spontaneous combustion. Each meeting was more like the brainstorm described earlier than the listless gatherings of earthly academies. Goran was one of the co-chairs of the STC.

The most difficult thing in communicating with the Martians was the inability to talk normally in real time. Light moved too slowly, from a little over three to twenty-two minutes in one direction and so only messaging with video or text was available.

Alex preferred text:

Hey Goran,

You must have heard about our project. You can probably imagine how unbearable it is, even considering that a mountain of money has fallen into our hands thanks to the will of fate. Currently we more or less understand how to organize the transportation and delivery of the cargo, but we can only vaguely imagine further what and how regarding what to do with it once on the surface of the planet. We (meaning those on Earth in general) do not have robots of the required level and even worse is the situation with in-laboratory reproduction of mammals. You seem to have moved much further in this aspect and your participation in the project, especially in its final stages, would be invaluable to us. Please discuss this issue there at home and if participation in the project is of interest to you, we will think about how best to coordinate all of our efforts. As for funds, I understand that you are not interested in our cash, but barter is also possible: we could arrange the delivery of whatever you want within the framework of the project.

Yours Alex

Goran preferred video:

Alex,

Hi! Glad to get news from you. I am terribly glad that such a project finally appeared. To be honest, I myself have been thinking about something like that at the level of relaxed dreams, when there is nothing else to occupy my head, but I have never been able to even imagine that someone would take it seriously, and the fact that you and Roland are initiating this is generally a delight! It's a pity I can't shake your hand, here's mine (I'm pushing it through the monitor).

Of course we will take part. However strictly speaking, I can't speak for the entire colony, but I will push the decision through the STC next week. I have no doubt that the people will approve, there are completely normal people on the council, and if anything starts to go wrong, I can punch the table with my fist. (Which Goran demonstrated as the image shook).

You are absolutely right about the fact that we should be connected with the work on the last stage of the project. We are currently creating the scenario for the recreation of Mars, designed for ten thousand years. As soon as we are finished, we will crawl out of our catacombs and join you. There's a lot in common in both scenarios. Coping with 47 Librae b will be easier, on the one hand because it already has a thick atmosphere, and on the other hand, more difficult since everything should be done through automation, and it will not be possible to interfere in order to correct anything. Nevertheless, we'll handle it! We don't have adequate robots yet and we ourselves desperately need them, so while you're busy with the transport aspect we'll handle it. It's a little more difficult with a person, but we had many more opportunities to deal with this and already have a backlog of ideas and plans. In other words, we have to, just do it.

Regarding the delivery of useful and pleasant things to us, that's a nice offer. We have things to wish for. We will give you a list. Please send me a draft of your project. Wish you happiness and every success! I am truly delighted. No fools allowed!

Bye then.

Alex switched to video:

Hello, Goran!

If only you knew the size of the stone that you have lifted from my soul! Oh, I feel like you have it good there on Mars! In terms of company and the atmosphere, but not the one on the surface which is ten millibars, but the one you have in the catacombs. However, it's also not too bad on our reservation, but as soon as we leave it, such a deep melancholy sets in!

If it's not too difficult, can you send a paper for the Park Council based on the results of your STC, they asked for it and said they need it for some kind of reports. The council really wants to appear to be the body leading the project, or at least as having a direct relationship with it. Well, let it appear to be so, you'll see, something additional will come from the Joint Council. So please make a paper with paragraphs and subparagraphs the way they like. I would be very grateful.

Most of all and in general at the moment I would like to drink with you to the success of our hopeless cause. Let's do so remotely. Here I'll pour, to your health! (Alex lightly tapped his glass on the video camera.)

OK Bye.

Goran a week later:

Alex, hi.

At STC everyone reacted to your project with a whooping hurrah. There was no need to punch the table. We will take on the most slippery issues that need to be carried out at the destination. There are no hopeless problems, at least not any that are yet visible. Volunteers have already been found for individual tasks. We have also written a paper with paragraphs and subparagraphs. If it's not right, edit it. Here, catch!

Alex took out the letter and called Roland. Here is the text:

From STC Mars

To the Council of the Mongolian Science Park

Dear Colleagues,

The Mars Science and Technology Council has carefully reviewed the preliminary version of the 47 Librae Ark Project and the many valuable contributions it has brought our community. First of all, we must state the following:

1. The project as a whole and its goals and concept deserve the highest praise. This is by far the most significantly important idea in the history of man.

2. Our analysis revealed some inaccuracies in the project at its current stage and a number of deviations from the optimum parameters. Our comments on this issue are given in Appendix 1.

3. Our community is enthusiastically ready to take a direct part in the implementation of the project.

4. Coordination of work requires a clear division of responsibilities. Our proposals boil down to the following:

4.1. The Party, conventionally referred to hereinafter as "Earth", provides everything related to the flight and preparation of genetic material: the development of the ship, power plant, magneto-rotary engine, magnetic biological protection, preparation and conservation of spores, seeds and fertilized eggs.

4.2. Earth is responsible for all matters related to navigation and will provide for the assembly of all structures in Earth orbit and the towing into near-solar orbit, launch and control of sustainer engines, then the automatic braking and maneuvers in the 47 Librae system, entry into the orbit 47 Librae b, selection of a landing site and the landing of all descent modules.

4.3. From the moment of delivery, the joint responsibility of Earth *and* Mars *begins, including:*

4.3.1. Mars: The deployment of a system of robots, equipment for their reproduction and the construction of the Central Complex of Structures.

4.3.2. Earth: The seeding of photosynthetic flora and necessary accompanying species.

4.3.3. Mars: The conservation of structures and transfer of equipment to dormant mode.

4.3.4. Earth: The control and biological correction of the chemical composition of the atmosphere during the period of primary modification lasting ten thousand years.

4.3.5. Earth: Sowing the second stage of marine and terrestrial flora with the addition of the simplest fauna to create a stable biocenoses.

4.3.6. Earth and Mars: The reproduction and distribution of aquatic and terrestrial fauna that does not require a special introduction program.

4.3.7. Earth and Mars: Reproduction and education of humans.

5. Further stages of the project, such as the replenishment of biological diversity, the control and correction of biocenoses, the introduction of mammals into the natural environment as a result of the execution of paragraph 4.3.7, will be carried out on-site under the control of a reproduced person.

6. For the implementation of Mars' contribution, no special funding from the Earth is required. However, our side will be extremely grateful if, as part of the project, the following biological materials are delivered to Mars as the first tranche:

1. Seeds from the following plants:

- The common dandelion
- The Shiraz and Carmenere variety of grapes
- Spores from mushrooms boletus and bolete boletus
- Apple trees of the varieties melba and white insides
- Adansonia digitata (baobab) trees
- Victoria Regia (Amozonica)
- Cloudberries
- Geraniums
- and 120 more items in Appendix 2.

2. Fertilized eggs of the following animals:

- European squirrels
- Common hedgehogs
– Dogs: large size, red color
- Indian elephants
- Bottlenose dolphins
- Crows
- Yellow-bellied snakes
- and 90 more items in Appendix 2.

"Yeah..." Roland said. "I knew they were having trouble drafting papers for the Earth bureaucracy, but not to that extent! In no case should this go beyond our small circle. Outsiders will perceive this declaration of needs as nonsense or a mockery of earthlings. Paragraph 4.3.7 which is supposed to be performed in automatic mode is particularly good as is the next paragraph, number 5."

"Okay, I'll edit it."

"And the list of biological materials? Any official from Interspace will immediately think that they are mocking him: a baobab with a dandelion! A pug with an elephant!"

"I suspect that something similar has already happened and that they have already tried through Interspace. Now they are turning to us as the saner people so that we can add everything through our own channels as part of the project. I have had quite a lot of contact with the Martians and I am absolutely sure that they need exactly what they have written. It is quite possible that, for example, some child of theirs ordered a large red mongrel, seeing one in a film, they have purebred dogs, but he decided he wanted just such a mongrel. And this application comes with the same priority as the rest of them. Maybe that's why they are so successful?"

"But the baobab, the elephants and the dolphins?! Where will they put all of that?"

"Do you know that they are now increasing the size of their world by thirty thousand cubic meters daily? They dig, they strengthen and they seal. Why not make a piece of savanna with elephants and baobabs? Yes, they have plenty of water. There are already lakes and artificial rivers with fish, apparently the time has come for a piece of sea. They already have twenty square kilometers of living space under normal pressure and there are about twenty thousand of them, imagine a city of twenty thousand in such a space, there is plenty of room to turn around. Or imagine densely populated areas of Europe with the same average density of one thousand people per square kilometer. There have everything there, fields, lakes, farms and parks."

"And what do you think about paragraph 4.3.7? Will they really do it?"

"That item and indeed item 4.3, was my worst nightmare. If you noticed, I have kept postponing and slowing down the discussion of the last stage. Not because I myself do not understand the subject, although I really do not, but because I was afraid of the hopelessness that emanated from all these cases, to deploy the most complex chain of actions without human intervention. I am afraid that the final stage discussion will kill all enthusiasm: Why are we here beating our foreheads against the wall, if at the end we will only meet a wall of armored steel?! And then Goran appears and says: 'Guys, calm down, this is all our part, we'll do it!' A great weight was lifted from my mind! And they'll do it! What they have already done seemed impossible. So they will do that too."

"Okay, let's take point 4.3.7. It also requires human experimentation, even worse, on children."

"Apparently it does and apparently they will. It would be impossible for us but they will do it, despite the risk of damaging the child's psyche. They have slightly different ideas about the ethics of human reproduction. Otherwise there would not be twenty thousand of them now. And they are all so stubborn too."

Together to Mongolia!

Stefan Mukha who had two weeks earlier defended his dissertation titled, "Destabilizing Breeding of Domestic Animals through Elements of Genetic Modification", walked along the embankment looking through passers-by at a point in space fifty meters ahead of him. They all looked at Stefan as he stood out too much with his gray, motionless face. He had never felt like such a badass before. If he was asked he would never be able to answer the question of what brought him to the embankment. He just walked because it was easier than sitting or lying down.

A couple of months ago he had been happy. First of all he had received a positive response from Eugene Cooney himself: he was then not just hired for a job related to the Ark, not only chosen to work in his own specialty, but was in fact hired to work directly on the topic of his dissertation with the possibility of choosing the object of selection. Second, his long and difficult romance with Susan had ended in a protracted honeymoon and they were ready to fly off together to Mongolia, where the headquarters of the Ark was located and to register a marriage there, buy a house and give birth to children.

The first blow that came was a quarrel with his parents: "You are leaving us in old age. What is the use of your material assistance to us! No, we won't go to this nature reserve of yours for any noble reason. We will stick out like sore thumbs. You are a bad son. Brought up with your own head..."

Then there was also something that had gone wrong with Sue two months ago: "I'm interested, are they all nerds like you? No, I understand that you are a zoologist, I mean nerds in a different sense... When you get together with your colleagues and talk about something I feel like a stranger. I will be like some beautiful doll there with you... It is clear that they are fun and cheerful, but that fun is somehow not for me, I'm used to another simpler kind. Well, let's see..."

Sue began to disappear more and more to who knows where, giving strained, unadulterated explanations. And then this morning she had announced: "Of course I have to say forgive me Stefan, but I will not go to Mongolia. It's better to say this directly and honestly: I found another person. He is not as smart and interesting as you, but it is easier for me with him and in the company of his friends I feel at ease. Go alone you will find your happiness there."

So Stefan walked along the embankment in a somnambulistic state. Some thoughts still kept running through his head: *Maybe stay? Engage in livestock breeding? Just wait, and Sue will come back* (a little warmth entered his soul). *After all, who could guarantee that he would be talented enough to be accepted as one of their own in the Mongolian Science Park? This is where the direction of your life will take place, one way or another and somehow it will take place even without the Ark...* (His heart grew cold again.) *No, no matter how you look at it everything ends in some kind of melancholy...*

A very unusual dog was walking towards him. First, it was unusually large, second it had tassels on its drooping ears, third it had combined black, white and red colors with a strong violation of mirror symmetry and fourth it had glimpses of remarkable canine intelligence in its kind brown eyes. The dog poked his wet nose into Stefan's hand and sat down. Stefan stopped and his face took on some human features again.

"Oh wow! Long eared and with smart eyes, come on give me a paw!

Oh wow! Well done. Where did you come from? Are you hungry? Want some junk food? I see you do." Stefan took a hamburger out of his backpack and gave it to the dog who carefully took it out of his hand, after which he furiously gobbled it up with a rumble in three seconds. "Hungry I see... You were obviously not born on the street. Did your owner abandon you? They also abandoned me... Come on, let's sit down and be silent together for a while."

Stefan sat down on the stone parapet and the dog sat opposite him, burying its head in Stefan's knees.

"You haven't betrayed anyone, and you're physically incapable of that I see. How did you end up on the street? And for such a long time, judging by your fur and ribs? Is your master even alive? Oh, I shouldn't ask such questions ... It's sad for you probably, to wander the streets, roam the garbage heaps and beg. And I'm not happy here either..."

Stefan's face gradually brightened.

"And so what, tailed one? If you want, we'll fly away together to the Mongolian Park!" The dog raised its head, tilted it to one side and wagged its tail. "Do you know what I'm thinking right now? On the new planet, man will also need a friend. Not for hunting and not for protection but just for friendship, for support, for everything all at once. At first there will be few people, but there will be a lot of space, too much so. Without a good friend with four legs, everyone will be oh so uncomfortable in the millions of wild square kilometers. Isn't that right?" The dog wagged its tail even more intensely. "I have been promised the right to choose, so I'm going to be breeding the best friend imaginable. Cows and sheep, I'm sure, will do fine without me. There are enough specialists there for them. But no one, it seems, has ever applied destabilization with elements of engineering to your brother."

Stefan's eyes began to sparkle. The dog looked on enthusiastically, his head cocked to one side. This is how students often look at a lecturer, simulating complete understanding and restrained admiration.

"By the way, how did you, such a handsome dog, come into the world? You poor thing, I suppose your mother was a border collie and got mixed up with a St. Bernard, is that right? Or, maybe the border collie was your father and standing on tiptoe, he reached where he had to? Excellent outbreeding: St. Bernard height and border collie ears and eyes. We will start a new tribe with you. Oh, yeah and that's the right name for you: Noah. You will be the forefather of the dogs of the Ark. All I need to do is wash and fatten you up a little first. Let's seeee... But how to transport you? I can't check in such a handsome dog in a cage that will go in the luggage compartment! You will have to fly first class. So, what about the money? I will have to write a new letter to Professor Cooney."

When changing at the Frankfurt airport, people looked slightly askance at Stefan and Noah and the crowd flowed around them at a respectful distance. The only thing was that some of children pointed their fingers at the dog, saying to their parents: "Look how big! A real dog. Let's buy one."

The parents dragged the children further away with words such as: "And who will walk with it at six in the morning?"

When they approached the exit for the flight to Khatgal, something changed radically. About a hundred people were waiting for the boarding and they somehow subtly stood out from the general passengers flowing through the airport. Perhaps it was their faces? The people in the chairs smiled, more at Noah than at Stefan.

The first to run up were two girls of about twelve years old, they sat down in front of Noah who was on all fours: "How nice! May we pet your dog?"

"Pet him if you want, he'll give you his paw and sit down or lie down or whatever else you want."

A tall man with gray Einsteinian hair approached them: "Oh, what settlers are going to our Park!"

"How do you know that we are going to the Park and that we are settlers?"

"There is nowhere else to go through Khatgal except to the Park. Everything here is going to the Park. And as for settlers, it's elementary: people don't fly with dogs on business trips."

A guy with large features came up, with big lips like Niels Bohr.

“What is your beauty’s name?”

“Noah.”

“What, is he intending on flying on the Ark?”

“Almost. The embryos of his offspring will fly.”

“Wow! Great dog! What is the name of the breed?”

“Librador, can’t you see?” a tall man answered for Stefan.

“Will his descendants also have tasseled ears?” one of the girls asked.

“Well, I don’t know, of course we will select things on other grounds, but who knows?”

“You have to really try, such beautiful brushes! It will be great if the dogs of the new planet have them.”

A man with standing black hair like the young Landau, approached them.

“And in what segment are you employed? And who are you exactly?”

“In Bio. Under Eugene Cooney.”

“Eugene? Wonderful! Let’s get to know each other, Rob Waxman.”

“Stefan Mukha. And you are the same Waxman, whose replica...?”

“Yes, sir! That’s me!”

“Why didn’t I recognize you right away? I’ve seen so many of your photos on the web!”

“So, is anyone meeting you at the airport?”

“They wrote to me (if I remember a Mrs. Svensson) that I need to take the number 32 bus to the main Bio building, and they will meet me there.”

“What bus? My car is parked at the airport and I’m going in that direction. Yes, actually half of the passengers *here* have cars in the parking lot and half of them are going there. A bus, damn it! Gene will be reprimanded to not entrust the meeting of important guests to Mrs. Svensson.

I'll call him now. By the way, where are you staying?"

"I guess at first time in a guest apartment."

"I recommend that you settle down with us on Khuvsgul-3. It is beautiful there! Are you alone or are there other family members?"

"No, I'm single," Stefan replied with a sigh.

"This is easily fixable, especially now. This year there is an unprecedented invasion of female graduate students into the Bio section, apparently in honor of the ten-year anniversary of the project."

"Why is our settler wearing a muzzle?" asked a thin woman with a highbrow like Marie Curie.

"Let me take the muzzle off the dog!" she said, turning to the steward standing at the control of the gate. This dog would rather fall into a hole than bite someone."

"I'd love to, but the rules don't allow it," the steward replied.

"And if all the passengers demand it? Everyone wants the muzzle removed from the new settler, isn't that the truth?"

The woman turned to the passengers, waiting for support.

"Take off the muzzle!" said the man with Einsteinian hair menacingly, shaking his fist above his head.

"Take off the muzzle! Take off the muzzle!" the girls chanted, bouncing to the beat of the syllables.

"Take off the muzzle, take off the muzzle," the passengers said in chorus under the direction of the high-browed woman.

"Well, I'll talk to the commander of the plane right now. This is our jurisdiction. If it's allowed, then so be it."

The steward went to the cockpit.

"The passengers are in an uproar back there demanding that the muzzle be removed from a dog flying on our flight."

“What kind of dog?”

“A hefty dog of an incomprehensible breed, seems to be kind. It has already become loved by all.”

“Okay, let them take it off.”

“And if one of the passengers complains?”

“Listen, I’m probably flying to Khatgal for the hundredth time and I know the peculiar people who travel back and forth on this flight very well. They are capable of funny tricks, but for one of them to snitch on such an occasion is unthinkable!”

The steward went out to talk to the passengers and announced that permission had been granted to remove the muzzle from the dog. In response, there were shouts of “bravo” and friendly applause. Noah flexed his jaws and smiled happily. Boarding had begun.

“Well, buddy, here we are at home. We haven’t even had time to fly away but we’re already home,” Stefan said quietly, closing his eyes to hide the tears that had welled up.

He finally let go, really let go.

The Missionary

Roland’s current successive educational raid was counted on lasting exactly one week: Beirut, Dublin, Portland, Sapporo and Irkutsk, a real round-the-world trip. It’s great to go around the world flying from east to west because you almost do not lose any time. He departed at 7 am and 8 hours later arrived at 7:30 am with the whole day ahead of him. The day ahead promised to be a cheerful one, with no time to rest. At eight thirty in the morning, he had to give a speech on regional television for a program called “Meeting at Breakfast”, then some kind of round table about some future or another, then a lecture at the university, then a live broadcast on the Cascade TV channel, then on Flight FM radio and finally a public lecture in the Central Library.

On the approach to Portland, the panorama on the left side of the plane was completely taken over by the Mount Hood volcano. Roland had deliberately taken a seat to the left by the window to admire the mountain which was a cross between Mount Fuji and Ararat. The plane descended flush with its top with the black ridges and snowy fields between them. In the basin below there was a glacier where the forest began and clearings for ski slopes. Actually, this volcano determined the choice between Kansas City and Portland: both are outback towns but here there was at least something to admire. So let Rob Waxman fly to Kansas City as he is indifferent to such beauty and always takes an aisle seat anyway.

How many years had they been flying around the Earth like that? Almost thirteen already, three or four times a year, several cities at a time, several appearances in each, as if they had covered the whole world, although what kind of world coverage? Just pin pricks. The cities were mixed up in their memories. Was it Sisyphean labor? Who knows? One thing was for sure: it would be impossible to create and send off the Ark in a mediocre, indifferent world. Even if there were at least a hundred trillion and even if they had to lay down bones, it was still impossible. But it is also impossible to change the world on your own. One can only do the right thing and hope that some underlying "chemical" mechanisms or reactions would then go to work. Here they are, the members of the team, and they have been stubbornly doing the right thing for a long time, and the world has actually moved from a dead point damn it! Maybe it was not because of their work but it had moved just where they had been pushing it. No, of course not everything was set in motion, only some of the upper layers, but they had saturated the atmosphere.

Mount Hood was now left behind and below there were hills covered with coniferous forests, a river with a cascade of reservoirs and farms and quadrangles of fields in the middle of the forest, then continuous fields with farms and omnipresent rectangles, as if the whole Earth was being cultivated. Once upon a time there were pioneers on Earth, and now it is all inhabited, like a big farm. After all, the Ark will give someone an exciting chance to become a pioneer again in the truest sense of the word. Oh, who would give them a gift such as an untrodden world?!

What works best, appearances on big time television shows where you always have to fight with the host who considers the audience to be idiots or these exhausting tours with dozens of appearances and meetings? Besides all of that, they are afraid of them on WWV channels. Everyone connected in one way or another with the Ark is feared after the scandal caused by Tall Jose at the "Court of Reason". It is of course much more pleasant to speak on your own channel but only a possible ten million people watch it. A handful against the three billion people in the WWV audience, and it is unlikely that this handful will grow by itself.

Yes, no one will ever replace direct meetings with people. They are also needed, these meetings. Without them, I would have been burned out already, and remembering the faces of the audience helps. At first, we flew more and more around the capitals, in most of them everyone knows us, and besides that, Ark departments were opened in many metropolitan universities, so why fly there? It's time to bring the unplowed outback up to speed. The strongest young people still grow up in the outback and they are more motivated and better tempered. God knows it is immense but we'll cover as much as we can. Forces have already accumulated. How many people are there on the missionary team? Perhaps forty people and young people are growing up and maturing. The worth of one Bill Pak is uncountable! So the water is wearing away the stone and how well it has taken seed. By the looks of it right in the middle of the city!

Oh, what a beautiful woman meets them with a sign! Yes, not just with a sign, but one that says "Professor Roland Wolf", an entire poster with his portrait. Nice to meet you! To the studio? Yes, so to the studio. Urgently? Yes, then urgently.

A "Breakfast meeting"? OK then, we'll have breakfast. Oh, so you're an ecologist?! Becoming one due to the influence of the Ark?! That's wonderful, but I remained the same as when I was a physicist, except that I learned some new correct words from ecology.

The studio was in some kind of a backyard but the people were nice and witty, especially the makeup girl. Now she would make a hero-lover out of a haggard looking image of a tired person who had not had enough sleep. Indeed, looking in the mirror was now no longer so disgusting.

Damn mic cord caught on something under my shirt. The host, cheerful and sharp-eyed, diligently went through the titles.

"Good morning," I said and thought: thank God I didn't make a mistake like yesterday in Dublin when I said 'good evening' at 8 o'clock in the morning.

"Can you please tell the listeners what the main purpose of your visit to our distant lands is?"

"The recruitment of youth: something I'll start right now at breakfast."

"What does recruitment mean? Who do you consider to be recruited?"

"To recruit means to interest and to ignite. I talk about all sorts of interesting things: where the Universe came from, about quasars, about planets and stars, about life in the Universe, and, of course about the Ark. Those who have a meaningful expression on their faces, especially those whose eyes light up and even more so those who ask a question, are recruited! Something turns on in people's brains..." Roland made a circular motion with his hand around his temple. "They make an effort and realize something new! That is a strong feeling and you can't erase it from a person. Even if they are not so young and have already decided on their occupation, or if they have or will have children, this infection is often inherited!"

"Do you ignite a lot of people in one visit?"

"No one has ever counted but I don't think it's very many. However even if my speeches in your city affect the fate of only one or two people, if at least one of them becomes a good scientist or a talented teacher as a result, then the trip will pay off many times over."

Next a round table in some downtown business center, a recording for a local WWV studio. Five participants, the most colorful one is a charming priest very large in diameter, moreover in a cassock, with a cross on his chest. Is he in any way Orthodox? Where did he come from? The subject of the dispute is the future in the view of contemporaries. What is seen there: homeostasis or a new scientific and technological revolution? Will there be arrangement or expansion, a cozy hearth or an interstellar Ark? Or maybe just darkness awaits us, where there is neither one nor the other. By the way, why has there been no utopia in world literature for a long time, only dystopia?

"Yes, because the very idea of paradise, both on Earth and in heaven, is false at its very core!" Roland blurted out and the priest stiffened. "What is a person to do in paradise? Suck up freebies? Won't they get bored? Sorry for the harshness, but a person is a creature, firstly they do not listen and secondly, they deteriorate from inaction. Yes, they will not leave a stone unturned from any static paradise and they will do the right thing. They will have no purpose there!"

"You see," the priest answered, "given your global goal is a kind of pride. And the Christian doctrine is humanistic and it denies pride and is based on love and compassion."

"And what does the Christian doctrine say about the development of the human race? After all, the modern world, whatever it may be, was in no way made by Christian righteous. On the contrary, people who possess such a virtue as humility are suppressed and the sin of heretical pride is developed, promoted and built upon. Without them, we would still be living in the Paleolithic era."

"If you mean science, then Christianity recognizes its role."

"Yes, retroactively and with a whimper. Why did God kick Adam and Eve out of paradise? How did he react to the construction of the Tower of Babel? He is not very friendly to inquisitive people and to creators. It's frightening to imagine how such a God would react to our Ark!"

"God is merciful, he would forgive you."

"And then at the Last Judgment he would deal with us as unbelievers!"

"The Apocalypse is not important for the description of horrors, they are nothing more than metaphors. The Last Judgment is the court of conscience. The main meaning of the Second Coming is the establishment of another, enlightened life. And this will give people completely new experiences, awakening the best aspects of human nature. People will be different."

"But all this has already been said throughout history. Let's recall the 20th century, the building of Communism, a grandiose experiment to create a new person, and the like? Again, we are relying on creating a new person, your version which I do not really like, to be honest. You want them to be obedient, without sin, with simple virtues but without the spark of God. Yes, slightly neutered."

The host, apparently, deciding that it was necessary to urgently move the conversation in a different direction, gave the floor to the participant who had been silent until then, someone whose name and profession Roland did not remember.

"But there are also positive trends! People really need positivity. We must fight for it! Here we have created a literary club, we publish an almanac and hold special evening events trying to make the world a better place, the world needs positivity."

The next participant spoke about how faith in the immortality of the soul helps him in life. Roland was a little despondent. And what about the future? Or is he physically incapable of thinking about a future in which he does not exist? Then the priest is again given a chance to speak and says that the most important thing that has come out of the discussion is "positive", and in terms of positive he means that they and their spiritual company are ahead of everyone. Roland winced a little. Why does the word "positive" make him flinch so much? Apparently, he guessed it was because the word had been impregnated with a sticky good-looking lie and then rolled in the dust.

Roland became lost in thought for a moment, lost the thread of the discussion, and did not immediately notice that the host was addressing him.

He had to repeat the question, "How do you imagine the future?"

"The world will remain the same (dazzlingly snowy and doubtfully tender were the words that flashed through his head). It will develop and then rot, catch on and then develop again, move towards disaster and heroically avoid it. New generations will create new dystopias and make pathetic attempts to create a new utopia. But the world will remain the same, except that the technological abilities of its inhabitants will grow, more and more they will move ahead of the intelligentsia. How might this end one day? Okay, well never mind... And in the future we will launch the Ark, which will greatly reduce the chances of the disappearance of intelligent life in the areas which are in the immediate vicinity to us in the Universe."

"Okay well it looks like the show is over." The host especially thanked Roland for his participation and looked at him knowingly.

Another University. The auditorium is close to half full with about a hundred people. There are five minutes left and the people keep coming in in a dense stream. Then there are two minutes left and it seems that there are no more free places. The people sit on the steps. The time has come to start, and they all go and stand along the walls.

"Well, perhaps let's get started. Right now we'll discuss the history of cosmology, and in the evening about the Ark. Wow, where have so many of you come from? Maybe you confused the auditorium from another ad? Which means you should all be waiting in another place... Please make room on the steps and in the aisle, maybe everyone will fit in. There are still seats along the edges of the stage... The youngest ones can sit on the floor in front of the stage... It seems they fit in, unbelievable, but it's true! Only if you are on the ledges and on the window sills, please be more careful, do not fall on the heads of those sitting below. Now let's start. First let me ask you some questions. What is the temperature of the Universe? There is no temperature? Zero degrees? Three degrees Kelvin? Who thinks it's higher? How many dimensions are there? Three, who thinks more? Four, good. Who is thinks even more? Eleven... Hands up, who's for eleven. Okay, you've heard of string theory. Yes, your level is above average. So I will give the average presentation, with simple formulas and graphs, but without equations. Questions can be asked during the lecture, including stupid ones..."

Roland went on and told the story of how Einstein did not like the consequences of his theory and then tried to spoil it, then about how

Hubble was wrong by a factor of seven and how the Universe had been demoted from the container of all things into a physical object. He looked from one face to the next, choosing a reference listener. His eyes ran all over the auditorium, there were so many magnificent faces, smart, attentive and benevolent. No less than at that very first press conference... But that was in the center of Europe, and here it was in one of the backyards of North America...

He continued to tell them about how Gamow had mistakenly received the correct temperature value but then he could not calculate it because there was not enough data. Then how Penzias and Wilson tried to get rid of cosmic microwave radiation for a long time, thinking that it was a defect in their antenna or the receiver...

He thought: Why are there so many of them here, such smart and beautiful faces? As if there were no educations reforms and the main TV channels of the world were not broadcasting nonsense twenty-four hours a day...

The coherent theory of the Big Bang turned out to be murky at the very beginning and it required delicately adjusted initial conditions. Who tuned it up like that? Of course, the Creator, and the churchmen triumphed. However, in the 1980s, physicists trivialized everything: they developed the theory of inflation, explaining how it happens by itself without the Creator... Then they laughed approvingly, where is the claimed eighty percent of the religious population? So, eternal inflation, you have to strain yourself, it's hard to comprehend this... You have to twist your brains into something like a ram's horn. Yet that is just another anthropic principle remains to tell about... As a result, we are tired, very tired, but we hold on.

"Well, that's all, and now the questions!"

"Where do all these universes fit into?"

"What was there before the stages of inflation?"

"Are new universes being born right now?"

"Can there be life in universes with different laws of physics, ones that are not similar to ours?"

“Are we also expanding along with the expanding Universe?”

“If you throw a brick into a black hole, will the black hole become heavier by the mass of the brick?”

“You talked about cosmological inflation. Does cosmological deflation happen?”

“How fast are we moving through the Universe?”

“Relative to what are we moving at six hundred kilometers per second?”

“What will happen to the Universe next? Will dark energy tear the planets away from the stars?”

“Will there be new vacuum phase transitions in the Universe?”

“If the laws of physics are different in different universes, then how long does it take for these laws to be established?”

“What was the temperature during expansion?”

“If we can never observe other universes, does this mean that they, in all reality, do not truly exist?”

The questions are not over but the time is over. Where to go next? Probably to the Cascade TV channel with its target audience of business people, white-collar workers and students. The backyards again but the host is a guy of about forty, smart and knows a lot about the Ark.

He starts: “I have what might be an unexpected question: How do you perceive the world when you travel outside your science park? A world where the vast majority spends all of their free time watching global TV channels and digesting advertising, considers science a suspicious and dangerous business, is guided by horoscopes and believes that you and your Ark have gotten into their pocket.”

“You know, I don’t see such a world. Everywhere I go I am met by people whom I recognize as being like-minded and I guess, apparently, they take me along special routes and lead me through special corridors, where there are completely normal people who understand everything perfectly. Wonderful inquisitive people come to the lectures but I know about the existence of the majority, about which you speak, but it seems to me that they are hiding from me. For a long time no one has asked why the Ark is even needed, everyone who would like to ask that seems to be hiding somewhere or is too embarrassed.

"Yes, and among the viewers of the program there are now our own like-minded people who clearly predominate and not a single question: 'Why is it needed?' But there are already more than fifty other questions..."

Let's continue. Damn it, how many times have I tried to stop putting my phone in my jeans pockets and there it is again, just try to get it out, sitting in a car.

"Professor Roland Wolff?"

"Yes, that is me."

"We have a proposal to reschedule your evening appearance. The library only has a total of one hundred and fifty seats and four hundred people have already signed up. We were offered a conference room in the banking center where there are a thousand seats, and there are bank employees who also want to listen to what you have to say."

"Well, okay, that's great. The curiosity of bank employees is also very inspiring."

"Excellent then. In an hour, our driver will pick you up from the Flight FM studio."

For some reason, they have all of their studios in some kind of backyards, around places that are something similar to industrial zones. Next a music channel, a fun host, a target audience of young people under twenty-five.

"I so want to get out of this wilderness," the presenter complains before the broadcast, "anywhere, even to your place in Mongolia, to be around smart people. The only thing that reconciles me here is the radio station."

That's interesting, I wonder if he would also broadcast radio programs for us. We don't seem to have one. Now you have to play the role of a sharp-shooter. Nothing concrete, not the first time.

Downtown again and everywhere they have the same face, but this one is perhaps smaller than average and more human than average. A hefty lobby with a huge screen, if even now they can't all fit into the hall, it will be possible to broadcast to here. Wow, almost every seat is taken. Perhaps a short presentation is better here. We wait five minutes. They have almost all fit in. Okay let's get started.

First slide: This is how the Ark would look like if all of the cables connecting its elements are shortened dozens of times. As you can see, there is nothing in common not only with the biblical ark, but also with the common ideas about how spaceships should look. There are no interior spaces as everything will be mounted in the void, the engine windings, the reactor, the radiators, antennas, landers, the superconducting solenoid and on and on... The people listen well, but perhaps we need to quickly get to the questions instead. There are some of the same people who listened at the university. I recognize ten people. I wonder how many bank employees there are. However, how can you tell them apart? Those who came are most definitely not wearing uniforms.

Well, here's the last slide. This is planet 47 Librae b in a little over twenty thousand years. It is an artist's conception. The young man and the girl look too glamorous really, reminiscent of advertising for world tours, and the mountains there are not so steep, but the artist tried hard so let's not find fault with him.

Now for the main part of the meeting: the questions: "Great, the first question is exactly the one that is asked most often. When? To be honest, I don't know. Not very soon. The ship itself, more precisely not the ship but the power unit and the engine, will be ready in the foreseeable future, but this is by far from the most difficult task ahead. I think that the actual launch is at least a quarter of a century away, and most likely thirty years. If I lead a healthy lifestyle, I have the chance of living to see it.

"Why are we sure that nothing will break? To be honest, we are in fact just the opposite, we are sure that something will break. In each of our bodies too, something regularly breaks down, little things, but that does not prevent us from functioning normally. However, we are sure that there will not be too many breakdowns and that they will not be fatal ones. In this regard the project has much in common with a living organism, especially in the fact that part of it that will develop on the planet itself. In order to obtain real confidence, it will take thousands, even tens of thousands of man-years. We cannot test the mechanisms in real time, but we know well what processes are going on in them, and we can numerically simulate their aging. In some cases, we can compress time and conduct direct tests, for example by using the accelerator to expose the electronics to a particle flux thousands of times greater than that in space, and then at the same time check how well our numerical models work.

"Yes, you are right the launch is the weak point of the Ranedo-Drake reactor. Indeed, heterogeneous uranium rods are required, ones which are fresh at the entrance and spent at the exit. It will take it five years to enter the full operating regime but it is possible to prepare the first rods on Earth by passing them through an identical reactor. Yes, it will take five years, but if the Ark's reactor is loaded with rods annealed on Earth it will immediately operate under its permanent regime.

"Regarding the first children. The first nine months are not a problem but the artificial uterus will have to be further developed. However, this is already part of a routine procedure. More difficult will be the first years. Currently a working option has been adopted and is being developed: this includes a cyber-nanny and replicas of parents. Both already exist and are being improved and worked on. Soon the first experiment, the first attempt, will be made on Mars.

"Yes, away from the eyes of the concerned public. This is one of the reasons that this will be done on Mars, although not only because of that.

"A cyber-nanny is also partly a replica, but it is not able to accurately reproduce the movements of a person. Worst of all are the facial expressions. Therefore, electronic visually flawless replicas of parents speaking natural speech are indispensable. They will be impossible to distinguish from living parents behind glass.

"No, not Adam and Eve. Psychologists say that the best option is first two girls and then boys.

"No, no, not a tropical forest at all. At first it was planned that way, but we found a more reliable option. The main producers of oxygen will be poisonous herbaceous plants related to hogweed, only much larger, with very large leaves. They will be poisonous in order not to rot after dying, and so they will be pressed into peat. This type of poison acts as a preservative. I should remind everyone that decay binds the released oxygen. There is no sense of obtaining oxygen from the photosynthesis of a plant which then rots as everything that the plant produced will be absorbed during decay. These super hogweeds are able to live at a concentration of carbon dioxide of at least two percent and of oxygen at no more than thirteen percent. That is, when an atmosphere similar to that of the earth is formed, they will die out and give way to normal plants."

Again, time ran out before all of the questions were asked. I've forgotten where they're taking me now. Some restaurant I think. The rector of a university has invited me. All the organizers of the lectures will be there, and that cute girl who met me at the airport. Well, here we are. Cozy place. Beer! Cold light beer! Wow, like water out on the hot sand.

Here is the hotel. Outside the window there is light, its reflections stretching across the river, up the wide valley, in some places the luminous panorama is blocked by dark hills. A good day, good people, it was as if he had never left the park. Yes, and it was a good day yesterday too. And really, where is that gray inert mass of humanity that the host talked about? Is really possible that this land covered by the scattering light is eighty percent inhabited by them? And what about these random passers-by, the passengers at the airport the fellow travelers on the plane? Yes, people are like people. Maybe this gray mass is a phantom, a myth? But then who orders the music? For whom are TV series filmed and mountains of meaningless consumer goods released? On whom does the power of C students rest? Alas, this is reality and what a reality! Two worlds are mixed into one in every city, every house, even in every single person. It's like in liquid helium, superfluid He II and inert viscous He I. It's impossible to separate one from the other! But that's enough of the philosophizing. All of this is complete nonsense, the world is much more complicated. It's time to sleep.

The Pusher

Alex, like Roland, preferred to fly around the world from east to west, although both of them had completely different reasons. The first stop on the trip was Voronezh. After having talked with the leadership of Kosmotech, Hank Orly warned him that there would most likely be no point in visiting there but Alex decided to stop by, plunge into the environment that spoke the language of his grandfathers and great-grandfathers and which he knew well from childhood, and at the same time see these eccentrics who refused to accept a golden order. In other words, it was a kind of ethnographic excursion with little chance of business success.

"Will you drop me or will you miss me ..." Alex whispered when the plane landed at the Mandelstam airport. Just like that, it had surfaced in his memory. The visit really did not have any fateful significance.

The director of Kosmotech was fifteen minutes late. Alex had to sit in the waiting room, where two women were talking apparently not knowing that Alex understood Russian, they called him some bigwig from Mongolia who had flown in to see their director.

"What model do you have?"

"I've had an F15 for five years now. I'm used to it and don't want to changc."

"F15? What do you mean? That is an Angel for low-lifes! In general, the F series is undignified. I have the S300. I lived with an S200 for five years, but my Angel convinced me to upgrade it to the S300. I had to take out a loan but now I have the coolest version!"

"No, I love my F15, no matter how outdated it is and I will not exchange it for another. I have no one else but him."

"Are you sleeping with him?"

"Well, sort of."

"But he is electronic!"

"Do you know how affectionate he is, how he whispers to me! Well, the rest I do myself..."

"I wonder if they all have such an option? My husband doesn't whisper anything to me."

"It is in the process of being developed. Imagine..."

Alex coughed a couple of times. He had no wish to hear the details. The women fell silent, suspecting that they had been understood. Just then a breathless director rushed into the reception room, profusely apologizing in Russian, asking the blushing woman, the owner of the F15 model, to serve tea.

"So, you probably already know that we want to order your gyrodynes for the Ark. Five sets. Hank Orly contacted you, but he did not quite understand your answer. That's why I'm here to dot the i's."

"Yes, I am aware of your order but to put it bluntly, here's the issue: as I understand it the gyrodynes will have to operate for twelve thousand years. We do not accept orders for such an extended service life."

"No really! What is the actual problem? Magnetic suspension removes all restrictions on the duration of operation."

"We do not deal with magnetic suspension. That is not part of our profile."

"So get busy with it. Is our order not important to you? It will overshadow your annual turnover many times over. You need to finally find a subcontractor for the magnetic suspension."

"How quick you are! Magnetic suspension is not rigid and our entire control software is designed for rigid suspension."

"Sorry, but we will pay so much for this that, for that kind of money, you can change all of the software ten times over."

"Yes we could do that," the director sighed heavily. "But we don't have the personnel. More precisely, they exist but they do not know how and do not want to master new software. All those who studied before the reforms have retired and all of those who managed to study well after the reforms have left for other lands. You see, now the only strategy for the survival of Kosmotech is not to change anything. As long as we have the same type of state orders, we stay alive."

"But that also means that your Kosmotech is doomed!"

"Of course we are doomed. Just like each and every one of us. Most of the staff and I are not that far from retirement. Yes, there is much that is doomed here. And not only here, you yourselves, I suppose have seen it, having traveled around the world. The reforms did not only take place in our country. Homeostasis is everywhere!

As soon as Alex left the doomed Kosmotech, one of the witnesses to his visit, the woman who owns the S300 model, asked the director about the strange Russian-speaking Mongol with the European face, and then sat down with her mouth gaping open. When she finally came to her senses, she immediately trumpeted on four social media networks that they had had a visit from the director of the trillion-dollar fund of the Ark and he had just left for the airport. The reaction from some of the Voronezh residents was excellent and timely and at the airport Alex was surrounded by a small but dense crowd. Up front were three people with microphones. All three used the word "trillion" in the first question (why does a person who manages a trillion dollars move around without guards, etc.). All three were politely refused answers. Then there were two inventors: one with a way to travel faster than light and the other with a mechanism for utilizing dark energy. He had to take a brochure from each of them. Next there were a couple of dozen people asking for autographs on popular books about the Ark and even on a monograph by Alex and Goran about exoplanets. There were quite nice and smart people everywhere, no matter how hard they were trying to eradicate them all.

Finally Alex heard: "Alexander Mikhailovich, Alexander Mikhailovich" from a voice which sounded as if it was coming from somewhere behind him.

Alex shook his head: who is Alexander Mikhailovich? After a few seconds he realized that it was him, he also had a patronymic Mikhailovich that he had never used.

Alex responded to him and the young boy squeezed forward. “My name is Vanya, Vanya Plotnikov. I am a fourth-year student on the Biology and Soil Faculty. Please take me for the Bio segment! I want to do phyto-engineering and Eco construction. I know the subject, I follow the literature and I am ready to go to work anywhere on Earth or Mars.”

“All right, Ivan, write a detailed application and send it to the official e-mail of the Ark, in the subject line indicate “For Alexander Selin” in Cyrillic, it will definitely get to me.”

Forty minutes left. It was time to say goodbye to these fast-moving people. No one ever knew what would end up being the bottom line of a visit. Who knows, maybe the most useful result would be this Vanya Plotnikov? Why not?

The next stop on his journey was in Toulouse at Electromechanika, the place where Roland’s corkscrew was being built. A full-scale layout of the outer contour had been mounted six months later than the deadline. The layout was not working. More precisely, it worked, but in such a way that it had caused Hank to laugh hysterically. Now it was Alex’s turn, it was time to use the heavy artillery. In reality it would be necessary to change the contractor, there was time, but first he would look and talk.

The building for the corkscrew was striking, even from the plane when landing, a cylinder-shaped structure of a hundred meters in height and fifty meters in diameter. It had been built quickly and the model had taken four years. It had required only six tons of copper and composites, but the dimensions...”

“Turn it on!” Alex demanded as soon as he entered the hall with his retinue.

“Maybe we should not? We will tell you everything. We will confess to everything.”

“Turn it on! It was turned on for Hank, I want to see it too.”

"Well, it's not the best sight, but if you demand it..."

It was like a cone-shaped bouquet of six strands of copper spirals and struts hanging down, which twitched and vibrated. The vibration then intensified until the windings began to dance convulsively and the hall was filled with infrasound, as if announcing the approach of the Day of Judgment. Then the structure calmed down and stabilized and after a while started dancing again.

"Enough," Alex said. "You have two mechanical resonances in the construction that are close to the operating frequency. That's why the dancing around."

"Yes, we got it."

"And obviously there are not enough external ring frames."

"Yes, there are not enough."

"So did you calculate the design at all or not?"

"We calculated it but only on a simplified model."

"You deal with alternating magnetic fields and mechanics all the time. Everything should be as easy as pie for you."

"You see, the parameters involved in this task go far beyond the input values of the codes that we currently use. We have never encountered such conditions. Our designers did not know from which side to approach the issue. What is worse is that we even tried to find outside specialists and there are none! So generally speaking, there is no one who will be ready to take on this task, even though we cast our fishing rods very far. It seems that such people simply do not exist. In the end, our employees decided to try it themselves using a simplified model, the result of their efforts is in front of you."

Alex fell silent. It was like the time of the fall of man in all its glory. Was it like this before the collapse of the Roman Empire? This was the second clear piece of evidence in one day. Damn homeostasis! What should be done about the order? Break the contract? Make it from scratch, recruit students, learn, form an enterprise... No, all of that would take too long. They had to be more humane.

"Do you want to keep the contract?"

"Of course, otherwise we fly down the tubes."

"Gather a team of those who can at least do something in terms of calculations and who have not yet attained a solid bone in their heads. Then send them to us on a very long business trip. We do not have specialists in electro-mechanics, but we have people who can take on any type of unfamiliar tasks and solve them quickly. Together they will cope with any issues in a year and a half."

Washington. Multi-colored people on the streets. A sad Minister of the Interior.

"How much land do you need and what type of land usage do you seek?"

"About five hundred square kilometers. Land usage being close to industrial. We'll have a polygon for testing robots and production, a runway and several square kilometers of transparent hangars with modified atmospheres inside."

"You have a healthy appetite!"

"So the task is really a no-brainer."

"I understand and support your goals, but unfortunately I am powerless here. The amount of land you want for this type of land usage is many times greater than the threshold after which a decision must be passed through Congress. That is the law. Even worse is that this threshold is also regularly lowered."

"If it has to go through Congress, then go through Congress. Or is that fatal?"

"Not that fatal, but sour soup. You know the story of how, a century and a half ago, Congress closed the funding for the record-breaking accelerator of those times, the supercollider, right in the midst of construction?

Many hundreds of millions had already been spent, many thousands of people had been employed or collaborated and they had built, planned experiments and had discussed new physics, which should have manifested itself at a new level of energy. And bam! Chopped off the funding suddenly and forever. Thousands of people were out of work, and the country is now inferior to Europe in fundamental physics. No one knew what to do with the tunnel that had been dug so they decided to grow champignon mushrooms! Why did Congress stop the funding? Pure roughnecks who said: 'These guys want to study something that played a role fourteen billion years ago and has not existed in nature since. Let them all go to hell!' The current composition of Congress is no better, and even the times are no better, if not worse."

"But we are not asking for money. On the contrary, we will pay for it directly into your budget."

"That is not an argument. If the congressmen get stuck on refusing something then no amount of money will help. And they can refuse here for a similar reason: 'These guys want to make someone happy after many thousands of years and ask for our land for this!'"

"Is that really their level?"

"Sometimes decent people end up there... Maybe we can find about twenty, other than that all I can say is: such times – such a Congress. The only thing I can offer is to write an application for the lease of ten square kilometers of desert. This I can decide to allocate within my authority. You will at least have a foothold, somewhere in Utah, Nevada or Arizona. Then, if fortune smiles down on you, you will be able to rent the rest. Maybe the mood in the country will change. It seems you are lucky."

Canberra, Australia.

At an open hearing in Parliament on the construction of a deep space communication station and a lander testing ground. In addition to the press, representatives of public and religious organizations were also invited. Alex's speech would be followed by questions and comments from members of the public.

Authorized Member of the Sovereign South Benjamin King:

"This so-called 'Mongolian Park' has spread its tentacles all over the world. Today they will build a station, and tomorrow they will build a university through which science-centrism, which is alien to us, will be introduced. These tentacles must not be allowed to dig into the body of our sovereign homeland!"

Secretary of the Indigenous Australian Council of Elders David Prince:

"Our land has endured so much from aliens! It has been terrorized by alien dingo dogs, eaten by imported rabbits and robbed by exiled convicts. Now two-ton blanks will be thrown at it right on the heads of living beings inhabiting the long-suffering land of their ancestors. The Indigenous Australian Council of Elders opposes the construction of the station and landfill."

Representative of the public movement "Green Australia" John Shoemaker:

"Do you know that the rays from your antennas destroy the stratosphere, causing heavy nuclei to fall on the ground?"

"Where did you get such information?"

"British scientists have proven that high-intensity microwave radiation destroys the stratosphere. Right here, in the Evening Sydney it is written!" The man shook a crumpled newspaper over his head.

Alex couldn't help but laugh. He looked around the hall and saw how about a dozen people in different places were hunched over, choking with soundless laughter. Okay only ten and the rest looked either approvingly or indifferently at what had been said.

"And how do you imagine heavy nuclei falling through the stratosphere?" Alex asked, and then about forty people laughed out loud. The author of the question looked around the hall in fright and bewilderment and silently sat down without announcing any verdict.

Australian Geographical Society Chairman Charles Taylor:

"On the one hand, the project deserves support. It is interesting and important in itself, but it will also bring some life in the most deserted corner of the continent, the south of Western Australia. Power plants, desalination plants, jobs, roads and a new oasis in the desert. On the other hand, after listening to previous speakers, I have doubts. Is such a project appropriate in a country that is rapidly running wild? Will it not lead to an increase in hysteria and all sorts of excesses? Therefore, I would suggest that, for a start, respected members of parliament decide how they see the future of the country, where it will have to move, backward or forward."

The speeches by the members of parliament were streamlined and unintelligible. Alex took a short nap, maintaining the air of a thoughtful listener, something he had learned as a student. The vote in Parliament would take place in a week. On the sidelines, they said that thanks to Taylor's remarks, there was a chance.

That's all! Alex breathed a sigh of relief on the way to the airport. This would be his last flight on the round-the-world trip. Just nine hours left! He needed to temporarily switch with Roland and let him be in his shoes for once and he would gladly fly around the light side of the globe.

Fatigue

Goran again jumped from the natural rock face into the cool water of the sea basin, swam about fifty meters out and returned, and again sat down on the stone. Again it didn't help. The sixth pair of babies had failed. The sixth pair... And again at eight months! Goran dried himself off, got dressed, got on his bicycle and rode to the Panoramic Hall. Oncoming cyclists nodded to him as they rode and he raised his hand in response. The bike path stayed out of residential areas and meandered through green squares where mothers walked with their children, past small shopping centers and crossed railroad tracks on curved bridges. Once upon a time, the walls had been decorated with earthly landscapes, now they were covered with climbing plants and huge mirrors, giving the illusion of volume. However, the volume was impressive even without illusions. Claustrophobia was not among the typical Martian ailments. It was noon, and the ceiling shone evenly with natural sunlight, which passed through the light guides that went through the thick and bulky roof.

"Why don't the ants maintain the shape of the wall? Why is it again something like a termite mound instead of a regular dome? When will they really be taught electric welding? Is it really impossible to make them normally weld two pieces of reinforcement to each other? However, the ants are nonsense, but the sixth pair... Joe and Tanya were emotional wrecks. Yes, and he himself...

The scoreboard in the Panoramic Hall showed ninety micro-roentgens per hour, plus twenty Celsius inside, plus five outside. It was hot, even by Mariner Valley standards. There were several more people in the hall, silently looking at the hills, at the mountains, at the bewitching desert, where giant walls with striped buttresses and scree crevices rose from behind the horizon in the haze. Goran didn't know any of the people that were sitting there. Apparently, they too were tired judging by their postures and motionless faces. They weren't sitting here for nothing, the view through the transparent wall usually brought Goran back into balance. And what a view it was! From the spur of the Capri plateau where the colony was located, the Mariner valley was visible up until the point where it turned at the forked canyon Koprat. It didn't take much imagination to imagine the sea that would overflow there in thousands of years, with the colony being right on its shore. The ridge dividing the Koprat canyon into two branches would stick out of the water for five kilometers and above would be snowy peaks, on which clouds would cling... When would that be...?

Aslan Schultz will deal with the ants, no need to fill your head with that. But with the babies it's much worse. They won't reboot... Why are they losing contact with Joe and Tanya? Is it possible that it really is just because they can't be touched?

Someday, instead of thick armored glass, there will be the most ordinary glass here, there will be a door through which you can go outside, go down to the water and sit on the shore. Even now, the panorama is breathtaking. It should be breathtaking... The babies do not scream, do not cry, they fall into a stupor. It's scarier. Right now, they are already being rehabilitated, they will soon be taken into a family and they will never remember the experiment. But there, on that planet, twenty parsecs away, there will be no family in the case of an unsuccessful outcome. What are we doing wrong? After all, there must be a way out! After all, every God pleasing problem has at least one solution.

Down below, some day in the future, a whirlwind would rise from the sea, grow to three hundred meters in height and move north, leaving behind a dark trail. Then two more whirlwinds would arise as the ground warmed up, and soon the distant slopes of the Mariner Valley would disappear in a dusty haze and the panorama would shrink. Oh, if there was already a sea, I would sail for three days on a yacht to the islands (those flat-topped mountains would have already become islands) and my brain would be cleared. The waves in the sea will be more serious than those on the earth, what is in the denominator, the force of gravity or the root of it? I could ride a rover, climb up the plateau. No too much time. It's better if I run along the Big Ring, although all twenty kilometers have been memorized down to the smallest detail. It's good on Earth, there are always places where you haven't been. You can always do something that you have not done before, sail on a yacht along a real sea, go on a white-water trip, wander through a forest, jump with a parachute... So you wanted something ready? Like a lullaby? That is fatigue. This is how our brothers break down.

What is worse: stress, constant crying, or such a dullness that they do not see the image of their own parents point-blank and do not hear their words? With complete indifference, they allow the Nanny to wash them, change their clothes, and only food causes some kind of response. Their eyes, in which a spark of interest in the world had already begun to appear, go out again. What happens if the experiment is not interrupted? Would they grow into vegetables? No, such an experiment cannot be... not interrupted.

Should I go to the nursery department and talk to the people? Everyone is tired too. What will I tell them now? "Let's cheer up!"? Perhaps now the sounds from my lips will not sound false, but simply funny, like laughter through tears. Of course, I'll go, of course, I'll talk, but first I myself must at least perk up a little.

Should I talk to Alex? If of course you can call that a conversation. What do we have with the Earth? Nothing but a twenty light-minute round trip. Goran sat far away from people so that no one would hear, he was lucky the hall was built on such a grand scale.

"Hi, Alex, I wanted to cry on your shoulder. I have been wandering around the catacombs and I can't find a quiet place by myself. We are completely stuck with the first babies. The sixth attempt in a row has ended in their stupor at eight months. This time we cranked up the nanny to the limit: a gentle voice, soft hands and she is a feast for the eyes! And still, these little devils recognize a fake. Up to six months, everything is fine; they smile at the nanny, google in response to the remarks of their parents. Then they start to get frightened of something and then just close up and turn into vegetables, with no reaction whatsoever to their parents behind the glass, no reactions to contact with the nanny, except sometimes some sort of sluggish communication with each other. Well, and then the only more or less lively reaction is to food. Moreover, this has been repeated time after time and all that has been achieved is to delay the stupor for a month. Maybe it's some kind of defensive reaction? That is what our experts say, they also say that tactile contact is necessary, that a robotic nanny is basically incapable of imitating a parental caress. They are probably right, but this is all fortune-telling, you yourself understand that there was no such practice at all before: for the first time in history, someone is trying to grow children without the participation of a living person. You know, it's getting scary. It's starting to look hopeless. I understand that the

task cannot be hopeless and this barrier must be overcome, otherwise everything loses its meaning. I'm just tired, Alex. I have grown so tired that at one point I actually wanted to go to Earth. I understand that this is a complete shame for a Martian, but there was such a case, a momentary weakness. Bye then. If I didn't scare you too much with my sour face, please say something."

Alex usually responded as soon as he received a message, but the light in this cottony space moved depressingly slowly. So, no matter what, it was necessary to wait the inevitable twenty minutes. Below, a dozen drunken dust devils were already wandering among the hills, leaving twisting dark trails to the north, where a seven-kilometer wall rose above the horizon. There is a road there and if you climb the wall, you will get to the Aurora Plain and from the cliff you can see across the entire Mariner Valley from edge to edge, much further than you see through the glass. The colony is visible from there only through good binoculars through which you can see the terraces, the roads, the outdoor greenhouses and the cone-shaped light receivers. But the canyon appears in full breadth: the confluence of the gorges of Capri and Eos, how wide is it, one hundred and fifty kilometers or almost two hundred? And you can see the opposite wall when the atmosphere is calm! A little imagination and in front of you is the dream of dozens of future generations of Martians, a real sea, islands, clouds and greenery. By that time, the Ark will already be at the target... A good thing for the descendants who will see this...

"Hi Goran. I come to you with a reciprocal cry and ask you to give me your shoulder. We have about the same thing, only worse. You are struggling with a specific problem that probably has a solution. And we are fighting with some indefinite viscous and sticky substance. We need polygons of thousands of square kilometers. Private land of this size does not exist. In Europe, where they treat us well, there are no such lands at all. All hope for public lands is on others continents, and this is just where it starts...

"Preliminary agreements on the lease of land have already been broken several times. First, they ask for exorbitant prices. Finally, we negotiate a price on moderately high terms. But then, when everything has already been agreed, the officials begin to divert their eyes from the table and mutter something about the difficult domestic political situation. It turns out that the population is against it. All right, we say, let's explain everything to your population, we will speak to

them, we will tell them everything, we will open an educational mission... And then the eyes of the officials begin to dart around even faster, these proposals frighten them even more. And without polygons, everything just stops. We can't develop the landing modules and we can't deploy a simulation environment. Maybe they just want a bribe? Imagine what I have to do! About longing for the Earth, I have a cure for that and it's being uploaded to your Martian mailbox right now. This is a four-hour selection of primetime broadcasts from the global television channel WWV with an audience of about three billion. You have to look through it all in one sitting. You will be sick of the news so be patient. Watch the talk shows, there are such characters! And they carry on about such things it's unbelievable! Including things about the Ark, so don't try to launch a boot into the screen, just watch and be patient. Also you will have to endure a portion of strained humor with the sonorous cackle of extras behind the scenes. There are two series of different TV shows, crocodile tears and crap on everything. You have to bite the bullet and watch both from beginning to end, remembering that all of this is being watched by billions of their own free will and with pleasure. After that, I guarantee you will be forever spared from relapses of nostalgia for the Earth. Now make sure you shake everything out. Go running, swimming or riding. At worst get drunk. Or better yet, burn yourself in a sauna and then wallow in the snow, you do have snow somewhere in the catacombs, right? Sometimes it helps me, but to be honest not right now. But what the hell, I'm not kidding!"

Alex looked no better than Goran, but by the end of the message he began to gesticulate intensely and it seemed that he felt a little better after speaking out.

Perhaps Alex was right, he needed to unwind a little. He was tired of running in circles, even though the circle is long. He remembered the snow, that's an idea! Maybe sit on a bike and go to the polar sector? It's winter there now. And recently, another ten hectares of forest-tundra were put into operation, with natural rocks, crooked birches and low pines. Go skiing... No, it's better to go and ride dogs, Tom now has four teams, wonderful fun dogs... Well, well, dogs, dogs... Funny fluffy dogs...

Bonfire and Space

Large rivers mysteriously affect a person, they relieve stress and depression like a magic wand and all you have to do is sit on the bank, watch the water and breathe in the river air. This was fully felt by Alex, Roland, Gene and the hefty dog named Jack already on their third day by the water after fleeing from civilization. Jack was one of the numerous descendants of Noah, but he had been rejected for the fact that he fought all males, regardless of size and breed, not that hard, only until first blood, but even this level of aggression was considered unacceptable for dogs for 47 Librae b. In the absence of males, he was the most gentle and friendly creature. In general, lines formed for the culled dogs of Stefan Mucha but Jack went to Alex, because as he had said, he was for "the big boss".

The three friends were sitting on a gray log, stripped clean by sand and river pebbles, and a fire was burning in front of them. The dog lay on the sand and just like them looked at the river and the reflection of the mountains in it and a river cruise ship passed slowly by.

"They've been sailing by here for ages," Alex said. "More than two hundred years ago, almost the same ships sailed here, only back then they were diesel and ran on oil-based fuel. Perhaps some of those are still floating around only the diesel engines have been replaced with reactors."

"You have already been here. Have you ever sailed on such a steel boat?"

"No, I only used a boat with oars, like now. Yes, and I was here only once with my grandfather. I was twelve years old, he was eighty-two. Feeling that he was weakening, my grandfather decided to show me this place as it meant a lot to him. He had taken a boat out here alone five years earlier. According to him he remembered his youth so well, and in such detail, including his dreams and thoughts, that it was as if he was having a dialogue with himself sixty years ago."

"Your grandfather definitely had a good childhood and youth," Gene said. "By the way, I also have Russian roots, even though I know only a dozen words in Russian. My name is actually Coonin but somewhere, three or four generations ago, the second letter N was lost."

"Yes, one could envy my grandfather. He also said that in the worst of times he warmed himself with memories, as if the warmth that he had absorbed here, lying on the hot sand, came back. I remember everything only vaguely, the mountains beyond the river and the smells. It's also been sixty years and everything also seems to have come to life, although I, unlike my grandfather, did not grow up here. Truly a supernatural place!"

The friends sat on the log, looking at the path that stretched along the river leading from the setting sun. It was not enough to say that they were tired, they were completely exhausted. Tiredness from good intensive work is pleasant, but fatigue from endlessly being pulled here and there, squabbles, urgent matters pouring in from all different sides, failures and promises that you do not have time to fulfill, is painful and destructive. It is not enough to say that the friends were resting. They were soaking in energy, retreating and reviving.

It was the twentieth year of the Ark epic. Usually a large project is difficult to start, but over time it seems to lift itself onto the rails and starts to roll along by itself, and is distributed among the participants, each of whom knows his own role. The Ark didn't have rails, and it didn't seem like it could. Everything was being done for the first time, there was a catch to everything hidden everywhere, and all of the failures were unexpected and seemed to be endless.

When the sun went down, a long-drawn-out whistle of a ship sounded from afar, low and aching, filling all space, as if not from this world.

"It's a metaphysical signal!" Roland said. "It sounds like it wants to tell us something important."

"Apparently, it is trying to cheer us up or stand up for us in front of the Cosmos," Gene added.

"As for cheering, we'll do it now," Alex entered. "So, the US Congress showed us the door, everyone saw this even before leaving and I asked you to leave all your gadgets at home, and did the right thing. But... I took a small electronic napkin just in case."

Alex took the napkin out of his shirt pocket, unfolded it out, flicked it, moved his finger along it and solemnly read:

"The California Vintners Association is protesting the shameful decision of the US Congress to deny a piece of federal land to the 47 Librae Ark Project. We are ashamed of the representatives of our people who do not understand either the meaning or the significance of the greatest cause in the modern history of mankind. We express our support to the participants of the project, the scientists, engineers and workers who do the most difficult work for the sake of the distant future of the human race. As a sign of support, we are sending ten thousand bottles of aged Californian wine of the best brands to the administration of the Ark."

"Damn! It just warmed my heart..."

"I wonder if the Canadian lumberjacks supported it?"

"We would build a whole building complex out of logs in the spirit of Auditorium B3. However, jokes aside. This is truly a wonderful sign. And they are no longer the only ones. It seems that the changes have gone deeper and that there are more and more signs of popular support. The winemakers are serious! Twenty years ago, they would have supported the US Congress and not us. Politicians still do not know how to relate to the Ark, and the people have already become numb from Homeostasis and have begun to wake up. Yes, and in the end all our wandering around the world with our lectures and speeches was not in vain. Why are we hanging our heads here? Alex, remember what you said at that dinner at B3 about despair in the middle of a hard road? Here it is, we are in the middle."

"Well, yeah, I remember. I also remember what Gene said: 'You have to live long to see the launch.' I definitely won't live long enough. Well, at least you and Gene..."

"Come on, Alex, you can be like a rock. Do you remember the night with the frogs, grasshoppers and stars in the Mongolian Park, the night when the idea first came up?"

"Of course 'the Bacchanalia of Life, the Omega Point', we covered it all! By the way, you put forward the idea, I just agreed with you."

“I don’t even remember who said “A” first, and it doesn’t matter. Here’s what’s interesting. That conversation had huge consequences. Thanks to it we decided to act. It turns out that it changed our lives, mobilized huge funds and hundreds of thousands of people, and there are far more grandiose consequences ahead if we don’t crack. What if the sky wasn’t so starry, or the frogs were silent, or if we had not been there? The conversation would not have taken place or would have gone the wrong way and farewell to the Ark! Those are the quirks of causal relationships.”

“Yes, if only! The idea had been hanging in the air for a long time. Even in the most miserable popular science programs it sometimes came up. It’s just that no one bothered to try to understand the problems and make a decision. Well, if it had not been us, someone else would have done it.”

“I think you would have done it anyway, a little earlier or later,” Gene concluded. “Not stars and frogs, then the sea and birds, not cognac, or whatever you had, then red wine. You were ripe for the Ark by then, and it was no quirk of causality.”

“Let’s sit silently for a while,” Alex suggested. “Let’s see how the stars light up. There, the brightest over the mountains, what is it?”

The brightest of the stars was Mars. When it got completely dark, it became so bright that a path stretched across the water from it.

“Our friends are there,” Roland said. “Goran and the others. How are they doing there? I wonder what time of day it is at the Capri Colony right now?”

“Let me look.” Alex again ran his finger over the napkin. “It is ten in the morning.”

“Let’s write something to Goran right now. Mars is getting close and the message will reach it in about six minutes.”

“No need for that. We are on vacation, he is at work. By the way, Goran has only seen big rivers in pictures. He was also born on Mars and they don't have big rivers there. Maybe in twenty thousand years but now there is no such thing."

"But they also don't have swindlers or boors and fools. They have naturally stupid people, but you can't call them fools, they are embarrassed by their stupidity and try their best to get rid of it. There are boors and impudent fools only on Earth. When big rivers appear on Mars, boors, crooks, and other riffraff will probably appear there as well. Apparently, that is the payment for open spaces, beauty and blue skies."

"What's up with Goran and the ant team?" Gene asked.

"It's moving forward. They taught them to cement pebbles and sand together and to build domes from them, and also to sniff out and collect particles of given ores and minerals. All this is needed on Mars. So far, they have not succeeded in the self-reproduction of ants. They will have to build a whole village and small workshops on that planet. Those that can be brought, ten to twenty tons, will not be enough. We decided that we would send ten tons of finished ants and thirty million chips for new ones. And they will make new ones on the site, for which the ants that are taken there will have to deploy some kind of miniature production facility which will be needed for other purposes. This is what they are fighting for."

Something squeaked softly in Alex's pocket. He took out the electronic napkin again and straightened it out.

"Wow, a message from Goran! Speak of the Devil. Video... What can I hang the napkin on so that everyone can see it clearly? Yeah, here's a bush back here, shine the light here..."

Alex hung up the luminous napkin, snapped it to the branches at the corners, moved his finger along it, and Goran appeared in front of his friends.

"Hello, colleagues! I have good news: the babies are fourteen months old, healthy and cheerful. They're already talking about something. If you remember, several times I had to interrupt the experiment at eight months due to self-sustaining depression. We have added only one innovation, a dog. Not a replica of a

dog, but a real live dog, which we already know how to reproduce autonomously. Until now, we have tried to improve the nanny and the replicas of the parents. The children quickly recognize that something is not right with the nanny, that she is just alien and it's impossible to make her better, and the virtual parents have been perfected to the limit. Tanya Meyers and Joe Sidorov are just heroes, almost five full years of recording, and your Waxman is a genius. Not a single word out of place, not the slightest falsehood, but they are behind glass, and here, a living soul, a warm, furry, kind creature... It seems that the critical moment has passed and they are beginning to understand what their parents say, it should become easier further on. I no longer doubt that it will work, although there is still about fifteen years of work to do. In the meantime, watch this short video."

In the video, children were crawling over a hefty red-haired mongrel. It rolled over on its back, folding its paws, then one of the girls sat on its belly and the other lay next to it imitating a dog. Behind the glass was a hologram of Joe Sidorov.

When the girl on the dog began to beat the dog, Joe said: "Kat, don't beat Magda, the dog hurts, better scratch her belly!"

"Jesus, how did Joe's hologram know what the girl was doing?" Roland whispered.

"Joe seems to have had a good time with kids and dogs live on record," Gene replied. "In general, the Waxman platform works wonders. No matter how much I watch it work, every time I feel a sense of mysticism, a miracle. Although, when Rob explains, it is clear that there is no mysticism. But I still can't get used to it..."

Magda moving from a position on her back reached out to the girl lying next to her and began to lick her cheek. And then Jack, who was watching the video along with the others, whined in a bass voice and rushed to the napkin. Apparently, he wanted to join Magda and the children.

"Wait, wait. It's very far away," Alex said and calmed the dog, patting the back of his head.

"They play like that for hours until they get tired," Goran continued.

"No signs of stress or depression. We are waiting for the system to make a decision to open the way for the girls to the large aviary, so far only Magda can get there. By the way, she is a descendant of the pack that you sent us in the form of embryos upon request."

"A big red mongrel. We considered her the best of the Martian varieties of dogs. But you on Earth can infer even better. I appeal to Gene: mobilize the best cynoligist. Or, if you think that the best of them, like Mukha, is already working for you, give him everything he wants. The dog has become a key element of the last phase of the project. You, apparently, yourself understand what is needed: an iron psyche, angelic patience, good nature and intelligence. Then there's the longevity of dogs and, well their love for people, especially for children of course. Let them be daring! You still have a lot of time and money that will seem fabulous to them. So let them make a fabulous creature: a dog with wings behind its back. It's easier than putting something like that on a person. Well, I'm sorry. Take care of yourselves and most importantly, take a break. You, as you appeared in the latest video messages, cannot be looked at without tears, a heartbreaking sight. Go out to nature in full detachment. Do you have somewhere...?"

The message ended and all three were silent, digesting what had been said. Goran was also not the best sight but still, the moment really became a turning point. Either the good news from Goran had an effect, or the petition of the winemakers, or simply the charm of the river. Yes, everyone remained exhausted, but suddenly they felt like travelers who had climbed a pass, beyond which there was a glacier, a valley, rivers. and a lake with a boundless blue space in the haze, a normal human panorama, and not the dark chaos moving behind their eyes.

Jack quickly fell asleep and was snoring peacefully. The rest spread their sleeping bags right on the sand and lay down next to the dying fire. They had not seen such a starry sky for a long time.

Gene broke the silence. "Will people really be able to populate this luminous abyss? Or maybe it is already partially inhabited by some intelligent creatures?"

"I don't know, maybe it's thanks to Goran, or maybe thanks to the river, but today I stopped doubting," Alex replied. "If we jump to forty-seven and then somewhere else, and then they in turn, jump to a couple of places, they will spread exponentially, which is something that nothing will stop. The time between jumps is, say thirty thousand years and the average distance is twenty parsecs. The settlement front will move at a speed of about one and a half parsecs every thousand years. The size of the Galaxy is thirty kilo parsecs, so some time in about fifty million years, all of it will be populated, that is, all planets suitable for life. But that's all a blink in time! It's several times less than the time it takes for one revolution of our solar system around the center of the Galaxy. Why is the Universe not inhabited by someone else yet? Because if it had been we would not be finding one planet after another that is suitable for life but lifeless. Otherwise, the abyss would not be as silent as a fish."

"Are we the first here? How many stars are there? More than a hundred billion! Or worse, are we the only ones in time? It kind of makes you feel uncomfortable when you think about it."

"If we are the first, or even more so the only ones, this whole 'glowing abyss', as Gene put it, is looking at us with hope, so chins up!"

"Hey, hey guys," Alex responded, "lower the pathos. The feeling of one's exceptional importance has not yet helped anyone to bring the matter to an end. Better to feel your microscopicity in comparison with what is above us. It disciplines one."

"Roland, please explain to the dense biologist what will happen to all of this splendor in hundreds of billions of years. In tens of billions, I know that all this will fade, but there will be red dwarfs that you can live with. So?"

"The smallest dwarfs will shine for hundreds of billions years. Further, if we are lucky, some galaxy from a local cluster will once again crash into us and a renaissance will occur, with billions of new stars created due to the compression of interstellar gas, but then everything will go out again! Life in its present form is doomed in trillions of years. There are other options, to adapt to the cooling of the universe, by cooling ourselves. If we follow the right strategy, life, while changing physical form, can exist forever. But there is another interesting possibility. Dark energy turned out to be the quintessence..."

"What?!"

"Haven't you heard of dark energy?"

"I heard it's what makes the Universe expand at an accelerating rate. Although I don't understand how, but quintessence?!"

"Well, these are the simplest differential equations need to be written down in order to explain. First of it's dark, and second of all I am too lazy. Let me try to explain like this: if dark energy is a hanging vacuum (and it weighs one gram in a cube with an edge of forty thousand kilometers) then its density does not change with time. Then dark energy will inflate through space for an unlimited time. Our cluster of galaxies is not going anywhere, it is bound by gravity. Later neighboring clusters will fly away beyond the horizon, and principally in tens of billions of years they will not be observable. Even during my childhood, it was determined that dark energy is not a vacuum, its density changes with time, it in fact decreases. How was that determined? Distant galaxies were observed until the observers were blue in the face, absolute brightness was calibrated for all sorts of supernovae and other standard "candles". Hubble diagrams were developed and they found that the density of dark energy decreases with time. This means that it is not a vacuum, but a physical field, the simplest one you can think of, a scalar but of a nature incomprehensible to us. This magnificent word "quintessence" was stuck to it. So, this field will weaken then it will begin to oscillate and crumble into some new particles, also of a nature unknown to us. New physics will arise and the Universe will be filled with new content. Who knows? Maybe new life will appear, of gigantic size, negligible density, unimaginably slow in movement or at an unthinkably low temperature."

"What will happen to the old content?"

"It won't go anywhere and it won't even feel the metamorphosis. Two levels of matter will coexist. Our level from the point of view of the new world will turn into some creepy exotic dimension. The cooled celestial bodies from the point of view of that Universe will be unthinkably dense compact formations, from which it is better to stay away. But this is all guesswork and divining coffee grounds. We do not know what physics will appear after the quintessence burns out. We only know that the moment of burnout will be something like a new Big Bang from the point of view of those who, perhaps, will appear there at the new level of physics."

"Let's go to sleep. Are hundreds of billions of years not enough for you?"

Three days later it was time to sail back. When they had collected everything and the kayaks were loaded, Jack suddenly decided he was not going anywhere. He did not want to leave there for any reason. He started whimpering and refused to go to any of the boats. He lay down and rolled onto his back then ran to the bushes and whined sadly. He seemed to be trying to say: "Where are you going? Finally, we found a piece of paradise where I can endlessly rush along the sand and jump into the shallow waters, splashing everything around us and you can look at the river and the stars endlessly and sit and think. What more do humans and dogs need?!" They tried everything and the only way left was to get into the boats and just sail away. Jack then rushed into the water and swam to Alex's boat, then he, as heavy as he was, was pulled out of the water by three of them in two boats which risked capsizing.

It was not only Jack who was sad to leave. The place was lost and far from the usual routes of the heroes of this story and everyone understood that it was unlikely that they would ever go there again. They were far from their youth, having reached the stage in life when a person becomes more and more difficult get up and when an encouraging "someday", as a rule, turns into a sentence of "never again".

In life it is impossible to indefinitely return to where things were good or became easier. Yes, and in fact there is no need to, just remember, and life will become broader and deeper.

In order to safely and logically approach some kind of epilogue, the narrative is forced to jump over large time intervals, omitting important events. Instead of a thread, a dotted line is then produced, but sadly there is nothing that can be done.

It is necessary to omit the part of the story of how the first tactical victories were won over the officials and the desired expanses of semi-deserts were leased. We also have to skip the descriptions of cyclopean structures, such as gigantic greenhouses with oxygen-free atmospheres where mats of algae grew, and others where rocks were overgrown with genetically modified lichens and mosses, and still others where fast-growing grassy thickets piled up on top of the compressed layers of trunks and leaves. Or the history of the flight of an experimental probe with a Roland corkscrew to the Kuiper Belt and back, in a year and a half.

It is impossible even to describe the scale of the work which consisted mainly of the routine goings on in thousands of laboratories, workshops and offices scattered around the world. How long would it take to describe the daily work of millions of people? We also have to skip the telling of how our heroes gradually grew old and lost their strength, but did not lose the ability to laugh and make fun of their own weakness.

Thus, having skipped an entire era, we jump forward twenty years. Twenty years, during which a lot of water has flowed under the bridge, during which the world has experienced another upheaval which managed to run out of steam a little. We have to skip over all of that and stop and focus on a sad, but alas, inevitable event.

Alex would be happy

Alex died when he was ninety-three years old. For the last couple of years of his life his legs had failed him. He appeared less and less in public and left all of his posts, but in spite of all that he began to work more than ever. His main activity was the creation of his own replica, a tool for communicating with the people on 47 Librae b many thousands of years in the future. Alex believed that they would have many questions for him and had already begun to quietly record on the Waxman platform many years earlier. However before now there had not been enough time to systematically record and work on his second self. Now he spent all his time talking to thousands of people, albeit remotely, but frankly. In the morning he sat down in front of the screen and a TV camera, connected with someone to an arbitrary point on the globe or with an entire audience, and he spoke and answered questions and even argued and everything was recorded and processed. By the middle of the day he was tired but an afternoon nap restored his working capacity. Then Alex spoke to himself, to his replica, checking his second "I" for lies, for indistinctness, inconsistencies and falsity.

There were almost no lies, but indistinctness and falsehood sometimes showed through. You can't fix a replica, you can't edit it, it is your model, it is something akin to your own reputation and in order to improve it Alex had to talk and argue with people again and again, avoiding falsehoods and indistinctness to earn a worthy replica.

As time went on there were fewer and fewer falsehoods, but Alex's strength was leaving him and he felt himself starting to fall apart, so he asked Roland, Gene, and Bill Pak to come and see him.

"So, friends, I increasingly hear persistent knocks from the other side and know that soon I will have to go. There's nothing more to be done here, yes the main things I have already done. In the matter of the final completion of the Ark, I will only interfere. I leave in my place a completely sane replica of myself for uploading to the Ark and I will try to die in the warm season so that you can adequately see me off. If I do not pass before mid-October, I will try to pull through until spring with all my might."

"Until what spring!? What are you talking about?! You will dance in your wheelchair at my funeral!"

"Until next spring, Roland, until next spring. All of my systems are failing one after the other, except that my head is still holding on. Almost like Professor Dowell's head."

"You still have your hands and you pound on a keyboard like a real secretary. And your mouth functions, God forbid it didn't. You're better off than Stephen Hawking, remember?"

"Hawking's internal organs worked normally, his heart, liver and lungs. I already have nothing but problems with them and my immunity has gone to hell. So either I'll hang on until mid-October, or try to pull through until next spring."

"It would be better if you tell me how you imagine a worthy farewell will be. Or should we guess or what?"

"Maybe on a carriage from an AX heavy orbital rocket, harnessed to a train of sixty-four Indian elephants. How's that for a decent hearse for you?

"Even that is something you scoff at. You never settled down... So this is what I want: no graves, coffins or priests, God forgive me. I have claustrophobia and I don't want to be in a coffin even as a corpse. And I don't need a grave with a monument, I have already inherited enough from the world to also have a monument. No need! So yeah! Just burn the body! It's much more hygienic than rotting in a grave and... listen carefully. Everyone gathers at Auditorium B3. Everyone hikes up with the exception of my wife and Roland who can be transported there by helicopter."

"Why me in a helicopter? I'll drag myself up, no doubt, and at the same time I'll sprinkle sand on the path. With my arthritis, the descent is more problematic for me. I will have to tie a heavy flat object to my back and hang it on a rope on the way back to take the load off the knee ligaments."

"According to tradition, there is sure to be someone drunk out of their mind, let that be a heavy flat object for you. But seriously, listen further. Rent a two-seater plane at the club. You will sit at the helm, Bill, since you are now the main boss and you have a pilot's license. The second one in the plane will hold the urn and will be my eldest son, Nick. When everyone has gathered, Bill flies out of Hatgal-2, flies up to B3, makes three circles over it, waves the plane's wings, and my son pours the ashes down over all of you. And then you will all rejoice and celebrate the successful completion of my turbulent life. Just like that. All of the little details are at your discretion. The only thing I regret is that I myself will not be able to enjoy the party."

Alex did not die by mid-October and dragged on as best he could until spring. He even exceeded his promise and lived until the beginning of June when he died in his sleep from a common cold which had set off a chain reaction of irreversible damage.

The official farewell took place in the columned hall of the Ark headquarters which was in the former main building of the physics department. It was a personable, meaningful and touching event in its own way, but we'll skip it for the less traditional event.

The day of the unofficial farewell was set for June 12, a week after his death. When choosing the date, no traditions or other wishes were taken into account, only the weather forecast.

On the path to Auditorium B3, people with backpacks appeared and they looked to be about the same types as those who had come to the brainstorming sessions forty years ago. The only difference was that now the average age had grown quite a bit, and now there were many more of them. The veterans were also hiking up the hill including most of the participants in that initial brainstorming session that were still alive and could move independently, including climbing uphill. It was clear that the rate of ascent became less on average as age increased. Roland was one of the slowest and he climbed, first and foremost, according to the principle: "Twenty steps, fifteen breaths in one place, then fifteen steps and twenty breaths". Roland was accompanied by Gene, who found his pace quite suitable, and Volodya Drake, who at sixty-eight years old could climb faster, but preferred good company and rejoiced when the people who overtook them shouted "Glory to the veterans!" Rob Waxman had started early and was way ahead. Stefan Mucha with his wife, younger son and their old dog Aram, one of the many grandchildren of Noah, on the contrary had started later, but they moved quite quickly and overtook the veterans halfway up the mountain. When Stefan met them, he offered Roland to give him Aram as a tractor. Roland did not refuse and a harness was fashioned for him from a long leash. Then the proud Aram pulled Roland the happy veteran up the mountain. He did such a good job that that Gene began to grumble and eventually fell behind. They waited for Gene at the observation deck and gathered together on a rocky ledge.

As soon as Gene emerged from around the bend in the path, he burst into another round of grumbling: "Here it is, old age, damn it! You sat down there at the bottom and you didn't understand what kind of a nag you have turned into. Haven't been here in five years but before, when they were building the auditorium, I could get all the way to the top at a run without stopping."

"You know, Gene, I think it's more important to be able to crawl here at eighty-something than to run up at thirty," Roland said.

"Even so, it doesn't make me feel any better now. Let's sit here and enjoy the view. Aram, give me a paw! What aaroma! The larches blossomed not so long ago..."

Only dozens of people could fit in room B3 but in fact there were thousands of people who had arrived. The people settled higher along the ridge or dispersed and spread into an alpine meadow overlooking the valley. Somewhere wandering around were five of Alex's eight grandchildren and nine of his twenty great-grandchildren. There were ten of his eleven disciples here. The eleventh, Bill Pak, was away on assignment. People sat on the rocks, on rugs or lay on the grass. They took food and drinks out of their backpacks, someone had set up a table on a boulder, someone else on a folding table, someone on the grass, there was no common table and there could not have been. The green meadow with protruding gray rocks covered with many colorful spots, had turned into a giant chaotic picnic. From below, two ravens rose from the forest, nervously yelled "caw-caw" and glided back down into the forest. They had never seen anything like this in their twenty years of life and did not know how to react to it.

The wild hamsters came running, knowing how to deal with all of it and they stood in columns, begging for food. They had been doing this for many generations. Thanks to the B3 visitors they had developed a peculiar culture of begging, unknown to the hamsters of other places.

People went back and forth, from "table" to "table", looking for acquaintances and found them at every step, including those who had been lost for a long time: "Rose, is that you? Hi dear! Yes, you have grown younger in all these years! Four grandchildren?! Wow! How is Paolo doing? All in their embryos? Are you interested in grandchildren? Occasionally ... Well, thanks for that. We are at that rock, come over."

"Oh, Chuck, hi! Damn, I haven't seen you in twenty years! Where are you working now? In Bio? What are you doing? Phytoexpansion that is, you are now a sower with us? And I'm still in radiation materials science.

We are fighting for durability. How long do you think the superconducting biosecurity solenoid will be functional? You offend us! If it's in the same intensity of space as the solar system, about a million years. Why a million years? Because a million is better than a hundred thousand. And then, and this is not a joke, suddenly in a million years someone wants to use the parts of the Ark that are still dangling in orbit. Of course I'll drop by. Write down my particulars."

"Excuse me, are you Hank Orly by any chance?" Oh, how nice to see you! Forty years have passed! Did you recognize me? Yeah, yeah, it's Uno Bjorn himself! Well, it's easy to recognize you, the entire Network is full of portraits of you, but how did you recognize me? Oh come on, I haven't changed... I'm one and a half times heavier. What do I do? We drop two-ton bricks from space then they parachute down and hit a two-meter bullseye. Yeah, you're right, it's a man's job. Oh look! Seems they're flying."

Indeed, the noise of the engine was heard.

"Look, look over there, to the left of that mountain!"

Indeed, a two-seat sports plane was approaching B3 from the side of the valley. It made three circles as instructed and then it made a movement as if waving its wings. On lap four, the front pilot pulled back the hatch and Alex's ashes were emptied out of the metal cylinder. The small ephemeral plume then quickly dissipated and all of the people got up. They stood up on stones, on the rock face and on the grass. No one knew in advance what they would do next. Should they now mournfully bow their heads in silence? No. They began waving their arms, their caps and shirts that they had taken off, silently smiling a little sadly. Probably, this was how long-distance sea expeditions were seen off in the eighteenth and nineteenth centuries, when the ship sailed, they could still see you waving but they no longer heard you.

Powerful speakers and a free microphone were installed on the open veranda of the B3 building, and people lined up to speak. Some people told funny stories about Alex, others remembered his words and made toasts. There was no mourning in the alpine meadow above

Auditorium B3. Alex would have been pleased.

A small turboprop aircraft flew high over the mountains and no one paid any particular attention to it.

Then after about three minutes one of the guys shouted: “Look, is that a parachutist heading towards us?”

Indeed, a red para-sail appeared high in the sky. A minute later, the most vigilant could see that there were two figures descending under the parachute.

“Logically, it could only be William Pak and Nikolai Selin,” Hank Orly stated.

It was them of course. Bill was piloting the parachute and the tandem landed right on the veranda. Then without even unfastening his straps, Bill went to the microphone, leading a smiling Nick with him by their bindings.

“I apologize for such an exotic entrance. The fact is that we wanted to get here as soon as possible, and climbing up would have taken two hours and taking the helicopter is not sporting and contrary to the charter of B3, so we chose a fast and sporting option. I see that the festivities are in full swing, and that you are all fine here. I must say that this is exactly what Alex would have wanted and what he in fact bequeathed: that we, and I quote, ‘You should properly celebrate the successful completion of my long and turbulent life.’ Therefore, we will join you and continue in the same spirit!”

The people ate, drank, got to know each other and even argued. Every one of them was surrounded by a circle of old or new friends. Even if someone happened to be restlessly wandering around the huge picnic, their minds could pick out a lot of interesting and unexpected pieces of conversation from the overall noise: “Yes, it is impossible only through the analysis of the chemical composition of the atmosphere to determine the stages of phytoexpansion! You are going to have to get your ass up out of the chair and do something, send probes, take samples... Got it? You’re going to have to think!”

“Listen, the incubator is not made of rubber! They have already crammed all of the electronic memory in there and you want to shove all of the ant chips in there too! The Arsenal has its own magnetic protection, so why?”

“It’s still too weak. Each chip must weigh at least three grams in order to survive inside the defense field of the Arsenal. Again these are extra tons! You have five hundred cubic meters of useful volume in there that can be used!”

“Hank, I’m sorry, is this your idea to build a nuclear power plant on the one hundreth year?” What were you thinking? They won’t even have time to scout out any uranium.”

“No, it was Mahmud’s idea. He is a known extremist! But for some reason this has not yet been included in the program. Let’s correct that!”

“Stefan, you are so religious with your dogs that the thought creeps into my mind...”

“That I love them more than people?”

“No, that you are preparing a backup option using them.”

And so on.

At the farewell picnic, about two hundred face-to-face new acquaintances took place, seventy-five upcoming joint cases were discussed, fifteen old conflicts were settled and not a single new one arose. Alex would have been happy!

The Preacher

When the last ends were finally made to meet, when the last inaccuracies were eliminated and any last doubts removed, it was necessary for Bill Pak to start traveling all over the world. Being the scientific supervisor of the project, as the work was nearing its end, he had to do the work of a polisher as there were still small nicks and scratches that were difficult to get rid of without personal communications and interference. No matter how telecommunications are advanced or improved, there is something indispensable in personal communication: breathing the same air, sharing the same smells and food and being inside the same walls all provide a common context which contributes to understanding even with only half a word.

This time, Bill was headed to the polygon of the phytoexpansion segment in the U.S. state of Utah. The purpose of the visit was to sort out the details in the end of the program final report. The U.S. Government had announced that it was terminating the lease of the federal land and was demanding that they completely vacate the area within a year. Overall, it seemed like everything that had to be done there was completed or almost completed. It was with the "seemed like" and the "almost" that Bill had to deal with and sort out.

The trip also had a second goal and for this he had planned the trip for the day when the so-called "keepers" would gather for a rally at the training ground. The "keepers" were a group that could be described as something between a social movement and a religious sect. They were gathering to protest against the whole "diabolical undertaking" and against mechanical ants, genetically modified lichens, fast-growing trees, the huge burdocks growing in the pavilions and the segment employees who they claimed were violating the moral code of a morally blameless state. As it was, the movement by the hard-nosed activists quickly gained strength and the lease agreement was broken precisely because of their pressure on the government, so Bill truly wanted to look them right in the eye.

After flying to the city of Green River by regular transport, Bill rented a single-seat plane. He could not stand being transported to a destination as some VIP and always got to wherever he had to go by himself. Besides that, he wanted to fly over some of the places that he had once visited and which had touched his soul, the main one being the confluence of the Colorado River and the Green River, and for this Bill made a small detour. Twenty-three years ago, he had sat on a cliff where two canyons meet, and watched the two rivers and their reddish and muddy green waters flow into a common channel and not mixing until the river bended. He then sat for several hours, looking at the slow movement of the currents and the same calm movement of the summer clouds. Time seemed to have stopped and Bill was thinking about something nice and good, when a curious gopher poked his nose into his hand and brought him out of a trance from which he could not remember anything except one simple thought: *Where do the waters of the two rivers finally mix?*

This time he saw the same scenery from a height of a couple of kilometers. The river flows were still the same and still did not mix, although it was clear that the boundary between them was gradually becoming more wavy as he went further, then in the distance the smooth waves turned into turbulent curls. Further on everything was hidden by a sharp bend in the canyon. Bill made a big circle and began to descend and flew right into the rusty colored canyon of the Colorado River. Once in the canyon he decided to fly low over the river. For some reason he needed to make sure that they really did mix and had to see it with his own eyes. Flying over the confluence point, Bill flew the plane directly over the dividing line. Ahead, the canyon turned sharply to the right, and Bill had to climb steeply to avoid the bend. Beyond it the dividing line itself seemed to collapse, breaking into patches of different colors that still did not mix with each other. It was then, only after passing the next turn, that Bill finally saw homogeneous muddy water where the waters had finally mixed. With a sigh of relief, he gained altitude and headed southwest to the testing grounds.

Somewhere about thirty kilometers before the testing grounds, Bill saw the "keepers". It was an eerie and creepy sight, all the way to the horizon the road was occupied by a column of buses, mostly black and yellow school buses.

"God, how many are there?!" Bill whispered.

Taking into account an interval of, say fifty meters, and the length of road visible to the eye, which was about thirty kilometers, it worked out to be that there were at least six hundred buses just in the foreseeable area. Everyone was headed to the soul of the Ark full of righteous malice and absolute inarguable self-righteousness.

After seven minutes of flying over a continuous non-stop column of vehicles, Bill finally reached the training grounds. Having made a turn over a nearby hill, on the slope of which the "righteous" men, who had come from many different states, had gathered and settled down on folding chairs and anything they could sit on (women were not accepted into their ranks). Flying over a stage which had been erected near the entrance, he then landed on the training grounds' runway. The concrete airstrip had been laid between the rows of arched greenhouses which were reminiscent of the size and shape of transparent aircraft hangars, and was suitable for landing heavy cargo jets. Against this backdrop Bill's little plane looked like a dragonfly that had accidentally flown in. On the runway, the Head of the Segment John Carpenter, the Head of Departments Ivan Plotnikov and three other employees were already waiting for him. Bill had forgotten their names, as his memory for names and surnames was full.

After landing, the colleagues went to John's office and immediately took the bull by the horns.

John assured Bill that the entire experimental part had been completed and all measurements were done. Only one problem remained, this was bifurcation at the period of seven thousand years, which concerned the intermediate flora of the humid tropical belt. As was shown it turned out that herbaceous plants competed with the tropical forest plants and could possibly displace them from the entire climate zone, or vice versa. In the first case scenario the achievement of the final level of oxygen would be delayed for three hundred years. In the second, the diversity of the herbaceous flora would suffer. Determining the outcome of a competition between wet savannah and forest plants depended on parameters that cannot be accurately predicted. They agreed that that they could simply give up on solving this problem as the option with the wet savannah plants leads to the same end result, only a little later. Afterwards any diversity issues can be retroactively corrected by the people of 47 Librae b.

While the discussion was going on, loud and powerful sounds were heard coming from outside, distorted by multiple sound reflections, layers of glass and the bad equipment of the "keepers". It was clear that it was a speech, although it was impossible to make out a single word from where they were.

"Boo, ba-a-ah, wow, ba-a-k boo-o-o!" the speaker said.

"WA-A-A BOOK OFF! a hundred thousand angry men responded powerfully in unison.

And again: "Uka-ha boo-wat you-y-y-uk-a-ak!"

"OFF AUCK DUC!" and so on.

"That reminds me of something," Bill said.

"It reminds you of old newsreel footage: Germany at the turn of the thirties and forties of the twentieth century," John replied. "But these are still a little calmer and seem to be more 'herbivorous' than those were."

"Let's take a look at them out in the light, I want to say a few words to them," Bill suggested.

"In my opinion that would be useless. Did you see them? Those kinds of people can't be convinced of anything."

"I don't believe that anything is ever useless. You might just not see the results right away."

"Okay, let's go."

Bill, John and Ivan reached the gate and then went to the foot of the stage, where another speaker was speaking: "God created the Earth and settled people and animals on it. They, these miserable people, imagine that they themselves are omnipotent and they want to repeat His work.

Who will benefit from their intentions, the Devil or God? The Devil or God?"

"THE DEVIL!" everyone on the hillside answered in a loud chorus.

"You're right," continued the orator, "the Devil: for no one has the right to encroach into a sphere where only God is competent, only the Devil could decide to do something like that!"

Seeing the approaching members of the Ark Project moving like parliamentarians, the orator became confused and fell silent, and the hillside started to rustle like foliage in a strong wind.

"I'm the Science Director for the Ark Program," Bill informed the moderator. "Since you're discussing us here, allow me to say a few words."

The host addressed the huge audience: "The leaders of the Ark Program have come to us and are asking for the floor. Shall we let them speak or send them on their merry way?"

In response, there was a lot of noise then a whistle and tomatoes, boiled eggs, sandwiches and juice containers flew at them from the front rows. Bill, Ivan and John, without flinching, continued to face the audience, dodging the flying food. Bill got hit in the chest with a hot dog with mustard and mayonnaise and thanked the audience for the treat but noted that he preferred ketchup. However, the food supplies in the front rows quickly ran out, and the three parliamentarians continued to stand their ground looking into the faces of the "keepers" who were quickly losing their resolve.

"Well, let them say a few words and then get the hell out of here," someone in the front rows said, and the host gave Bill a microphone, an act he soon regretted.

"I see so many good honest faces here," Bill began, "and I don't understand your aggression. Good people, do you know that there are more stars and planets within reach of our telescopes, than there are grains of sand on all of Earth's ocean beaches put together? Did you know that? Yes or no?! Yes or no?!"

“No,” the slope rustled discordantly.

“So now you know! Then how is it, in your opinion, that among these countless planets there are those that are inhabited by intelligent beings no worse than us?” Everyone on the slope responded with low indistinct sounds.

“Then let me put the question this way: Could God, having created a myriad of planetary systems, populate only one of them? Only the Earth? Would that be wise of him? Yes or no?” the slope responded with a lot of noises in which a “no” stood out slightly.

“That’s right, there are a huge number of inhabited worlds in the Universe. Now know this: among the myriad planets there are a lot like Earth: with oceans and land, with mountains and plains, with clouds and rivers, but they are without life. They are not inhabited and we know this for sure, we can see these worlds, several of them in fact. And what about this fact: once upon a time this continent, the one on which we are now, was also not inhabited by people. But people came here on their own, first on foot through Alaska, then thousands of years later on ships from Europe. Did people have the right to populate what the Europeans called the New World? If by the will of God, the Europeans appeared only in the Old World? Did they or not?”

“Yes they had!” those on the slope of the hill answered, a little more distinctly.

“So, the settlement of people on a new planet is just as pleasing to God as the settlement of people in the ‘New World’. He probably had a reason and it was not for nothing that He left most of the planets empty because this was space for new settlers. So that those who have reached a higher state of mind can send their sons to new lands, who will initiate a new human race. What did God create man to be: a helpless child, not able to take a step without the permission of a parent or responsible mature male? Child or mature male?”

“Mature male!” the people on slope of the hill answered, this time firmly and coherently. The leader became nervous. He asked the people into his microphone: “Maybe that’s enough? We have given them the floor and that's enough! It's time to end our meeting..."

"Let him talk until he's finished... Let him continue..."

"Thanks everyone, I don't have much left to say," Bill continued. "That's right, God created us to be real men. That was the intention. So, if we can overcome sixty light-years and populate a new world, God will be happy. It means that his creation turned out to be worthy of him, the Creator. So, in that case the plan was a success and man worked towards glory! Let's look a little further: are you grateful to the Lord for giving you the opportunity to see this world, one created by Him and rejoice at how good it is? That world out there, also created by God, is just as good, and we should let people see it too and rejoice. So as it turns out, the settlement of a new world is actually something that would be pleasing to God or not? Godly or not?!"

The hillside responded with indistinct noises. Tens of thousands of people were suddenly being tormented by a most severe case of cognitive dissonance. Bill peered into the faces of the people in the front rows: they were biting their lips, their eyes were fixed on the ground, they were holding their heads in their hands and some had their palms covering their faces to the bridge of their noses.

"Brothers, have you thought about it? This is the best thing that could happen to human kind. Think about it! Let me continue. The settlers carried tools, domestic animals and cereal seeds on ships to the New World. What you see behind the fence is the same! The mechanical ants that seem to be like monsters to you are just building tools. They have no wills of their own, only a simple program and they need to be periodically charged from special devices. They can do no more harm than the lawnmowers you keep in your garages. And those plants in greenhouses that scare you so much cannot take over the world, they require more carbon dioxide than we have in our air, and they would die in the open. Their purpose is to saturate the air of the new planet with oxygen and then give way to ordinary terrestrial plants. I believe that you are all good people, although you arrived here with malice in your hearts. Your only problem is that you lack certain knowledge. Fill up on knowledge and you will see the world as a bright place and enemies will become your friends."

Bill, John and Ivan left the stage as the people on the hill made a sound like the sound of a forest when a squall is passing. There was no applause, no whistling, no yelling, no heckling or swearing, just a steady uneven noise. The leader tried to calm the people down and wanted to make a final speech in order to return the flock to its former basic state, but it was in vain. Then he decided to round everything off and deliver his closing speech without waiting for silence. The silence never came, even as people were folding their chairs and rushing off towards the giant parking lot.

"Bill, the talent of a Christian preacher is being lost in you," Ivan concluded.

"Maybe. I always believed that a good preacher should be an atheist who puts man at the forefront, not God. I simply stated the Purpose Postulate in a language they could understand."

"Listen, these 'keepers' are far from the only ones in the world. It is as if a wave of ignorance is rising around the world, one with which parliaments and governments are trying to reckon with. Are you not afraid that it will overwhelm the Ark Project? Now we have to close the polygon, but thankfully everything has been done here, but what about the other places?"

Yes, I have thought about that a lot. Everything, including this wave of darkness, has its own characteristic time limit. Believe me we have time to launch the Ark. It may be at the very limit of our window, but we'll make it. If we had been stuck for a couple more years, then maybe we would not have enough time. In three years, the start and the Ark will fly away before it is overwhelmed by the wave of ignorance. Another thing is that after that this dark wave will then come and engulf us. But we will worry about that after the launch"

At dusk Bill was flying back to Green River and again had chosen to fly along the same route, he flew over the column this time marked by an endless series of red parking lights as everyone left the area of the polygon.

Now, in these hundreds of school buses, instead of righteous malice, other feelings were percolating: confusion, bewilderment and anger, of course, but now it was not righteous but just ordinary.

The Launch

When Black Waxman had already long since become White, Roland had already long become a bald ninety-five-year-old man, Gene was ninety and also bald, Alex had already been gone for ten years and Tall Jose had been resting in peace for a quarter of a century. The Martian soil had also long since become the final resting place of Goran Kirk when the launch finally took place.

Any epochal event must have a most solemn moment but in the case of the Ark, such a moment did not emerge during the natural course of things. The number of launches from Earth to deliver the components of the Ark into orbit exceeded a hundred, plus there were several ships that had arrived in orbit from Mars. The number of launches of refuelers for space tugs exceeded three hundred: these tugs, in groups, took the caravan of the Ark out of the Earth's gravitational field. The main systems of the Ark were assembled and put together and then one after another were activated and put into operation millions of kilometers from Earth. So what could be the most solemn moment in all of that?

Therefore, it was determined by a forced decision: the main celebration was to be the launch of Cargo Flight AX 220, which carried the last twelve modules of the Incubator which contained the cryopreserved embryos that were being sent, including human ones.

The ceremonial launches were usually carried out from the historic complex at Cape Canaveral which had long served as a museum and only in exceptional cases a spaceport, and not from the usual working launch site in the Bolivian highlands.

Unfortunately, they were unlucky with regard to the weather. On the day of the launch there was a low cloud cover and cold drizzling rain. The launch had to be planned eight days in advance and the forecast had been for good weather but then deteriorated in days leading to the countdown. It was impossible to transfer the event to another date as a lot of people were already working in orbit and they would have to wait around in space for an extra period of time. The weather may be the weather, but many tens of thousands of people who has arrived from all over the world still gathered in the stands and on the field. The vast majority of these were veterans of the Ark Project itself.

Among them were even five Martians. Five people who were seeing the Earth for the first time. They had arrived because they were given the opportunity to accompany and install the Martian piece of equipment on the ship and they stood out for their tall statures and the joyfully-astonished expressions on their faces. It wasn't the people or the landscape that amazed them, it was the smells! At the moment, it was the smell of the sea, the fresh smell of ocean mist carried by the winds mixed with rain.

It was then that the speeches of the officials began. Present were the presidents of two large countries, the head of the administration of Interspace and the president of the Ark Global Coordinating Committee. They talked about the giant step for humanity, the outstanding feats of scientists and engineers, the triumph of cooperation between Earth and Mars, the exit to the expanses of the Galaxy, and so on and so forth. Fortunately, everyone spoke briefly, keeping within a five minute time limit.

After the officials' speeches, a video message from Paul Dors, recorded shortly before his death nine years ago, was played. The image was projected directly onto the low-lying clouds which were solid enough but uneven in form so for those who stood far from the projector, the image of Paul's face flying on the clouds constantly changed shape and expression.

"I would like to greet everyone who is listening or watching this recording of mine. Since it is physically impossible for me to live to see the launch of the Ark, I want to address you posthumously on the day of the launch. I hope, well I am sure that I have earned this right by my contribution to the project. I won't take much of your time.

"Many out there consider me to be a cynic, and I have nothing to say about that. I understood that I was earning money on what were not the best properties of human nature, mental laziness, unwillingness to make decisions and refusal to take responsibility. To be honest, I was aware that the object which brought me my success, that thing with the affectionate name 'Personal Angel' exacerbate these flaws. Did I atone for the harm I caused by disposing of my capital in this way? You be the judge of that. If you're watching or listening to this recording at the launch, I'm hoping for a positive verdict.

"I had been thinking for quite a long time about whether or not to use the trillion I earned for something that would be the opposite of a Personal Angel. For a cause that mobilized the best aspects of human nature. I waited for years and finally the Ark appeared.

"I remember the first press conference very well. Listening to Alex Roland and Gene, who outlined the essence of the project, I paid more attention not to what they were saying but to how they were saying it, how they reacted to the audience, followed by the expressions on their faces. And at that moment I stopped doubting, because I saw in front of me... How can I say this? I saw what might be described as a kind of hybrid, an intellectual and devotee, a scientist and a pioneer, experiencing amazement that this type of people had not yet died out. They seemed to glow! After reviewing everything that was in the public domain about them, I discarded the last doubts and knew I was not mistaken.

"There were no doubts even for the first two decades, when it seemed that things were standing still. Alex and his comrades pulled as best they could, but sometimes fell into despair. In fact, there was an inevitable latent period and from the outside it was clearer to me how the project was overgrown with the same luminous people, how the general atmosphere and the attitude of the world towards the Ark were changing. The world has also changed, obviously for the better, and not without the influence of the project. Even the Personal Angel business fell into decay, which did not upset me at all, especially since I had gotten rid of it long before that. Things went by so quickly and powerfully that there was hope to live to see the launch, but this was really too much. Things like that don't happen. There is no such thing as a long golden age and then a few years ago I felt the first signs of depression, a kind of rot that started developing in the head. I appealed to those who are a couple of generations younger than me: I pleaded

that if they were ever covered in darkness that they would become keepers of the fire! The fire that accompanied the Ark.

"Alex, peace be with him, also had no chance to live to see the launch. But he lived up to the moment when it became absolutely clear that the project had already taken off and nothing could stop it. We met a year ago and talked exactly about this topic. 'Life has happened,' he said. I answered 'mine too'. To this we drank.

"I am not with you now, but I envy you a little and I am sure that each of those who devoted themselves to the Ark, having returned home, has the right to drink to the fact that life has happened. That's actually all I wanted to say."

Paul Dors watched silently from the clouds for another half a minute. The veterans then rendered their verdict. Applause in an open, ventilated space cannot be called thunderous or stormy, but it can be an even volumetric noise that fills the stands and the field, audible for several kilometers, and that is what it was.

The last to speak was the Science Director of the Ark Project Bill Pak, whose speech was the shortest.

"So the work is finished, to which many of those present, including myself devoted their entire adult lives. We may be a little uneasy about the fact that our offspring maybe entering the darkness and we will not see the result. But this is not so. Yes, we will not see the result, but the result is known: there will be a new living world, a new chance for life and evolution. If our knowledge, our experience and our science are worth anything, everything will work out in the end. The guarantee that it will succeed is the labor and talent invested in the Ark in such a volume that it itself grew into an animate being. There is no need to worry about the fate of the Ark, it is not just traveling into the darkness, but to its destination, and that is clear as day.

"It's been half a century since I was a teenager and listened to a taped press conference during which Alex, Roland, and Gene first talked about the Ark Project. Half a century is too long for determining a human destiny. Many of those who helped start the project have not survived to this day. For example, Alex Selin who is no longer here with us, but that doesn't mean that he doesn't exist. He is embodied in the main ideas of the Ark and lives in its gigantic memory. In thousands of years, he will speak to the people of the new world, answer their questions and

be able to teach them a lot, in the same way that he taught me. He's there, aboard the Ark. He's its captain. Happy travels, Alex!

"Goran Kirk, José Ranedo and many other veterans are also not with us any longer. They too are on their way. Just imagine that the Ark has a captain's bridge, that's their place. And with them on the bridge are Roland Wolf, Gene Cooney and Rob Waxman. Bon voyage, founding fathers!

"Look how many of us are here right now! Everyone put a part of themselves into the Ark. Yes, a part of each of us leaves the Earth as a member of its huge team. Happy journey to us! And may the job be finished with honors in thousands of years!"

With these words, the last ten seconds of the countdown began, and then came the usual launch of a heavy rocket with its related sound and visual effects. In a matter of seconds, the AX 220 disappeared into the clouds, leaving behind its subsiding thunder and a fading glow.

Tens of thousands of people stood silently in the drizzling rain. Suddenly, one after the other, they began to bare their heads, take off their hats and caps, throw back their hoods and fold their umbrellas. A sea of people stood silently under the drizzle with bare heads, lush-haired, gray-haired and bald, with the vast majority being bald.

"Did something go wrong?" an embarrassed WWV commentator giving a live report asked. "No, everything seems to be in order, the flight is absolutely normal. Why did they bare their heads? This is not a funeral ceremony, but something quite the opposite, when people should shout joyfully, and if they take something off their heads, then in order to throw it up. Look," the commentator continued, "and the officials, after a pause, have also bared their heads, apparently out of solidarity. I do not understand this mourning gesture, nothing of the kind was planned or called for, they all did it suddenly and without agreement..."

After a long minute of silence, one by one people began to put on their hats, open their umbrellas, and started to leave. To understand what he called a "mourning gesture", the commentator would have had to try to put himself in the place of all of the people, which he could not do because of his lack of years. At that moment, the people who made the Ark were saying goodbye to what was for many the main thing in their lives and for others important content in their lives. Most of them now had only the hope of living out the age as pensioners. The caravan left, and they are left, with nothing ahead to catch the imagination. It was truly a mourning gesture to them personally. Thanks to Bill for finding the right words: "Have a nice trip!" People were leaving in a long continuous stream. Survive the age or keep the fire? Everyone had their own path.

The solemn ceremony lasted a couple of hours, but the real launch several more weeks. Launches from Earth continued: rocket fuel for the tugs, crew changes and fitters who had to cross the radiation belts several times. All of the parts of the Ark were pushed out of the Earth's gravitational field in a swinging motion, by the pushes of the tugboats refueling at the perigee. The orbit of the Ark became wider and wider, until it was moved into a near-solar position. There, the Tractor, the Power Unit, the Arsenal, the Headquarters and the Incubator were coupled into a caravan forty kilometers long and pushed for the last time by the tugboats, the reactor was started, the radiators were unfolded, the first hot hydrogen was driven into the circuits, then hot liquid gallium, and finally the main engine was turned on. After that, the last people, making sure that everything was working properly, went home.

Behind the Ark, a luminous trail from the plasma jet stretched out for many thousands of kilometers, visible from the Earth through amateur telescopes and strong binoculars. A year later, it was still visible in good amateur telescopes, and two and a half years later it was observed for the last time with a fifteen-meter reflector telescope on a Hawaiian volcano. But the Ark continued to regularly send daily messages: its exact coordinates, reports on the operation of the systems and data on the interstellar environment.

Following the caravan of the Ark, our story now leaves Earth and the Solar System, leaving the old world to its next decline after what was another rise. We will not know its fate or what happens further, but as always, we will hold on to the hope that everything will work out in the foreseeable future. Of course, it is a pity to leave the aged heroes and the settled world, but in the interests of the story it is impossible to just sit still, in the same way as the leader of a sled team setting off on a journey cannot sit still, trying to free the brakes of the sled in order to quickly rush off beyond the horizon.

PART TWO

Reversal

After seven thousand years had passed, the caravan gained a speed of three thousand kilometers per second, becoming the fastest free moving massive body in the desert-like empty spaces of the Galaxy.

Such a speed was far above that even obtained by pulsars, which had received powerful kicks capable of throwing them out of the galactic gravitational field during the explosions of a stars. We speak about this quite confidently, believing that at that moment not a single creation of intelligent beings, launched from star to star, was moving about the Galaxy, maybe not a very optimistic assumption, but one that is quite plausible.

So, at this point seven thousand years of darkness, emptiness and cold, at minus two hundred and fifty Celsius, have passed and there were still five thousand years of the same thing lying ahead.

Bill Park had a reason for calling the Ark animated. There are some products created by human hands that seem to us to be able to reason, such as automatic probes that operate on the surface of other planets. Apparently, we perceive them this way not only because of their complex deeply thought out behavior, but also because the creators have invested parts of their souls into them. That being the case, the Ark was loaded to capacity with souls although it had been in a state of half-sleep for seven thousand years, keeping track of only the simplest things using just a tiny bit of the edge of its "consciousness": coordinates, orientation, the mode of operation of all of its systems, nevertheless it was still an animated creation.

The reactor was the part of the Ark that carried the heaviest load and all seven thousand years it had worked smoothly, without the slightest failure. The only moving parts in the reactor were a uranium rod feeder. There were no control rods or other moving parts in the core either, just a tricky system of metal membranes that responded to pressure. The reactor breathed slightly, increased reactivity: there was exhalation of the moderator from the active zone and inhalation of the absorber.

Seven thousand years earlier, in the first brainstorming session, "Tall" José Ranedo was put in charge of the development of the reactor. He was instructed to "gather adequate reactor experts and workers" and supervise the task of its creation. José failed miserably and explained this by citing the fact that all reactor experts and workers are pathologically touchy people, as soon as you say anything to them directly, they become mortally offended and run off to hide in the bushes. The only opportunity he had left was to become a specialist in nuclear reactors himself after having mastered all of the intricacies of the craft. However, he was not completely alone, the former post-doctoral student Volodya Drake and the only person on Earth to whom Jose did not say nasty things, joined him and they made up a pair.

Everything worked out with Jose constantly grumbling things like: "What did they imagine themselves to be? Did they really think that no one except them would be able to properly model the active zone! Quasi-linear Monte Carlo, oh I'm searching for wisdom! They act as if no one except them knows where to get cross-sectional data for uranium fragments! They go around as if no one else knows where to get public codes and can figure them out!"

He and Volodya found everything, figured everything out, modeled everything and on top of that they even came up with a couple more innovations, thanks to the fact that they were not subjected to the professional prejudices which limit nuclear reactor designers. Jose died before all the other veterans of the Ark, but he had lived to see the time when the "Ranedo-Drake Reactor" beat all other competitors in the field of deep space expeditions and it had already been put into full use twenty years after that very brainstorming session. Volodya lived to see the launch and was present at the launch ceremony of the AX220. By that time he was not even eighty years old.

The caravan moved in the utter darkness, one only slightly diluted by starlight. It also remained absolutely dark, only by using infrared rays could one see a reactor with huge radiators. No signal lights were required on its path and only the faint ghostly glow of ions in the plasma jet trailing behind the tugboat could be detected by a good photodetector at high exposure.

The Ark flew absolutely silently and this was not because sound does not propagate in space, even if you attached a microphone to the structure of any module it would not help you to hear the workings of machines. The power unit worked without making a single sound: apart from heavy water in the primary circuit, the gallium in the second and membranes that breathed slightly, nothing moved in it all. The engine of the Tractor did not make a single sound either, nothing in it trembled nor did anything move that was noticeable to the eye. The fixed windings were connected together and placed right out in the void, twelve cylindrical copper windings forming two truncated coaxial cones: the wider one in front and the narrower one behind. They consumed the lion's share of the reactor's power, but this could not be seen or felt: all the energy was pumped into a rotating magnetic field. All fifty megawatts produced by the reactor went into the generation of the magnetic field and its lines of force, reached out almost to infinity, forming an expanding spiral. Twelve injectors at the exit of the windings constantly injected plasma which was extracted from the substance of the spent uranium rods into the magnetic field for thousands of years, only one and a half milligrams per second but they were very important one and a half milligrams. They gradually took on the energy of the magnetic field, and somewhere in the distance most of the power was transferred to the plasma jet, which drilled a channel into the calm interstellar medium. Only fifty megawatts and a jet with a flow rate of one and a half milligrams per second, but this was enough for the curling field to "press" forward on the windings with a force of a little more than a kilogram, the light pressure of a finger on a colossus that weighed more than a thousand-tons. The acceleration rate was only ten microns per second. If there had been a cosmic Angel on the Ark, and a glass hung motionlessly in front of them then in a couple of minutes the Angel would notice that the glass had shifted ten centimeters along the Ark towards the back, in another two minutes it would have moved noticeably another forty centimeters from the initial point, and so it would be for thousands of years. Incredibly great power, obtained through the microscopic consumption of matter and negligible thrust, nothing else would work if the ship was to accelerate to thousands of kilometers per second.

That was how Roland's corkscrew worked. Of course, Roland's contribution to the Ark was immeasurably greater than only the drive apparatus. If we recall the long ago conversations at night in the Mongolian Park, it turns out that it was he who usually struck the first spark and got the fire of ideas started. He then continued to constantly set off sparks. One might say, he in fact served as the leader of the project. The people felt it, and when Roland appeared at the launch ceremony in a wheelchair, he was greeted by hundreds of people who shook his hands which were clasped above his head. Gene arrived on foot and stood for the whole ceremony, holding on to Roland's chair.

"You were absolutely right about the project participants having to live long," Roland stated at the end of the ceremony. "Well, we may be in this condition but we survived! Alex would have been a hundred and three... Let's go please, we'll fulfill Paul's covenant, at least in a hotel restaurant. I can still do so and you even more so."

That was seven thousand years ago. At the present moment, the part of Roland's soul that was invested inside the engine, was probably celebrating its triumph. The part of Gene's soul was still asleep.

Now, having accelerated to three thousand kilometers per second, it was as if the dreaming Ark opened one eye and turned over on the other side. The complete turnaround took three months. Into the outer windings of the two gyrodynes of the Tractor a small electrical load was applied. The rotors which had been rotating for thousands of years in a vacuum with no contact with matter, held in place only by a magnetic field, slowed down a miniscule amount and the multi-ton Tractor, under the influence of their rotational momentum, began to turn around at a speed that was a hundred times slower than the hour hand of a clock. The rest of the sections of the caravan obediently followed the lead of the Tractor and after three months the entire chain of the Ark completed a one hundred and eighty degree turn and then began the almost imperceptible process of slowing so that in five thousand years it would arrive at its target location at the required minimum speed.

The Ark's systems had perfect positioning data and always knew its exact orientation using data from three bright quasars and observing the few stars whose trajectories and velocities were best known. The cruiser-like navigation system of the Ark was one of its simplest elements. Its creation had been supervised by one of the simplest of people, the scientist Hui Li, who during his life only knew how to do two things well: developing navigation systems for spacecraft and growing cabbage in his garden. He was not interested in politics or women, was faithful to his wife, did not enjoy modern art and if he read something outside the framework of professional literature, then only the simplest of detective stories. He never told anyone anything nor did he do nasty things. Regardless, it would have been difficult to expect compliments or gifts from him. He constantly grumbled and complained to his children and grandchildren that they shouldn't get involved in all sorts of nonsense and that it was necessary to live simply. His favorite delicacy was a juicy fleshy tomato on a piece of black bread, and he could not physically stand alcohol. He was known as an excellent professional, although the navigation systems of spacecraft are not that complicated, it is of utmost important not to make mistakes in them, and in that regard during his entire career he did not make a single mistake, mainly because he never allowed himself to get distracted by anything. Hui Li died five years before the launch of the Ark, having lived a life filled with the simplest forms of happiness.

There was now a weak star on the direct course of the caravan as it traveled backwards. Had there been a cosmonaut with decent vision on the Ark, he would have easily seen it with the naked eye. At the moment its brightness was that of a 4.5 magnitude star.

Arrival

When the caravan was illuminated by 47 Librae with light that was just a little more than that of the full moon on Earth, the Ark began to wake up. The observatory in the Headquarters module was the first to come to life. There the main telescope opened like a flower bud and began to slowly turn towards it target, to which there were still many years of travel.

From the very first observations, it was clear that there were not only the five planets in the system that were observed at Darwin, but in fact nine. There were what appeared to be two scorched brothers of Mercury, a sister of the Earth, a twin of Mars, a twin of Jupiter, a super-sized Saturn and three Neptune-like fiends on the cold gloomy periphery. The planetary system turned out to be even more similar to the solar system than it had seemed from the observations at Darwin. Was this a coincidence? Or is there such a standard type in the hundred billion systems of the Milky Way? Was it possible that Venus was born in the 47 Librae system, or had it been knocked away in the course of a gravitational game of bowling which marked the birth of the abundant broods of planets?

A few months after awakening, the Ark knew the exact orbits and masses of the main celestial bodies in the system. The super Saturn turned out to be the record holder in size, it had almost four times the mass of Jupiter and Jupiter's twin had both the mass and the orbital radius of the Jupiter in the Solar System. The mass of 47 Librae b was only ten percent less than that of the Earth. However, now it is time to move from the astronomical name to the standard given name of the long-awaited goal of the Ark. We recall that the Selin dynasty by all means possible resisted any moves towards naming the planet after them, but the name Selina was chosen by the people.

Shortly before his death when Alex was asked to finally bless the inevitable, he sighed, waved with his hand and answered: "Yeah whatever! Call it a pot if you want... The main thing is that everything works out."

So the Ark, more than a hundred billion kilometers from its goal, was convinced that for earthly creatures, the force of gravity on Selina is quite comfortable, but for a more thorough study of the planet, it was necessary to get closer. The task of how to go about getting close to the planet in the shortest possible time using only a sustainer engine at constant thrust was solved by the Ark System in half a second. It would be necessary to perform three gravitational maneuvers near planets e, d and c. Subsequently it would have to gradually regulate the orbit of the Ark in order to approach the vicinity of Selina, something which would take half a year.

Such a quick decision by the Ark System was preceded by five years of hard work by Lisa Hansen, who had long been begging the boss for a task she could do independently that was connected with the arrival of the Ark at 47 Librae Before that he had rejected her two previous proposals with the words "this is not a woman's business", explaining to her that for these types of operations, which are carried out in real time, nerves of steel are required, and on top of all that the use of "dark" programming.

She persisted and finally one day he himself approached Lisa, saying: "Here's some woman's work for you, and just the job for such a malicious perfectionist as yourself. We have to optimize the approach of the Ark to Selina at a minimum speed, and do so without changing the operation mode of the engine. The key point of the optimization is the travel time. This is vitally important, since it is not guaranteed that during the approach it will be possible to maintain windings responsible for biological protection in a superconducting state. Keep in mind that for gravity maneuvers, there are two giant planets and at least one other terrestrial-like planet."

"But this task is too easy. We already have 'Rock and Roll', which everyone uses to optimize ballistic calculations and tasks."

"To be honest 'Rock and Roll', is full of hacked up, unkempt code. The source code looks like it was written by a crowd of graduate students. It often gets stuck in the local minima. So far, we have put up with it because we can just correct the trajectory to offset any errors. The problem is that out there, there will be no one to correct it. Therefore, be daring and go for it, so that there is perfect code, fast and error-free. We'll call it 'Waltz', and 'Rock and Roll' can be thrown in the trash."

Actually, that's exactly what happened. Lisa spent several years perfecting the parametrization of the trajectories, and "Waltz" really replaced "Rock and Roll" in the sphere of space ballistics. When the Ark was launched, Lisa was only sixty. In the moment of silence, her chestnut hair stood out sharply among the uncovered gray and bald heads. She could not handle the moment and burst into tears. Twelve thousand years have passed since then, and her 'Waltz' solved the problem in half a second. That's the entire prehistory of the gravitational maneuvers of the Ark.

The caravan approached planet e in order to lose a calculated amount of its speed and then pass into the plane of the ecliptic of 47 Librae. It turned out that near e lies a huge system of planets, not just a super-Saturn, but a Saturn squared. From afar, it looked like a family of worlds: in the center was the Saturn-dad with luxurious wide rings, at a distance there were three satellite children, also with rings, and then ten to twenty other smaller bodies similar in size to the Earth's Moon. These "children" themselves were rock and ice subgiants, all having a mass from three to seven times that of Earth and with thick atmospheres. Each of these, in turn, had its own satellites, but they were of a "normal" size and without rings.

The huge rings were made up of thousands of thinner rings and resembled an ancient plastic record on which music was recorded in the twentieth century. The similarity was enhanced by gaps that would serve as pauses that separated songs or compositions. The rings were also slightly wavy, like sound recording tracks. It would have been interesting to hear what kind of music they would have played.

When flying out of the dark side of the planet, the Headquarters' wide-angle telescope recorded an amazing color-show in detail, an aurora storm caused by a flash in the star's magnetosphere. The ring's usual ultraviolet glow which was about two Earth diameters in size, slowly flashed into the visible range in a matter of minutes and became several times brighter, overgrown with what looked like luminous "wool" and serpentine tentacles stretching down to the lower latitudes. Green and red highlights were added to the radiance and the tentacles either shrunk or contracted, in certain spots green and red lights scattered about and flared up, as if someone was setting off a gigantic fireworks show from below.

The day side of planet e on which it was day looked like a carefully decorated ball, despite the fact that the artist did not abuse the use of bright colors, but spared no effort in drawing numerous belts decorated with fine ornaments, ovals and rotating curls dancing in pairs with anticyclone curls. The "painting" seemed to be static, but in fact everything was moving, spinning, and flying about at speeds of hundreds and thousands of kilometers per hour.

The Ark circled the planet from north to south, and towards the end of the flyby, the view obtained by the wide-angle camera, revealed a phenomenon that was much easier to attribute to the imagination of the artist than to the whims of nature, the camera recorded a perfect regular hexagon framing the south pole of the planet. The hexagon was created by powerful atmospheric currents separating a giant polar cyclone and six anticyclones, located at the same distance around the pole at exactly thirty degrees of longitude. Looking at it, it's hard to believe that such fantastic and exact geometry is nothing more than a simple weather phenomenon.

In the center of the hexagon gaped a huge "eye", right over the very pole, and having the same nature as the eye of a hurricane but comparable in size to Earth's circumference. There was no surface area, the crater dipped deep into the dark brown layers of the atmosphere which gave the eye a sinister look. The Ark completed its maneuver, leaving behind the hyperbole on the side of the southern pole and the giant dark evil eye watched the departing caravan for a very long time.

If the planet e could cause delight in a viewer of earthly origin, then planet d would cause shock and an eerie feeling of deja vu. The fact was that it appeared to be Jupiter itself, with the same red spot and the same vortex stripes and white ovals. It also had the same Io, Europa, Ganymede and Callisto. The sister of Io was similarly violently volcanic, and a long-range telescope recorded a fountain of eruption the size of a quarter of the diameter of the satellite in perfect detail. Only accurate measurements could show that the red spot was slightly further to the south, and that the Galilean satellites differed from our counterparts in their masses only by about ten percent. The flyby around New Jupiter was able to cut a significant part of the Ark's azimuth velocity, after which its orbit became highly elongated. The next step was planet c, the passed by of which was designed to make the Ark's orbit almost circular but much smaller.

The planet seemed to have jumped out of the pages of a long-standing theoretical paper by Goran Kirk and Alex Selin called, "the Evolution of Terrestrial Planets at the Far Edge of the Habitable Zone with an Increase in the Luminosity of the Host Star." It was a cold but revitalizing world, mostly icy and snowy, but with its first rivers and a sea. 47 Librae, like any star following its evolution, had become slightly brighter with age. Previously, planet c had strongly resembled Mars, although it was twice as heavy. However, as heat increased a little, and all the solid carbon dioxide buried in the polar caps evaporated, the atmosphere became thicker. Then the greenhouse effect turned on, and now the water which had before been ice began to melt, at first near the equator in the depressions of the planet. Rivers now flowed, and in the lowest place on the planet, in a deserted rocky bowl-like depression, the first sea appeared, a real sea with open water and waves.

Once open water appeared, it meant that its cycle was automatically turned on. The lowland, in fact a geological analogue of the Earth's oceans which occupied a quarter of the planet, became an oasis where cumulus clouds floated above and it rained. Another hitherto dry ocean, smaller, also began to show signs of life and lakes appeared at its bottom. The continents remained as snow-covered highlands and glaciers flowed from them into the oceans where rivers originated from their melting ice and flowed into the lakes or the sea. It was a beautiful world in its own way: very transparent air, dark blue sky, dazzling snowy mountains, reddish rocks, blue glaciers, sand dunes, beaches and a blue sea, where the only thing that was missing were seagulls. In the landscapes of 47 Librae c, the joy of coming to life was evident. If it were possible to teleport a painter here to adequately convey the spirit of the planet, then Rockwell Kent would have been chosen for this mission.

In the article by Goran and Alex, the awakening of frozen planets was reflected in temperature graphs, measurements of atmospheric thickness, and precipitation volume calculations obtained by numerical simulation. It turned out that if, on a planet with deposits of carbon dioxide and ice, there are deep lowlands several kilometers below the average surface level, then when the host star heats up, they turn into oases with a stable positive temperature and open water. This happens abruptly, over tens of thousands of years, but as soon as the seas appear in the lowlands, further warming is inhibited: fresh snow falling on the continents reflects light and as a result the planet holds less heat.

Now that the thawing planet had been filmed in detail and studied top to bottom, all of the data was sent to the Earth's solar system. If there was anyone left who could receive the data, either on Earth or Mars, then in sixty years there would be a great holiday there, the discovery of a new, and in its own way, wonderful world. And that would only be a prelude.

Finally, the Ark arrived at the end point of the journey. Selina's two satellites provided it with a perfect harbor: a high resonant orbit. The moons were at a level of 1:4 resonance with each other, as done on purpose to maintain a stable 1:2 resonant orbit for the Ark. Of course, on Earth they had known nothing about these satellites and without them, the Ark would have had to have risen to a slightly higher orbit, but why not take advantage of such a wonderful surprise as orbital resonance?

The main engine stopped, but the reactor continued to work for the sake of the transmitter, the amount of data to be transmitted to the solar system required many megawatts of power to send it all. The first data to be sent were pictures of the planet at a resolution of one hundred meters per pixel with the geography of the planet being very well recorded on them. The ocean covered three-quarters of the surface and there were three continents: one in the North which was the size of Eurasia, one on the southern meridian similar in shape and size to South America, and one at the south latitudinal, stretching for eight thousand kilometers from east to west between thirty-five and sixty degrees south latitude.

Soon the Arsenal came to life and three probes separated from it which entered into a low circumpolar orbit and began to go about their main business, namely a detailed survey of the planet. Their first task was taking wide-angle images of the entire surface, the continents, the oceans and the polar ice. In three weeks, a virtual globe of the planet with a resolution down to five meters was ready. Selina turned out to be a tectonically active planet, like the Earth: there were island arcs, young mountain ranges and active volcanoes. And it was just as wet with most of the land being crisscrossed by a well-developed network of rivers. It was also just as warm, even a little warmer than Earth and Selina's cloud cover looked like the Earth's with the same cyclone coils, cirrus and cumulus clouds. The only significant difference was that Selina was biologically dead since its creation. And yet, if the presence of the souls of the creators of the Ark on board was not just a metaphor, these souls would have now rejoiced.

When the virtual globe was ready, the Ark transmitter sent it towards the solar system, spending about a terajoule on it alone. Then the probes began to photograph the continents and islands in greater detail, taking especially close looks at rivers and seashores. All the data was immediately transferred to the Ark, whose System began the process of selecting a landing site.

The landing site strategy had proven to be one of the most contentious tasks that had to be carried out in the entire history of the Ark Project. The main battles unfolded around the so-called "weighing factors": What would be more important, proximity to an ocean or proximity to a river? What's better rocky ground or low seismicity? How important was the proximity of mountains and what type should the mountains be? Would the proximity of mountains be fatal if glaciation begins? What is the optimal height above the nearest water line? The questions went on and on. There was no consensus reached on any of these issues, on the contrary, controversies and arguments only occurred more and more and even crossed the line of decency. Voting in such cases never provided an adequate result, as neither did the drawing of straws which the desperate parties were forced to resort to in the end.

Finally Bill Pak, who at that time was the head of the Arrival Problems Segment, declared that the task had failed completely, and that they had to start everything from scratch: change the approach, build models; study and comprehend the data on exoplanets that had accumulated en-masse; sort through everything that was known about geology, about the climate of the planets and about climatic catastrophes, then go through all the conceivable states of 47 Librae b, and work through all climatic and geological scenarios, and finally when all of that was done, they had to optimize all weight and cross-correlation coefficients on the entire set of models.

There were objections to Bill's approach: "In principle, the risks with the choice of location are not so great. You are the boss, in the end put on a judge's robe, hit the table with a gavel and announce the values of all the disputed coefficients yourself; no one will utter a word against you because everyone is tired. What you are offering us to do will take years, and the quality of the choice will improve only by maybe five percent. Is the game worth the candle?"

Bill replied: "What are these years compared to the thousands of years to come? And what is five percent when it is multiplied by the price of a new world? Therefore, consider that I put on a judge's robe, hit the table with a gavel and said: 'We start from scratch, damn it!'"

The new approach took ten years. It was much more difficult to teach the System to choose a site under conditions of complete uncertainty than it was to train it to play chess at the level of a world grand champion...

In one way or another, the Ark finally chose the coast of the northern mainland, at forty degrees north latitude, on a flat granite area to the left of a river's confluence with the ocean. This was the very place where the salty sea licks the warm sand and an unforgettable rock formation that looks like a dog's fang sticks out from a dune.

A Migratory School of White Wings

In the early morning hours, the sea was mirror-smooth and the mountains seemed to have their start right behind the dunes due to the fact that the air was so transparent. As for sounds, only the slight sound of the river could be distinguished in the distance on a rift a kilometer from the confluence with the sea. Mornings like this were very common here. Millions and even billions of times the day had begun in this exact way. The first subtle difference between this morning and the previous ones were three dots which appeared in the sky from out of nowhere.

The three points began to gradually diverge away from each other and off to the sides and then turned into the red wings of small parachutes carrying radio beacons. One landed on top of one of the dunes, the other two about three kilometers from the sea on outcroppings. The beacons immediately turned themselves on, then the probes accurately recorded their own coordinates and transmitted them to the System, making it possible to determine positioning with an accuracy of half a meter.

To make further observations, an imaginary observer would have chosen the crest of the last dune with relation to the side of the mountains, a little to the left of a cliff and directly in front of an almost completely flat granite area the size of a good airfield. Farther beyond the field towards the mountain range, a gentle rise of outcroppings began, turning into a wide spur, a moraine ridge of boulders ran for a kilometer to the left and an even descent to the river below began to the right.

An hour after the landing of the beacons, a large white parachute-wing appeared in the sky. Beyond it, above and to the right, came the second, the third and the fourth... And if you looked closely, then high in the dark blue sky, slightly to the southeast, a whole chain of white wings was beginning to appear. It was as if a school of giant migratory birds was descending, having found a suitable nesting site, after a very long journey.

When the first parachutes dropped low enough, it would have become clear to the imaginary observer, that their cargo was wedge-shaped container modules covered with a dark gray ceramic coating, a bit like small space shuttles. They slowly glided towards the granite field and, in the silence, one could hear the sound of the wind in the wings and along the lines. The first one dropped to a meter, decelerating to a decent speed along a gentle glide path, then the rear lines pulled up sharply, the wing immediately increased its angle of attack and all speed was extinguished.

The two-ton container, having braked successfully, gently set down on the shock-absorbing cushions which automatically inflated under its belly, and having settled in a little, stopped. Simply masterful! The slings connecting the wing immediately separated from the load and a miniature rocket carried the folded wing three hundred meters to the northwest, lowering it at the edge of the dunes. The next "bird" was flying in after it and set down in the same way, leaving the exact same load seven meters from the first, and then the third and the fourth...

The containers landed and were released at thirty second intervals. The silence was broken only by the noise of the rushing air, the occasional rustling sound of shock-absorbing cushions and the whistle of small rockets carrying away the wings. The most striking aspect of the base camp landing scenario was the accuracy and coherence with which it was carried out. Thirty seconds after landing the previous module transmitted: "landing OK" or "missed by one and a half meters to the north", so that the next one had time to correct its approach. The dark gray containers, these were the Arsenal Modules, were brought in quite tightly, within an interval of six to seven meters from each other in several rows forming a large semicircle.

Then came the containers, covered with a yellow ceramic coating and blackened on the underside, they landed even closer to each other in the center of the semicircle. These were the Incubator Modules. Two hours later, the entire "migratory school" of landing modules had touched down. A large semicircle of dark containers sprawled across the granite field, with a yellow circle in the center and a mountain of white wings off to the side. One hundred and forty dark gray and fifty yellow containers, three hundred tons of payload, were now ready to immediately take on the task of transforming an entire planet.

There was not a single collision or missed target during their descent or landings, even when the modules entered the atmosphere from the high orbit or during the aerodynamic braking of the wedge-shaped containers in a luminous shock wave or during the parachute descent from a height of ten kilometers, everything went off perfectly. Still: the "planting of the seeds" was rehearsed many times on Earth until it turned into a dull routine with no surprises.

As is almost always the case, in the end even bold ideas turn into routines. First, they thought of launching the modules according to a classical scheme, using traditional round parachutes, something as reliable as a sledge hammer. However, landing with them is like dropping something from three meters. The choice was then: either make the payloads indestructible, or use soft-landing rocket engines that eliminate the last meters per second near the ground itself, it seemed simple but there were plenty of headaches with regard to their layout and the payload. In addition, their reliability did not coincide with their handling characteristics. In a strong variable wind (Who could make an absolutely reliable weather forecast there?) it would be very difficult to land all the modules using round parachutes on one patch (Who would collect those that had fallen into the surrounding gullies?) The people from the Arrival Segment got together for a meeting and thought about it long and hard.

The first to overcome the reverie was the most silent and phlegmatic member of the Academic Council, Uno Bjorn, a tall man who showed signs of fighting a losing battle with being overweight: "Have you ever seen how athletes land using small high-speed parachutes?"

Nobody answered. Then Uno offered to drive everyone to the nearest sports airfield on the following Sunday and arrange an off-site meeting there. The weather turned out to be wonderful and the field meeting out on the grass was great and completely changed the concept of landing. For a long time, the colleagues watched in amazement as the paratroopers and parasailers descended one by one and as they approached, picked up speed, then went into level flight near the ground, then sharply increased the angle of attack of their parasails, and slowed down to a stop and calmly stepped onto the ground, as if stepping off an escalator.

"This trick is called a pillow," Uno said, "horizontal speed before landing is important here. The most experienced ones manage to land on a dime using a four-square-meter parasail. So why the hell does anyone need soft landing engines if we can land in the same way? Look at the speed they have on approach, they don't care about the wind."

"But this is done by a person whose intelligence slightly exceeds the current modest achievements with regards to artificial intelligence."

"This is not intelligence, these are trained reflexes. Can't we copy these reflexes and then program them to do the same thing?"

The following years Uno and three colleagues engaged in throwing dummies of landing modules from aircraft and landing them by remotely controlling the lines. They did not crash very often. Gradually, more and more of the procedure shifted to electronics. Fifteen years later, the monumental Uno, with his arms folded on his chest, stood at the edge of a field, watching with a grin, as one hundred two-ton dummies, dropped from a height of ten kilometers from a heavy transport plane, set down one after another in a circle with a diameter of fifty meters. With this came the time to drop them from space, but not dummies, but real prototypes with ceramic thermal protection and proven aerodynamics. Once again, Uno, with his trademark smirk, set down an entire "flock" of containers. By the way, he was awarded the title of "Honorary Master of Parachuting" although at the same time, he never made a single jump in his life, he claimed to have an inappropriate build and mild arthritis but to be honest, he was just scared. That was twelve thousand years ago.

Several minutes passed and the one hundred and ninety modules showed no signs of life. The imaginary observer would have begun to worry, but after a quarter of an hour it all started! A crowd of rat-sized robot ants poured out of one of the Arsenal Modules and split into several teams. One of them took on the task of carrying out the most urgent business.

The ant foreman ran to the container in which the power plant was located and signaled on the radio "give me a cable". A lid opened up on the wall of one of the sides, from which the end of a cable with the connector protruded. The ant grabbed onto it with its dorsal grasping limbs and pulled. Behind him a second, third... tenth ant joined him and a chain of small pullers dragged the cable to the nearest yellow container of the Incubator Module. The leader stopped in front of the wall, saying "take the end", a lid opened, a gripper came out of it which pulled in the cable in, then the connector lock clicked and the electrification of the module was complete.

After that in the same way, the ants powered up all of the yellow containers from two more power plants and connected them to each other, but this was only the beginning. Here, in the warm environment, the Incubators needed to be replenished with liquid nitrogen. There were liquefaction plants in only three of the fifty modules, the rest had to be connected to them by thermally insulated hoses which were light but thick. The brigade coped with this task in about an hour and then all ran to recharge. The most urgent task was now completed.

Meanwhile other ant crews set up a network of charging stations and began sticking rolls of temporary solar panels a little off to the side on the convex surface of the outcropping. The midday heat had set in and work was in full swing. The area, seeming to sway from the rising hot air, was filled with an eerie rustle made by the chirping and scraping of hundreds of ant appendages. The ants periodically ran to recharge points, where they froze for about ten minutes, resting their heads against the charging socket. Some of them ran out of charge before they made it to the charge points and with their "last breath" signaled to other ants to "give me a jump!" the nearest charged ant would then run up to them and pressing their heads together would give them a small charge and they would be rescued. The power cables lying on the surface everywhere did not get in the way of the ants, and nothing could damage the cables, since nothing heavier than an ant would cross them. Later they would be covered with armor, poured over with concrete and preserved for millennia, but so far this was not required. All of it together gave the impression of highly intelligent action, although the robot ants were no smarter than their natural prototypes.

Twelve thousand years ago, such scenes as the one taking place now had unfolded many times over on the Martian plains. The ants built low-pressure greenhouses, these were open structures covered with a film and a strong web of polymer fibers on top of it. On these relatively simple construction sites, the "civilization" of mechanical ants, spiders and dragonflies was debugged.

In any worthwhile business, a unique master always appears, usually one, and Aslan Schultz became the main debugger, reminiscent in his appearance and mannerisms of a Hollywood cowboy. He watched the construction site for hours, narrowing his eyes slightly as he leaned back in his chair in the rover's cockpit. He could, noticing a slight under-static, for example, determine when too many ants responded to a command and immediately change the desired parameter, and he always knew which one. He would stop the construction and restart the entire network, after which the work became more productive without aimless ants that turned out to be superfluous. If after work he had a free hour, Aslan enjoyed driving the rover through the desert and over the dunes. He had a craving for speed and open spaces in his blood. His friends joked that his great-grandfathers must have been cowboys and rushed around on horseback over the prairies. He knew nothing about his ancestors who lived on Earth, but he believed in jokes and adored the expanses of Mars.

The construction of greenhouses was the final act of polishing up the ants. Prior to that, Aslan had put ten years into the preparations. At first, he and his colleagues trained individual robots, then more precisely, one robot: all of the ants were loaded with only one version of "intelligence" and behaved identically. Then he taught them to interact with each other and correctly respond to the commands of the System and only a few years after that did the stage of complex debugging during real serious business begin. When the entire mechanical army learned how to perfectly build greenhouses and other structures without human supervision and when they could make the equipment needed for the self-reproduction of robots, it was time to transfer the technology to Earth for the Ark. Aslan Shultz, as a unique master in his field, went to the cradle of mankind along with the technology and equipment he had developed.

The debugging of the "Rooting Program" that unfolded at the Selina Granite Field was first carried out in the semi-desert of Utah on the border with Arizona. Aslan fell in love at first sight with this almost Martian landscape, one which didn't require either a spacesuit or a pressurized cabin to move around in. All his free time he rushed around Arizona, Nevada and Utah, either on a motorcycle or on an ATV, as if he could not get enough of the wind blowing on his uncovered face. And he even had the real opportunity to stay on Earth forever. His children had already grown up and lived independent lives and the possibility of his wife moving to Earth was fixed into his contract. What was not included in the contract was the return of the couple to Mars after the wife flew to Earth; this was because a "return ticket" for two, cost about twenty million. His wife Helga really wanted to visit Earth and to travel across the continents, sail the oceans, breathe the air in open spaces and swim in the sea and at one point the issues seemed almost solved, but something made Aslan wait to send for her.

When it was no longer possible to postpone making the decision any longer and he had to give her an answer as to when, Aslan Schultz sent the following message to his wife: *"Hi Helga. I have had time to think and to travel around the cities, and I realized what was bothering me: there are completely different people here. They are good in their own way, but they are very different. I do not understand the goals that drive them, I cannot relate to the moods they are in. They seem to be kind of 'demagnetized' or something and I quickly have nothing to talk about with them. There is even nothing to argue with them about, they seem to have a different kind of logic. Helga it's wonderful here, of course, the expanses of Arizona are magnificent, the air is incomparable, and the expanses of the Earth are huge. However having had enough of all this, you and I would howl from longing for our Martians, those we know and those we don't. I already miss all of you. So sorry, but I'm going back."*

Meanwhile, the clouds blowing in from the side of the mountains darkened. The system issued a squall warning. The ants gathered in dense groups and grappled together with their legs, clinging to each other. The squall flew by without causing the slightest harm to the construction site and the rain poured down closer to the mountains, only a few drops fell here. The work continued, now it was necessary to establish a water supply, and a double brigade of barge haulers pulled a hose to the river along the path already laid by the scouts. The first day of rooting at the Granite Field went according to plan.

The Logarithmic Chronicle

A week later, an irreversible event took place. At a miniature river water intake station, a check valve opened, and water poured in from a hose in the river. In the water that spilled out there were ten million live, already dividing, blue-green algae cells and many other bacteria. In another half an hour they would enter the ocean, where nothing would stop them from multiplying exponentially, as long as the resources allowed it.

That's all! The planet will never be dead again, even if tomorrow a large meteorite falls on the Granite Field. It can now be said that an act of directed panspermia, in its simplest form has successfully taken place and the minimum program has been completed. There is a chance that the prokaryotes poured into the river will overcome the battle with evolution and evolve into higher life forms in a couple of billion years, although we cannot say anything about the likelihood of such an event occurring. We have one positive result before our eyes, but we do not know how many more were negative. But one way or another, there is no way back, if hundreds of millions of years from now distant observers look at the spectrum of Selina's atmosphere, they will see oxygen, the green flag of life.

Of course, the minimum program is hopelessly far from what the fathers of the Ark fought for. On its own, it would cost twenty times less, but it would not inspire anyone, and Paul Dors would not have sent everyone to hell if he had been offered to finance such a thing. Therefore, all the most important tasks remained ahead and the Granite Field turned into a construction site, where work went on in full swing.

In a week's time, the System had already deployed serious transport vehicles, an all-terrain vehicle, three trucks and two ships. All the transport was slow-moving as you can't accelerate very much on solar batteries, but there was no particular rush. The all-terrain vehicle explored the contents of the river valley, clay, gravel, pieces of ore were required for analysis. Everything was in the valley. Trucks hauled gravel and minerals back to the edge of the Granite Field, where an industrial zone quickly developed, there was a miniature cement plant, a small chemical workshop and a metallurgical complex. The ships then went to sea to extract raw materials from the salt water.

The containers of the Incubator Segment were pulled in close to each other and began to be surrounded and enclosed by a reinforced concrete wall. The wall was built slowly, as the production of steel for rebar and cement occurred at a rate of about one teaspoon per hour. This was because it had not made sense to carry heavy equipment from Earth. Slowly but surely, so that it would last for centuries, more precisely for millennia, the sarcophagus was erected around the Incubator Segment. "A sarcophagus for the Incubator": how contradictory this combination of words sounds. The ants erected the structure that had been designed by man, in a way that only ants can: bring a rod, weld it to others, carry a handful of gravel, pour a glass of mortar and then vibrate it to mix. The ring wall around the Incubators swarmed with ants and sparkled with hundreds of sparks from electric welding.

The work went on at night, and was interrupted only by a siesta in the afternoon, a time when usually a squall came up and the entire mechanical army rushed into a shelter specially erected for this purpose. There were also some cloudy days without squalls and showers, on those days work continued around the clock.

A month later, balloons filled with hydrogen soared up into the sky from the Granite Field. They carried with them "land", blue-green algae and lichens, on which genetic engineers had done an excellent job. The system determined the launch time with the help of orbital probes which had built a radar map of the planet's winds: the balloons were supposed to fly over the mountain range and then deep into the continent. Three weeks later, the forecast showed that atmospheric circulation, with a probability of eighty-five percent, would carry the balloons to the South Meridional continent, and then another batch took off. The launch of the balloons would not have been a spectacular sight: they were all light gray and quickly lost sight of as they rose in the sky. However, the contents of the small capsules suspended from balloons in potential exceeded the equivalent of megatons of TNT. Only the potential here was the opposite of destructive. Dispersed in the atmosphere of Selina a gram of the simplest organisms would eventually digest mountains of rocky soil and turn thousands and thousands of square kilometers of rocky desert into fertile plains.

Back in the early days of the Ark, they had considered a squadron of solar-powered drones for primary seeding. John Carpenter the head of the Phytoexpansion Segment was staunchly against the idea: "Each of these little drones of yours will sooner or later be destroyed or torn apart by little bits of strong turbulence. Will they be able to fly in the stratosphere? You still have to get to the stratosphere. How much extra weight do we need to carry? And why do all that when simple balloons can be replicated on the spot. The polymer shells are easily made from air and sea water, as many as you like, thousands, tens of thousands. Tell

Gene Cooney that you want to use drones, he will laugh and ridicule you, because in the scenario they are working on, tens of thousands, if not hundreds of thousands of flights will be needed for seeding. Yes, that would be a whole fleet of drones! Produce on site? Yes, balloons are an order of magnitude, even two orders of magnitude easier to produce. What is needed? Hydrogen, carbon, oxygen, chlorine from sea water, and there you have it, is that vinyl chloride for you? What is the problem? If you want silicone, throw out the chlorine, add silicon from the sand."

"We need a good 'targeting' for sowing," objected the head of the Department of Bio introduction, Ivan Plotnikov. "Your balloons will pour out whatever they have, wherever God decides to blow them, and what will grow out of that?"

"That's the only way things grow. Ask Jean. How do you think new volcanic islands are populated? The carefully aimed throwing of seeds and small vertebrates?"

Ivan did not give up, despite the clear superiority of John's arguments. The fact was that drones, especially those powered by solar panels, were his longtime and passionate love. While still a schoolboy, he himself assembled small lightweight models and flew them for hours over cities, forests and mountains, without looking up from the monitor. Now his passion came into direct conflict with his professional conscience. Ivan continued to resist, but gradually began to back off, realizing that John was right. He became gloomy and withdrawn. Then once at a meeting, Gene Cooney said that selective monitoring of vegetation is definitely needed, and the balloons are not able to provide that. Ivan immediately brightened up! Just a few drones were enough for monitoring every ten years. They were brought to the Ark and were stored away in one of the modules of the Arsenal.

Thus John Carpenter and Ivan Plotnikov remained best friends twelve thousand years ago.

A year later, the ants closed the dome of the Sarcophagus. All that remained was to increase the thickness and reinforce the walls well so that they become too tough for sands of time, and would exceed the age of the most ancient terrestrial ruins.

The change of seasons did not affect the work in any way – the thunderstorms stopped in the winter, and in the spring there was a series of prolonged rains. Within a year, the Granite Field has turned into a full-fledged industrial complex. Between the Sarcophagus and the descent to the river there were already several miniature production workshops. In the last newly built hangar, there was a facility for the reproduction of artificial insects. On its casing was the brand marker: Made on Mars. It was placed there on the grounds that the location would one day eventually become a local museum exhibit. Well, the Martians were inferior in number to the earthlings by five and a half orders of magnitude, but they were ahead in creating unique single devices and were not lacking in a healthy dose of patriotism. The Ark brought the equipment itself, but all the raw materials needed for constructing the bodies of the new robots had to be found locally. The ants dragged metal ingots and briquettes of various organic substances and minerals to the receiving trays. Once every half an hour a new ant came off the assembly line, less often a long-legged haymaker spider. The last operation in the process was the insertion of a chip produced on Earth and the download of data. After that, the high-tech fruit of human engineering skills ran away on its six legs and joined in the work.

There was no end to the work. Plant nurseries were next in line. The simplest bacteria could be revived and forced to multiply right inside the yellow containers, and the spores of fungi, lichens and ferns could simply be scattered across the expanses of Selina in the form in which they were brought (only half a ton), but with the seeds of higher level plants everything was much more complicated. The Ark was not able to carry all of the seeds of hundreds of thousands of plants in the basic package, many of them were simply too heavy. Only microscopic rudiments of heavy seeds arrived on Selina. It was necessary to first grow the seeds into an artificial fruit, then plant them again, grow grass, bushes, and trees, then take several of the new crops and launch them into the sky for sowing. That is why nurseries were required, open and closed, with and without irrigation, but all with soil and climate control.

In order to sow such seeds in dozens and in hundreds of years, it was necessary to start construction and growing now. So, on the edge of the

Granite Field closest to the sea, at the foot of the dune, electric welding flashed as the ants were welding the frame of the first nursery. Haymaker spiders with two-meter leg spans covered the structure with a polymer web and then put a film over it, trucks carried in fertile grayish loess, which would eventually turn into black soil, bulldozers the size of a large boar moved the earth and leveled the floor of the nursery. They had also built a compressor station nearby. Was it reminiscent of earthly construction sites? Only remotely, the buildings had both the features of hangars and the appearance of gigantic cocoons or wasp nests. They would not survive in this form until the advent of the civilization of Selina, but everything would be carefully filmed and stored in the archives.

Ten years later, the balloons still soared into the air, although less often than in the first years, satellite probes still flew over Selina, and two blocks of the Ark continued to still operate in orbit. These were the Power Unit and the Headquarters with an antenna aimed at Earth's solar system. The probes took many eloquent photographs: the growing village on the Granite Field around the Sarcophagus and the nurseries, which were similar to Earth's greenhouses, sitting on the river floodplain and at the edge of the sand dunes. Then on many pictures of the surface of the continents, the first dirty green spots began to appear, these were mats of cyanobacteria.

The sea was still calm eight or nine days out of ten. Sometimes the receding waves now left green lumps on the sand, although the water remained clear and the sand clean as before. The ecological catastrophes that the planet was to go through still lie ahead. Unfortunately, they are inevitable if a planet is going to go from being a desert into a flourishing world in a short time. Yes, and the Earth, having passed a similar path for a billion years, did not escape them either.

For ten years, the probes broadcast images and data to the Ark radio station, and the twenty-megawatt transmitter sent them in the direction of the Earth's solar system. Pictures were sent of the selected landing site, the landing of the containers and all stages of construction. Now here were the first pictures of life on the new planet, and again, willy-nilly, the question arises: was there anyone there to take in all this wealth of information? Are there still living people there? Do they still have radio telescopes? Do they know where to direct their dishes? Do they remember Ark 47 Librae? Are they interested in its fate? Please ask something easier!

If the answer to those questions is yes, then you can imagine the delight of the inhabitants of the Earth and Mars. If humans had not arranged an apocalypse for themselves and have not gone wild, then they will undoubtedly appreciate the gift prepared for them by their ancestors more than two hundred generations ago, but who knows what they really did there...? It is impossible to know what has happened on Earth since it is sixty light years away. Instead of guessing, let's return to our chronicle.

A hundred years later, all construction stopped, and all action moved to nurseries. It was time to harvest the seeds. This was done by miniature harvesters and the smallest of the ants which were the size of mice.

Then the first percent of oxygen appeared in Selina's atmosphere.

There were no flags on the Granite Field, there was no problem in planting them, but the staff of the Rooting Segment could not come up with such an idea in principle. They treated flags and other symbols only as vestiges of past centuries, as a way of asserting some sort of power over others or as a sign of belonging to a certain population. What the hell is the population here? Before whom did the Ark affirm its status? By the living before the dead? What use were flags here? However, nature and chance seemed to have decided to correct what the staff had missed long ago.

At the entrance to the village from the side of the river, there was a dump of waste rock piled there from the metallurgical complex. An ant with a malfunctioning orientation system that had worked in the coniferous nursery ran through it and a few months later, at the top of the dump, a tiny pine sprout began to grow. In the rocks the pine found everything it needed to grow and flourish: nitrogen, potassium, phosphorus and trace elements, and it began to grow at an unprecedented rate. Besides everything else it also needed some oxygen but only a little, and to provide this a thick dirty green blotch spread out near the dump in the lowland, adding two more local points to the global percentage of oxygen. Ten years later, the pine tree, towering over the industrial domes and arched nurseries, was visible from everywhere. Fifteen years later, it gained the strength of a lone adult tree and rustled in the strong winds from the sea. It served as the banner of the Granite Field raised in the bare landscape.

By that time, the probes had burned up in the atmosphere, due to the fact that the fuel required for them to maintain their orbit had simply run out. The hypothetical people in the solar system no longer saw the surface of the continents of Selina with sprawling patches of vegetation. However theoretically, they would still be able to see the Granite Field and its surroundings for a long time: an antenna has been erected and had started working here, transmitting a signal directly to the Ark. The transmitter of the Ark was still alive, only it had long ago been switched to power from solar batteries: the uranium rods long ago passed through and burned out and the reactor had stopped. The rate of transmission dropped dozens of times, but time on Selina also slowed down, events began to occur many times less often, however they did not in any way become less important.

Most of the ants and machines were preserved in airtight boxes filled with argon at zero humidity and kept at a constant temperature. Once every ten years, the ants briefly interrupted their sleep to stretch their limbs and reboot. In the Incubator Segment under the dome of the Sarcophagus, nitrogen liquefiers continued to operate, and in one of the hangars, for many years, a simple installation produced and inflated balloons with hydrogen, which one after another were released to fly away.

The time has now come to check how the primitive life is mastering the land. Maybe it's time to correct something in the Program? Two drones named after Ivan Plotnikov were removed from their places in mothballing and put on alert. They were small propeller-driven drones, sized and shaped like albatrosses. They, also like albatrosses, could fly for weeks and months. During the day, the drones were recharged, and at night they simply hovered, saving their charges. One of them flew along the coast of the ocean, the second over the mountains and deep into the mainland. We'll follow the second one.

The apparatus travelled along the river bed and recorded that the pebbly floodplain was now gray-green, and the oxbow lakes were a rich green. Seeing this on Earth, they would conclude that it was an "environmental disaster!" The valley gradually narrowed and its slopes became higher and steeper. The drone took a course towards the pass that led it along the ridge. It flew as if it was controlled by Plotnikov himself, it searched for updrafts and circled in them, gaining altitude like a glider, then it continued its horizontal flight in the right direction, found a new updraft... However, one has to ask why "as if"? In the memory of the drone were all of the reflex experiences of its predecessors, drones which Ivan had flown over the Andes, the Caucasus Range, the spurs of the Himalayas and the ice domes of Greenland. Therefore, it was in fact so, the drone was being led by the firm hand of Ivan Plotnikov, and being thus it headed for the pass.

At an altitude of about four thousand meters, a strong rising stream of tailwind picked up the apparatus and carried it to the top. On Earth, such air flows dump butterflies and other flying insects onto the snow of the highlands. This trick is used by jackdaws when motionlessly gliding against the wind over the dazzling snow of passes and slopes, and they catch delicacies on the fly. There were no butterflies or jackdaws here yet, but the wet snow covering the glacier that was under the pass was pink – apparently some algae had already drifted there.

And then the drone cameras opened up onto a panorama on the other side of the ridge, the bluish expanse of the huge mainland: immense, untrodden, and never once seen by anyone. The spurs of the main ridge quickly lowered to the northeast and for forty kilometers led into a hilly plain. An almost completely straight valley with steep sides and a flat bottom stretched from the pass to the plain. Under the pass there was a glacier, further the land turned to granite and even further cobblestone. From the glacier, a river flowed down into a valley where it flowed into a long mountain lake which was a deep blue and cold and which filled the entire valley where a slope had once collapsed, blocking the path of the river. Further on, about a hundred kilometers out on the plain there was another large lake, so large that it was unlikely that the opposite side could be seen from the shore. The path of the drone lay first to this lake, and then five hundred kilometers further.

The craft began its descent into and along the valley, flying high giving it a bird's eye view of the river. Having flown over the waters of the long transparent lake, it immediately dove down after the area that served as a dam and ended up in another world. The bottom of the valley was covered with a thick layer of dark green slime and overgrown with lichens. Farther down the spurs became flatter, and the bushy lichen looked like some kind of cauliflower thicket.

Less than an hour after the start of the descent, the drone reached the plain. What it saw there would hardly have pleased the human eye, the same thick dark green carpets, brown domes of disgusting looking meter-wide mushrooms and lush lichen, as far as the eye could see. A huge inviting lake, which looked blue from afar, turned out to be so blooming with plant life that even the white caps of the waves were a deep green. Yes, the planet, a hundred years after the arrival of the Ark, was alive, but it was very unpleasant. Was it like the Precambrian Earth? It is unlikely, however, who knows...?

At night the drone gained altitude, after which it continued flying to the northeast, and by morning it had reached its main goal – the great river that crosses the vast inner plain of the Northern continent. The river was green, although maybe not as green as the lake. The beaches along the coasts and on the islands were clean, apparently the recent flooding had washed their coarse quartz sand well, but a vile-looking dark green bubbling substance was spread all over the floodplain.

The device descended, flying at a low level and took a sample of the water and then rose and set off on the return journey. It was very important for it to return home safely. It had not been possible to transmit data from such a distance, and even the heights of the mountains blocked the signals, so that not a single bit, out of the hundreds of gigabytes of recorded information, had been sent. Actually, for a drone that had gone through the Plotnikov School this was not a particular problem, the main thing is not to try to cross the ridge in the afternoon, when thunderstorms raged in from the sea.

Upon approaching home, the drone uploaded all of its records to the System from the air, while circling over the Granite Field. Then it safely set down and was sent for maintenance. System, after having processed the optical and infrared records, the air analyzer data, and having studied the water sample, issued a verdict: "It's time to sow!" The algae and lichens had filled all of the available niches and processed mountains of rocky soil into a kind of soil suitable for the first higher level plants and the oxygen content in some of the locations of the lowlands exceeded five percent. The Granite Field seemed to have been waiting for this moment for a long time: several tons of seeds and spores of thousands of plant species were already stored in one of the argon boxes.

Mosses and cereals were the first to be sent on the attack. The seeds and spores were carried by the same balloons, and there were thousands of balloons for thousands of kilometers. The very next year, the first grass sprouted on the flat rocks among the lichens, and the shady side of the boulders of the moraine were overgrown with moss.

What was happening now on the half-asleep Granite Field at one time had completely passed through the head of Eugene Cooney, who by the way, became one of the founding fathers of the project almost by accident. When preparing the first brainstorming session, Alex suggested calling some kind of biologist just in case, although the topic was purely engineering. Gene, thanks to his acquaintance with Roland, turned out to be that "some kind of biologist" and from the very first gathering in room B3 he was hopelessly involved in the project. He had been engaged in evolutionary biology, bioinformatics and nothing caused him grief. Then everything that he had only known before by hearsay fell on top of him: ecology, planetology, dendrology, embryology, and a dozen other different disciplines, a literal sea of tasks. And since he had taken the bull by the horns, he urgently needed to hunt for heads and look for and attract professionals scattered around the world. In order to successfully attract prey, you must be able to clearly speak their professional language and for this alone, he was forced to delve into dozens of problems associated with the rooting of life on a hitherto empty planet. In this way a certain amount of flair was developed, not erudition, but flair. In his case the ability to smell true statements from erroneous ones, identify breakthrough ideas from dead ends and recognize reliable results from bullshit. It was a flair in such a wide area that it could not be kept in his head.

Gradually, the Bio Segment of the Ark was assembled head by head, but even when the powerful team had been formed, Gene remained a plug to all barrels, in any large endeavor there must be a glue man who puts everything together, a frame man who keeps everything essential in his head, no matter how plump it is. How to grow seeds of thousands of plant species, how to prepare soil for nurseries in the absence of natural soil, what, when and in what sequence to sow across continents? Thousands of questions arose, forming an incredibly wide field of knowledge. There were specialists for each issue, but someone had to somehow integrate it into themselves – that was Gene.

His head was swollen, but it managed to hold on. Perhaps all of the leaders of the Ark Project had had to somehow change their area of expertise and master many methods and concepts from different spheres. The myth that the future belongs to narrow minded specialists who know everything about nothing is not worth a damn. The era of the Renaissance remained in the distant past, but life keeps demanding and demanding people like Leonardo. By the way, they have not gone away, they have just become less noticeable.

A thousand years later, the dunes were covered with pine forests, the former outcroppings and glacial moraines disappeared into the greenery of forests filled with broad-leaved plants and trees. Under the canopy of the forest it was already possible to breathe a little, although not for a person, but at least for less whimsical and oxygen consuming little creatures such as earthworms. The balloons kept landing and taking off, except now instead of seeds and spores, they carried all kinds of protozoa, and the eggs of worms and arthropods.

The afternoon thunderstorms over the foothills had almost stopped and the cooled down forests did not allow powerful updrafts to develop. Now there were often long drizzling rains and the drops, slipping down from the leaves of trees, fell on last year's foliage. In the ravine, where after downpours once rushed streams of water on bare granite, now a transparent eternal stream murmured.

Never again would Selina's water cycle be empty! Anytime it rained here it would give water to at least one living thing. The grass, the trees and the living creatures teeming among the fallen leaves, all of this was indestructible as long as 47 Librae shone!

The new world was already beautiful in its own way. Maybe it was already worth stopping? Leaving the revived planet to itself and not driving forward the hands of time, compressing it hundreds of thousands of times over. Where were they hurrying to? Maybe these worms would give rise to vertebrates who in their turn... Well, you see... There was the goal of the race of man, what a risk factor! What could it do here?

But, alas, this world did not perceive or observe itself. When we say something like "the world is beautiful", we mean it is beautiful to the observer. Even if they do not know how to describe what they see in words, they are at least able to admire the view of the valleys for hours, lying on the edge of a cliff while resting their heads on their paws, or perhaps just looking around the floodplain of a river, or at the soaring cliffs ascending over a stream, or even just simply enjoying the rising sun, like a dolphin jumping out of the water and spinning around like a dervish among the waves.

The program didn't provide a stop point for nor was it designed for one, following the Postulate of the key goal which was: "As many intelligent beings as possible should see and perceive this beautiful world." Yes, and in fact the lands of the continents were ready for more and seemed to be waiting for something or someone.

They seemed to be saying: "Someone must graze this lush grass, cutting and fertilizing it; someone must live in the cozy hollow of an old oak tree; and someone should build houses on the high banks near the bends of the river."

The sea, not lagging behind the land, threw tangled tentacles of branches of algae out onto the shore, then strips of kelp, demonstrating that it was no longer barren and that it was now able to shelter not only primitive unicellular life and was ready for more.

On the humid plains of the southern part of the northern continent, across the monsoon belt of the South Meridional and in the northern part of the South Latitudinal continents, towering poisonous grass-filled herbaceous jungles had appeared and were spreading, and in these were neither worms nor insects, only the hard trunks, standing and fallen and huge carved leaves both living and dead. The roots of the trees, which were creations of genetic engineering, went down for many meters through layers of their dead compressed predecessors, finally reaching sedimentary soil and rocks, from where the lush plants fed on elements that they could not get from the air. Bright green leaves covered the sky in several tiers, so that on the surface (if you can call the surface a gradual transition of layers from living to dead vegetation) it was dark, as in dense twilight. An eerie sight of dense thickets of giant hogweed, standing over a layer of last year's dead plants and their leaves. Yes, the planet's main oxygen factories may have looked repulsive but there was no one to admire them except for a few drones that happened to fly along their borders during the thousands of years of their existence.

By this time, the Ark had long ago fallen asleep, forever turning into a space memorial, but so far there had been no visitors. An archive with information about the Earth, mankind and the Ark itself was preserved on board. All the information was stored on metal disks, in the form of engravings large enough not to suffer from the heavy high-energy nuclei that leave damage visible only under a microscope. Much more information was stored in more vulnerable but permanently maintained form, and had been sent to Selina where it had been placed in the shelter under the dome of the Sarcophagus.

After ten thousand more years had passed, the Granite Field began to come to life again. The ants poured out en masse from the conservation boxes into the industrial area, onto the gentle slopes of the ridge and then to the river and to the seashore. The Granite Field then began to grow rapidly in all available directions. Thousands, then tens of thousands, then hundreds of thousands of ants and spiders of all shapes and sizes set to work.

The frequency of the flights of the balloons also increased several times. Now they carried the eggs of fish and amphibians, collected in nurseries that had been set up by the river, in an artificial harbor. The balloons dropped units of thousands of eggs into the right environments and they soon developed into fish and into frogs, right out in the wild

where there were not yet predators. Some of them would find mates and the process would continue... In some of the closed and protected pavilions of the Granite Field , for the first time in the history of Selina, the squeaky voices of chicks could be heard and in others: knocking sounds, chomping and indistinct bleating. Then chickens poured out of the pavilion into their pen, following an ant in a light feathery cloak, from another pavilion a flock of young crows flew out into the open and from a third pavilion calves came out into the their own spacious corals and, looking around, immediately set to eating the fresh grass.

Maybe this all seems completely impossible? After all, neither the first eggs nor the first roe were on the Ark as they were too big, everything was grown on the spot from microscopic immature eggs. Then someone or something had to shove worms down the throats of the chicks, feed the calves grown in artificial wombs, spread the roe in a suitable place and build and equip the enclosures. How can all this happen without human intervention? It seems that it would have been easier to reach the speed of light, fold space, teleport and deliver the administrator and controller, than to design something like this.

Here it would be a good idea to repeat: in our Universe, where only in the visible part of it there are more stars than grains of sand on all the beaches of the Earth, no one has yet been able to break the prohibitions that prevent the above methods of movement, but to carry out the most complex chain of actions without supervision and guidance and with excellent results? Yes, please, as much as you like. Each of us was born as a result of such a chain of simple events. Nowhere is there a complete and total centralized program or blueprint for the development of the human body from a fertilized egg. There is no master plan for us! Everything is programmed at the cellular level in the form of simple instructions such as "if the concentration of such and such a substance exceeds such and such a value, produce such and such a protein", a set of such instructions as these is much simpler than the act of growing a person on their basis.

In the same way, the Granite Field and everything that happened on it did not have a detailed master plan. The actions unfolded with the help of a set of simple instructions, "conditional statements", a long chain of which produces a surprisingly complex stable result. An ant that finds itself in the zone of the bird incubator receives the beacon signal "download the reflexes of the chick feeder", then "take it into cell 3.17 and put the bird head manipulator on the front top connector. Then the reflex action dictates to the ant: "Catch the green fluorescent line, move to its source, grab the fluorescent worm." Then "select sound from the noise bank with such and such a Fourier profile and in the region of five kilohertz, move it to the nearest source", "put the worm into the sound source with the manipulator". And so on. The ant acts without knowing what is going on outside its narrow field of its assigned task. The system itself does not control any one individual ant. It only sends each one the necessary code upon receiving a request.

It is from these simple steps that a grandiose scheme is formed and carried out. The principle of life in fact is thus, there is not a centralized command post that directs life, it is the sum of simple local instructions. Not even a generalized plan, but a genome which landed on Selina with the Ark, the genome of a new biosphere.

The "development" of the human genome took billions of years, while the development of the "genome" of the Ark only took decades. Even though the time was much less, people, even if acting by trial and error, are able to reduce the number of erroneous trials by orders of magnitude less, when compared to Nature. In addition, he created excellent tools for accelerated modeling of reality. And, finally, Nature endowed humans with something that she herself does not have, and that is flair. That is why they managed to complete the Ark in half a century, actually creating and sending the embryo of the Nature's biosphere daughter to its new destination. Looking ahead, we can add that not only was the biosphere sent, but also civilization.

PART THREE

Magda's Strange Children

Magda did not understand what Joe wanted from her right away. He pointed his hand at the open door in the wall, and said: "Magda, there," but it was not clear what "there" meant. Could he mean the door? She was scared. She was used to her own space, to her own little room, the neighboring room of Berta and the yard which was covered with grass and overgrown along the edges with bushes. Berta had eight children and Aunt Magda adored them all and played in the yard with them for hours, either running in circles or freezing in ambush. Being a mother, Berta had a higher status, which she used from time to time, to drive her sister away from her beloved brats, at which times Magda went to her own room and felt sad, putting her head on her paws.

"Go, go, don't be afraid, it's okay," Joe said. For some reason it stopped being so scary and then Magda, with her tail between her legs and her head bowed low, went up to the door, and stuck her head through the opening. The smell she smelled was unfamiliar, but it seemed alive and harmless. Magda entered the area beyond the opening and found herself in a corridor at the end of which another door opened. Unfamiliar but interesting sounds could be heard coming from it and the smell became even stronger and more attractive. Magda, overcoming her fear, went ahead passed through the second door and found herself in a large room, much larger than her own. Joe was also sitting in this room, but, most importantly two strange children were crawling around on the floor: they were large but had the clumsy movements of small children and not those of their size who should have been running around the yard and not crawling. They did not smell like Berta's children, but it was clear from their smell that they were helpless and in need of care.

Magda approached one of the children and licked his face. The smell of the child changed as if they liked it. Joe said something in an approving voice, Magda licked the second child. It made cheerful jerky sounds and also began to smell joyful.

"Well, did you like the pets?" Joe asked. For Magda, this phrase was too complicated, but she realized that Joe approved of her and that everything was fine. She lay down and one child crawled up to her and grabbed her by the ear.

"Kate," Joe said.

Another child crawled up behind him and tried to climb onto Magda's back.

"Lisa," Joe said.

Just then a large door opened in the wall, and someone came into the room in a wheelchair, vaguely resembling Tanya and Joe, but rather strange. The scent and face of the strange creature were lifeless. Magda was frightened and growled.

"What's wrong, Magda? Don't be afraid, this is Nanny. She's good, don't be afraid. Magda calmed down, went up to Nanny and sniffed her. She smelled strange but not dangerous. Nanny stretched out her hand and stroked Magda, not exactly affectionately, but soothingly. Tanya then appeared next to Joe.

"Magda, now these are your pets!" she said. Magda did not understand, but for some reason she was delighted and stretched out on her back folding her front paws on her chest. The children crawled along the floor to the kind warm woolly creature and lay down beside her. In this position, all three fell into a deep, serene sleep.

Time passed happily and slowly. Magda played for hours with Kate and Lisa, who began to stand up on their hind legs and walk around holding on to her tail. Nanny fed the children, cleaned up after them and washed them, and Tanya and Joe spent more and more time talking with the little ones. Magda at first understood everything they said to the children, for example, “take a cube.” Sometimes she would grab the cube impatiently herself and they would say to her: “Wait, let Kate get it.”

A new form of entertainment had appeared, living creatures and children had appeared on the wall. They were very similar to real ones, but they were not real, no smell emanated from them. Joe and Tanya were looking at the living wall and telling everyone what and who appeared on it. As time went on Magda understood everything less and less but the children got better and better at it and tried to repeat the names of the creatures on the wall.

Magda could still take a walk in the courtyard but Kate and Lisa could not enter it yet, the entrance was blocked by what was an impregnable barrier for them, which Magda easily jumped over. Through the courtyard it was possible to get to Berta, whose children had already grown up and gone left here. Their voices came from somewhere beyond the fence among the dense thickets of bushes. One day the barrier that had protected the children disappeared and all three went out into the yard together.

Now Magda had the highest status with her two children who were so big and funny. Berta approached them, her head bent down and her tail wagging along with her rear end. She was generously received by the children who pulled her by the tail and pulled on her ears, while Magda calmly lay on the sidelines and watched, screwing up her eyes. The children kept growing and they soon became taller than Magda when they stood on two legs at their full height, but they remained children, with their childish movements, their falls, crying and disobedience. When Joe or Tanya called everyone home, for dinner or bed, the children often did not react, but continued to dig in the sand or pick at things in the grass. Then Magda had to push them to the entrance with a bark, the children walked home, sometimes whining and protesting but once at home they were quickly calmed down by licking their faces or making them laugh.

Thus the months and then the years of the happy lives of Magda and her unusual children flowed by. The idyll scene did not even remotely resemble what it really was: the most dangerous and risk filled moment of the entire Project, a bottleneck called “the barrier of the first babies.”

The people of Mars had to practice this stage for thirty-five years, having conducted more than a hundred experiments in which more than two hundred children participated. At first there had been continuous failures and there was a moment when the entire Martian Ark team had fallen into despair. In the end the number of overall failures had been in the dozens but none of the children died. Many survived with the effects of severe stress, possibly imprinted for life. What could they have done? On the one hand, experimentation on children was one of the most severe taboos in the developed world. On the other hand, without such experiments the Ark would not have been possible and the rug would have been pulled out from under their feet. So you be the judge!

The people of Earth did judge them and it did not go well! They screamed on television duels, wrote devastating articles, started mass petitions and filed appeals in the courts. Social networks seethed with indignation and bubbled with mutual hatred for the disputing parties, but all of that happened on Earth. On Mars, outside of all earthly jurisdictions, the people worked on, stubbornly and silently and continued to experiment, looking for a way out.

The problems with the children started at five or six months. They ceased to perceive the nurse as a real mother and at that moment their attention had to be switched to the replicas of their parents. Sometimes it worked and sometimes it didn't. If not, the experiment had to be interrupted to avoid the children panicking or causing them runaway hysteria. If that happened the experiment continued, but later other problems would begin and due to the lack of tactile contact with their parents, untold stress developed which turned into a complete loss of interest in everything around them and in the end a catatonic state.

Who had first suggested giving the children a real dog remains unknown with at least three people claiming it was their idea, including Goran. However regardless of authorship, the idea turned out to be not just successful but saved the mission. The children clung to the dogs as if it were both their mother's skirts and their favorite toys and the dogs perceived the children as their own and gave them all the tenderness they could.

There were no more stress related stupors or issues but then another problem arose: they would eventually lose their connection with the parents behind the glass and their lives with the nanny and the dog turned out to be sufficient. With weak or no contact, they mastered speech poorly and grew up as cheerful, joyful savages. This was not as fatal and unamenable to subsequent correction as other issues but it still remained a problem. There could be only one way out, to close the gap and achieve full contact not only with the dogs but with the human replicas. For this, the dogs needed an innate ability to perceive and correctly interpret the image of a person, whether holographic or flat. Stefan Mukha and his team resolved the problem and fulfilled the task in just seventeen years. After that, one after another all of the experiments began to end in complete success.

In that regard the idyll life that unfolded in the Children's Complex among the dunes did in no way really resemble the most difficult stage of the Program. Then at four years old, Kate asked the question: "Mom and Dad, why are you always behind glass? Why can't you come and be near Lisa and me? Why can we only touch only Magda and Nanny and only can only play with Magda for real? Well, and with Berta. We want to play with you too."

It was agreed in advance that Joe Sidorov would answer this question: "Kate, Mom and I are really far away. It just seems like we're close. You see our images, not us. Here you can see yourself in the mirror, that is also an image, but you cannot touch it, your hand only rests against the glass, but your image in the mirror is actually close to you but we are far, very far from our image and from you."

"And when will you come to us here so that we can touch you?"

We're not coming, Kate. We can't. We are so far away that we can neither visit nor fly there but we will see you all the time and our images and voices will be with you always. We will never leave you alone."

"And in the movies we saw other people. Will they come to visit us?"

"No, Kate. All other people are also very far away but you will have little brothers and sisters. Then you will grow up and become mothers yourself and there will be many of you and all of you will be close to each other. And you and Lisa will be the elders, and everyone will obey you. Now go and calm Lisa, look, she burst into tears. Magda! Where is Magda? Magda, go to Lisa!"

The foregoing was enough for a year and a half to maintain a holistic picture of the world in the children's heads.

The following radical question was then asked by Lisa: "You promised that we would have little brothers and sisters. Where are they? Why aren't they all here?"

"They will be with you soon. But you and Kate should be able to take care of them, help Nanny dress them and play with them. You have little dolls. Now take a big doll from the closet and learn to babysit it. We've been waiting for one of you to ask about this. Now you have to get ready."

Kate had her another question. "Dad, how did it happen that you are very far from us? Where is this far place? Why did we end up alone with the dogs here?"

"We live in a different world, Kate. It's called Earth. Your world is called Selina, in which you and Lisa are the first people. Before you, your world was empty, and we who live on Earth, decided to populate it. Between the Earth and Selina is a huge empty space that an adult cannot overcome. Only a small fetus of a human or dog or other animal can survive the long journey through the void. Therefore, people sent embryos of people and animals to Selina. You and Lisa grew up first. Others will grow up soon and there will be many of you. We will always be here behind the glass with you, and we will help you. Lisa, why are you crying?"

"I'm scared that we're alone here. We are alone in the whole world, and there is no one who can come and rescue us! There is no one to protect us."

"Lisa, nobody and nothing is threatening you in your world. You have a very calm world. Magda, Nanny and robots always come to help you. You don't see them, but they are the ones who give Nanny food for you.

We monitor everything, and if something goes wrong, we will tell you how to behave and instruct the robots how to fix everything. And now I ask Kate and Magda: please calm down Lisa!"

"Magda, let's make Lisa laugh," Kate suggested and got on all fours and barked at Magda. Huge Magda, with her tail between her legs and whimpering, ran in circles from Kate, who followed, continuing to growl and bark. For half a minute Lisa, biting her lips, kept a mournful face, but then she could not hold back any longer and burst out laughing.

Then not much time passed, and Tanya asked the children to enter the room beyond door, one which was always locked and almost invisible. In the room behind the door two little brothers were crawling around and Berta was sitting proudly. The barrier of the first children had now been crossed and left behind.

They are All Dead!

After dinner as usual the youth gathered on the veranda of the dining room to talk and to admire how the sun sets beyond the sea making the mountain tops light up and then watching them go out. There were very few of them in this world, so at least once a day it was required for everyone to get together, sit down closely and have a leisurely conversation. Thanks to the System, they felt like they were in Christ's bosom on their patch of habitable space, although all around them lay huge uninhabited expanses, from which they could sense only threats and danger. Mentally at least they wanted to populate these expanses, so in the evenings they composed and told each other stories about non-humanoid aborigines living behind the mountains, and about an alien ark that had landed in the North many years ago in order to populate the planet with giant black creatures. These sweetly creepy tales, as they were, served to emphasize the comfort of their reliable abode.

There were truly really only a very few of them and it was a tangible fact. Not counting the dogs, minus the smallest and two kitchen attendants, there were seventeen. This time, however, in addition to the already small number, Jan was absent, as he had returned to the class room before dinner. At the time he had been about to go to the dining room along with everyone, but suddenly stopped halfway there, said he urgently needed to go to back to class, and then proceeded to rush back across the lawn at a full run. He did not show up for dinner and they were discussing how it would be nice to go get him, when he appeared in person. He apparently had been running again and his face looked strange, his mouth was gaping open and his eyebrows were raised, which made his face seem elongated, kind of how witnesses to a catastrophe that has just happened looked.

"Listen, listen!" he shouted. "They're all dead! They died thousands and thousands of years ago!!"

"What are you talking about? Who died?"

"All of them. Joe, Tanya, the professor, the teachers."

"What do you mean they're dead? How do they talk to us and teach us then?"

"I mean they are all long gone. Their old recordings speak to us. But it's not just recordings, but as the professor said, replicas of themselves made from recordings."

Everyone was quiet trying in vain to comprehend what had just been said. Magda and Berta, who were lying at the feet of the now pale Lisa, raised their heads anxiously.

"The Professor just told me all this," Jan finally continued. Yesterday he was talking about the theory of relativity, you heard it yourselves. He said that no signal can travel faster than the speed of light. And then I asked him today: 'How are we talking then? There are sixty light years between the Earth and Selina. That means that the time between the question and the answer should be one hundred and twenty years and not a second."

"Yes, I also had a similar thought, but somehow it slipped by me," Jules muttered. "Indeed, it is very strange."

"Their records and replicas were made twenty-two thousand years

ago and brought here on the Ark. Our parents and our teachers have been gone for more than twenty thousand years!"

Silence fell again, interrupted only by indistinct interjections and indistinct muttering.

The pause was interrupted again by Jules: "What is this? So we were brought up and taught not by people, but by their recordings? And all this time we thought that they were people and believed their every word! How is this possible?"

"The professor said that he was waiting for this question and that he who is able to ask it will be able to handle the truth. They didn't tell us this before for fear that the truth would frighten us and that we would stop listening to them and remain savages. He also said that we need to talk to the head of the entire project, Alex Selin. He said just go to class and say we want to talk to the Project Manager."

"Shall we go right now?" Jules asked.

"Better tomorrow. Right now you can't face it. You need to calm down and think things through first. Let's go tomorrow morning. But not all of us, from the old girls we'll take Kate, she has a strong psyche. Well, and then Jules and I. And that's enough, the small fry will be a hindrance."

Kate was on duty in the kitchen, otherwise the fourteen-year-old Jan would have gotten told off for his "old girls" comment. Lisa sat with a stony face and did not react to anything. As for the twelve-year-old and younger youth, they accepted the verdict with humility: Jan in their eyes had suddenly become a leader as the person who revealed a terrible secret.

The next morning, they dressed nicer than usual and combed their hair carefully. Jan, Kate, and Jules entered the classroom, locked the doors, sat down, and Jan said: "We want to talk to the Project Manager."

An old man appeared on the screen, it was Alex from the time when he was already confined to a wheelchair and had retired.

"Hello, friends. I have been waiting for a long time to be called. Let's get acquainted. I'm Alex Selin. Let's start with you, young lady."

"My name is Kate."

"Kate, do I understand correctly that you are the eldest on the planet? The very first?"

"Yes, my sister and I are the oldest."

"Where is your sister?"

"We decided not to bring Lisa to this conversation," Jan answered for Kate. "She is a nervous crybaby, although she is very kind and loves all of us."

"Then all the more reason you need to call her, especially if she loves everyone. Maybe that would make her the most important person with you."

"Can she come with the dogs that nursed us?" asked Kate. "They are already quite old and go everywhere with Lisa, she almost never parts with them."

"Well, of course you can, call them quickly."

Jules ran to go and find Lisa. A couple of minutes later they entered, the young Lisa and the decrepit Magda and Berta. The dogs sat down at Lisa's sides like guard lions, expressing their full attention with their heavy gray muzzles.

"Hello, Lisa, hello dogs. What are your guys' names?"

"Jan."

"Julien."

"I understand you are next in the order of precedence. And how many of you are there?"

"Counting the very small ones? Twenty-eight people."

"Okay, now let me tell you about myself and how and why you ended up here. The fact is that the parents and teachers told you everything as if you were children, hiding part of the truth and simplifying a lot. They were forced to do this to protect your psyches. You should not have had any doubts that a direct conversation was going on. But from now on, you are adults. Therefore, I will speak frankly."

At one time, Alex had made it a condition that his remarks "turned on" only after the first children find out with whom, or rather, with what, they are talking to. He insisted that it was absolutely necessary that one of the mentors of the matured Selinites be a person who had never twisted the truth and had never had to prevaricate."

"I can't lie to you," Alex said. "My replica will spoil everything at the first stage: if I cannot lie convincingly, then it will not be able to either."

Alex told them all about how the idea for the project had come about and about the visit to Paul Dors. He told them how the Martians solved the problems with the first children, their problem. He repeated a lot of what the children had already been told about the Ark, only the context was different, in this context, the whole story looked much more complicated.

The now former children listened to Alex without moving. Not only because their entire world view had suddenly changed but because bridges or tunnels that go far through time, often hypnotize us. We might peer for a long time at photographs of the nineteenth century, at people who have long been dead or cities and places that have become completely different. We are fascinated by structures that have endured thousands of years of turbulent history and changing climates. Now, in this case, on one side of the tunnel is an old man with clear eyes and unhurried speech and on the other, children who have just grown up. They seemed to be very close to each other but there were twenty-two thousand years between them.

Alex talked about the Mongolian Park, about the Purpose Postulate, about the silence of the cosmos and finally about how important it is to populate new planets. The youth were frozen in some place out of time, lost in hundreds of thousands of centuries. Waxman's platform recognized perfectly the state of the current audience, their emotions and their ability to perceive. Alex, working on a cue, had also provided for a similar reaction, it was absolutely vital to break their hypnosis and bring the audience back to the real world.

“Well, what are you standing there with your mouths open for? Either people, or dogs ... Come on, snap out of your trances! You are not listeners, you are participants. Now I will say a few more words, and you may ask questions.”

Everyone except Lisa came back to reality and looked at each other.

“There, that’s better,” Alex said and continued. “Until now, everything depended on us, how well we foresaw everything, how smart and flexible the System we created was. From this day on, things begin to depend on you, and the further you go, the more it will be so.”

“For a while, you will still be dependent on the System for everything related to food, housing and clothing. But the possibilities of the System are limited, it cannot feed more than a hundred people. Therefore, all of you will have to work, to become farmers, metallurgists, builders and engineers. But above all we need educators and teachers. If it comes to metallurgists and engineers in the next generations, then teachers are needed immediately, and you should become them, despite your young age. Right now. Please note that now the younger ones, knowing the truth, but not yet acquiring a sense of responsibility, will lose contact with the replicas of teachers. They will lose an important lever, shame in front of the teacher. What is there to be ashamed of before a recording a long-dead person? You have to become those before whom the younger ones will be ashamed of unfulfilled or poorly done tasks, of laziness and of lies. And I will become the one whom, if anything, you will be ashamed of. Do not forget that the fate of the future civilization of Selina depends on you and to be honest, I envy you. We live here in a populated and equipped world, where very little depends on each of us. Everything important that my colleagues and I managed to do on Earth is connected with your world, the planet where you were placed with such incredible difficulty. Now it’s up to you.”

Alex then fell silent and the young people also became silent. Chaos still reigned in their heads, from which unfinished questions tried to rise, but immediately crumbled and returned to their original substance.

Only Lisa, suddenly waking up, blurted out what seemed like deliberate stupidity: "What is happening on Earth right now?"

"Lisa, no one can know the future. What is 'right now' for you is the distant future for me. I can only say that the sun probably shines in the same way and the Earth moves in the same way in its orbit. I can't even tell you how the launch of the Ark went, because I didn't live to see it. Someday your descendants will make a big antenna and point it at the Earth. Then, if you're lucky enough to contact the earthlings, they'll know everything, but that will not be soon. And now let's finish, I think your questions will mature in a day and tomorrow I will tell you about the Program: it is a chain of actions that must be performed in order to quickly, and without loss, reproduce the Earth's civilization on your planet."

The "small fry" were waiting for the elders in the clearing in front of the class and immediately pounced on them with questions: What did the most important person from Earth tell them?

"He said," Kate said, "'more than a million people worked on Earth and thousands on Mars to get us here. And now it depends only on us that their work was not in vain. To do this, we must study well and not be fools.'"

"He also said," Jan added, "'that when there are more than a hundred of us, we will have to work hard to provide everything we need for ourselves and the children and to do this, we will have to become farmers, engineers and builders.'"

"But first we, the elders," continued Jules, "'must become your teachers and educators and you should be ashamed before us for tasks not done and for all sorts of stupid things.'"

"Not quite like that," objected Lisa, suddenly becoming calm. "He said: 'the main thing is that as many people as possible see this wonderful world. Therefore, we must take care of each other and protect and love each other, especially the little ones. And also in every way possible help them to be born.'"

When evening came, it somehow happened by itself that everyone had gathered on the veranda, all twenty-eight people on the planet, including those on duty in the kitchen and the kids. Kate and Lisa each held a baby on their laps, four more, barely able to walk, crawled over the dogs at Lisa's feet, and four more settled down under the table. That evening, as in all subsequent ones, they no longer told each other sweet and creepy tales. They discussed going to the north along the coast and up the river, arguing about how farms should be set up and how to fish for themselves in the river and in the sea. When the disk of the sun completely sank into the ocean, they saw a green ray of sun light which appeared here a little more often than on Earth. And then the mountains seemed to slowly fade away, going from hot pink to maroon to purple. The evening turned out to be warm and all of the kids fell asleep, some under the table, some on knees. And the elders, suddenly matured beyond their years, could not talk enough.

The Pioneers

On a high dune, where the pines parted, revealing an expansive view of the sea, two people were sitting on a bench in front of a fire, a man of about fifty and a younger man of about thirty.

"I have finally decided, at the end of April I am going through the mountains to the Volga. If I don't find some to accompany me, I'll go alone," the younger man said.

"Mark, why are you in such a rush? The program is moving forward, in nine years we will have a hydroplane and it will take two or three hours to reach the Volga."

"Why should I wait nine years, when it's just seven hundred kilometers away? Over the ridge a great river flows, one such as none of us has ever seen with our own eyes except in films about the Earth. Only seven hundred kilometers one way, people on Earth have traveled much longer distances without seaplanes. In short, I'm going."

"Which way do you want to go?"

"First I want to go up the Rhine, then from the place where the Rhine exits the canyon up the left branch and traverse the glacier, then to the White Pass. From the pass straight down to the nameless river that flows into Lake Chad. Judging by the pictures of the probes, there are no canyons or waterfalls. I'll float down the river to the lake, cross it in the boat to the source of the Hudson. Then along the Hudson to the confluence of the Volga, it's a direct route over water."

"These images from orbit are more than ten thousand years old. During all the time that has passed everything could have changed."

"Yeah sure, forests have grown, it has become a little colder, but the river valleys and ridges could not have changed over such a period. And how can you get lost with such clear topography: there is a simple mountain range separating the basins of the ocean and the huge river."

"Okay, good. What will you eat?"

"Food from the pastures. I will hunt and also fish."

"Okay. But there is no way that you are going to go alone. Don't forget that on the way back you will have to row six hundred kilometers up the river. There must be at least three of you. I can recommend two fellow travelers for you. Not long ago they also started talking about an expedition to the Volga. You know them, but let me talk to them myself first. Take a shortwave transmitter, a roll-up solar array, an inflatable boat, we have it all."

That conversation had taken place at the end of March, and now at the beginning of June, the four travelers on the pass fell backwards into a snowdrift, removed the straps of their backpacks and staggering in the snow, went to the eastern slope. With every step they took, a panorama slowly unfolded in front of them that no human had ever seen before, the inner plain of a huge continent opened up before them. Only birds had seen this view and even the seasoned mountain goat, who watched them from high on the pass, looking hard at the mainland distances, turned around and went back. It didn't like something there.

A strong wind from the other side of the pass ruffled their jackets and puffed up their hoods. Above them a flock of jackdaws maneuvered in the wind, now diving down into the valley, then soaring up in the updrafts back to the pass. All four stood at the edge of the steep drop, arms outstretched, leaning forward as the wind supported them. They all imagined that they could fly, gliding down like the jackdaws, over steep snowy slopes, over the grayish glacier, the black moraine, the green meadows of the valley, and then over the turquoise mountain lake, down again along the river to the blue plain, to silvery Lake Chad, from which the unexplored Hudson is within easy reach of the Volga. Yet alas, the laws of physics would not allow this. The guys had to go back to their backpacks, re-harness them while beginning to experience the symptoms of mountain sickness, hike over the pass. However, the laws of physics did allow them to experience another kind of joy: that of sliding down the packed, slightly soaked snow on the soles of their boots, astride their walking sticks like children's horses. Mark even managed to stand up to his full height, sliding down while slightly leaning forward and spreading his arms with sticks. In two minutes, with joyful cries, they finally reached the end of the steep slope and stopped as it began to flatten out at the bottom, finding themselves five hundred meters below the pass at the head of the glacier. It was much warmer and quieter here and the signs of altitude sickness went away in a few minutes.

Catching their breath slightly, the travelers set off down the gently sloping even glacier, where it was easier to walk despite their fatigue. However, closer to the end of the glacier, a continuous, sharp moraine of large boulders began to form. The way around it was found at the edge, between the glacial moraine on the side and the steep slope of the valley there was a moraine pocket, a ravine covered with real soil like an oasis along the edge of the glacier. Short dense grass, yellow buttercups, and here and there small transparent ponds and real warmth: a mountain paradise. Soon the travelers passed the glacier and arrived at the flat grassy bottom of the valley, where a river flowed, originating from a cave near the base of the glacier. They decided to spend the night there.

When the crescent of Deimos appeared over the side ridge, the stars began to light up and they boiled tea, and with it was time to talk about the past day, about their plans for tomorrow and just to talk about things in general. With a pleasant feeling of healthy fatigue, the conversation guided itself. Moreover, the day had been wonderful, they had conquered the ridge, had seen the Inner Plain, and were full of impressions of the sliding "glider-like" descent from the pass. Finally, the conversation turned to the next day and the topic quickly jumped to that of the river: Wasn't it time to use the boat?

"By the way, this river is still unnamed, and we have every right to give it a name," Alex said. "Mark, you are our senior, it's your right."

"To be honest, I'm lost here..."

"What is your nationality?"

"I was named Mark in honor of Mark Selin, and he was Russian. That's why I decided to become Russian. I already read it quite well, although I speak it horribly.

"So remember the name of some Russian river. You know the geography of the Earth well."

"The Neva... But wait, no. The Neva is on flat land. Let it be the Biya, it also has a mountain lake called Teletskoye as its source."

"Stop, stop!" Goran screamed. "You can only name the river, let someone else name the lake."

"Okay, name it yourself. And what is your nationality?"

"Italian. Even my father decided so after watching Fellini's films. So it's already hereditary."

"Come on then, an Italian lake. Mark will help if you want."

"I can do it myself... Let it be Lake Como, it's also in the mountains and on a mountain river."

"Beautiful."

"So, it's decided: the Biya River and Lake Como," summed up Gene, who had been silent until now. “By the way, Alex, what is your nationality?”

“I don’t know, to be honest, I don’t like this whole idea of nationalities, although I was also named after Selin... So Mark, I am in a sense your grandson, but I decided to remain without a nationality. On Earth, division by nationality did not lead to anything good.”

“I think,” Mark replied, “that people, if they want, will always find a sign by which to divide in order to destroy each other, but in this way we will preserve the national flavors of the Earth and, most importantly the languages. True while we are few, too few to reproduce real nations.”

Phobos emerged from behind the main ridge and headed towards Deimos. It got very cold and the guys climbed partially into their tents and into sleeping bags, with their feet inside and their heads out and continued the conversation.

“Now there are few of us, but there will be a lot, great numbers will come with time.”

“Be fruitful and multiply and fill Selina! God bless us.”

“Why shouldn’t we breed if we have fifty thousand square kilometers per brother? To each, a kingdom the size of Denmark!”

“We will multiply and we will not back down! Now let’s go to sleep. Tomorrow we should reach the beginning of Lake Como.”

Indeed, the next evening they reached the lake and spent the night there, pumping up the boat in advance and in the early morning quickly rolled up their tents and set sail without having breakfast. The mirror surface of the lake, where the mountains and the sky were reflected, was breathtaking. Ahead of them the valley narrowed, and the rocky slopes, dotted with the odd pine tree, rising up out of the water got so steep that they became a vertical gorge, making the river look like a portal to the expanses of the mainland. Sailing through that place, the travelers stopped rowing and experienced an almost religious reverence, with the turquoise water of the lake, the Gothic rocks on both sides, and the sound of waterfalls only emphasizing the solemn silence.

After narrowing, the valley then split and the slopes became less pronounced and instead of pines along the banks, broad-leaved forests began to grow. A tail wind was blowing making progress easy but soon they had to lean into the oars seeing the dam that had blocked in the lake in front of them, beyond it they could only see open sky with warm summer clouds.

Although they looked, they did not find the place where the river flowed over the dam, it in fact did not exist. Only a low guttural rumble could be heard. The waters of the Biya River made their way onward only in the depths, among the fragments of rocks. It took them three of the hardest hours imaginable to descend from the dam and reach the bottom.

"It would have been easier to deflate the boat, pack it up and inflate it again," Alex concluded after they had reached the bottom. But of course it was too late.

Having escaped from the blockage of the dam, the Biya became more full-flowing and even but it remained too fast and was unsafe. Therefore Gene, as he was the most nimble of them all, was put on the bow position and had the landing rope tied to him, and as soon as something suspicious appeared ahead, they rowed with all their might to the shore and Gene jumped out and moored the boat while someone went on ahead to investigate. A couple of times they avoided real meat grinders but gradually the river calmed down and thickets of reeds began to appear along the low banks. Finally, the river turned into a channel filled with shallow water overgrown with reeds. Then the channel in turn forked and the guys realized that they were already on Lake Chad, although they could not see anything as the reeds covered everything around them and blocked the view. After conferring, they chose to take the right channel as the path to the Hudson was shorter than the right bank of the lake. The reeds gradually became lower and thinner and finally, the wide distance and expanse of the lake, stretching beyond the horizon, appeared.

It took them four days to get around the lake, one of them which they had to sit out because of a storm, but they continued following the shore with its low hills and strips of lakeside sand, which in some places was covered with reeds and driftwood. Finally, behind yet another cape, the source of the Hudson appeared in front of them.

The character of the Hudson turned out to be what could be described as cheerful and hospitable. Lush meadows and clean unobstructed pine forests filled the spaces along its high banks, the river's waters alternated with thundering rapids and ones with large permanent waves caused by obstruction under the surface and on which it was a hereinto unknown pleasure to the people of Selina to ride on. Gradually granite cobblestones and boulders gave way to sandy beaches and the fish were caught easily and willingly. The journey along the Hudson took two weeks, and when it was possible to drive the thought of going back upstream from their thoughts, these were the most serene days of the journey. Downstream, the rapids stopped, and on the fifteenth day of rafting, a low blue ridge appeared along their course. They traveled onward and it turned out that the Hudson Valley cut through it. Along the right bank the ridge descended to the river as a rocky cliff and along the left it descended as a gently sloping wooded mountain. As soon as the travelers sailed over the rocky cliff area, they found themselves on what had been named the Volga.

"Wow, yeah..." was all Alex said.

"Wow!" Mark added.

An innumerable mass of water moved swiftly almost straight ahead, as far as the eye could see, along a line of gray cliffs which jutted out from the wooded ridge. The left bank was sandy and low and some large trees were growing on it and the guys decided to camp there. Then while crossing the river, they realized that its width was much more than it seemed, and that the trees that had appeared to be merely big, were in fact huge. After landing and getting out of the boat, they ran for joy along the shore and clean coarse sand sang under their feet.

Okay! That's all!" Mark shouted and stopped. "We don't do anything until tonight! Now we rest and unwind."

He then went up to one of the gigantic trees and lay down in its shade. It was a black poplar with a trunk about three meters in diameter and at its heights branches a meter thick growing in its own rustling grove which spread across the sky and quickly lulled Mark to sleep. When he awoke everything seemed to have changed. The place was no longer one that was unfamiliar to him. The rustle of the leaves, the smells, the huge river and the reflection of the mountains in it, everything now seemed familiar, as if he had grown up in this place and had simply been absent for some time. It seemed to him that even as a child he had run along the narrow pieces of land sticking out into the water and the sand that had the shape of icy sastrugi near the spraying water. For some reason it seemed to him that on the right bank, in the valley, was the house where he had grown up, that he had many times laid on his back under this tree, with his hands under his head, and thought about the future.

Of course, it was all an illusion. Many of us have experienced a similar feeling when we find ourselves in a place that, for some unknown reason seems to enter and calm our souls. A person may not have genetic memory, but there is an innate instinct, akin to a sense of beauty. Our ancestors, relying on this instinct, chose places for settlement and rarely made a mistake. For modern man, bound by circumstances on a densely populated Earth, fate rarely provided such an opportunity. However if suddenly you feel that you are in the very place that was created for you, and the opportunity to make it your own exists there is no need to hesitate. Say “here it is!” and drive in a stake, build a home there and settle down until the end of your days. You will not regret it.

Mark got up. Alex was lying on the sand not far from the boat, Gene was drifting lazily with the current in shallow water, pushing off the bottom with his hands, and Goran was plodding along the wet sand at the water’s edge, looking for something near his feet.

“Hey!” Mark shouted. “Listen to what I have decided.” The guys all gathered near the boat.

“I’m going to live here! Right over there in that valley on the right bank! I will settle down with my girlfriend and invite everyone who wants to settle on the Volga. I’ll gather a group and come here next year with axes and saws and build houses. We will return to the Base for the winter and a year later, at the beginning of summer, we will finally move here with cattle and dogs. Who is with me?!”

"How will you transport everything necessary for life here?" Alex asked. "According to the Program, we should settle deep into the mainland only after hydroplanes are built. Just imagine how much junk you have to carry by yourself!"

"Why junk? Tools plus knowledge, that's all the junk we'll need."

"And when your shoes disintegrate into tatters, what will you do with your tools and knowledge?"

"I'll sew them up. What did the first colonists in the Americas do when their shoes fell apart? They were not very comfortable and things were not easy. So let it not be very comfortable or easy for us, but at least it will be for real. Otherwise, it all seems that we are like children, being led by the hand by earthlings who lived many thousands of years ago."

"But the Program exists not only for our sake. We ourselves must do a lot for the future of Selina, to grow and resettle hordes of mammals and plants."

"Well, let's settle here. Especially in such a strategic place, as they said in the earthly films about important rivers it's 'a transcontinental water artery.' If we go beyond the framework of the Program, it will be development and not a violation."

"We shall see what we shall see. The program seems to only prescribe certain actions without forbidding others, but what you have in mind is too radical an action. Let's assume everyone follows your example, then who will carry on following the plans of the Program?"

"If there are too many followers, then it will be necessary to think of something else. It's just not likely to come to that. Here's what I'll do: I'll talk to Alex. No, not with you, with Alex Selin, and follow what he has to say. I will ask him directly about going beyond the parameters of the Program and find out how he relates to it. For some reason I think he'll be okay with it."

"So," said Goran, "perhaps I like this place too. I like the idea too. I will go with you next year. The truth is I don't have a girlfriend yet. But maybe there is a crazy one..."

“I’ll stay at the Base,” Alex said. “Being a hermit for me is useless. I prefer to be in the midst of people. Yes, and there is a lot of work to be done.”

“Me too,” Gene said. “I like it here, but I don’t want to move from there either. I will become a traveling merchant. I will establish a trade route from the Base to the Volga. I will bring goods here and sell them, and when a hydroplane appears, I will become a pilot and I will do the same thing only a hundred times faster.”

“And what currency will you use to sell your goods here?”

“Boots made by Mark. They will be in great demand on the Coast as handicraft souvenirs, but seriously, sturgeons should immediately be seeded here. I will supply black caviar to the coast! Let’s feed the entire Coast with black caviar, which none of Selina’s people have ever tasted before!”

“Agreed,” Mark concluded. “We’ll have supper in three hours. Yesterday’s catch is more than enough. In the meantime, let’s take a break a little longer. I want to think in peace.”

Mark returned to his spot under the black poplar and lay down. He tried to visualize the millions of people who worked on Earth on the Ark so that he could simply lie here and think right now. Nothing... it did not work. Then Mark tried to imagine the descendants who would appear here thanks to him. This time something happened: he saw descendants sailing along the Volga on yachts, swimming and walking along an imaginary embankment of a future city in the valley on the other side of the river. Will they remember Mark and his friends as the first people to have reached these shores as the first colonists? Why not? The main thing though was that the descendants were here and that in this very place, after thousands, tens of thousands or even hundreds of thousands of years in the future someone could also lie under a huge tree, look at the river which reflected the mountains and perceive it all as their own.

The Sentence

The flight left the Base for Troy half empty, and Chris settled comfortably in the wide aisle by the porthole, his legs outstretched. The weather was good and the view was breathtaking: mountains with glaciers, lakes, waterfalls and Lake Como. No matter how much he flew here, Chris never got tired of this panorama, every time he admired it clinging to the porthole, and always found new details below. However, this time he was not up to details: he was furious and confused. Confused because he had just discovered a terrible fact, and furious because this fact should have been discovered a long time ago by those who had access to the data.

Regardless, the panorama was still beautiful. To the east, the plain was covered with a light haze through which the gleam of distant lakes broke through; to the north stretched the Coast Range, jutting out from the haze in all its majesty, as if from water. About two hundred kilometers to the north, the ridge curved to the west, then again to the east and somewhere in that mountain bend, the Mekong, one of the largest tributaries of the Volga, originated. To the south, the ridge became wider and bifurcated into the Coastal and Continental ridges and at the fork was the radiant Pyramid, the only the only eight-thousander in Borealis still unconquered due to the fact that Selina's people had a host of far more pressing challenges.

As Chris pondered the terms with which he would begin the non-telephone conversation, far to the east, the shiny ribbon of the Volga emerged from the haze.

How lucky we were with our world! How everything had started so well, and here we are, such outright meanness! thought Chris.

The plane crossed the Volga twice during the descent. This was how planes always landed at Troy airport when there was a westerly wind. Chris checked the forecast before each flight and is always glad if a west wind is promised, as he liked to fly over the wide river with the green island from which a long sandy spit stretched downstream. Troy's airport seemed too big and pompous for a city of fifty thousand but there was logic behind it, everything had been built for growth. Moreover, Troy was the second most populated city of Selina after Baza.

The flight was met by only fifteen people – among them was Ruben, a former classmate of Chris'. For some time they had studied in the same mathematics group. Ruben turned out to be rather weak in mathematics and other exact sciences in fact but he caught on like fire in sociology, a subject which became more diverse and interesting as the transition from a mobilized way of life (following the Program) to a free society continued. Now he is one of Selina's ten main heads, a member of either the Council of the Central Administration, or the High Council of the Administration, Chris could not remember the exact name of the nascent authority.

"Well, shall we go to my office?" Ruben asked.

"Let's go somewhere neutral, for example somewhere on the Mark embankment. Let's sit on the veranda of the restaurant and order beer with black caviar as usual, cheap and cheerful. That will make it less likely that I'll tell you all sorts of nasty things."

So they went there. The embankment was empty. It was the height of the working day and there was a cold wind. They were the only visitors on the veranda which had a peaceful view of the Volga and several sail boats and moored fishing boats and a formation of huge black poplars on the opposite bank.

"I have bad news," Chris began the conversation, "very bad news."

"State it. What is the news about?"

"About fertility."

"That doesn't seem to be your thing. You are a mathematician, not a doctor. Not even a biologist. As for the birth rate, well, hasn't it grown over the past fifteen years?"

"Why didn't the doctors or biologists think of breaking down the birth rate by generations counting from the embryos of the Incubator?"

"Why is the global genealogical database closed? I only gained access through my friendship with Bruno Levich. Who in general from decent researchers had access to it? Sorry, I'm furious. We have lost at least thirty years, for a long time everything could have been found out and the alarm raised!"

"Stop, stop. Calm down for a start. The genealogical database was closed because it contains data on infertile couples and surrogate mothers, which is a personal secret. And let's calm down: what did you find there?"

"How many years have passed since the birth of the first incubator babies? One hundred and forty years. Seventh generation women should have already been born but they have not been. There is not a single person beyond the sixth generation in the female line! There are women of the sixth generation, including those that are not the first youth and they don't have a single child! In all couples where a woman belongs to the sixth generation on the maternal side, there is not a single child of their own, only surrogates or donors. Half of the fifth generation are also sterile and from the fourth, fifteen percent. In the first three generations everything is normal. Everything points to the occurrence of infertility as not being a Markov process."

"Wait, I can't remember too clearly what a Markov process is..."

"It is a process without memory. Like radioactive decay. The nucleus will decay in the next time interval with a constant probability, regardless of how long it exists. The death of a passenger in a car accident is a Markov process, a brick on the head too. Even mutation is a Markov process, although I am a layman here, but the process of death from old age is not a damn Markov process. With each passing year after sixty, the probability of dying the following year increases. What we have is similar to death from old age, only instead of years lived we have generations of women, counted from the embryos of the Ark. That is the whole problem, the entire population of Selina is waiting for inevitable death from genetic or generational old age! What else to call it? True, it can be delayed as long as frozen embryos remain in the Incubator."

"But why has the birth rate increased recently?"

"Yes well, because forty years ago they "extracted" a rather large batch of embryos. Those people, their children and then their grandchildren and great-grandchildren are fertile, which is why the birth rate has grown and will continue to grow until it starts to fall again. Please try to understand, if it were not for this generational old age and if infertility arose only by chance, believe me, it would be much better than this. If a third of the offspring are sterile, regardless of the generation, it is enough for a couple to give birth to an average of four children for the population to grow exponentially, or three to maintain the population at a constant level indefinitely. Oh, hell, if only! Yes, if only..."

A tourist ship sailed along the Volga along the deserted embankment (the fairway passed close to the shore) tourism as a normal activity was just coming into being on Selina. The passengers, seeing Chris with Ruben, shouted joyfully and discordantly, the waved "hello" and the captain gave a double low beep.

"Okay, I'll ask them to check your results right now. If you're right, something needs to be done."

"Don't check me, Ruben. I'm not out of my mind, I don't smoke anything, everything is so transparent there that it's better to punish everyone who had access to the data for not seeing the obvious. We've already activated a bunch of embryos with far fewer offspring than we should have. The question is, can this be fixed? And what is the reason? Something tells me we can't fix this. But it's better to talk to a biologist. Do you have a reliable competent biologist within reach? I don't."

"Perhaps there is. Amir Bakkar. He should be within a twenty-minute walk from here. True, he is not entirely versed in this topic, he examines genomes for all sorts of changes in comparison with terrestrial genomes, but he is a literate person and I think he will be able to help clarify some things."

"Did he have access to the base? If so, leave him alone, please."

"Calm down, I didn't mean that. Access to the base has been strictly limited, and logically, Bruno Levich should be given a good kick for giving you access."

"It's you who needs to arrange a nationwide sit-in or actions against whoever blocked access to the base. Bruno will still be thanked. Call your biologist!"

Ruben called. While they were consuming their second beer, Amir appeared at the end of the embankment and arrived just in time to catch the waiter bringing him the same classic order. He was a short, thin man with delicate features, whose modest geometric dimensions were offset by lush, curly hair and a beard, all together which formed an unforgettable whole. On top all of it was crowned by a hat with a turned-up brim.

"Doing well I see, my dear conspirators! Happy to join you! So what happened that was so important that you suddenly needed an armchair geneticist?"

"Here's Chris, he's a mathematician and he got into the genealogy database. Let him tell you.

"In a nutshell: the sixth generation of women, if you count the generation from the embryo of the Ark along the female branch as the first, is completely sterile. Well maybe not completely, but at least ninety nine percent. For the fifth generation half, the fourth, fifteen percent and there are practically no cases of partial infertility, either they have normal fertility or zero. There are also no correlations between other health factors and generations. The impression is as if some kind of error accumulates during the changing of generations, leading to a sharp irreversible breakdown. The clinical picture appears to be that: the embryos seem to die after a few divisions? Ruben, you should know."

"Yes exactly. They die almost immediately, so it is not possible to fix the pregnancy. So Amir, can you finally say something! You are the only one of us who understands this."

The biologist looked silently at the river for a long time, pursing his lips. The others were also silent, waiting for an answer.

Finally he said: "Yes, it really smells like something went south. I somehow tried not to think about the problem of fertility, drove away those thoughts like thoughts about old age, and tried not to delve into them too much. What can I say? A kind of cowardice I suppose... Now, what it looks like at first glance... Well it seems that then telomerase in the female reproductive cells is not working. None of the women on Selina have telomerase that works. Do you know what telomerase is?"

“Is that what the ends of DNA complete?”

“Something like that. How is chromosome DNA duplicated during cell division? A so-called polymerase rides along the DNA strand, formally a protein molecule, but in fact a whole mechanism, and builds exactly the same thread. So, this mechanism cannot reproduce DNA from the very end, it needs a piece to “get on the rails”, and this piece is not reproduced. So the copy is shorter than the original. Nature gets around this problem with an extra piece of DNA at the end that contains no information and serves as a rail for the polymerase. These rails are called “telomeres”. Naturally, with each cell division, telomeres shorten but this is where telomerase comes in, it is a protein molecule, but in fact it is also a mechanism. It brings the telomeres to their original length. Now is it clear what will happen if telomerase do not work?”

“Understood,” Chris replied. “A catastrophe when telomeres are eaten to zero. Why six generations? Why is there a scatter, for some infertility occurs in the sixth generation, for others as soon as the fourth?”

“Why six? That should be clear, the typical length of telomeres is calculated to be at somewhere around sixty to seventy divisions, if they are not restored. With a change of generations, female eggs divide thirteen to fourteen times, for the sixth generation that is five shifts, starting from the earthly embryos with normal telomeres. So they are just eaten away, for some a little earlier, for some a little later, since the initial length may have different lengths. If telomerase did not work in men, it would be much worse since we have many more germ cell divisions. If men had the same problem the telomeres would be eaten up in one generation. However, there is nothing worse that could have happened and whether it is possible to fix it is the question.”

“What could have caused the telomerase to stop working?”

“Exposure during the flight?” Ruben suggested.

“Irradiation could have knocked out the telomerase in some of the embryos but if only a few had remained intact, they would have given the seventh and subsequent generations. And then all humanity would have been healthy. It is unlikely that there could have been total damage to only one mechanism. In everything else people are being born normal.”

"A magnetic field? They spent thousands of years in a Tesla 10 field."

"So what about the field? Molecules, when they simply lie without interacting, are not affected at all by it, especially at low temperatures. I'm afraid that something completely different affected them. It has nothing to do with mutations. It's worse."

"What could be worse?" Ruben asked.

"A human is not only a human. It is a symbiosis of a huge number of organisms. Each of us has one and a half kilograms of bacteria, without which we would not be able to digest food or live. In addition to those countless viruses exist and function in each of us, including ones that are necessary, although we understand their role even less. Did you know that in addition to the embryos, the Ark also brought a supply of human feces and other waste products? All the necessary intestinal flora was there, but where is the guarantee that some necessary ones, for example viruses which live in the human body, were not forgotten on Earth? For one reason or another they might not have gotten into the embryos. If so, I'm afraid the problem is hopeless, but I'm not sure yet that this is the case."

"Wait, are there other species besides humans facing the same problem?"

"Let me think... All of our human-like great apes have died out... Their generations change faster... They thought it was a problem of introduction into the environment, and waved it off, but it looks like our whole family is having such troubles."

"I read that all hyenas mysteriously died out."

"Does any of the viverrid family live with us? Mongooses, genets?"

"Mongooses, it seems are not present here, although they were probably in the basic package. I don't know about the rest."

"It's as if the attack is decimating entire families. This, perhaps, confirms the idea that the problem is in the missing organisms."

"Suppose we're doomed," Chris continued, "but everyone is doomed, the sun will go out and so on. The question is timing. My question is: How many embryos are left in the Incubator? That is for you, Ruben."

"About five thousand six hundred."

"How long can they keep?"

"At least ten thousand years, if everything is kept in order."

"So, there have never been problems with spermatozoa and never will be. What about eggs? How many can one woman produce?"

"A woman has tens of thousands of immature eggs from birth, but only hundreds of them actually reach maturity. Somewhere on average of about three hundred ovulations per life cycle, as a rule one matures per ovulation."

"So, is it possible to get a hundred descendants from these three hundred for the most part through IVF?"

"Theoretically, it is possible but where are you going to get so many surrogate mothers?"

"What do mean where? If each generation is a hundred times larger than the previous one, then the last would be the sterile one and would outnumber all the others by a hundred times. God himself ordered the women of this generation to become surrogate mothers. Now look, if the breeding factor is one hundred, the number of fertile generations is four and a half, then the number of descendants that can be obtained from each incubator embryo will be ten to the ninth power. A billion! Ruben, do you understand why a billion?"

"Well, you don't have to take me for a fool, a hundred to the power of four and a half or ten to the ninth power."

"Multiply a billion by five thousand, we get five trillion and we get more than the entire population of the Earth from the Paleolithic to the launch of the Ark, a huge and powerful civilization. If five billion live for a hundred years at the same time, then the lifespan of mankind will be one hundred thousand years, as much time as has passed from the inception of homo-erectus until the creation of the Ark. During that time, the problem that we are talking about will surely resolve itself somehow, either scientists will find a solution, or there will be mutations which will correct the error, it is not possible that a way out will not be found among such a gigantic population."

"Wait," Ruben said in objection, "if you stretch out the embryos so they last for a hundred thousand years, you will have to activate one every twenty years and all of its descendants will be forced to interbreed with each other. What is that called? ...Inbreeding?"

"That's not a problem," said Amir. "Part of the embryos of the second and third generations can be preserved and put into use later, this is how you can cross family trees that 'sprout' at different times."

"Perhaps, everything does not look as hopeless as it seemed to me in the morning. A hundred thousand years of developed civilization, even earthlings could not dream of this. If some other dirty trick is not found then..."

All three fell silent. A group of children from a kindergarten walked along the embankment, three dozen multi-colored children from four to six years old. *Surely some of these girls were sterile purely by the will of fate. But even so they are normal children, they have normal lives ahead of them, perhaps even happy ones. What about the girls who are infertile? Soon they will be the vast majority and they will be forced to raise other people's children. Can this be considered a misfortune when that is the fate of the majority? How will the news that the human race is threatened with death, albeit a distant one, affect these children?* That is exactly what the silent visitors of the Mark's Place restaurant were thinking about while slowly sipping beer.

"Excuse me, gentlemen scientists," Ruben broke the silence, "neither trillions nor even billions will turn out. How do you imagine a society where every woman has to go through the painful procedure of egg extraction every month for the sake of the future of civilization? How will billions of infertile women feel, who are obliged, not by the dictates of the soul, but by rules, to endure and raise surrogate children? It is possible that such a thing is possible but it will not be a society, it will be a beehive or like something else from the insect world. Not even the most ferocious totalitarian regimes on Earth ever dreamed of such control over the private lives of citizens. To impose such an order, you need to turn the planet into a concentration camp. So what would there be then, five trillion slaves? Yes, this world should be inhabited by as many intelligent beings as possible, but not slaves! Free intelligent beings that act according to their own free will and live by their own rules. So forget the multiplication factor of a hundred."

"Yes, Ruben, you are most likely right here," Amir continued. "We thought about the theoretical possibility. In reality, of course, it looks idiotic. And what factor do you think is real? Ten?"

"Maybe ten and even then, that must come with the right social policy. If egg donation is honorable and paid and if surrogate motherhood becomes the norm. Lots of 'ifs'..."

"With ten, we have thirty thousand from one embryo and one hundred and fifty million in total, that gives us a thousand-year-old civilization with a population a little more than ten million. Well, modest, but for the sake of that it was still worth launching the Ark."

"And if, thanks to a wonderful social policy, it would be possible to reach a factor of twenty? That's over a hundred million in two thousand years."

"If, if only..." Ruben answered. "One thing can be said for sure here, more than half of the Ark Project involved biological problems. Now the fate of Selina's humanity becomes, for the most part, a sociological task. Alas, on Earth, sociological problems were solved very poorly."

"To be honest," Chris concluded, "we most likely are faced not with a problem, but with a verdict."

"Even so," Reuben said, "we don't have to convince people that this is a sentence. The people won't believe it anyway. We must honestly tell them that there is such a problem, and then the more clearly we pursue the proper demographic policy, the higher the reproduction rate we will be able to achieve and consequently the more likely it is that the problem will be solved. Yes, in fact, that is the way it is."

The kindergarten group walked past again, the same one that had passed earlier only this time in the opposite direction, apparently returning from a walk. They were all well-groomed children who had everything ahead of them, a great and interesting life, no matter what social policies were to be implemented. They already had the luck to be born, unlike the billions of potential children that the planet would be able to take in and feed.

"Chris," Ruben broke the silence, "did you, by any chance, check my girl's generation in the database? I don't know her whole family tree exactly..."

"Yes, I checked. She is fourth generation and you have children in common with her. So you have a chance to have grandchildren."

"Did you check yours too?"

"Yes. She's sixth, Ruben. Sixth..."

Silence

Which Cyclopean structure was the first to appear on Selina? Of course, the hundred-meter parabolic antenna capable of staying directed at one point in the sky for eleven hours a day. It is not really necessary to point out that this one point was the Earth's solar system. Day after day, like a sunflower, the huge radio dish on the semi-desert plateau of South Borealia, turned to the sun. Not the blinding sun that was above it but a primordial Sun, a faint star, visible at night through binoculars. On all the standard frequencies, the Solar System has been silent for the entire hundred and thirty years that had passed since the building of the Great Antenna. There had never been a regular signal, nor noise that distinguished the target from other star systems. At other frequencies, it was silent too: several scans at wavelengths from one and a half centimeters to a meter excluded any signal at a level one hundred thousand times less than what an antenna sixty light years away is capable of transmitting to another similar antenna with the same type of receiver.

Every ten hours for a hundred and thirty years, it transmitted a call sign followed by a data packet. In fact, it was an SOS signal sent out every ten hours for one hundred and thirty years. The request for help was repeated: "In order to save the human race on the planet, it was necessary to compare in the smallest detail everything related to female cells here and on Earth: their structure, chemistry, process of division and especially the behavior of telomerase. It has long been clear that there is no other way to understand why the latter is not fulfilling its purpose on Selina."

Imagine having the most complicated non-working mechanism, which seems to be an exact copy of another one which is working. How do you fix the one that doesn't work? Of course, to begin with, you need to find differences that are not noticeable at first glance and then try to eliminate or correct them. Selina's biologists sent packet after packet of information about the eggs to the solar system so that the earthlings could understand the difference without asking additional questions, each of which would take one hundred and twenty years to answer.

Having finished the night shift, Aristarchus Shen went out onto the balcony. The sun had not yet risen, but the antenna was already turning pink against the background of the dark mountains.

It was nice in the early mornings, cool and quiet. During the day, you couldn't go out very much as you would fry in the merciless heat, and the silhouette of the antenna sways in the drafts of hot air. One might wonder if a bird flew between the transmitter and the dish: would it be fried? Maybe not, but it would definitely feel the heat, like being in a microwave. Lord, what am I thinking about? What birds for God's sake?! How much energy had been pumped into space in the span of one hundred and thirty years? Into the emptiness... This was something useful to calculate: one hundred and thirty years, the total transmission time of thirty years is a billion seconds, ten to the sixteenth joule. How many large cities could have been built by putting this energy into the work of construction equipment? But for whom would the cities be? There are eight million of us on the planet and there are almost no new additions. Enough has already been built for everyone, so there is no one to build for. First you need to contact the Earth to remove the curse. Then, you'll see, there will be someone for whom to build cities. My thoughts are going around in circles. Not enough sleep...

People had had ten years to receive the signals and respond. At least by simply saying: "message received, wait for a detailed answer." What is going on with them there? Did they fall asleep? Are they running around wild? Or are they simply no longer there? Isn't it time to turn out the lights? Reduce the number of transmissions by an order of magnitude? But most importantly, stop hoping for an answer from the Earth. Do something ourselves, finally start to give birth to more children. Poor women...

What happened on Earth? And why does the entire known history of earthlings end with the launch of the Ark? After all, its antenna worked for another twelve thousand years! It did not only work for transmissions but could have also received signals and data. People could have sent twelve thousand years of history at almost no additional cost. Why didn't they do it? If something happened to them, then it didn't happen right away. We would have a much better understanding of their fate, if they had made sent even the simplest message. Why don't you ask Alex Selin about it? It is not clear whether the replica can answer such a question, but he could provide some clues. You just need to sleep first.

Just don't sleep here. Charge yourself with caffeine for two hours of driving and go home, to the wife, the dog, the greenery, the shade, the pool, the coolness and the view of the Tiber and, even more important, the peace of mind that you need for the conversation.

Aristarchus drove up to the edge of the plateau and the panorama of the wide valley below opened up before him. He felt a surge of warmth from within. He had traveled this road hundreds of times and each and every time his soul felt a warmth when after the endless brown hills the blue expanse opened below. Down there was the place that he himself had grown roots along with centuries-old trees. The valley was like a magnet, which after three days would pull anyone back home from anywhere in the world. Sometimes in dreams he would find himself living in some distorted city from a past life and think: *What brought me here? Why do I live here? Why the hell did I leave the house? Hurry home! Where the hell did I park my car? Where is my car?! It seems to have been here. Has it been stolen? How will I get home without it?!*

Then he would wake up and breathe a sigh of relief: *Okay, I'm home, the car is parked in front under the window. Many neighbors had also firmly put down roots nearby. There was a biologist, an artist, even a professional philosopher living on the next hill. Would this valley be empty in hundreds of years?*

The descent from the plateau begins with smooth turns winding down the semi-desert slope. At the top, there are only trees near smooth rock face of brown sandstone. In the morning moisture condenses on them then it flows down the slope and waters the trees that have taken root under the rock. At night, small owls sit on these trees and seem to be talking about something in their eerie language. The lower you get the greener it becomes even though rains are rare here. The dew condenses and the lower you go the more abundant it is. Sometimes, when returning early in the morning, the valley is filled with fog. Despite the fact that you have to dive into this fog, you rejoice: down there, it gives water to all living things and even lower it is as if you are entering the humid subtropics, at that level there is simple drip irrigation.

He arrives at his house and of course, Klaus is the first to run out to meet him and barking happily, stands on his hind legs and throws his front ones his chest (with enough force to knock a man down), then he licks his face, spins around (still standing on his hind legs) and licks his face again. Finally, after a few moments he calms down a little and then runs off towards the side path where he stops and makes a movement with his shoulders and head pointing towards the river, meaning "let's go there now!"

"Wait, Klaus, we'll swim to the other side of the Tiber tomorrow, I need to get some sleep..."

His wife sleepily comes out onto the balcony, still in her dressing gown and half asleep marking the occasion of Sunday.

"Oh-oh-oh, look who came to visit! What will you have for breakfast?"

"You mean dinner? Let's have ham and eggs and something to put me to sleep."

"Cognac or whiskey?"

"Whiskey. That Australian cognac gets worse every year. The

southerners are starting to hack things more and more, and not only the cognac. Well, God bless them, I urgently need to sleep. Then I have to have a difficult conversation and need a clear head."

"Who are you going to talk to?"

"With Alex Selin. Yes, *the* Alex Selin or rather with his replica."

"Did you lose hope of contacting the Earth?"

"That's exactly it. You do have a good sense of things!"

Aristarchus fell asleep instantly. He dreamed of Earth, where he asked everyone he met why they don't answer Selina.

"It is forbidden to listen and it is forbidden to answer," they say.

"Why is it forbidden, who forbade it?" asked Aristarchus.

"Look, he doesn't know who banned it! He's not one of us, grab him!" shouted the people, the number of whom increased rapidly.

Aristarchus rushed to the nearest doorway and the crowd followed him, he started to climb up a multi-story building, climbing up the balconies and on one of them he was met by a girl he loved in his youth who pulled him by the hand into the room.

"Why didn't you wait for me?" asked the love of his youth.

"You chose someone else."

"But you should have waited, I would have preferred you in the end, and you didn't wait."

What am I doing here? thought Aristarchus looking around the cramped room with the bed and the wardrobe cabinet. *Why am I not at home? I need to urgently get out on the street and quickly go home to my wife and Klaus. Where did I park my car? No, not here! Probably on the next street. Where did the next street go? Where is my car, how will I get home without it?!*

After a panicked search for the car, Aristarchus always woke up well rested and with a clear head. Then he immediately logged in and called Alex.

"Hello, Alex. My question may be an idle one since the answer to it is unlikely to help us in any way. Yet, I need to ask it: Why did the Earth not tell the Ark what was going on there while the Headquarters antenna was still working? And why did it only work in transmission mode?"

"Do I understand correctly that you are asking this question because you are desperate to contact the Earth?"

"In general, that's right. And yes, I am desperate."

"It's not easy for me to answer your question. I will answer for myself first. I never thought about it but since you're asking, that means it's bad that I didn't think about it. In my defense, I can say one thing, this issue seemed insignificant and very simple: what could have been easier than adding a receive mode and allowing the archivers to receive messages from Earth. That could have been done at the last minute. You see, we were concentrating on how to launch the Ark, land the cargo, transform the planet, raise, educate and train your ancestors. The rest of the details just did not fit in my head. I can also say in my defense that I did not live to see the launch by at least seven years. Therefore, it is better to ask Bill Pak, he definitely lived to see the launch."

"I'll ask him today. Do you have at least a vague idea of why this might have been?"

"Alas I do have a vague hypothesis, but it's not a happy one: my comrades who launched the Ark probably did not trust those in whose hands the transmitters would end up in the future. Before my own eyes, the first bad symptoms appeared in the world, a kind of insinuating stench of the Middle Ages. At that time the problem seemed to be a mild one. You see, the Middle Ages still did not let us go. I don't mean the historical period, but the concept of the Middle Ages with obscurantism, servility, witch hunts, green aliens and other primitive delights. Sometimes it seemed that there would be a breakthrough and that finally intelligence would win and there would be a triumph of humanism and enlightenment that would have been irreversible, but no, as it turns out, it was reversible...

This has already happened in recent history and, it seems, is ready to repeat itself again. As if as soon as you relax, some bony hand from distant times grabs us from behind and pulls us towards it. Or is something like a Middle Ages infection sitting deep inside of us? It sits there quietly and suddenly becomes active when society weakens and runs out of steam."

"There hasn't been such a relapse here on Selina in nearly four centuries. Maybe there is more to come? How can we avoid this infection? Maybe she is dormant in us too, waiting for the right moment to activate itself?"

"Of course, it has been dormant in all of us since the time of the anthropoid primates. Dormant in the form of a secret animal craving to rule, execute and pardon, a craving to belong to a ferocious crowd, ready to tear apart all strangers. The recipe for reducing this infection to zero is simple and well-known: culture, education, upbringing, you probably understand this yourself so I have nothing new to add. That is why we put so much effort into the education and upbringing of the first colonists. Continue in the same spirit! It is easier for you, unlike us you have space in which you can develop and expand. Problems will start to occur when things started getting cramped. We are overcrowded, therefore suffocation begins. But enough! Stop whining! Talk to Bill, he'll probably be able to tell you more."

Aristarchus did not pause and immediately called Bill: "Hi, Bill. This time I have a difficult question for you. I already spoke with Alex, and he advised me to contact you. Why do we not know the history of the Earth after the launch of the Ark? Why didn't anyone report..."

"Aristarchus, I understand what you are asking and I can answer your question: this is a consequence of the panic that was taking place during the last moments before the launch. Everything that the Headquarters antenna would receive from the Earth had to be carefully encapsulated and put under a reliable lock, so that only now you, who raised the issue of such data for the first time, could open it. Yes, even after passing the maturity test. Do you understand why?"

"I guess I do. Moreover, Alex suggested the hypothesis that those into whose hands the transmitters fell might not be trustworthy."

"Yes, Alex really missed a lot. Right now I'm talking from the time-frame of the launch plus one hundred and thirty-five days. The Ark is already flying away and its antenna is still working for reception. In Spain, where one of our communication antennas is located, a kind of Christian caliphate of Orthodox Catholics is already brewing. In Bolivia, where the second antenna is located, the parliamentary elections were won by a party calling for an end to the centuries-old dictates of Anglo-Saxon civilization. They want traditional values and true religion! In Australia, where the third antenna is, elections were won by the Green fundamentalists, who consider the Ark a crime against the virgin Galaxy. Imagine what kind of hands these antennas will fall into and what propaganda slop will be poured onto the Ark if we leave the receive mode active."

"Alex called it 'the infection of the Middle Ages'."

"Exactly! Alex always knew how to find the right words. You understand how important it is to get rid of this infection in the first colonists who will not yet have independent historical experiences and thus will not have immunity. How important it is not to allow all of this gloomy trash to grow by leaps and bounds and give it the opportunity to harm the project. Everything that would have been transferred from Earth after us would be useful to you, but not before civilization matures on Selina. Not before the person who receives this data perceives it as a researcher, and not as a student.

"It would be correct to receive everything and then keep it under lock and key, but right now this lock is not ready and there is no agreement on how it should be organized. This is a consequence of the final panic and too much has collapsed onto our heads. So now I will issue a command to block the receive mode. And to do so completely. Forgive me for this, Aristarchus. This is the wrong decision but we don't have time for the right one and I have to accept this to ensure the safety of the project and for the sake of the mental balance of your ancestors. Farewell, Aristarchus. Besides my words, none of the interlocutors will be able to tell you what happened here. We're going through bad times, but we'll get through it! I'll be glad to talk to you again, but only about what was before the current moment: December 20, 2195, 22:30 GMT. Now my last words are to be added to my replica, after which there will be complete silence from the Earth. Forever or not, I can't say."

"Goodbye, Bill. You have given me an exhaustive answer. I won't say that it has calmed my soul, but at least now I know what to do."

In fact, this is precisely what Aristarchus did not know yet. It was clear that it was necessary to tell the people the whole gloomy truth and that it was no longer worth waiting for an answer from Earth. They had to rely only on themselves. *But how? A press conference? A TV appearance? What would he say? How to tell them the truth so that it does not paralyze people but mobilize them?*

Aristarchus decided to take a break and to swim across the Tiber and back with Klaus, especially since he had promised him.

The dog's joy at the words "let's go to the river" turned out to be so complete and contagious that it violated all of the precepts of the lofty tragedy of reality.

There are three hundred meters of shady paths and stone steps to the river, things that are conducive to correct thoughts. Perhaps I should call Pete Chub and have me interviewed in front of the Antenna for the weekly newscast. For five minutes.

"Klaus, damn it, leave that pheasant alone!"

After that I can have a press conference. Yes, it is necessary to speak during the prime time news as it is watched by about three million people, almost one in three. What exactly should I say?

"Klaus, wait, let me undress."

So, my glasses in one of the sneakers and the phone in the other. My T-shirt and shorts on top, and it would better to put a stone on top of everything in case the wind blows.

"Well, let's swim!"

What should I say? We must stop relying on someone else and depend only on ourselves. We have to imagine that we are alone, as once the earthlings were all alone. They gathered their strength and launched the Ark, but could not cope with their own problems. Wait, that's going to be a risky statement about "couldn't cope." Use the subjunctive. The main thing is to stick with the fact that we must cope with our problems and misfortune ourselves, and if they cannot be overcome, then we have to minimize the effects.

"Klaus, slow down, you're not a speedboat, swim slowly alongside me."

How does he manage to overtake me swimming like a dog, even if I am swimming the crawl, I'm a good swimmer after all? There are still two hundred meters left. The saddest thing is that no one has any idea what to do with this damn telomerase. I have nothing to say in that regard either. And won't, I'd rather tell them about Alex's warning about the medieval infection. They have already begun to cut mathematics and literature. I will say that in all ages, as soon as mathematics, astronomy and literature were reduced in schools, the bacilli of the Middle Ages became more active, they have to learn Earth's history. Well, finally here is the beach. It is better than ours, it has pure sand.

"Klaus, let's go up there."

We have to go up six hundred meters to get to the starting point. At the same time I will say that the Australians should stop making hacked cognac. Yes first cognac, then cars and ships, because degradation begins with trifles. There are no competitors, so they abuse that. We are not enough in number to have competition everywhere! It must be said that without mobilization now there will be no free competition in the future. Although you should not get off topic, you need to focus on the main issue.

"Klaus, let's lie down on the sand. It's not too hot but you can warm up. Stop running around, damn it, I don't need your sand in my face, calm down, lie down next to me!"

The main thing... The main thing, of course, is the birth rate. There may be more of us, many more, even with this malfunctioning telomerase. Yes, and almost all of the burden falls on the women. What can men do? Nothing but provide economic and moral support. Maybe take wives. We already have four children living their own lives. Sophia is still in her fertile age. She is third generation and her eggs are precious. We can give birth to a couple more of our own children, and she can donate a few more eggs to the bank.

"Klaus, why are you digging under me? Lie still."

Yes, this is her burden, can I share it somehow? Sophia wanted to go to Atlantis. Should I take a vacation and go to Atlantis with her? I could go there endlessly, one trip for each donor egg. At least I'll contribute somehow and I'm not an unknown person. They will look at us and someone will take an example from us. They will do so and perhaps here will be someone to build new cities for. This is how we should respond to the silence of the Earth.

"Klaus, let's go home quickly, I think I understand what to do!"

Boarding Pass to Carthage

The home of the Rudnick family was located on the side of a mountain overlooking the Volga. The huge river with green islands, wide sandy beaches and sand bars traveled southeast for about thirty kilometers, where it turned right as it passed a long blue ridge made up of wooded hills. Victor Rudnick had been ready to sell his soul to the devil for such a view, but fortunately this was not required, he got off with having to survive several years of austerity and repaying a moderately heavy loan. Right now, he and Elsa were drinking wine on the veranda above the view of eternal peace, admiring the evening river and dreaming about their upcoming cruise. For several years in a row, they had planned a long peaceful journey by ship along the Volga to its confluence with the ocean but again and again, something didn't work out.

"Well, the vacation is delayed," said Elsa, "and it's already the middle of October. It's too late, and Chuck has to wait another week with his practice."

"What if he suddenly has an internship in the middle of the semester? After all, he already had practice in the summer. Who did they monitor, beavers or what?"

"He said it was extra practice. The urgent monitoring of raccoon dogs was needed, and well-performing students were allowed to go on an expedition for two weeks."

"Did you call him?"

"He said there was no phone coverage there."

Chuck returned a week later.

"Well, how are the raccoon dogs doing?" his father asked as he waited for his son to finish his bowl of soup and two portions of fried turkey.

"They're doing well, they're breeding and multiplying, there's been a three percent increase in their number in the last year," Chuck said, looking at the table.

"Your face doesn't look very expeditionary, you look as if you've been sitting in a room for the whole two weeks," his father remarked.

"The weather wasn't very good, it was cloudy," the son replied, looking at the wall.

"So what is this?" Elsa asked slowly with an unpleasant tone in her voice. She was carrying Chuck's jacket in one hand and shaking a small rectangle of thick paper with the other hand. "Here, I was checking the pockets before washing it. What is this?"

"It's a boarding pass," Chuck said, looking down at the floor.

"Well, well look what we have here," Elsa said, handing the ticket over to Victor.

"Wow! Imagine that! Flight A675 Troy-Carthage! Airline Pan Selinium! October 4, 1109. Charles Rudnick, Seat 21A. Our son traveled twelve thousand kilometers to the southern hemisphere at the height of the semester. So, Chuck, I feel for you. You just got caught in a huge lie. This is, of course, one of the most unpleasant things that can happen to a person. Well, now. So tell me..."

"There's nothing to tell... Well, I have a girlfriend there, in Carthage. In the summer, she came here for practice. She had received a private grant for a trip to our university for an internship."

"And what grant did you use to fly to Carthage?"

"Half of it earned doing promotions, and the other half I borrowed.

Don't worry I'll pay it back myself."

"So, a girl in the Southern Hemisphere is, of course, a strong incentive. But remember: there is no incentive that warrants being caught lying because of it!"

"Yes, Dad, I understand. Can she stay here with me when you go on vacation?"

"Well, you should get married or something then. Otherwise it will not be clear in what capacity she will live here."

"Yeah, that's possible, although the idea hasn't crossed our minds yet..."

"Did you ask her what generation she is?" Elsa asked.

"Didn't have to ask, she told me herself. She said she is sixth."

"Oh, our grave sins..." Elsa sighed heavily.

"Come on," Victor responded, "it's time to get used to this. Just think grandchildren from an unknown woman. Life will continue anyway! Never mind. Chuck, go! You obviously need to sleep off the work of the righteous! Otherwise you will fall off your chair."

The next evening as usual, the couple sat drinking wine on the veranda.

"Well, it's getting dark quite early. And the black poplars have all flown away. And we are sitting here with ideas flying around inside our heads of sailing to the ocean."

"Listen! Why are we so obsessed with that cruise? Frankly, it's an old-fashioned way of traveling. We are still young, not even fifty. Look at our youngest offspring, he took off and hit the road to Australia without any fanfare. So what if there's a girl there. Don't we have an incentive? We have never been in the Southern Hemisphere in all of our lives, although we have been drinking wine from there for so many years. Most of all we have never been to Atlantis. Besides, down there it is now like the end of

April. Why is there no money? We've already reserved a cruise. So what, let it be twice as expensive. We'll borrow. In the end, I will teach an extra course. Or in an extreme case I'll do tutoring."

"Do you have any idea how to get there?"

"You need to fly there through the same Carthage where Chuck was, then take a local airline to the Western Port, then either by ship or by a tourist charter across the sea to the North-Eastern cordon. There we'll pay for a tour, sign an oath, rent a car and Atlantis is at our feet!"

In mid-November, Victor and Elsa, having paid all the required fees, signed the necessary papers where, among other things, they pledged not to: feed bears or cuddle with lions. They also received: a flash drive with instructions and maps, a satellite phone, a GPS navigator and a small SUV, which they drove out through the opened gate.

Finally, before them was Atlantis, stretching from the equator to the southern polar tundra with: glaciers throughout all of its climatic zones; mountains and endless ranges; steppes, tundra and plains; savannahs, jungles, taiga and forests with an almost endless array of marine fauna. Eight hundred years ago, Atlantis had already received the status of a global nature reserve, where any activity was prohibited, except for research, ecological studies and tourist activities. Selina's people could afford to set aside an entire continent for a nature reserve, for every inhabitant on the planet there were three of the one hundred and twenty million square kilometers of land, by November 1109 there were then four.

This does not mean that no one lived in Atlantis, in fact quite the opposite. Personnel were required to repair roads, serve tourists, conduct research, introduce new animals into nature, teach children and import goods. There were at least two hundred thousand people who lived on the mainland and were scattered throughout all of the small villages and stations.

So, Victor and Elsa left through the gate and in front of them was the hospitable mainland, where everything except alcohol had already been paid for a month in advance. After having driven for only a couple of minutes they pulled up at an intersection with a simple sign: north (right), south (left) and west (straight). They chose west as they were eager to cross the mainland and the two mountain ranges and the inland basin which stood between them and the Great Western Ocean. After the intersection there was a sign with the most vital information: Refueling 70 km; Groceries 150 km; Beer 250 km and Accommodation 300 km. The road was not wide, but straight and smooth as a pencil lead, it cut straight through the hills, over bridges and embankments and through the lowlands. A desolate well-groomed road with bright markings, clean gravel shoulders and wire animal fencing. It was a hypnotic road that required driving and driving without turning back.

"Why did they make the road so straight?" Viktor thought out loud. "Such perfection has almost no benefit but it does cost a lot."

"In my opinion, the road is a kind of a symbol. It makes an impression on us. Relax and try to understand what this road brings you."

"An arrow of time and we're heading into the future? No, perhaps not exactly, but something like that I suppose."

On either side of them were expanses of savannah, where three or four species of antelope grazed and even rhinos and groups of giraffes could occasionally be seen. The "Groceries" turned out to be a small kiosk at a gas station, but the beer at around 250 km was quite decent, tasty, cool and bubbly. The couple spent the night at the 532nd kilometer in a self-hotel (without servants) you insert the universal key issued at the initial cordon, you entered, took your bed linens, make the bed and then in the morning you throw the linen into the washing machine processor and press the button. During the day they came across two people (in the kiosk and behind the beer counter), a dozen and a half oncoming cars, thousands of artiodactyls, hundreds of baboons, and dozens of rhinos and elephants the last of which were usually only found to the north.

The next day did not offer anything fundamentally new, but on the third day mountains appeared on the horizon. The road went uphill just as straight as it had over bridges, interchanges and through tunnels. The last tunnel they went through was twenty-kilometers long and led them into the rocky semi-desert of the Inner Basin. Once there had been a sea there but tectonics had raised the seabed to a height of three and a half kilometers. This slightly hilly plain did not resemble yesterday's savanna, just as the llamas grazing in small groups did not resemble antelopes. At a gas station, getting out of the car, Victor felt how much colder it was here. He suggested climbing the nearest hill to stretch out their muscles and take a break. This was when the couple was hit by the feeling that they were not so young anymore.

"Never mind, don't worry about it," Victor said, "we just haven't had enough time for acclimatization."

The next day, the road still stretched endlessly forward in a straight line like a pencil lead and it was hypnotizing, cutting through the psychedelic landscape. On the sides of the road there were strange pointed statues, similar to drunken monks in hoods, obelisks, arches and domes. It was like something out of a dream, and in order to get out of the semi-hypnosis, Victor took a sip of strong coffee from a thermos, shook his head, massaged the back of his neck and cracked opened the window.

"Say something," he asked Elsa. "Anything at all, even nonsense, only be expressive."

"Oh, it seems that this is not all some kind of stupidity at all: look, everything seems to be breaking apart ahead of us and there is only haze, and behind the haze, something strange."

Victor looked at the navigator.

"So this is the Central Canyon already! Looks like I went overboard."

"You were driving one hundred and eighty until you had your coffee."

Before entering the canyon they came across the first real village on the way located to the side of the main road, there was a road service for cars, rescue services with helicopters, a canteen and a real hotel. The entire staff of the hotel was sitting on a bench at the entrance, two people with two dogs lying at their feet. Victor and Elsa did not linger there, they did not need rescuing and they had enough food rations for five days in advance, so they moved on. The road led straight off the side of a cliff.

Victor reflexively pressed the brake, but when he saw a speed limit sign saying 120, he let off the brakes and continued straight ahead believing the road service. The ground on the left and right suddenly dropped far down, and the road began to gently descend straight through the air. It was supported by openwork reinforced concrete pillars, rooted deep into the layered slopes of the canyon.

The road turned smoothly to the right and continued its way in the air over the abyss to a rock-outcropping with vertical slopes and a flat top where there was an observation deck. Far, far below, flowed a muddy rusty river, which the reader may have already guessed, was called the Colorado. It had three times the water of its earthly sister, since it originated from the glaciers of the Northern Range and was filled by constant monsoons. From there, at a great height, the river seemed quite narrow as the canyon was much deeper than its earthly counterpart. It was listed as the ninth natural wonder of this world and the ten-kilometer bridge across the canyon was the first among man-made miracles on Selina. It was held up by a web of openwork supports and it seemed to be hanging from the sky above the canyon, only slightly bending downward. In fact, not a single support was longer than six hundred meters, and the monolithic web consisted of powerful, stressed reinforced concrete beams, vertical, inclined and arcuate. The central arch spanned over the river at a height of one and a half kilometers, locked in place by the high cliffs on the banks of the river.

"Listen, the road over the canyon could have been built ten times cheaper! For example going over there and traversing down the slope over that ledge. As you can see there are two bridges there, a bridge over the river and one over the gorge which goes up again along the slope. Why was it necessary to construct such a miracle?"

“You just answered the question yourself. It’s a miracle. Consider it a work of art. In this bridge we can see that aesthetics and challenge were of higher value than rationality.”

“How much money and effort was invested in it!”

“How old is this bridge? Somewhere around five hundred years old?”

“I think perhaps closer to six hundred.”

“Well, how many people has it attracted here in six centuries? How many people have visited the mainland in order to travel over the first wonder of this world? How many people have experienced this delight? There is no rationality in this. Do you need a rationalization?”

“I am delighted myself. It’s just unusual. Usually, in engineering structures, aesthetics is subordinated to rationality. Here, the lion’s share of the costs was invested in the aesthetics and in the grandeur of the structure. Can you name any earthly counterparts?”

“Of course, cathedrals, palaces and even the great pyramids, which all had different motives behind their constructions. On Earth, they were built in the name of a god or a monarch or to display wealth. Here it is more like a challenge to fate: “There are few of us here, we are doomed but look what we can do. Heads up!”

“Head up? So heads up! Higher and higher! Forward and forward!” Having stopped they decided to continue. “Let’s go, there is also an observation deck with a transparent floor on the central span which I want to see.”

After a ten-kilometer flight over the abyss, they stopped and they wanted some beer. Elsa took a stack of travel brochures from the entrance to the bar which was in the tourist structure and laid them out on the table they had occupied.

When Victor held out the second glass for a toast Elsa exclaimed: “Here, I found it! Listen: ‘The architect of the West-East road crossing the northern part of Atlantis, Simeon Shama, called his project ‘the Way of Reason’. In his concept, he conceived it as the antithesis to postmodernism, and believed that the path of reason should be straight... People wander around the truth and believes that the path to knowledge is tortuous,' said Shama, 'but in fact it is just like the arrow of time.'

"Oh Victor, you almost guessed it! Listen further: 'In the same concept, the Central Canyon was considered to be something like fate, like an abyss that cut off the human history of Selina from the future, at the time of the road's construction it was already clear that the problem of fertility was insurmountable. According to the architect's intention, the bridge, running almost completely straight at a great height above the canyon, symbolized the belief that the human mind would miraculously overcome the abyss and continue on its straight path into the future. A proper name could not be thought up and the concept was forgotten. For a long time, the road was called Simeon's String, but over time, the road along with the bridge, having received the status of the first artificial wonders of the world, lost this name as well.' Victor, how dense we are not to know such illuminating facts!"

"And how to keep in our minds everything that is forgotten by history itself? Especially in a case like this where the idea is clearly not deserving of being forgotten."

"Oh, wait, wait, it gets even more interesting: 'The southern road, crossing the continent in the latitudinal direction and designed by Simeon Shama, was named *the Path of History* by him. The road is famous for its dizzying slanting turns, sharp bends, steep descents and ascents and the abrupt changes in landscape'."

"So it's like this: we proceed by the way of reason, but we will return by way of history! Don't go crazy on those bends..."

"We won't go crazy, let's keep going, we still have more than two thousand kilometers of a perfectly straight road ahead!"

Three days later, Victor and Elsa had crossed the Western Range and had found themselves in humid blooming subtropics, among palm trees near the ocean. After spending a couple of days in a coastal hotel and swimming in the cool ocean, they decided to move south. The road ran along the sea, an ordinary seaside road with the usual seaside attractions.

After a hundred kilometers they began to come across small villages more often. The subtropics became a little drier, and the road headed upward and continued along the sides of the mountains. Having come across a branch of the road which led downward, they saw a sign that said 'Biostation 48', the couple decided to try their luck and turned off the main road and headed down. Soon they found themselves in a neat little village with eighteen houses with small mowed lawns. They had been placed in a semicircle around a central lawn with a transparent pavilion on it and judging by the abundance of office equipment in it, it served as an office. As soon as they stopped, a dog ran up to the car and, standing on its hind legs, stretched its muzzle into the window and licked Victor on the cheek. Then the dog sat down and let out a bellowing bark in a bass voice, shaking its raised head and wagging its tail.

On the street there appeared a slightly limping man who was in a hurry: "Welcome!" he shouted from afar. "Do not be afraid of Agatha, she invites all good people to get out of their cars and welcomes them to visit. I will join her request," said the owner of the dog slightly out of breath and coming up and holding out his hand. "Welcome to our biological station! My name is John Smoot. You are the first visitors here in a whole month. Please follow me to our dinner table, which my wife is already setting."

"How does your dog recognize good people?"

"Very simple, they roll down the window or leave the window open when he runs up to the car."

John, who looked to be in his seventies, led them to one of the houses and a woman of about the same age as the owner came out to meet them.

"Meet Mary, my wife."

Victor and Elsa introduced themselves and marched into the dining room, where the table was already laid with wine, cheeses, fruits and vegetables.

"Oh, you shouldn't have really!" Elsa protested. "We recently had lunch."

"Yeah, sorry," Victor added, "but at such a table I can't legally refuse."

"Are you going to go somewhere else today?" asked the owner in a low voice.

"I wouldn't want to trouble you... We are going to spend the night in a self-hotel, which is about half an hour away," Elsa mumbled uncertainly.

"God, what self-hotel! Before you are fifteen empty houses waiting for you, where every comfort is covered, where there are hot showers, and in the refrigerators there is light beer for weary travelers."

"What about the owners of these houses?"

"There are no owners. Some left, some died. We are alone here. We mow the lawns and look after the houses. What you see is not the whole biological station, it is only the central platform, but there is no one on the other sites either."

Victor and Elsa took a long look at each other.

"All right," Victor said, "with only one condition: tomorrow we will eat our food together from our food supply and drink the contents of a special box in the trunk."

John and Maria talked all evening about the introduction of marine mammals, about the rearing of ungulates, about how the first wolf cubs were taught to hunt, about how Biological Station 48, over the six centuries of its existence, achieved the harmony of the wildlife on the area entrusted to it, a stunning half a million square kilometers. They talked about how the children of employees left forever 'for the mainland', and how they gradually curtailed work as the program approached completion and finally how they ended up there all alone.

"We receive a pension and a small salary for so-called "permanent monitoring", which does not involve any obligations, we write regular reports on the life of the local fauna, and in fact this is an addition to our pensions. With the fauna as a whole, everything is in order, it lives and thrives. The task is done."

They sat together for a long time, the hosts could not talk enough, the last inhabitants of an outgoing world with a glorious history, such as Biostation 48, had something to tell. In the house where the owners brought Viktor and Elsa to spend the night, wonderful photographs hung on the walls. Portraits, group shots, people bottle-feeding animals, games and touching goodbyes. Sweet faces, funny stories, adorable babies and excellent print quality.

"The former inhabitants of this house?" Victor asked.

"Yes, there were more than ten generations here. Here is a picture from three hundred years ago, a group involved in the adaptation of cetaceans against the background of pets. And this is Sophia Chen with a puma, she is alive and well on the mainland. Maybe the puma is still alive as well since the picture is only twenty years old."

"Who printed these pictures? It is clear that they are made by the same technique."

"We did," John replied. "Laser ceramic printing, expensive but it will last forever. Shot of course, by different people, we collected all of this from all kinds of electronic archives, online and local. The fact is that in this form these photographs will far outlive their electronic versions. And in thousands of years they will hang here in the same capacity."

"Do other houses have similar pictures?"

"Of course, you will see everything tomorrow. We also recording our own replicas, which will receive visitors after us. There was once a biological station and then there will be a museum-shelter."

The next morning, Smoot invited the guests to get acquainted with representatives of the friendly local fauna. Everyone, including Agatha, went down the stairs to the shore and walked along it to a small bay with a concrete pier. John went out to the pier and whistled so loudly several times, so that Victor, who was standing next to him, almost went deaf. About three minutes later, a heavy crackling sound came from the bushes at the edge of the water and a huge wild boar proudly emerged from the thickets, as if from behind an open curtain.

Agatha rushed over to him, whimpered and twisting her tail, got up on her hind legs, growled, lunged and rushed around in loops along the beach, the boar following her. Then vice versa, the earth was shaking, stones and sand were flying everywhere and God forbid anyone got in their way, whether a man or a pillar. Finally, boar was out of breath and lay down on its side, and Agatha, having made a couple of fruitless lunges, began to bite the grunting boar's bristles. But then two fins appeared, and the boar and Agatha ran to the pier. Two dolphin heads popped out of the water near the pier. The wild boar ran up to one of the dolphins and rested its snout against its beak, distant evolutionary relatives shook their shifting muzzles, as people shake their hands at a joyful meeting. Agatha, meanwhile, was playing with the second dolphin, rushing back and forth along the pier growling and lunging down, the dolphin rushed about in the water and jumped toward Agatha, landing with its chest on the edge of the pier, the dog dodged back and forth and then jumped back. Out of nowhere, two pairs of ravens appeared in the air. With cries of "caw-caw" they swooped down onto the pier and then soared up again. Both pairs were gliding, synchronously making circles and loops while touching each other with the tips of their wings. Suddenly one of the ravens folded its wings and began to fall backwards, the other caught up with it in a sharp dive, after which both spread their wings and again gained altitude, they repeated this trick several times, changing roles. The other couple descended to an altitude just above the water's surface and began to fly in circles. All of a sudden two gray-white torpedoes noisily erupted from the water, trying to strike the ravens with their noses, one of the dolphins almost succeeded and they kept trying. Agatha roared and rushed into the water with a running start, and swam to the noisy company, and at each jump of the dolphins she beat her paws on the water, trying to contribute to the ongoing riot.

Finally, the friendly fauna calmed down. The dog came out of the water and shook herself off. The dolphins swam up to the pier and stood up to the waist to be stroked by John and Mary, the couple of ravens came down and landed on the lying boar, then one got on John's shoulder and another walked next to the lying Agatha.

"Well, so you see, we are not at all bored here," said Maria. "You haven't seen everyone. Sometimes the boar comes with a girlfriend. Different dolphins come, sometimes a whole school. There are other places where other animals come when we whistle, but this group is the most fun."

The Rudnicks spent three nights and two full days at the Smoots', visiting other sites, climbing the mountains and getting acquainted with the local representatives of the fauna of Atlantis.

"Say hello to the mainland and don't worry about us. We will live here happily ever after and die on the same day," Maria said in parting.

Victor and Elsa continued their journey along the ocean to the south. The subtropics gave way to dry steppes, then the landscape began to turn green, and finally lush broad-leaved forests began to appear. One morning they decided to stop and walk along the foothills to a waterfall they could see in the distance. On the way back, they got caught in rain, and not just rain, but the warm front of an oceanic cyclone.

The lingering rain got stuck in the foliage of the upper tier then merged into large drops which rustled down the leaves and drummed onto the hoods of Victor and Elsa. Victor threw back his hood, reasoning that the warm rain was something friendly.

This is good, he thought, *why don't we like to get caught in the rain? Well, okay, maybe if it's cold and there is a piercing wind... But this one is alive and warm, and even fragrant...*

"Pour, pour rain," Victor muttered, "rustle in the foliage..."

"What are you mumbling about under your breath?" Elsa asked.

"Ode to the water cycle! I'm like Winnie the Pooh, composing on the go... Oh, here it is: Pour, pour rain. Rustle in the leaves... Having soaked the humus, drive the striped worms out into the light... And having had a sip of adventure in the woven roots, make your way into the shady ravine!" Victor sang in a singsong voice.

"Yes, Winnie the Pooh can take a seat. It seems that you have not shown such talents before."

“Who knows, maybe because it started raining, or maybe I heard it somewhere, then forgot it and then it re-surfaced.”

“Come on, my Winnie the Pooh, what else did the rain give you?”

“Wait,” Victor replied, continuing to walk and waving his arms. “Hold on it’s coming. Oh jumping stream, break away for a moment from the blind attraction of the sea and allow yourself a little sleep in the pool where the pine needles drop. And from there, through the crowns of the trees, look at your cradle in gray tatters flying south!”

Elsa looked up into the gap between the crowns and saw that the clouds were really flying from north to south.

“Wait,” Victor continued, “there must be something else. Any ode without a sad note is false, and an ode to the water cycle is even more so. Here it is, a sad note.” Victor thumped his chest.

“Time will soon sweep us away like the brushing of a hand. This is the peaceful grave prepared for us, and the grass, like a child, drinks eternal juice! And the flow of running water will not run dry! That’s what was dictated to me either by rain, or by a leaky memory! After us, the world will not go anywhere, it will do just fine. So let us bless it, when leaving and the soul will feel better.”

“It reminded me of something else: *‘And Spring herself when she woke at dawn would scarcely know that we were gone.’*”

“Yes, I remember that: ‘There will come soft rains and the smell of the ground’ a good poem, but I didn’t want to say that. I meant that it’s not worth it to shed tears for us, let them, and the willows and the birds, and the others do their job: live and develop while the water flows and the sun shines. They will have a lot of time ahead of them, and something worthwhile will surely come out of all this.”

“Without people, this world would have remained a desert. Even without us, who were born here, it would have remained much more miserable.”

“Even more so. It is much easier to leave with a sense of

accomplishment, although it was not you and I who fulfilled our duties but the Smoots and people like them. You know, perhaps I quite foolishly considered the Archive an empty business. Having visited the Smoots, I think we should do our bit. Prepare lectures properly. Collect photos and films. Sign and comment on material and now, when we return home, we will mount all the footage under the heading "Atlantis in the Beginning of the XII Century" and show something about the Smoots and ask them for all the photos in electronic form, we will upload everything to the Archive. Maybe people somewhere out there, among the stars, are still living and will suddenly look over here."

"People from the sky... The only thing left is to hope for a miracle."

"Why not hope? Hope is not only empowering, if followed through in life, it makes miracles more likely. See what a powerful symbol Simeon Shama built with engineers and workers. Looking at the bridge, do you really believe that the history of intelligent life on Selina should not end with our disappearance? Okay, a bridge with a road is still a symbol, but the Archive is no longer a symbol. It is a sort of calculation to bring about a miracle that can then in fact materialize hope. And what about plutonium 242, for which the working parameters of several nuclear power plants had to be changed? I, like most, did not see the point in these costly actions but it all finally came to fruition: plutonium is like the pillars of a bridge across an abyss. A plutonium heating pad is a source of energy for hundreds of thousands of years. perhaps a weak one, but reliable and constant. There are hundreds of thousands of years of life in the gigantic electronic memory of the Archive, hundreds of thousands of years of eternal readiness to recognize intelligence and turn on the uranium capsules that power the libraries and the beacons and hundreds of thousands of years of constant readiness for a miracle that will, in the end, make it happen."

"And what do you think this miracle will be? That baboons get smarter? Another Ark lands from somewhere?"

"I don't know, Elsa. Maybe something like that, maybe something else, be that as it may, we must leave a memory of ourselves, of human history. Do you know what came to my mind after visiting the Smoots?

It would be nice if Chuck got busy making arrangements for the world that will be after us. These beavers and raccoon dogs of his are just from that area of arrangements. And yes, he has potential. Like it or not, not every student is able to secretly and suddenly fly to another hemisphere. He will come to his senses. He won't be an idiot all his life!"

The Rudnick couple successfully completed their journey across Atlantis, having successfully traveled across the Path of History without compromising their sanity, and five years later they fulfilled their dream of sailing along the Volga to the ocean. On this we say goodbye to them, although the name Rudnick will come up again.

The Last Old Man

Five years ago, the last living people on the planet moved to the Base which was the cradle of mankind on Selina to live out the rest of the century. No one wanted to die alone and the old people stayed close to each other, just as the first children of the planet did one and a half thousand years ago. The old man, slowly walking along the wide ocean beach had just such a fate, as he turned out to be the very last person alive.

Six years ago the old man and his wife moved here along with the last three families of Troy. They had made sure that before leaving they had "turned off the lights", giving the command to shut down the last unit of the local nuclear power plant: his wife, armed with thick glasses had dictated passwords and options from a paper and the old man had typed in and sent the commands to the plants control network. They had reached the Base in one day. Heading out before sunrise the old man had driven a truck with the belongings of the four families while the rest drove their cars. Toward evening, their small column emerged from the tunnel under the White Pass and headed towards the calm golden-blue ocean. At dusk, at the entrance to the Base, they were met by dogs grazing a herd of cows that energetically waved their tails and ran along the road behind the column barking merrily. Now every car on this road was an exceptional rarity and was a cause for merriment for the dogs in the surrounding area.

Having collected sixty passengers from all over Australia and Atlantis who had gathered in the southern capital, the last flight from Carthage had landed at the airport of the Base three years before the arrival of the old man, his wife and their countrymen. They had been flown here by a lone eighty-three-year-old pilot who despite his age had been as strong as the bush in the outback and died only six months back. Before that flight a ship had landed a year earlier with almost a hundred people from all over the coast of Borealia on board. They had all boarded the ship after all of the remaining inhabitants of the inner cities had been notified that they had to arrive at the nearest port by a certain date. All in all, it was a rather large friendly grouping of people – there were those who could still walk, those in wheelchairs, those with clear minds and those with fading memories. The group was slowly thinning out, but those who were there were holding on as long as possible, helped by unlimited food and medical supplies, a working infrastructure and a fully operational hospital with robotic nurses at their disposal.

The old man sat down to rest. Three months ago, there had been two left and when they had celebrated the past New Year, there had been four. The tumor in his right side kept growing, with the pain becoming more and more severe, requiring injections which had to be done more and more often. There was really no point in dragging this on. Why spoil a generally good long life with a brutal and painful end? Even the final years they had spent here had been good ones: they had regularly gathered in the gazebo on Pine Dune, and drank fine old wine, remembered the past, told each other jokes and laughed together. The last year and a half, since his wife had died had been much harder, but the time flew by quickly...

For what would be the last time the old man checked for messages regarding a reception trigger on the Great Antenna. If such had been the case he would have delayed his departure for a few days. Twelve years ago there had been a reception trigger when the antenna had registered a signal from the Earth's solar system. It had been a very weak signal but it had corresponded to the standard structure and frequency that would have come from Earth. Sadly the data turned out to be unreadable, although the very fact of signal transmission left little doubt that someone had tried to transmit information from an antenna that was either too small, could not be aimed accurately or was equipped with an insufficiently powerful transmitter. It had been the only trigger in the more than one thousand years that the Great Antenna had existed and which had regularly transmitted signals to the Earth's solar system.

There were no messages so the old man walked towards the water and when he got close he made his decision: here!

He recalled the words of Joseph Brodsky:

"...I will not bring hurt

To anyone, lying on in the coastal sand..."

Brodsky helped but another thin syringe helped even more, so much so that the old man was able to dig a hollow in the sand as long as his own height. He was, however, in no real hurry to lie down, let the sun go down first. Watching the sun going down below the horizon, the old man saw a green ray of light!

A good last gift, he thought, and then he heard chugging and stomping. Polundra and Athas were galloping towards him along the beach. They ran up, twisting their tails like propellers, whining and licking the old man's face.

"Oh, brothers, I didn't want to call you so that as to save you from the shock. Well, since you've come running, lie down next to me. Thanks, I don't have to die alone. In peace it will be easier...

The old man lay down in the sandy hollow he had dug. The dogs then quickly dug holes on both sides of him for themselves and lay down in them, clinging to the old man and warming him. It felt good and calm, but not for long, the pain in his side erupted again and became stronger with each breath.

"Now, guys, this is your planet," the old man said. "Now you are in charge here. Don't let me down... I guess that perhaps it's time."

He took out a thicker syringe and injected it into a vein. Polundra and Athas lay quietly for several minutes, then suddenly jumped up and began furiously licking the old man's face in vain. The old man did not come back to life and the dogs sat down and howled. A few minutes later the whole flock of creatures came running, a mournful song spread along the coast, which was picked up by distant relatives across the river and beyond the Northern Cape. Beyond them, in turn, the dogs of the foothill steppes, the floodplain meadows and the South Bay also started howling. They did not know whom they were mourning, but they felt that something very sad had happened. However, life went on and the dogs gradually quieted down. At night, a small atmospheric front came, causing a short, but quite noticeable storm and the surf covered the body of the old man with sand. The next morning, after checking the herd, the dogs went to the beach to play football with a leather ball stuffed with grass, fun and noisy. Atas broke the rules and grabbed the ball with his teeth and ran with it, for which he was battered by his relatives and earned another scar on his face.

It had been easier for the elderly to live out their last years with the belief that people had prepared the world well for their departure. Not a single animal remained homeless, all of the ones capable of independent living were released into nature and the incapable ceased to be bred many years ago. The dogs, the distant descendants of Noah with tassels who chased the ball around the beach, from time to time had fed the old man and his friends with fresh beef.

The Base's nuclear power plant had been switched to low-power autonomous mode ten years ago and would operate for another ten years. The last old power engineers had set it up for twenty years of autonomous operation as it had not been known in advance when the last people would die. After the reactor shut down automatically the load would fall on the radioisotope generators. The most powerful of them designed for an antenna that would continue to transmit and receive signals for hundreds of years and was there to send an answer if there was ever a message, which was in fact never expected.

Perhaps the most important thing that people had done before they left the world was the setting up of the archives. At least, they themselves thought so. They truly hoped that one day someone would read them. They had thought that the most important things were the micron engraving on discs made of precious metal alloys, this data would survive until they were erased by geological processes, such as being flooded over with lava or swallowed up and buried under the sediments of the sea. That is, not only tens but rather, hundreds of millions of years. However, you can't write much with micron engraving. The main body of information was stored in electronic form on different media with periodic re-writing. The radioisotope power sources that kept the main archives alive were designed to last seven hundred thousand years. Yes, people really believed that during such a length of time there would come along someone who could read what they had left behind...

PART FOUR

UhirrMuhh and SirriSill

UhirrMuhh (pronounced in a guttural bass as low as the pronunciator is capable of) finally chose a place for the calf house, leaving a mark close to the wall that was a phenomenon of stone with a rectangular shape and square holes in it. The dogs saw quite a few of these strange rocks and often used them: the walls went quite deep into the ground and insured that at least one side of the calf house would not collapse. Late autumn was fast approaching, and the winters were getting colder every year. Last year's calf houses were not enough for this winter, especially since some had crumbled and collapsed in the spring. Therefore, it was necessary to dig new ones otherwise part of the late offspring would not survive the winter.

UhirrMuhh was the leader of the dog tribe. He was not distinguished by exceptional strength, but he was known as the most intelligent, and the elders of the dog tribe had long figured out what was more important. Actually, he had revolutionized the digging of the calf houses. Before, digging had been done using the front paws and the dogs were already masters of this, but the problem was in transporting the soil outside. Previously, it had been carried out by using a bull hide which was spread near the wall and two dogs dug the ground with their two front paws, as their ancestors did, with the earth flying back between their hind legs onto the hide. Then two other dogs grabbed the hide by the edges and, backing out, dragged it to the exit. For the second pair of dogs, the work was hard and quite vile.

What had UhirrMuhh come up with that revolutionized digging? He gnawed two large holes in the hide on the side where the head had been then crawled under it, stuck his head into one of them, after which pulling with his chest he dragged the earth much easier and faster than even the two fastest could. "Look," he shouted, and several of his fellow tribe-dogs came nearer and at first glance completely understood the idea. Another dog joined him and the two of them pulled the hide so hard and fast that all of the dirt that had been on it fell off. They instantly found a solution tying the two hind legs of the hide together along with the tail. This time they loaded even more dirt onto it and rushed off with a cheerful joyful bark, which in human language is closest to a "he-he-he-he!" Out of joy the dogs did not stop at the dump and rushed onward, the first dirt dragging team in the post-human history of Selina disappeared into the fields with a fading canine "he-he-he-he".

The dog tribe then began to use the same transport method to deliver hay to calves. Using the old method, dry grass was collected with the help of a hawthorn bush. Backing through the grass, the dog pulled the bush with its teeth and the grass clung to the thorns and got stuck between the branches. Over time, the dog tribe replaced the hawthorn with a withered spruce tree, which proved to be a more powerful technology. The spruce tree was easy enough to drag and the grass got wrapped up in it perfectly. Most importantly, this process was much more fun and was always accompanied by joyful growls and barks, especially when the tree went rolling downhill by itself.

Spruce trees were actually a rarity as a team of a dozen dogs had to be sent twenty kilometers up the river to get them. Not being beavers, it was quite difficult for the dogs to chop down spruce trees with their fangs alone, but in a day they could manage chopping down a dozen or two small spruce trees. Then the trees were floated down the river and the dogs followed close behind on the shore, watching to see if any got stuck or went aground. When they reached home the trees were pulled ashore and dried until the next autumn. The most unpleasant task associated with the expedition occurred during the next couple of days during which the dogs cleaned the spruce resin from their muzzles.

UhirrMuhh and his comrades were in a hurry digging the new calf house when suddenly the overseer said, "That's enough for today."

Everyone was sent home but the overseer himself immediately returned to the hole that was being dug and stared at the lower part of the wall that had been exposed. It was something absolutely incredible: as usual the stone wall they had been digging under broke off the deeper they got but here further down was an unprecedented shiny hard material with a strange faint smell. He sent the rest home because he had to figure out what it was by himself and it was important that no was getting in the way. He tried to expose more of the surface and saw that the material continued down without any sign of an edge marking its finish. He then called out to his wife SirriSill (pronounced with a slight whine in "Si") for help.

"Look," UhirrMuhh said.

"That's scary looking," whined SirriSill.

"Interesting," said UhirrMuhh. "Let's dig."

They dug quickly together and in just five runs using the ox hide they got to the level where the unusual material ended and the stone continued. What they uncovered was a shiny rectangle. UhirrMuhh then noticed that a darker square, divided into even smaller squares, stood out on the shiny material. UhirrMuhh ran his paw over the square. On one of the small squares a red light immediately flashed.

"That's scary," whined SirriSill again.

"Will you stop with your 'scary'! Of course it's 'scary'! Look, how interesting!" UhirrMuhh touched the blinking square.

Just then another blinked. Without thinking for a second the leader touched this point as well. Then a third blinked and repeated the process ten times. After the tenth press, there were clicking sounds inside the wall and the shiny material began to detract itself inside and an entrance opened up.

"Very scary," SirriSill said again.

"Wait here!" UhirrMuhh barked and went through the opening. Before he had gone ten steps, the lights inside flashed on and the wall of the room in which he found himself glowed and another world opened up in it and there was somebody in that world... He spoke, but UhirrMuhh did not understand a single sound.

What a good guy! thought the chief of the dogs. He couldn't explain to himself why this someone was good but he knew.

"Come here, it's not scary at all," UhirrMuhh shouted to his wife. SirriSill entered on half-bent legs.

Seeing the heretofore unknown creature, she sat down and stared at him: "Oh, what a good one!"

"Yes, good. I've never seen anything like him... How do I know he's good?"

It was really a good question. Why? Why had dogs not lost their attachment to humans after a hundred thousand generations on Selina? After all, this love and devotion had appeared only in thousands of dog generations on Earth. How was it that this reaction to the appearance of a person fixed in their genes? Of course, it would be better to ask an evolutionary geneticist about this, but they could say anything, for example, that this trait turned out to be linked to intelligence, or maybe not say anything at all and just shrug. In any case, in this context, the continuation of this discussion is clearly unnecessary.

The man continued to speak and the couple listened with their mouths open and their heads tilted to one side. The man was clearly pointing to something in this world from his place in his world. This something turned out to be several stones lying on the floor. All of the stones were different from each other with the only thing they had in common being that each had at least one sharp edge. However, analogues to any of these stones could be found upstream near the river. The dogs went up to the stones and sniffed them, nothing suspicious. UhirrMuhh touched one of them with his paw and then the man said something, nodding approvingly and took a stone from the ground, an exact copy of the one that the paw had touched. It was an elongated stone, almost black in color, with a sharp edge.

"Can you also pick up the stone with your paw?"

"Yes, I can," SirriSill replied, walking over and grasping it with four fingers.

A slight digression may be required here. SirriSill was not only the first lady of the dog tribe, but also the first beauty and not only because of the luxurious tassels on her ears. The main criterion of female beauty among the dogs was the possession of long flexible toes on the front paws. They did not interfere when running fast and now it was no longer fast legs that fed the dogs. With such "fingers" it was possible to milk cows and pull hay out of branches and comb the fur of husbands who had returned from work. Oddly enough, the length and flexibility of the "fingers" slightly increased from generation to generation across the entire tribe. On rare encounters they had to listen to ridicule about this from dogs of other tribes which used other criteria for beauty. Ridicule may be ridicule, but the tribe of the long-fingered (pronounced as "ArruSihamm" with a squeal on the third syllable) was the largest and most prosperous on the entire coast. Remember this name!

The world behind the wall suddenly changed. The same man was there, and two others were with him along with the carcass of a bull. The first man held the same type of stone in his hand and stuck it into the carcass in the lower abdomen and began sawing a smooth cut with the stone.

"He does it well," SirriSill approved of the man, "but when you tear things apart it's bad."

"R-r-r," said UhirrMuhh.

The three of them, helping each other, skinned the carcass rather quickly. And the hide turned out to be surprisingly nice, not like the ones the dogs ended up with which had uneven edges with tatters and tears. But at the very least, they were able to primitively handle the task. Then something happened which caused UhirrMuhh's ears to perk up and for him to straighten up and become tense like a piano wire. The man went to another hide that had already been dried and sawed it exactly in half along the ridge. Then, with the same tool, he cut off a long narrow strip from one of the halves. Then seven more strips which he then tied into two with the simplest knots and then made loops at the ends. UhirrMuhh cocked his head to the side and parted his mouth. The man went to another dried skin, cut four holes in it at the front edge. UhirrMuhh whimpered and leaned forward, he had begun to understand... The man then passed one of the straps through a hole and tied it to the hide. At this point UhirrMuhh understood everything, he could not stand it and with a cry tried to rush into that world, "Do not dare without me!" but there was only a loud crack, then a red light flashed and a transparent wall stood in front of them. UhirrMuhh realized he couldn't go there! While the man was tying the other three straps, he cooled off and thought.

The man whistled, and a few strange-looking dogs came running.

"Oh, look, how shabby and low-browed. But they're still cute and funny!"

"Wait, let me think." UhirrMuhh seemed to have lost interest in what was happening as the man put on a loop on each of the four dogs, sat down on the hide, whistled and raced off through the grass behind the team waving goodbye.

UhirrMuhh sat and thought. He was having what could be called a technological revolution going on in his head and one after the other thoughts came of new uses for these straps.

Meanwhile, the show continued, but without the main character who had sped away with his team. The world behind the screen was almost unchanged and in it, somewhere in the background, other people started passing by and "shaggy low-browed" dogs also ran past. There were houses for people and pine trees grew everywhere and there was something that strongly attracted the couple who were staring at one spot. In this spot there was a shiny rectangle with small dark squares on what could be seen of the basement area of one of the houses.

"That's our entrance!"

"It's the same as ours, but it's not ours. It's not crumbling apart. The wall is a bit similar too but it's still different. It's covered with red on top and there is something strange in the holes and the terrain is also similar, but very different."

"UhirrMuhh, look at that! That is our rock! Our fang!"

"Yes, our rock ... A very similar world! How is it possible, both ours and not ours? Here, look where that thing is, we also have a similar wall. It's like the whole top has been blown off. And here there is nothing in that place. Interesting, but if you dig there? Maybe that world is..."

UhirrMuhh stopped a millimeter from a brilliant guess. Only his grandson would finally say: "This other world is our world in the past."

"Never mind, this is nonsense... Let's go home. Soon it will be morning and we need to think about how to deal with all this."

When the couple stepped out of the opening, the door quietly closed behind them. UhirrMuhh ran his paw over the dark square again and one of the little squares blinked. So, everything was in order, tomorrow the door would open again for them.

The next day, UhirrMuhh gathered the council of elders and delivered a speech: "Yesterday I found a passage which led to a very important place. Unfortunately, I don't have enough words to explain everything but there is someone very good there who can teach us very useful things. Every one of you will see it with your own eyes. Today you, and you, will come with me. We also need guards to protect the passage from the curious while we are in there."

"How is it that you know that he is good and teaches things that are useful?"

"How do I know he's good? I cannot explain, but you will see and you will understand. Why are the things useful? I saw myself and I regret that I did not think of such things earlier. For example, he taught us how to cut hides evenly. Is that useful?"

"Useful, useful," the council of elders agreed...

Thus UhirrMuhh with two elders and the first lady, whose fear from yesterday had been replaced by iron perseverance, repeated yesterday's procedure with buttons and went inside. The elders only said "Yes-ah-ah!" while staring at the talking person and UhirrMuhh went up to the stones and poked the biggest one with his nose. The man took his copy of it with both hands and swung it. UhirrMuhh also took the stone, standing on his hind legs, and swung it, an action that turned out to be quite impressive. The man then walked up to a small pine tree and struck the trunk at an angle with the sharp end of the stone. It produced a good cut into the tree. Then he hit it again close to the first cut and then higher, and the cut had grown considerably. Then he went to the other side and did the same thing, then on the back, until the notch encircled the whole trunk. Then he casually rested against the trunk and began to lightly push up against it until the tree collapsed with a crash.

"That's good," UhirrMuhh said, "we won't have to clean our muzzles from that muck anymore!"

The elders never uttered a sound. Only the position of their backs and heads, and the movements of their eyes, ears and tails betrayed the feverish workings of their thoughts and the boiling cauldron of their feelings.

The sessions went on and on. Around the clock sentries sat at the entrance, letting in two dogs at a time for a session following the decision of the council of elders and the leader. It was absolutely impossible to show the sacrament to the entire huge tribe, so visiting the Room was seen as a reward for successful labor. The man did various manipulations with stones, sometimes resorting to the help of his fellow tribesmen, sometimes alone. He always operated using the first stone that the viewer touched, but each time he did something different.

The most zealous and grateful member of the audience was, of course SirriSill, who took advantage of her position as first lady. Her whole appearance betrayed what that was happening was affecting her to the point causing her to tremble: she leaned her head this way and that, then leaned forward, then had one ear sticking up, then the other, then both at once, or her tail would start waggling joyfully, then it would nervously knock against the floor.

Suddenly she said: "I understand what the other world is talking about. And I even know his name: Rrghhakh Rudrnighkh. He always explains what he is going to do: 'I'll take a stone, I can cut the hide with it ... I will chop a tree down with this stone, I will twist a hole in the skin with this small sharp stone and put a strip of skin through it ..."

The tribe immediately rushed into the Middle Paleolithic Age at full speed. Every day, detachments of dogs, each with a pair of leather bags tied together with a belt and thrown over their backs, went to the upper reaches of the river. The bags, of course, were intended for stones that would be used as knives, scrapers and axes. The detachment usually went along with a cheerful road song, from which the blood in the veins of the wild animals of the foothills froze. They did not understand that these lingering sounds, which had terrified their ancestors, were just a cheerful song.

When the number of tools and instruments became sufficient the dogs felled a young pine grove in order to train themselves and test the stone axes. Then they started to think about what to do with the fallen trunks, and immediately invented enclosed pens for the calves, using the trees to form roofs which they then covered with earth and which greatly facilitated an end to endless digging and attempts to do away with the threat of arch collapses. Even the puppies switched from sticks to stones in their games.

Chuck Rudnick was constantly asked why he put so much energy into the Paleolithic training sessions. After all, a creature capable of typing a code using illuminated buttons could itself master all of the tools in a matter of hundreds of thousands of years and as a result, it would be stronger if it had come to the knowledge of everything in its own.

"Then what will happen to this when we disappear?" Chuck pointed at the Archive dome which was under construction. "You are so easily scattered over hundreds of thousands of years, but can you create a power source with a lifespan of, say, ten million years? Nonsense? Yes, there are only ten to the power of thirteen bits of engraving, just a dry sample of the main achievements. In addition, this "nonsense" still needs to be launched and then read, but first they need to be able to read the tablets with instructions. In the active memory there are ten to the power of eigthteen bits of a living human civilization, our ancestors and us, the Earth, people moving and talking, animals, landscapes, sounds, music and so on. If no one sees this, then everything about us will die completely. If that's the case is there any point in our existence in the here and now?

"Yes, the main principle here is that as many intelligent beings as possible see and perceive our world, but not only in its current state. It is important that intelligent beings see and know those who preceded them. Then their lives will have... Broader and deeper meanings, or something like that... Yes, and so we do not sink into oblivion... However we have no more than seven hundred thousand years for all this. There is no power source for more. We have nothing but plutonium 242 and uranium capsules. If during this time no one touches the touch lock, then it will be our deaths. Who will touch them? Yes, maybe at least his descendants." Chuck pointed to his Shustrik, who as if understanding what he was talking about, stood up on his hind legs and proudly lifted his head. Yes, most likely it will be his descendants. Primates, including us, have completely soured on Selina, and for them it has been the other way around. It's good that they graze livestock with us. They do the same thing without people in the North Bay where they graze herds, protect them from bears and slaughter young bulls for their food. In just a thousand years, they have turned from natural-born predators into independent herders here! That is real culture! Why did they make such a leap? I don't know, maybe one of the earthly scientists could explain... Apparently, the planet treated them much more favorably than us. Or the radiation dose during the flight had the opposite effect on them. Or Stefan Mukha successfully conjured something up on Earth? I don't know, but look: he is already seventeen years old but the dog is in its prime! They have even begun to live much longer here. There are now fewer and fewer of us. However, we still have at least three hundred years left. We should be able to finish!"

Chuck Rudnick, his team and his followers set up over a hundred and three "schools" at key locations on the planet, near the mouths of rivers, on their high banks and near the bays of the seas. Mainly in locations where there were cities and human settlements. Chuck, having mastered all of the primitive wisdom, recorded thousands of hours of lectures on the Waxman platform. Of course, the Paleolithic Course was only the first class. UhirrMuhh almost immediately noticed another door in the dark corner of the room and even ran his paw over the sensor, but the latter did not respond. The time had not yet come.

Beyond the Snowy Mountains

The mountains draw one to them most strongly in the early morning, when they are clearly visible in all of their purest colors. In the morning light, the ridges seem closer and more reachable than their dirty blue contours which appear through the daytime haze. For several mornings GaurGrimm had been coming and sitting on the gently sloping smooth rock rising above the boxwood thickets and looking at the mountains. This time he smelled the snowy peaks, the scent being brought by the morning breeze. It was a formidable fresh smell of rocks, snow and ice. Despite the most complex bouquet of fragrances picked up by the wind along the way, the smell of the mountains clearly stood out through the aromas of the nearby meadow with its cows, the smells of the deciduous forests filled with spur firs and spruce, and the invigorating smells of alpine meadows. This smell, being at once disturbing and inviting at the same time, was the last straw for him.

GaurGrymm went and found his wife in the meadow: “ArilSirr, that’s it, I’ve decided: I’m going. I can no longer live in peace until I see and feel with my own nose what is there, beyond the ridge.”

“I won’t let you! What if you don’t come back?! It’s very far and dangerous!”

“It’s not that far. And what is dangerous there? My head is in place, I am an adult Arrusikhan. How much can you possibly be afraid for me?”

“No, I won’t let you go! I won’t find peace! I’ll howl at night and scratch my back out of nervousness! I won’t let you go!”

“What do you mean you won’t let me go? What if I just pick up and leave?”

“I will follow you! I will follow you and howl until you turn back.”

“Yes, that’s an idea! If you can just walk and not howl, we’ll go together.”

“What about Arukhkh, Umyrr, Arsil and Sillar?”

"Why do they have so many aunts and uncles? The children will only be too happy to have some time without parental supervision."

"Well, if we go together, then it's not as scary as letting you go alone. What should you take with you?"

"We won't take food. We haven't quite forgotten how to hunt yet. We need to sew shoes and gloves with slots for our claws, they will come in handy on the hard snow. I will make patterns from bovine and sheep skin and you can sew them. Let's take a set of flints, I like a fire and baked fish. A small fishing net wouldn't hurt either. Yes, and perhaps that's all. We'll travel light."

Three days later they left.

How wonderful it is to climb up mountains when you are going light and in your prime! Every grade is a joy, when the legs seem to spring and push off on their own and the headwind brings with it an increasingly distinct smell of snowy peaks. Nowhere can you see so many new and unexpected things in one day as when climbing mountains, the vegetation, the air, the panoramic views and the feeling of being alive!

On the third day of their journey, GaurGrymm and ArilSirr quickly, with soft, precise jumps, overcame a heap of boulders that had blocked most of the valley, and reached the glacier. The fog was rolling in but they continued walking up the glacier, guided by the slope and direction of the wind. The path became easier, the wind died down, and the fog suddenly disappeared and the view opened up before them!

They sat in the middle of the most majestic mountain spectacle one could imagine. On the left, a smooth snowy slope rose, turning into an equally smooth, dazzling white dome with a sharp cliff on one side over which a loomed a menacingly blue curtain of blowing snow. To the right was a rocky ridge which rose higher and higher, culminating in two gigantic crenellations, between which nestled a small hanging glacier, ending in a greenish-blue cleft. And right in front of them, a snow-covered pass opened up, leading into the deep blue.

The couple froze in complete awe, absorbing the smell and sight of a hitherto unseen world that had nothing in common with the image that their imaginations had painted when viewed from afar. Something strange happened with time, as if the life on the coast that they had abandoned three days ago, their relatives, the village, the cattle, games and children were something from ancient times or from another era. All the passions of that era, quarrels with parents, a fight with a cousin, the envy for a neighbor who managed to make a boat out of rods and skins, seemed like some shameful trifles! What on earth are envy and anger for when there is something like this?!

It was quiet in the amphitheater, but the snowy flags fluttered over the mountain battlements, which meant that a strong wind was blowing from the other side, passing over the summit. It was easy to walk along the glacier, but when the steep ascent to the pass through the dense snow began, the travelers began to feel how thin the air was. Below, they would have galloped up such a rise with no problem but here even simply walking was hard and they had to constantly stop to catch their breath. Finally, they reached the saddle point. It was also on this side of the pass, where approximately five hundred thousand years ago Mark and his comrades fell into a snowdrift and dropped their backpacks. GaurGrymm felt the air from the Other Side and stood up to his full height and turned up his nose, expanding his nostrils. Yes, it was the smell of the Other Side, exciting and a little unusual. What was not in the smell was the question! Melting water, grinding stones, wet ice, lichens, goat droppings, small-grass meadows with buttercups, pines, spicy foliage of unknown trees – it was impossible to list everything that GaurGrymm's nose easily recognized in the gusts of the eastern wind.

"Do you sense it?" the husband asked.

"I do," the wife replied.

"Let's go take a look at all of it!"

"Let's go!"

The panorama was the same as it had been five hundred thousand years ago, with the exception of the mountain lake which had turned into a flat meadow, in some places overgrown with sea-side buckthorn bushes. The same wind blew, raising the fur on their backs and cooling their bellies. The same jackdaws made aero-acrobatic somersaults, catching butterflies brought up by the wind. Only this time the sentient beings overlooking the Inner Plain looked different. However, the feelings that they experienced were still almost the same.

"Let's go?" the husband asked.

Aril Sirri had wanted to persuade her husband to turn back from the pass, but when she saw and felt the new world, she realized that it was completely useless.

"Let's go," said the wife.

With long leaps, slipping and sliding through the dense snow, they quickly descended to the glacier, then crossed the glacier at a light trot, crossed the moraine in leaps and bounds and finally finding themselves in a high mountain meadow, felt terribly hungry. There was a lot of food around, hamsters, marmots and pikas, all of them fat and not scared. The couple really had not completely lost their hunting skills but they had lost the habit of eating raw meat and it turned out to be quite tasteless, but still satisfying. Such a dinner was enough for a couple of days in advance. The couple descended to the upper border of the forest, dug a lair under the roots of a twisted pine, raked dry needles into it and instantly fell asleep, curled up without waiting for the spectacle of the flashing stars and the rise of the two small moons.

The next day, coming out onto the plain, they came across was appeared to be an endless swamp where the river disappeared and decided to bypass the swamp on the right along a chain of hills. This took a couple of days and they eventually they again came to the river, which flowed further on between hard dry banks. Now their main diet was GaurGrymm's favorite dish, baked fish. Everything went well and the only thing missing was one important component in a journey in an unknown land, a sense of danger. Without it the path seemed dry and empty.

One evening ArilSirr became extremely alert: "There's a bear somewhere nearby, can you feel it?"

"Well, I feel it and what's more, I think we should just let him go his own way."

"What if he attacks us while we're sleeping?"

"Won't you wake up from the noise and smell of a walking bear?"

"I'll wake up, perhaps, but it's still scary."

"Why would a bear attack us? They are afraid of us. They all strive to secretly steal the calves when we are not around. And as soon as they see us, they immediately run away and leave their prey."

"Well, we have scientific bears there, they know who it's better not to mess with, but how can the local bears know?"

"They'll try something and find out. I know how to scare them away and here there are two of us."

"What if two bears attack at once?"

"Have you ever seen bears doing anything together? So that's it! Sleep well, you can snuggle closer."

A bear did not appear, neither in reality, nor in their dreams. So the spouses had to go on without a disturbing sense of danger. Otherwise, the path along the river was pleasant and interesting, but Aril Sirr increasingly reminded him about home.

"How far will we go? It's good here, but we have already seen all the interesting things, and at home the children are waiting."

"Wait, I'm sure that the most interesting and the main thing is still ahead. Soon."

Another couple of days passed, and GaurGrymm, sniffing the air, stood up to his full height.

"Do you feel it?"

"I feel something. Something related to water, but unusual."

"Yes, but not only with water. It still smells of the ruins left by people. Like we have across the river, where the walls with holes are and the piles of stones and the Big Dome."

The bank of the river became higher and steeper. The slope was overgrown with dense forest, and a fragrant steppe with feathery grass, flowers and luxurious thistles stretched to the side. It was full of gophers, but the travelers had no time for them as they walked along a slightly sloping hilly steppe, rising and gradually moving away from the river, to where something light gray could be seen on the horizon. It was the Dome. The same Great Dome that stood across their river, only this one did not have trees on top and the entrance was high above the ground.

"Eh," said GaurGrymm, "no one has been here yet, but without a good log we can't climb."

"What for? Surely the same thing will be shown on the wall here, but you won't be able to open the second door again."

"I wonder why people made the second door that we can't open. It is necessary to press the buttons correctly, but no one has yet managed to do it. People probably thought we were fools who could only be let in through the first door."

"Maybe we are fools if we can't press the buttons correctly. People might have expected someone else to come here, someone smarter than us, and open the second door, behind which there is something important."

"Where have the people gone? Gone somewhere? But why? It's so good here, both here and on the shore and beyond the mountains."

"Perhaps they have found a place where they are much better off? And where did we come from? After all, in what the Dome and the School show, we are not there, only dogs that look a little like us. Where are the dogs now? Gone with the people?"

"Listen, maybe the second door will be opened not by some aliens, but by our descendants? Look, Arukhh is so smart at the age of four! Oh, you feel that? Again there was a scent of some sort of unusual water, from over there."

Where GaurGrymm pointed, a ravine began, which in the distance became deeper and then turned into a valley covered with forest. The travelers preferred to travel along the top of the gully over a flat field, holding their course in direction of the smell. The field ended and they entered an oak forest, where a steep descent immediately began. Through the trees, an intriguing space shone through which had not yet formed into a single picture. However, the gaps became wider and soon merged into an unexpected panorama: in front of the travelers lay a wide meadow-like valley, an arc enveloping a mountain that looked like a lying human fist, the top of which was covered with forest, with the fingers being the steppe, and in the hollows between the fingers were strips of shrubs and trees. However most importantly, the valley spread outward to a wide body of water from which the enticing smell came.

The couple went down into the expansive peaceful meadow, where old oaks and lindens grew and a small herd of deer grazed in the distance. GaurGrymm and ArilSirr crossed the meadow and on the other side of the valley ran into a wide ravine with a fresh-looking cliff. There were walls at the bottom of the ravine, solid monolithic walls with rectangular windows. The same walls went straight into the slope of the cliff.

"People lived here, many people," concluded GuarGrymm. "Probably, their houses were all over the valley but then they went underground and here the water washed out the ravine, and the ruins of houses were on the surface."

"Maybe people left these places because their houses went underground?"

"You think that that they were just swallowed up by the ground? No, the people left first, leaving the houses and the Dome up there, and only then did the houses gradually become covered with earth. My great grandfather built stone corrals for livestock. So its walls have also been covered by the earth since then. Everything from below is covered by earth. The one on top is not, which is why people built domes on high places. They wanted us to find them."

"So they left something very important inside behind the second door? I don't understand why they left it? Why leave something important? For whom, for us? Why doesn't the second door open then? What could possibly be so important?"

"I wish I knew at least one answer. Let's go, there is such interesting water! Probably a big lake."

They trotted towards the mouth of the valley. On the descent to the water, ruins protruded from the ground, as in the ravine, the remains of walls, rickety monoliths, an arch that miraculously survived and finally, the pebbly beach...

"Look ArilSirr, it's a river!"

"How is that a river? How big can a river be?"

"Look, you can't see the shore either there or there. And it's flowing fast! Look! See it flows just like a river!"

"It's flowing all right... And oh, how it smells! What a powerful smell! It's so heartbreaking! After all, none of our kind knows that there are such rivers!"

"Look, what a sandy shore there is, what big trees."

"Let's swim over there!"

"Are you kidding?! That's too far to swim!"

"And so what if it is far away? The water is warm, we won't freeze. But I promise you that the other side will be the last place. From there we will turn back and head home."

The last argument worked. The couple went further upstream and then swam, leaving slanting waves on the smooth water. Swimming was fun at first, the mountain shore was rapidly moving away but then everything seemed to freeze, the shore they left stopped receding and the opposite sandy shore still did not appear to be approaching. All they could see was the current carrying them down stream.

GaurGrymm and ArilSirr, being excellent swimmers, did not panic, but they fully felt the entire greatness and power of the river. Finally, the opposite shore with the large trees began to approach rapidly and soon the tired spouses, having emerged from the water, shook themselves off, emitting clouds of spray. Then, seeing the purest quartz sand under their feet, they rushed at a gallop along the water's edge, then again into the water, sending out fountains of spray with each jump! Then with a growl they rushed at each other, imitating a struggle and fell down with a screech, after having gone under the water with their heads. However, fatigue took its toll and they again shook themselves off on the shore and climbed up to the huge tree, in the shade of which they fell asleep peacefully.

When the sun passed its zenith and the shadows were gone, GaurGrymm awoke. He lay for a long time, with his head in his paws and looked at the river and at the mountains. Having waited for ArilSirr to wake up, he said: "You know, it suddenly seems to me that I was born here, that I have already inhaled these smells and ran here on the sand in my deep childhood. And the mountains and that valley seem familiar."

"You couldn't have been born here. You just feel good here, because it seems so comfortable. And I'm good here too."

"So let's move here! Let's go back, pick up the kids and get the calves and the sheep. It's crowded on the coast there, that's why quarrels occur. And here you can have as many pastures as you like, as many fish as you like, and as many children as you like. We will settle in the valley where people lived, we will dig spacious dugouts on the slopes and we will swim here from time to time, and I will finally make a boat."

"It's hard to move, but I think I agree. Not now, but next summer. Let the kids get a little stronger."

"Could be so. It would be better if two or three more families moved here with us. It is easier to graze cattle, and the children will have someone to marry."

"And how will we lead the calves through the glaciers and the pass?"

"We'll have to pull them over with ropes one at a time. This is why we need adult helpers. I think let's spend the night here and go home in the morning. Over there in that channel, judging by the smell, it's full of fish."

When the couple had dinner and settled down for the night under the black poplar, ArilSirr asked again: "Still, what is so important in these domes? Why did people build them?"

"You keep asking questions, and I think the most important thing in the domes is the answers. The answer to the question: Where did the people go? And some more things: Where did they come from? Where is the end of the world? How did we appear here? And most importantly: Why? Probably, people did not appear here by accident but had some kind of common cause and there must be more important business in the world besides herding cattle and eating. It seems to me that there are answers to all these questions in the domes. I think when we get smart enough to understand the answers, we will be able to open the second door."

Lighthouse of Atlantis

The first ocean-going ship in post-human history, the Atlantis (commonly pronounced Ardlanchida), was preparing for its first ocean voyage to the mainland after which it had been named. The existence of the mainland was only known from maps and books left by people in the library of the Dome. Being a little clumsy and quite heavy, the three-masted ship was not a marvel of shipbuilding art but it was stable in the waters. It was built with the knowledge of the theory of shipbuilding, but without the practice or the knowledge of many necessary details that are difficult to convey in writing. Therefore, it took a long time to build as they tried to master the craft along the way.

The choice of the type of ship to build had been an extremely simple one and they chose a schooner as the only option. This was not because schooners sail better while tacking at steep angles, the reason was much simpler – they had slanting sails and only slanting sails can be directed and adjusted from the deck. To steer a ship with straight sails, a horde of sailors with the agility of monkeys had to climb the shrouds at the same time. The Arrucihanes were not monkeys at all, they were digitigrade creatures, unlike us plantigrades. Their feet, if you can call them that, are much more difficult to use to grab or balance on a rope than our hands and feet. Of course, it was possible for them to climb the shrouds, but only slowly and carefully, so that any captain who gave the command to "reef ahead" would have had a fit of rage at their progress.

The Atlantis was being loaded at a high log pier and the stocky longshoredogs, auburn-haired and black-faced, rolled trolleys loaded with supplies and gear up the long ramp in teams of two. On board a winch creaked, lowering the trolleys into the hold and the captain stood on the bridge, watching the loading. They had to hurry in order to sail no later than at three in the afternoon. The captain was a tall, middle-aged sailor with a torn ear and scars on his cheeks and under his eyes, the results of duels of honor. The captain's ear was injured in a duel with the owner of a commercial coastal fleet, who denied the existence of Atlantis and Australia.

"These are all inventions of people who slipped us fake maps with two non-existent continents," argued the owner of six wretched vessels, on which no one dared to go farther off the coast than to the point where it was still possible to see land.

Unfortunately, he said it once in the presence of the captain.

"Life will punish you for your stupidity, and you will answer to me for slandering people!" said the captain in the presence of seven witnesses. Refusal to fight threatened one with the loss of reputation for life, which was much worse than losing life itself. The ship-owner accepted the challenge and tore the captain's ear, which was considered a vile trick. Again, his actions were unfortunate for him. Enraged with pain, the captain dodged and grabbed the ship-owner by the side by the neck, knocked him down and pulled him along the ground but his enemy did not give up and kept trying to bite the captain's legs from a prone position. It was all in vain, feeling all of the movements of the prone opponent, the captain avoided the enemy's teeth, and firmly pressed the head and shoulders of the ship-owner to the ground. The most he could have done was to raise his buttocks and rotate jerkily, moving his legs around. Having exhausted the enemy, the captain let him go and allowed him to stand up. Then he grabbed him by the back of the neck with his teeth and gritted them so hard that the ship-owner whined and sank to his knees, a sign of defeat.

That had been about seven years ago, when the fundraising for the construction of Atlantis had just begun and now the team and the those escorting them were gradually gathering on the pier. The participants of the expedition could be recognized by their leather harness, to which all kinds of pockets with small things in them were attached, folding knives, awls and other personal tools. The sailors did not need much so they all had small bundles on their backs. Only one of them had a heavy bundle, a student named Ruank Uxarr, who took at least a dozen books on the expedition.

"Do you think you will have the time and desire to read all that?" asked the sturman. "You are an optimist!"

Ruank was the only rookie from the whole team. However, no one had any experience in ocean navigation and until now, ships only sailed from port to port along the coast. Ruank was hired on the team thanks to the erudition he showed during the interview, his knowledge base contained a lot of heterogeneous information gleaned from a wide variety of books, everything from the Myths of Ancient Greece, translated from the languages of people to The Path of Bears to the Polar Snows, diaries of the famous expedition of Vyra Agraujarra. The navigator liked Ruank and promised to take patronage over him. Needless to say, sailing to Atlantis had been one of Ruank's fondest dreams and now he was glowing with happiness.

The loading was finally completed and the team assembled and a miracle of technology would see the ship off to Atlantis, namely the first and so far the only steam tugboat in the world. Usually, ships were towed from the pier by six-oared boats, but the Atlantis deserved a special honor and the tug was launched just for the occasion. Its weak point was its two cylinders motor, the specifics of processing large parts had not yet been given to the craftsmen. Therefore, the consumption of steam and oil was horrendous and the efficiency approached zero with the entire harbor being covered with gray smoke from a peat furnace, where frantic, dirty-red stokers with scorched whiskers were slaving away. The tug puffed and clanged, but pulled the schooner! It actually pulled much stronger than even two six-oared boats and the craftsmen promised to make much better cylinders in six months.

A large crowd had gathered on the beach. Ruank's parents and his friends were there. They waved their farewells as the water hissed behind the stern of the tug as the Atlantis slowly moved away in a puff of smoke. The crowd on the shore sang a song of farewell for distant travelers and the sailors sang along.

Most were a little sad but not Ruank. *What a pity they are left on the shore,* he thought. *They have ordinary lives ahead of them, in which there will be nothing bright nor any adventures. How good for it was for him and what happiness lay ahead! Everything would be new, the ocean and the new continent, never before seen animals, untrodden expanses, unfamiliar mountains, new rivers and even the unknown stars of the southern sky.*

The tugboat pulled the Atlantis out of the harbor and the long-awaited command "raise the sails" sounded, the sails caught the wind and the water rustled along the sides. The heavy vessel was finally moving smoothly towards the southwest.

After a few days of happy sailing a strong storm arose and all the sails had to be removed except for the mainsail and staysail. Ruank soon understood that the ocean was not to be trifled with and while he was wondering if the onset of nausea would ever go away, he vomited right onto the deck... Fortunately, his comrades, who themselves had all once experienced something similar, cleaned up after him and brought a basin but he got worse and worse. There was no longer any food left in the stomach and he vomited yellow foam, and excruciating spasms began. Ruank felt like he was completely broken and he couldn't even get up. He was ready to curse the moment he had decided to join the expedition but he could not curse, because he could do nothing, even mental exercises were beyond his strength.

All of this went on for what seemed to be an infinitely long time. With the ending of the storm the pitching subsided a little but did not stop and only on the fourth day was he able to drink some water. On the fifth day, he raised his head and looked around at what was going on. Nothing was happening: the deck was empty and only three sailors from the night watch were snoring on the sidelines. On the sixth day, he raised his head again and sensed that the other dogs were having dinner. He shuddered at the smell of food. On the seventh day he asked his comrades to bring him some food. On the eighth day he got up for dinner and actually walked, his legs far apart. He didn't look like a pale ghost for the sole reason than his fur hid the color and texture of his skin. The team greeted him with a stormy greeting and congratulated him on his initiation as a sailor.

A couple of days later, Ruank was already on duty and his happiness had returned. It was a sun filled happiness in a fresh blue space full of salt spray. A steady west wind blew and the schooner was on the left tack so there was not much work to do. Ruank even had time to read. He tried to master the knowledge in a useful translated book called *Sailing Equipment of Ships of the 17th–19th Centuries*, but broke off somewhere in the middle and decided to take up another translated work titled: *Fauna of the Equatorial Belt of Selina*.

On the fifty-fifth day of the journey, Ruank Uxarr smelled dry land. You don't sense the smell while living at home, but only after spending many days on the ocean, having been weaned away from it. After a while you cease to feel that something is missing in the sea air so you easily recognize the familiar smells, barely peeking through the scents of the ocean and the ship, even if the land is completely different and has different smells. Ruank immediately reported the smell to the captain.

"Maybe I ruined my nose twenty years ago when I worked as a tar miner in a shipyard as you can see. The wind is from the southeast, which is about where Atlantis should be. Too bad we can't say for sure. Maybe by using the azimuth of the sunset we can get a clear picture of where we are. The magnetic declination is not exactly known here either. Let's keep following the left tack to the south for the time being and if we don't see signs of land, closer to nightfall, we will switch to the right tack and we keep a course to the southeast. Atlantis is big, we won't miss it.

Soon five more sailors smelled dry land.

The sun did not come out until right before sunset because of high thin clouds but at night the sky cleared and the sea calmed down.

The navigator brought the instruments on deck and called Ruank:

"Come on, you will point at the stars that I dictate to you. You have better eyes than mine. Do you see the horizon?"

"No, it's too dark. If Auarr, or at least Gownorr, were in the sky..."

"Okay, then we don't need a sextant. In this case, there is a quadrant with plumb lines. The accuracy is worse, but at least we'll determine our location within ten-minute accuracy. Bring a couple of cups of water for the weights."

The navigator slowly turned the screws, aligning the tool, and continued: "Have you seen the map of the sky that people have made?"

"I saw it hanging at the entrance to the second circle of the Dome but I didn't look at it."

"Just so you know it is not at all like this sky."

"Yes, I understand that the stars move, that's why the constellations have changed."

"They are moving, what else could they do? Everything is moving, and we aren't sitting still either..."

"Of all the constellations, only the Flock survived, it became a little wider. People used to call it Pleiades."

"Why didn't it break apart like the rest?"

"Read the book 'Principles of Astronomy'. The Flock is very far away – they are bright young stars that were born together and move together. Then they will eventually all scatter to the sides but very slowly. All the other constellations have disappeared. The Polar Triangle disappeared but the Polar Pair appeared instead. It is very convenient to measure latitude using it, but now the Fox has gone below the horizon since we are very close to the equator and the Hare barely shines through the haze. We will use the Navigator's Triangle, Diamond, Emerald and Ruby, there they are. Come on, point the pipe at Ruby. The people called it Betelgeuse. Good point? You didn't disturb the base, did you? So, fifty-three degrees and twenty-three minutes. Oh what inconvenient units of measurement were invented by people. In some places everything is in tens, in others in minutes, which by the way for some reason are sixty and not a hundred. Why three hundred and sixty degrees, and not a hundred or a thousand? Well, it could have been at least four hundred, one hundred per quadrant. Then three hundred and sixty... Where, what inspired them? And where should we go? Borrowed something without thinking, now it's too late... Come on, now the Diamond... Two, in principle, is enough, but three is more accurate. Point at the Emerald, people called it Rigel... Now let's go to the cabin. Here are the tables, look at the Navigator's Triangle. The height of the Diamond, in the second column is the Emerald..."

The navigator wrote out numbers on a piece of paper with a pencil, multiplied something, added something up and announced: we are at zero degrees thirty-something minutes north latitude. The local time is two hours thirty-five minutes at night, not now but ten minutes ago when they had pointed the pipe at the stars. How to determine longitude now?

"Take a chronometer and see what time it was ten minutes ago in our port. Then do some recalculation..."

"Somehow we count. Our time at the time of observation was eleven forty-five in the evening. We translate the damn hours into stupid degrees. Multiply by fifteen and more idiotic minutes divided by four and then added. Who came up with all this!? So, our longitude is east, forty-two and a half degrees. We are here... The nearest point of Atlantis is only two hundred kilometers away. So that you were not mistaken when you smell dry land. Wow, look what a bright star has risen to the very south! On the very horizon. Apparently, it is very close to the south pole of the sky. No one has seen it yet! No one except us has been so close to the equator. It's so low and already so bright!"

"No way, is it the brightest star in the whole sky? And look at the reflection on the water!"

"Yes, being higher above the horizon , it will outshine all the other stars. I'll bet my tail that it's the brightest and much brighter than the rest. There were no people from that star on the celestial map. On it the Diamond was the brightest. Apparently, some of the stars from the times of people have flown by close to us."

“Listen, do we have the right to name it?”

“Who can stop us? Unless they rename it later.”

“Do you have any idea?”

“I’m kind of a nobody. To name the brightest star in the sky is too great an honor. Who am I?”

“You are one of those who first reached the equator. A pioneer! So chin up!”

“If I were a man, I would call it Aphrodite (Ruank pronounced it ‘Achrodida’), the goddess of beauty, born from water as this star rose from water. We have already borrowed too much from people. Are our imaginations so much worse that we can’t come up with anything of our own?!”

The calm continued all night, but in the morning a fresh west wind blew. The Atlantis ran briskly south-south-west at a speed of nine knots, which was an excellent result for such a floating pot. In the evening, the watchman barked and yelled with all his might: “Land, land! I see a mountain, fifteen degrees to the right of course. The captain ran up to the bridge and aimed his spyglass.”

“Mountains. There’s a whole range there. Change course for fifteen degrees steeper into the wind. We’ll be there by morning.”

The whole team went upstairs. Gradually it got dark, but no one was in a hurry to leave the deck. Who could possibly sleep? And besides, the brightest southern star any of them had ever seen had risen, one which none of the sailors, except Ruank, the navigator and the captain, had yet witnessed. While everyone was admiring the star, one of the sailors shouted: “Directly on course! A storm! I just saw a lightning bolt!”

“Strange, the sky is clear and the wind is fresh and even. There shouldn’t be a storm. Oh, really! Lightning again.”

Everyone stared ahead as the flashes continued straight ahead.

"Stop! That's not lightning!" Ruank shouted. "They repeat at regular intervals. Every eleven seconds! If you don't believe me count for yourselves."

"Yes," said the navigator, "not eleven, but exactly ten seconds. This cannot be the work of nature. There is someone there!"

Half of the sailors had the hair on their backs standing on end and the youngest growled dully. The crew was frozen, looking ahead at the mysterious lightning, experiencing muffled fear, as if it had leaked from the distant past. An under tensioned staysail clapped in the wind, and the water rustled along the side of the ship and to the right in time with the rolling waves. The schooner moved like a ghost ship, with bewitched silent sailors on board.

Only when Auarr ascended in the west did the Navigator break the silence: "Are there people left?"

"Then why didn't they come for us? Why is there nothing in the Dome's library about people left on Atlantis?" Ruank objected.

"Then who, if not people?"

"Something new, like us. There's nothing about us in the Dome's library either."

The sailors thought. Maybe their brothers are there? But how do they arrange such outbursts of light? The Arrucihans are incapable of such a thing. Maybe they have leaped ahead in their development? Or maybe there were still people who decided to hide on Atlantis? Or maybe it's someone else completely unknown because the world is huge.

Everyone looked ahead. The lightning became brighter it became clear that it came from one point just over the horizon.

"I see a flashing fire!" said the duty officer from the foremast.

"Maybe we should go around this fire and land to the south?" suggested the captain's first mate. The team murmured in approval.

"That's enough!" the captain growled. "Why do you think this fire is a threat? Why are you afraid of the mysterious and incomprehensible? This fear is an atavism inherited from our wild ancestors! A hundred chances to one that there is no threat there but a hundred chances out of a hundred that it is unusually interesting. Everything unknown is interesting at first, and only then can it turn out to be dangerous. We are not cowards to think otherwise. Urahamm," the captain turned to the navigator, "let's go look at the map."

"What's this?" The captain jabbed his claw at the long, curved headland at the northeastern tip of Atlantis.

"That is a cape," answered the navigator. "It is the nearest edge of the mainland to us."

"I can see that it's a cape. What does this star on the cape mean?"

"Rock, I think."

"And there, on the reverse side, isn't it written what kind of asterisk it is?" the captain asked.

The navigator turned over the map.

"Yes, there is an asterisk here, and something is written, but I do not know human language."

"How do you chart a course on human maps without knowing the human language?"

"Yes, everything is clear here. In addition, I learned a lot in translation. Do you know their language?"

"No, I don't know either," the captain replied conciliatorily.

"I think Ruank knows. He has a head stuffed with all sorts of human goddesses and the devil knows what else."

They called Ruank.

"Can you translate?" asked the navigator, pointing to the caption for the star.

"I don't know the language of people very well. There is something strange here: a house of light, but it is written together, as if it is translated in one word. But I don't know that word."

"Light house, light house..." the captain muttered. "That sounds like something like the truth. We see the flashes of light but what does the house have to do with it?"

"Oh, we are idiots! How did we not guess right away?" the navigator exclaimed. "Yes, it's a lighthouse! Even sheep would understand. Remember our old lighthouses! This lighthouse was made by people and put on the map."

"Wait," said the captain, "can you imagine a beacon as bright as lightning? And how long has it been working on its own? Scientists say that people left the world no less than a hundred thousand years ago, and maybe all of three hundred thousand and all this time it has been emitting such flashes? For whom? Surely, they had to go out of their way to make something that could work for so long."

"It seems to me that I understand for whom the people made this eternal lighthouse," Ruank said. "For us!"

"You're right! For us! You, me, the captain and the team?" the navigator objected. "Wouldn't that be too much of an honor?"

"Not exactly for us, but for anyone who would sail here in the times when there would no longer be people in the world. We were the first of these. Therefore, the lighthouse shines for us. This is its purpose."

"Imagine yourself if you were in the people position: full of things to do, but not such difficult things and then here is a much more complicated matter for someone unknown, who perhaps will only appear in the far distant future. Would you do that?"

"It all depends on the future of my own kind. If I knew that many generations would come after me, then I would leave such things for them, and I myself would work for myself, for my children and grandchildren. If I knew that our family was ending and that there was no one else to take care of the inhabitants of the distant future, I would think about it.

Most likely I would have made up my mind to do it too, otherwise life seems to lose its meaning."

When the last doubts about the nature of the flickering light had disappeared, the captain ordered the crew to change course for five degrees to the left of the lighthouse in order to go around the sharp long cape and enter the bay that was being protected by it. The ship slowed down so as to pass the lighthouse when it was light. After the sun started to come up the flashes stopped and in the pinkish morning twilight, the sailors saw a pillar, a dark gray monolith twice as tall as the Fang, slightly tapered at the top standing on a high rocky promontory. The captain ordered the crew to drop anchor and lower the landing boat. Then the sailors rowed to the base of the lighthouse. The pillar was of a very hard unknown stone that went straight into the rock and its top was crowned with a dark shiny cylinder. The surface of the pillar turned out to be so smooth that it became obvious: this structure was too tough for any cataclysms, tsunami or even time to destroy. The lighthouse tilted only slightly, as the rock layers of the cape also tilted slightly.

"Human beings were far more powerful than the ancient gods they themselves imagined," Ruank concluded.

"But why did they put the lighthouse far from the shore? It would have been necessary to put it on the most extreme rock surface near the water so that no one would run into it."

No one on the ship came up with a single sane idea of how such a thing could work. How could the crew know what a uranium capsule, capacitors and heavy-duty LEDs were. This knowledge was in the Dome, but in those departments where no one had yet reached.

"I have an idea!" Ruank suddenly exclaimed. "Let's call the bright star Lighthouse! Or even the Lighthouse of Atlantis."

"Atlantis? In honor of the ship or the mainland?"

"Let everyone think that the star is named after the mainland, and we and all our friends and relatives will know that this is our ship immortalized in the southern sky."

The Atlantis anchored in the bay about five hundred meters from the sandy beach. The navigator and two sailors, who were punished for improper cleanliness, remained on board. Two boats were lowered into the water, barrels for water, axes and guns were loaded into them. The sailors, except for the captain and those who were assigned as rowers, poured into the water and swam to the shore themselves, enjoying the light coolness of the unusually clear water.

On the shore, the team divided into three groups: the first group led by the captain, went north to a ravine in the coastal hills in search of fresh water. Another group, the largest, went deep into the savannah to replenish their food supplies and the third, the smallest, headed south along the coast without a specific task instructed to act at its discretion and carry out reconnaissance. Ruank was in the third group and it seemed that the beaches, which had no end in sight, did not promise anything interesting. The sailors were about to turn away from the shore and head inland when suddenly, three hundred meters away, three lions came out of the bushes onto the beach.

"Wow, what big kitties!" Vyuramm, the senior member of the group, said. "However, they are not anything compared to our bears. They don't seem to like us."

Slowly the lions, growling menacingly, approached the sailors.

"Why should they like us?" Ruank replied. "This is their territory. They consider themselves in charge here. We are just arrogant aliens to them."

"Let's just do our job, sail away, and they will once again be the main ones here. Right now it would be useful to scare them off so that they don't interfere."

"Shall we perform a bear march for them?"

"Let's do it. Take my flask, you be the drummer. Graxurr, just don't try to shoot these beauties with your cannon. If anything, shoot in the air but I think it won't be needed."

All six stood up to their full height and, shaking their hands over their heads, moved in a line towards the lions. The drummer beat the rhythm with two brass flasks, two others loudly barked to the beat, two heart-rendingly squealed out of rhythm and two more, including the drummer, howled continuously.

The lions stopped, flattened their ears and bristled. The male's mane stood up so that the drummer and Ruank could hardly restrain themselves from bursting out barking. Suddenly, the drummer switched to a fast beat, and six sailors crouched and jumped, roaring in unison, and then did it again.

The first maned macho could not stand it. He backed away, turned around and ran away. Almost immediately behind him was one of the lionesses. But another lioness, apparently the main one, remained. Crouching to the ground with her ears flattened, she continued to snarl, more in desperation than in menace. Apparently, some kind of lion's honor did not allow her to take flight, despite all the horror of what was happening.

"She is in shock and capable of doing something unpredictable," Vyuramm said. "We need to bring her to her senses. Ruank, let's play double claws with her, just be careful and you come in from the right."

The two sailors began to slowly come at her from different directions. The lioness quickly looked from one to the other. Vyuramm made a light lunge, the lioness rushed towards him, at that moment Ruank rushed forward, grabbed her thigh and managed to shake her with clenched jaws a couple of times while the lioness turned around, raising her paw to hit him. The blow fell into empty space where Ruank had already not been for a long time, and at that moment Vyuramm was already tormenting the other thigh of the lioness. While she turned around again, the sailors slightly jumped back, opening the way for the lioness to retreat, which she immediately took advantage of, rushing to catch up with her relatives.

The lions ran across the yellow sand of the beach. Simply put, they fled in confusion, having lost the status of kings of the local nature. Now they will watch the terrible aliens from the thickets, trying to stay unnoticed. But the aliens will disappear, and the lions would not be able to pass on their dormant fear to their children, who would again become kings of the shore of the bay until the next expedition arrived.

All three groups returned with trophies. The first one found water, however, it tasted disgusting. The second shot down five weighty antelopes. ("Unsportsmanlike," the captain grumbled, "as if it wasn't possible to hunt them down honestly, being as there are so many of you.") The third group gathered a wealth of impressions and stories. There was however one victim who returned walking on three limbs after trying to catch a porcupine.

Then they had a feast. A month and a half of dried meat soaked in water, and finally here was fresh game... The journey to the south along the coast promised to be a like holiday tour but the holiday was spoiled at the very beginning and the feast proved to have been a mistake. The whole team was struck down by severe intestinal infections. The regular latrines could not cope with the constant usage and the fittest had to build a platform at the stern hanging overboard: on the edge of the platform, five to seven sailors at a time suffered in a characteristic pose with arched backs and a raised tail. The doctor ordered that they open a barrel of disgusting liquor: a frothy drink brewed from barley and malt made worse by being fermented. To add to everything this muck affected their coordination and made them choke, but in accordance with the strictest orders they drank it. Oddly enough the swill helped. The doctor explained that, most likely, their sickness came from the new water and gave strict orders that it be boiled in the future. The crew slowly got better but, alas not all of them. One of the sailors died from the intestinal scourge. He had been a cheerful, efficient sailor, almost all black with a white stripe from the crown of the head to the top if his nose and had white "socks and gloves". Actually, he was the only sailor who did not live to see the return of the Atlantis. One of seventy-four, which was a phenomenally low loss for similar expeditions, phenomenally small... But just try to tell that to his wife and parents!

Probably, the crews of sailing ships of all planets bury their comrades in the same way. The body, along with a couple of cobblestones, is placed into a bag, then a team lines up on the deck, stands at attention and sings a farewell tribute... Under a volley of fifteen guns, the bag is then released... Thus it was on the Atlantis.

As the ship was heading south it was sometimes accompanied by curious dolphins. A couple of times a herd of elephants appeared on the shore and several times they saw giraffes. Ruank recognized all these animals thanks to a book he had just read. The entire crew listened to his comments tilting their heads to the side with open mouths.

The abundance of events was so much that the captain was unable to cope with keeping the ship's diary and appointed Ruank as a clerk. "September 12, 12:00. Twelve degrees forty-five minutes south forty-one degrees thirty-four minutes, depth one hundred and twenty meters, bottom soil gray sand. The distance to the coast is three kilometers. The landscape is hilly. The type of vegetation is savannah. We observed two rhinos and a flock of baboons. We maintain a SSW course. And so on. Ruank kept his personal diary as well, making notes before going to bed every night by the light of a kerosene lamp.

The temperature was getting cooler and soon, on land, the savanna was replaced by desert, then the desert turned into forests which, as they moved south, became more opulent and greener.

The expedition had to return no later than eight months after sailing to avoid the tropical storm season and according to the navigator's calculations, they should not travel further than fifty degrees south latitude in order to avoid any unneeded haste on the return trip. At that exact latitude the Atlantis anchored in a wide bay with pebbly shores. Here a fast flowing river filled with clear water flowed into the bay. Beyond the pebbles were meadows with short dense grass, then a pine forest began, covering the slopes of the coastal mountains. The team landed on the shore to replenish supplies, rest on the cozy shore and then set about on starting the return journey.

Ruank relaxed by lying on his back on dense grass and sliding around while the other members of the team rested in their own ways, some lying on their sides, some on their backs and some just lying and rubbing their heads against the grass. Everything was peaceful and then their ancestors came out of the forest!

Yes, they were wolves. The pack stood in a line at the edge of the forest. The wolves were curious but scared. Ruank wagged his tail and the leader wagged his just a little in response, but fear outweighed any friendliness and the pack disappeared into the undergrowth. This was the first such meeting in history. Wolves were not found in Borealia. If they had been there at one time, they had long ago assimilated among the Praarrusihan hundreds of thousands of years ago. Just in case, the commander ordered them not to go out alone, even though the wolves were inferior to the sailors in size and strength, who knows what they had in mind.

In the evening, after the next shift was sent to ship duty, a fire was lit to roast the roe deer. They decided to spend the night right there on the grass and sat and talked about the way back, remembering the lighthouse. All of a sudden Ruank heard a whine behind him and turned and saw two glowing orange eyes in the dark, only twenty paces away. The creature behind the eyes whimpered again. Ruank turned, wagged his tail, and whined in response. The creature took a few steps forward and appeared in the firelight. It was a slender young she-wolf. Ruank wagged his tail even more intensively, then the she-wolf carefully bent her paws, flattened her ears and wagging her tail between her legs, slowly approached. Ruank allowed himself to be sniffed (a ritual that had gone out of use in the Neolithic era and was now considered indecent) and it had a striking effect as the she-wolf calmed down and sat nearby.

"Wyuramm, toss me a piece of meat!" shouted Ruank.

He caught the flying piece of meat with his teeth and placed it in front of the she-wolf. She hesitated a little and without taking her eyes off Ruank, took the piece and began to chew with obvious pleasure. Having finished with the treat, the she-wolf opened her mouth, as if smiling, and then something incredible happened.

Ruank, not knowing why (he just suddenly felt like it), stretched out his hand to the she-wolf and said "give me your paw."

She responded but how was it that she knew what he wanted from her? The she-wolf put her paw into the open palm of her distant evolutionary descendant. The wolf's paw lay in a hand covered with the same hair and the same callouses but with a wider palm, longer fingers ending in wider and shorter claws, and an opposing fifth finger. They were relatives, separated by half a million years, when one had been kicked out of its natural environment and had gone through a whole series of ups and downs and metamorphoses, the other had stayed in safe homeostasis and did not even notice the relocation to other planets.

"Here we meet!" Ruank slightly squeezed the outstretched paw and shook his hand.

The she-wolf did not leave, and when the sailors settled down to sleep, she curled and peacefully fell asleep next to Ruank.

In the morning, Ruank was awaken by the she-wolf gently licking his ear and the sailors chatted animatedly: "So, we have a new crew member?"

"Yeah, a ready-made permanent kitchen attendant!"

"Yes, right! A woman on the ship! What could be scarier?"

"Look, she's seriously in love with Ruank!"

The she-wolf did move a single step away from Ruank and rubbed against him, turned over on her back in front of him, flirted and tried to lick his ear. Ruank liked it but he was embarrassed by the certain unnaturalness of the situation. He gently rejected her caresses, but willingly played with her. They rushed around in circles, rolled over on their backs, then one lay on their back and the other pounced with a growl and carefully grabbed the other's neck.

Soon it was time to sail. When the first boat loaded and sailed away the she-wolf became alarmed. When the last landing boat, the captain's boat on which Ruank would sail away in, was being prepared, she whined and ran back and forth along the shore. Then when the boat was pushed away, she entered the water, as if trying to swim after it, but realizing that everything was useless, she sobbed and then howled. Ruank was sitting at the stern, feeling uneasy.

The sailors, of course, began to make various jokes about the couple in love but then the captain stood up to his full height. "That's enough!" he growled at the top of his voice. Everyone went silent. After a pause he sang a farewell song. The sailors in the boat also stood up and heartily sang along with the song. The she-wolf seemed to calm down and silently looked at the sailing boat, watching the sailors climb on board the ship. She then watched as the schooner raised its sails and headed north. Only after the ship had disappeared behind the cape, did she slowly wander back into the forest with her head down.

Time passed and the mountains of their native coast finally appeared on the horizon and then the Fang appeared in the haze. The ship slowly entered the harbor and a huge crowd on the pier sang a long-awaited meeting song. When the ladder was lowered, no one shed a tear (for the sole reason that the Arrusihan do not have lacrimal glands) but the whining, whimpering, sobbing and furious hugs were overwhelming. A light turbulent breeze even rose over the pier from many hundreds of tails waving with all their might.

The expedition brought home a lot of things, from a collection of insects to unprecedented types of shells, but it was the ship's diaries, drawings and maps which became the main booty. Researchers immediately began to check the new data with the old maps and descriptions of people and as it turned out the coastline had changed markedly and Atlantis had actually risen a hundred meters above sea level. That is why the lighthouse was on a high rock at some distance from the coast.

After he finalized and published his diaries, Ruank Uxarr was forced to go through an ordeal of being famous. His book had the obvious title of the Lighthouse of Atlantis.

Monument to Man

Ahar Zu Mrim tightened the lacing of the leather brace on his hand: his weak fifth finger was tired of supporting the chisel. It had already slipped out of his left hand a couple of times and had hung by the safety string. It was easier to work with a brace, but accuracy was lost, perhaps imperceptible to the casual eye but absolutely noticeable to the conscience of the artist. Ahar continued to work on the right eye and tomorrow, with fresh energy, he would finish the job. Three of his assistants, all hanging on ropes, worked with electric cutters and pneumatic perforators, removing large volumes of excess from the rock from which the face of a person would soon look into the ocean. The rock was the Fang, and the man was Chuck Rudnick, who lived a little over five hundred thousand years ago.

It was much easier to work hanging from a rope in a comfortable sling than standing. When standing Ahar got tired of working after only three hours and had to put on a corset that supported his hips. He yelled for the boom to be extended as he needed to take a look at today's results. On the one hand, thank God that the apprentices did not cut off anything other than what was superfluous with the perforators. Nevertheless, they must be moved away from the chin area starting tomorrow. The right eye was not entirely good. It looked sad and even doomed. Chuck wasn't looking at the ocean like that in his famous entry. Ahar looked at his watch: it was time to finish. There was no sense in working further today and besides he wanted to be in time for the lecture, one which for him was of no idle interest. The well-known anthropologist Khrumm Vyr Arukh, who spent many years in the Archives was scheduled to speak. He called himself an archive worm and probably knew the history of the world and human culture better than anyone on the planet. The lecture was called: the Arrucihans and the People: Major Differences and a Common Road.

Ahar left half an hour before the start, risking being late but fortunatcly, thc usual traffic jam at thc bridgc ovcr thc rivcr was abscnt and he managed to arrive five minutes before the start of the lecture and get a good seat. By the beginning of the lecture, the thousand-seat-hall (marked with squares on the floor) was full. The professor with noble gray hair on his face stepped on stage, according to etiquette, on two legs and received a friendly applause.

After bowing and squatting in front of the microphone, the anthropologist began his speech: "Good evening, brothers and sisters! My lecture today will be slightly anthropomorphic in structure and mood. People often started their speeches with the words 'I have two pieces of news: good and bad' and always started with the bad news. I will probably follow this tradition.

"Did you know that it takes us, on average, twice as long as a human to drive in a screw with a screwdriver? It also takes us sixty percent more time than humans to verbally communicate the same information. Do you know why we have practically only one language, while people on Earth had thousands of languages? Yes, because due to the structure of the larynx and tongue, the set of articulate combinations of sounds, that is, the words that we are able to pronounce, is incomparably less than that of people. Almost all of them are involved in our language but there are simply no sound combinations for other languages! There are dialects where the meanings of words are slightly shifted, but in general we lack those that are, so we often have to use two words where people got by with one.

"By the way, we ourselves are a refutation of the mainstream theories that mankind had about the origins of the mind. Those theories claimed that bipedalism was one of the necessary steps for the emergence of the mind, others being the structure of the hand, where the fifth finger was opposed to the rest, and then vocal abilities.

"Well, let's take me, I seem to have a mind, otherwise I would not be sitting here in front of you, but I still have big problems with upright walking and I can't give a lecture standing on two legs for more than two hours. It's also hard for me to walk more than two kilometers using only two legs. Look at me! I'm sitting here almost like a man, on a small stool, with my hands on my knees. To be honest, this is uncomfortable for me, I would rather sit on the floor with my hands on it but etiquette, apparently borrowed from human culture, instructs the lecturer to sit in this way. It's good that etiquette does not force us to wear clothes by analogy.

"Going further: the use of our hands and wrists is also still a big problem. Our ancestors had a fifth finger which generally only dangled without a joint, like a rudimentary object. Our joint has somewhat recovered and the thumb is slightly stronger and has grown, but still it is not optimally positioned and is rather weak. Therefore, we twist a screw twice as long as a person would."

At these words Ahar looked sadly at his left hand and shook his head.

"About our vocal abilities I have already made mention. Here's a question for the audience: can any of you pronounce the names of two people, Rudnick and Mukha, the well-known benefactors of our big family? Listen to how they sound from the mouth of a person (the lecturer turned on a recording where a human voice loudly and clearly said the names several times: 'Chuck... Stefan...). Now let's try again."

Clumsy sounding combinations were heard in the hall, from which everyone started to laugh. Short, abrupt barks could be heard, their sound expressing laughter.

"Well, you see," the lecturer continued, "it's funny. So, the prerequisites for the emergence of reason in our kind were very deplorable and remain so. Where did this intelligence come from then? There are several theories here, and they all take into account that we do not come from the wild, but from human civilization. There is such a thing as the pickup effect.

"Our ancestors were involved in human activities, including grazing livestock and when people began to disappear, they were left with only one way out, to survive by themselves, without teams of pastoralists, to maintain the livestock population as the main source of food. Here a powerful evolutionary stimulus arose: expansion. Tribes that could breed cattle better easily mastered new territories on the sparsely populated planet and could multiply faster, this was how useful qualities were fixed upon with the main one being intelligence. So, two factors: the capture of human practice and vast free territories gave us an unprecedented evolutionary push, such that the development of our intellects far outpaced the development of the anatomical features associated with it.

"But let's get back down to earth and continue to cover the bad news. Has our intellect reached that of a human? Alas! In some ways we are superior to man, for example, in orientation to terrain, but we are inferior in abstract thinking. We have been able to understand and master many man-made technologies, but there is not a single Arrucihan in the world who understands string theory. I don't mean being able to develop such a theory, just to be at least able to understand it. True, even people could not get a single clear prediction from string theory, but the theory is beautiful and majestic. But it's not about us ... Apparently, imaginative thinking is a great interference for us, and where it begins to slip, we give up. However, it is worth clarifying: we are inferior to people in the highest examples of intelligence. If we take the average level, then we concede much less, and almost do not concede at all, but on the other hand, we have far fewer outright idiots than people had.

"And now it's time to move on to the good news. I'll start from ancient times, when people were just beginning to explore space. Even before orbital launches were made and only short space jumps in space were practiced, the first astronauts were not humans but their ancestors, monkeys. Nothing worked with them; the monkeys under the conditions of the experiments instantly succumbed to stress, escaped from their chairs and smashed everything around them. Then they tried to work with our ancestors, dogs. Immediately everything went smoothly, our ancestors, inferior in intelligence, were far superior to monkeys in the ability to maintain rational behavior in difficult and unusual conditions. They were not afraid of belts or sensors, they calmly endured the restrictions in mobility and even understood well what people wanted from them."

One of the listeners in the hall raised her hand and waved it impatiently.

"Yes, please, I'm listening."

"Tell me, when will we ourselves fly into space, and who will fly first, the Arrusikhan or some other animal?"

The lecturer liked the question and its author so much that he involuntarily waved his tail, which was considered a violation of etiquette, since tradition dictated that lecturers keep their distance from the audience.

"Thanks for the great question. We will fly into space in ten or fifteen years. If we were human, we would have already flown with a high chance of accidents, out of impatience. One of our main differences from people is that we know how to wait. We know how to act slowly and carefully. Therefore, we do not need to insure ourselves by launching animals, we will fly ourselves when everything is absolutely reliable.

"I continue with the good news. We are generally less aggressive towards our fellow creatures. It may not be that we are less aggressive, sometimes we don't even mind a fight, rather we need to talk about the limiters of aggression, which are strong in us. Many researchers believe that the limiters of aggression are the result of better armament: our ancestors fought only to first blood otherwise the fight could end in the death of the vanquished. This forced our ancestors to work out a certain code of honor which included things like: not to beat those lying down and letting go those who surrendered. Of course, any family has its black sheep, but in our entire history there has not been a single bloody war. At maximum grandiose mass fights. In our society less than a thousandth of the population works in law enforcement, ten times less than people on Earth and with much better results.

"Moving on... Our ancestors hunted together, coordinating superbly with each other. Just try driving a deer or an elk in a hunt! Here, in addition to strength and speed, the utmost coherence and discipline are required and we have preserved and strengthened these qualities. Now we build bridges, roads and ships with the same teamwork and enthusiasm that our ancestors used to hunt deer. At the same time, no one is forcing anyone to do anything. If earthly socialists, including Marx, saw our cooperatives, they would shed tears of joy.

"So to summarize: the main differences between humans and Arrusihans can be easily traced even at the level of distant ancestors, to monkeys and wolves. Our ancestors inherited more severe living conditions, where endurance, patience, altruism meant a lot. The way of life demanded good cooperation, and sharp fangs demanded a code of honor that restrained aggression. Yes, our ancestors were less developed and we are a little behind in development ourselves but the qualities inherited from them, believe me, will over vast historical times outweigh the advantages of a person in intellect. And now, before proceeding to the final part of the lecture, I am ready to answer questions, if there are any."

Ahar was waiting for this moment and raised his hand first.

"You said that one of our advantages is altruism. But what could be more altruistic than the activities of Chuck Rudnick (he said "Ghaka Rudnik"), who devoted his whole life to schools intended for unknown sentient beings of a distant future?! And isn't the Ark itself an example of the highest form of human altruism?"

"Yes, you are right there are many other examples of genuine altruism in the history of mankind. Just like true enthusiasm, nobility and other qualities, but there are almost more examples of the opposites in humans: self-interest, meanness and baseness. The fact is that humanity was (although excuse me, I don't know, it's probably inappropriate to talk about humanity in the past tense) very heterogeneous. The positive qualities of a person, which aroused admiration, are the norm in our country and do not surprise anyone. Another thing is that the highest human achievements are inaccessible to us, for now anyway. We have enough altruism to spend a huge amount of energy on a new Ark, but not enough talent to conceive, develop and implement such a project from scratch. However, I will talk about this in the final part."

"Tell me, is it true that people, even when they flew into space, believed in a wonderful omnipotent being and the immortality of the soul?"

"Paradoxical as it may seem, they believed in all that. Not everyone of course, those who flew into space and built ships, hardly believed in such things, but most did believe in a deity. Why? It was probably because of the lack of strong mentality. What would they do if life suddenly went wrong?"

"What do you mean what would they do? Try to figure out what they did wrong and fix it."

"And if it does not depend on you and you cannot fix it yourself?"

"I will call my friends for help."

"What if your friends can't help?"

"I will be patient and try to minimize the damage."

"That's right, you will act this way, because you are a being with a strong psyche and are able to maintain presence of mind in a difficult situation, but many people, instead of gathering strength, or instead of calling friends, called for help from a powerful but fictional creature. And guess what, it helped them! It helped by removing stress, giving strength, after which a person became able to act rationally and minimize damage. With our stronger nervous system, we do without such a psychotherapeutic trick. But let us be indulgent to human weaknesses. They are compensated by a higher creative potential. Just a few perhaps, but that's enough.

"However, I will continue and move on to the second part of the lecture, in which I want to make a strong statement: we share a common road with people. Here, in fact, there are two strong statements at once: the first is that for developed forms of life there is a certain 'highway' leading to prosperity, and the second is that we have it in common with people. It is clear that the very concept of 'highway' is pure metaphysics, so let's make a clarification: this very path consists of development and expansion. Actually, it can also be traced to pre-intellectual biological evolution where at some stage, expansion must move to the cosmic stage in order to protect life and mind from irreversible catastrophes.

"So, we perfectly complement each other along the way. A person has a huge potential for rapid development, for revolutionary leaps and for breakthroughs. Human civilization is unusually creative, but at the same time unstable, contradictions are embedded in a person that can destroy them and everything around them. Man is a sprinter, capable of a quick climb, but also a tragic fall.

"We are stayers. We are also capable of independent development, those who say that our entire civilization came out of that are wrong." The lecturer pointed with his hand towards the glazed wall, behind which could be seen the dome of the Archives. "In order to understand and master human culture, we had to reproduce it ourselves, not to learn, but to reproduce. We were developing more slowly but we have plenty of time. We are unable to cause world war, we are not in danger of drowning in unbridled consumption or ruining the planet and we generally do not have the ability to get hooked on drugs, chemical or psychological substances. It's easier for us in this regard. And I have no doubt that time will pass, and our descendants will send a new Ark. I'm sure not because we already have a recipe for how to do it, but because we have the time and energy for long distances. We'll do it, and not alone.

"So, some make breakthroughs, others cross the open spaces, this is how life is affirmed, for billions of years or forever. This is the general path. Let me answer questions."

"Do you think there are people left anywhere in the universe?"

"If a new breakthrough is required, who will come up with it?"

"How can I know about the people of Earth? Everyone has probably heard that more than twenty thousand years after the launch of the Ark, there was an unsuccessful attempt to establish communication from the solar system. After all, someone tried to do it, although the resources that they had were clearly not enough. Why didn't they try again? Perhaps simply because they learned about the extinction of people on our planet, because everything that happened on Selina was broadcast to Earth for more than a thousand years. So that connection attempt gives hope, but nothing more can be said.

"How about a new jump? Evolution continues, its ways are inscrutable, but the more we send arks, the more likely it is that a new extremely creative species will arise somewhere."

"Even if a person is no more, then we have the complete genome of many people. Will it be possible in the future to recreate a person from a known genome?"

"Yes, there is not only a genome, but also well-preserved tissues specially preserved by people. However, man himself was never able to recreate the mammoth, despite the fact that its genome was completely known and its closest relative, the Indian elephant, was alive. At least, it did not succeed during the known history of the Earth before the sending of the Ark. There may be no fundamental obstacles to collecting human DNA and even packaging it into the correct set of chromosomes. But it is also necessary for the genome to work, for this you need a suitable living cell. Somewhere I read about the idea of turning a baboon into a human by gradually changing pieces of monkey DNA, not so much needs to be changed in relative terms. Maybe it's not serious maybe it is. Someone thought that this would take thousands of generations, tens of thousands of years but do not believe that this will never be done. At least our descendants will have these tens of thousands of years. So, although not soon, not very soon, but our distant descendants will recreate a person."

There were many questions, but Ahar switched to his thoughts. With the right eye of Chuck Rudnick, perhaps, everything was in order: first, there really was a hint of sadness in his look in the records, and second, the whole expression of his face would come through later. Another thing was interesting: how was it possible that Ahar, who had never seen people alive, could feel emotions so subtly in the images of their faces and even reproduce people's feelings with the help of his crude tools. Is there a universal language of emotions? Or did Ahar subtly master the language of human feelings by watching a huge number of archival films? Why do faces, both people's and Arrusihans' convey emotions so vividly with subtle movements of small muscles? People did not see the Arrusihans but they perfectly understood the emotions of their ancestors the dogs.

The lecturer is right, we and the people have a common road, and his task is to convey this in a monument. How to do it? He imagined the Fang from memory, how it looked from the ocean shore ... A dog! There, on the left, approximately in the middle of the height, there is a ledge. This is a direct hint! Remove a little extra and there will be a dog, an ancestor, looking at the ocean with Chuck.

Distant Farewell

Arzuh Gra Urman was the heir to a dynasty of cosmonauts, rooted in antiquity. His ancestor from eight generations ago sent a probe to the solar system. Now the probe is flying somewhere a light year away and in five thousand years should shed light on the fate of mankind and life on Earth. Something would surely be brought by its radio beam directed back home: either triumphal news or grief or timid hope, who knows?

His great-great-great-grandfather and his team had first visited the old Ark, examined it and proved that it was suitable for launching life into space, to the 53 Bowl, if all the electronics were replaced and major repairs were carried out. He had spent a lot of effort to convince the World Council that it could and should be used and he proved that the use of the earthly Ark would reduce the time of dispatch by half a century and reduce the cost of the project by forty percent. This was not enough. The members of the Council were afraid to make such a decision because the age of the Ark frightened them.

And then Arzuh's great-great-great-grandfather when speaking before the Council asked them: "Do you honor the memory of mankind?"

"Of course we honor it... And how we honor it! Is it possible not to honor the memory of people... Without them, we would still be running around the earth's steppes and tundra..."

"So, the best way to honor their memory, the best way to pay a moral debt to humanity, is to use the creation of people in which they put their souls and send it on a second voyage, and let it serve its purpose again!" said the great-great-great-grandfather of Arzukha.

After these words, the Council melted away and immediately unanimously decided to restore the Ark.

The dynasty continued its mission. Arzuh's great-great-grandfather was building a space service station to repair the Ark. The great-grandfather changed the thin elements of the radiator, which had become unusable more than half a million years before. Then the grandfather transported and assembled the uranium rods of the reactor, repaired the feed mechanism and installed new thermoelectric converters. His father changed the electronics of all the systems.

Then Arzukh arrived at the Ark, which was now called the "Ark of the 53 Bowls", and was the commander of the group escorting the caravan. It was necessary to see it off to about a hundred million kilometers, until the main engine was turned on and a little further, until all systems were checked. To do this, they would have to spend a whole year outside the Selina radiation belts, the maximum allowed by the rules of radiation safety for emergency cases.

A year ago, during the installation of the Arsenal blocks, an event occurred that almost cost Arzuh his career and his life. The brigade was in a hurry, fifteen modules arrived at once. Once, towards the end of the watch, he hastily put on a spacesuit without combing his hair. This was considered a serious violation, and the service ship had excellent combing equipment, an air suction cabin with rotating cylindrical brushes, flexible brushes and automatic slickers, all this made the procedure not so much mandatory as pleasant, but this time Arzuh was in too much of a hurry. In principle, there was nothing wrong with that, this happened often: if you didn't comb the hair out, then it was enough to properly blow out the spacesuit using a vacuum stand. But that time, Arzuh had started molting two weeks ahead of schedule and he did not notice it, again because of his haste and so when Arzuh was mounting the next module, he suddenly felt that he was suffocating, the exhaust air path was clogged, and thus the fresh air stopped flowing. It had become clogged by his own undercoat, but there was no sense in determining the reason for the problem, it was necessary to overcome about three hundred meters to the service ship and take the suit off without losing consciousness. Three hundred meters is at least three minutes of flight, then you need to press the remote control of the airlock gates, then get into the gateway and press the remote control again, and only after that can you lose consciousness. One of the crew members was on the service ship, but he did not have time to put on a spacesuit to come to the rescue. The rest were far away. Arzuh managed to report the problem and started towards the living compartment at the maximum possible speed, which was artificially limited to two meters per second relative to the ship. And then the release got stuck. In order not to lose consciousness, he counted the pulse beats in his temples, but this did not help...

Fortunately, Urmykh, a member of the crew on duty in the ship, did not lose his head. He managed to answer Arzuh so that he would not twitch and fly in a straight line, without touching the control sensor, and he himself undocked the service ship, opened the port of the airlock and, controlling the maneuvering micro thrusters, orienting on three television cameras, and caught the flying Arzukh with the airlock, like a beetle with a net. After which he closed the port, restored the pressure and, dragging him inside, removed the helmet from the chief. Arzuh regained consciousness on his own and only cursed heavily.

If Arzuh had had a slightly poorer reputation, he would not have seen the current mission being launched, something which he had dreamed of for many years. Oh and how the mission began! The ceremonial launch, when the last modules with the embryos and the team of escorts were sent off, became the event of the century.

The team, dressed according to the old tradition in spacesuits with their helmets off, stood to their full height on the platform at the entrance to the ship's cockpit. From above, he could see all of the assembled crowd, five hundred thousand, and a huge choir on the hill with about three to four thousand singers. The speeches ended and the choir began. Powerful polyphonic vocals filled the space of the Cosmodrome and the support mast seemed to vibrate slightly. The choir performed the most solemn, and at the same time, the brightest and life-affirming music of all peoples and all times, it was the Mozart requiem.

Arzuh was shaken to the core. A man in his place would have welled up with tears, but he only whimpered thinly, restraining himself so that no one would hear. And down there, when the choir fell silent, many could not restrain themselves, some whined, some sobbed, but the voices quickly organized into a growing song of the ancestors, at first similar to an ordinary howl, it became more and more harmonious and melodic, a simple folk song of send-offs on a long journey. When the choir picked it up and led five hundred thousand voices, from the low tones of this song the support mast clearly started vibrating from the platform where the escort team stood.

A few hours later they entered high orbit and parked in front of the Headquarters, where the Incubator assemblers were waiting for them in a small tow. Picking up the modules that had arrived on the last flight, they went to fit the two-ton wedges covered with yellow ceramics into their places, a quick matter, after which they would be going home.

Meanwhile, Arzuh's team connected their ship to the System and began testing the mechanics and electronics of all the devices. Soon, the tablet floating in the cockpit slowly moved towards one of the walls, the main tugboat turned on the engines, shining like a small star at the head of the caravan. Four days later, the tug did its job, sending the Ark to the second location at plus three kilometers per second, and then returned home. Only the escorters who had months of work ahead to bring the Ark to its fully operational working condition remained. The work was not as intense as it was tedious, especially the launch of the reactor. First the pressure testing of the radiators, then filling the second circuit with gallium, then removing the jamming rods: hundreds of operations, the correct execution of which had to be monitored and double checked. Finally, the reactor began to revive itself.

Arzuh tried to adjust the mode: "How softly it works! Nothing thrown off and no fluctuations of any kind! They wrote that the designer was a tough, unpleasant person in communications... Like him... Jose was either Big or Long, and he made this, a purring kitten, and not a reactor of clean uranium two hundred and thirty-five: Could he have even imagined that someone would re-launch his brainchild again half a million years later?

It took another month to bring all of the systems to permanent operating mode, a viscous month of monotonous tests and idle disputes about the past and the future. Then a load was applied to the thruster windings, and Roland's Corkscrew began to work again, as if it had stood idle for only a few days. For the first time, the plasma flow rate was increased many times, in order to quickly take the Ark away from the star and from the plane of the ecliptic: only when the temperature of the Incubator windings dropped below thirty-two kelvin would they go into a superconducting state.

Weeks passed, the team completed the farewell. The Ark, on its second voyage, carried a new genome of the biosphere and civilization. There was a depressing gap in the genome, but a new find of stubborn Nature was also firmly sewn in: a biological species that for the first time had carried out the advancement of the mind, similar to passing a relay-fire.

Well, that's all. Having crossed a long and difficult path along the bright side of being, our weary story is coming to an end.

In the end, Arzuh gently undocked the ship from the Headquarters, but did not turn on the engines, suggesting: "Let's hang out a bit. Let's sit here and watch the Ark leave."

For the first minute, nothing seemed to happen, but after another minute, the Headquarters docking device moved a couple of meters. Soon it became clear that the Headquarters was moving a little, and in fifteen minutes it was already a hundred meters away with its huge antenna.

"Let's wait some more, let the Incubator pass by us."

The shiny umbrella covering the ship from the sun, invisible in the shade, passed by. Next would be the Incubator, which was still far away. They had to wait about an hour until the last part of the caravan passed at the speed of a camel running at a light trot.

"Well, are we going home?" Arzuh asked.

"Wait a minute," Urmykh replied. "Let me see some more. This is really something sad. We devoted half our lives to it and now it is leaving forever. And why is it leaving?"

"Why, why...?" Arzuh drew a circle above his head with his hand and glanced around. "So that as many curious creatures as possible, like you, can see and feel what you saw and felt, and so that they have the intelligence to be delighted by it."

Acknowledgements

The author is grateful to his wife, Valentina Safronova, who took on the heaviest burden as the first reader, and is also grateful to the second and third readers, Evgeny Stern and Alexander Polnarev for timely moral support. Special thanks go to the first critic, Elena Kleshchenko, who had a positive opinion about the book based on the first chapters (how a paleontologist determines the appearance of an animal from one jaw) and who expressed this opinion publicly.

The author is also grateful to the founding fathers of the Schrödinger's Cat Magazine, Alexei Torgashev and Grigory Tarasevich, who on their own initiative, published the first two chapters of the book.

When writing a book, it is very useful to have qualified advisers and we were lucky to have wonderful ones! In particular Stanislav Gubin who found seeds that had lain in the permafrost for tens of thousands of years and then sprouted them in a laboratory. He explained how to quickly develop soil on a hitherto bare planet. Leading Russian radiochemist Boris Zhuikov selected a suitable isotope for a long-term radioisotope source. Someone may have noticed that the biologist Amir Bakkar looks a lot like the famous biologist Mikhail Gelfand. The similarity, of course, is purely accidental, but it was Mikhail who formulated the essence of this character's assumption about the cause of the fatal problem of the colonists. The author expresses his heartfelt gratitude to his consultants and another expert, Valery Rubakov, who advised us on any problems of cosmology and fundamental physics, if it were necessary, and presented a small vivid story from life, for which many thanks to him.